Read

DREAD CHAMPION

Also by Brandilyn Collins

Color the Sidewalk for Me

Eyes of Elisha

DREAD CHAMPION

Brandilyn Collins

ZONDERVAN™

GRAND RAPIDS, MICHIGAN 49530 USA

ZONDERVAN™

Dread Champion
Copyright © 2002 by Brandilyn Collins

Requests for information should be addressed to:
Zondervan, *Grand Rapids, Michigan 49530*

ISBN 0-7394-2977-9

Interior design by Susan Ambs

Printed in the United States of America

For Ryan Matthew Collins.
This is my version
of a single white rose.

For me the word of the LORD has resulted in reproach and derision all day long.... I have heard the whispering of many ... watching for my fall, say: "Perhaps he will be deceived, so that we may prevail against him and take our revenge on him." But the LORD is with me like a dread champion; therefore my persecutors will stumble and not prevail.

JEREMIAH 20:8, 10–11 NASB

PREFACE AND ACKNOWLEDGMENTS

Many people generously gave of their time as I wrote this book. I'd like to thank these professionals for granting me interviews on myriad subjects: Gery Sterling, D.D.S., good-naturedly answered some rather strange questions about teeth. Lynne Jacobs, executive director of Adopt International in Redwood City, took time out of her busy schedule to talk both about the procedures of adoption and about her personal passion for her work. Charles Robinson, assistant administrator for San Mateo County's Private Defender Program, went over many details of how a defense attorney would handle a case such as the one presented in this story. And James Wade, San Mateo County deputy district attorney, gave me the prosecutorial side of things. Redwood City police officer Todd Hurst outlined the various jobs of law enforcement professionals in regard to missing persons and murder cases.

These folks know their stuff. If you find errors within these pages, *mea culpa.*

A special thanks to my wonderful friend Jacqueline Clark, who drove around Salinas and nearby beaches with me, helping me note exact driving times and details. Jacqueline also critiqued the manuscript, along with my respected writer colleagues Niwana Briggs and Randy Ingermanson.

As always, special thanks to my agents, Jane Jordan Browne and Scott Mendel of Multimedia Product Development, and her team. And of course my utmost gratitude to my editor, Dave Lambert, and all the terrific folks at Zondervan. They are heaven-sent.

Most of all, God, omnipotent and full of mercy, saw me through the worst days of writing this book, when I thought I had no more to give. May he be glorified by this story about his ultimate power and grace.

And now a word of explanation about the locations within these events. As with *Eyes of Elisha,* the first book in this series, I have begun with real places, at some point jumping off into the chasm of fiction. Breaker Beach is fictional but all surrounding beaches are real. Latitude and longitude and information about currents and tides are based on nearby Moss Landing Beach. The general areas of Salinas are true to life, as are some of the streets mentioned. And the exact location of Darren Welk's house is real, although that rich plot of earth is certainly not owned by the "Salad King." As for the hardworking ranchers of Salinas and surrounding areas in Monterey County, they are indeed larger than life. We have them to thank for most of the vegetables and salads on our dinner tables. In fact, it is true that ranchers in Salinas are credited with creating the ready-made, bagged salads in today's grocery stores. However, my character Darren Welk, who is given the credit in *Dread Champion,* is in no way based upon any real rancher in Salinas. Nor is the character Enrico Delgadia based upon any real person. Of course the San Mateo County Courthouse in Redwood City does exist. People familiar with it will recognize most of the description. Occasionally I have made some changes, adding a door or bench as the story required. Finally, Channel Seven (ABC affiliate) is a respected source for news in the California Bay Area. But they do not employ a Milt Waking, nor is the character of Milt based on any Channel Seven reporter.

To quote the character of Geoffrey Chaucer when he was caught fictionalizing in *A Knight's Tale,* "I am a writer. I give the truth—scope."

So allow me some scope and come on, get in. Let's go for a ride....

DREAD CHAMPION

PROLOGUE

After twenty years of midnights among the dead, Victor Mendoza didn't spook easily.

The graveyard shift at the graveyard. His superstitious mother had shaken her head when he first took the job. Victor didn't care. You want to talk fear, he'd told her, fear was the night he was four years old, clinging to his papa's bony back as they scuttled like rats across the U.S. border.

"But the dead," she'd said.

"They don't scare me half as bad as the living."

Brothers Memorial Cemetery was oddly shaped at its rear, one corner crooking like an arthritic finger around the edge of Darren Welk's sprawling backyard. A single line of ancient gravestones formed that finger, an incongruous add-on years before the Salinas Valley sprang to life with ranches and crops. Victor didn't typically patrol the crook; no need to. Whoever once tended those graves had long passed on. His job was to protect the graves of those whose loved ones still visited Brothers Memorial—folks whose money greened the cemetery and surrounding valley. Rich folks like Darren Welk, whose parents were buried on the eastern hill.

But that night something caught Victor Mendoza's eye, and he ventured in for a look.

Chilly air wafted around Victor's face as he stealthily drew near the edge of the crook, his breath puffing in a fog. A crescent moon slung itself against a hazy sky, stingy with its light. He hunched, fists curling and uncurling, about three feet from the rusty barbed wire fence running the perimeter of the cemetery. His eyes widened as he realized what had caught his attention. A shadow. Grotesquely tall and skinny—a warped silhouette spilling across the entire driveway leading into the Welks' garage. The aberration moved in steady rhythm, spindly arms stretching, pulling back, stretching, pulling back. Victor stopped breathing and tilted his head, listening. A vague sound rolled toward him, then sharpened into pattern. *Crunch, hiss. Crunch, hiss.* In beat with the shadow's movement. Slowly Victor's eyes followed the shadow's extremities to its bent shoulders, along its narrow torso, down a stick-figure leg. There it connected with a stocky man on the far side of the driveway, feet wide apart, shovel in his hands, digging. He extended his muscular arms, and the skinny silhouette arms slid across cement. *Crunch.* The shovel connected with ground. He arced the shovel back and to the side, shadow arms mocking. *Hiss.* Dirt and tiny rocks flowed off onto a growing pile. A large potted bush, similar to others already planted alongside the driveway, sat a few feet away. Victor's eyes fell on a blazing lantern on the ground behind the man—the cause of his shadow. The light illuminated the man's trousers, haloing his back, fading into an umbra behind his head. But Victor Mendoza saw just enough of the features to recognize him. Anyone in the valley would know this man.

Goose bumps popped down Victor's arms. His neck warmed with sweat. A man with money to spare for gardeners planting a bush at 4:20 a.m. was odd enough, but it was more than that. Something about the man's posture seemed depressed, heavy. Victor's thoughts tangled, almost as if a disjointed consciousness from the figure flowed into his own. He forced himself to gaze, pay attention, record. One of the man's feet was turned in slightly. Was that a shifting of weight or a half stagger? *Crunch.* The man threw his weight behind the shovel, his shadow dancing. *Hiss.* He swung his arms, dirt sliding. He did not raise his head; his shoulders curved inward, neck bent.

Victor stepped back and twigs crackled beneath his boot. The man's head pulled up and hung there, adrift. Spiders crawled down Victor's spine. He froze, willing the night to blanket him. Seconds ticked by. Finally the head lowered. Digging resumed.

Crunch. Hiss.

Victor Mendoza let out his breath and faded into darkness, creeping around ancient gravestones. He could not shake his uneasiness. When morning dawned hours later, his back muscles still twitched. As he crawled into a warm bed at 8:30 a.m., his workday over, the *crunch hiss* still reverberated in his head.

Two days later Victor heard the news. Darren Welk's fancy wife was missing.

HARSH LIGHT SPILLED FROM the naked bulb, lancing Darren Welk's eyes. He winced.

"Sorry to bring you in here, but this holding cell's the quietest place at the moment," Detective Draker said, motioning for his partner to take a seat. "We had a little altercation in here a few days ago. Haven't gotten around to replacing the fixture yet." Draker settled his bulky frame in a chair opposite Darren. His thinning blond hair was clipped short, a matching mustache bristling under an oversized nose.

"No problem." The words sounded hollow to Darren's ears. What hadn't been a problem the last two and a half days? He grasped for his last ounce of energy, willing his face and body into placidity while every muscle tensed, every fiber hummed. He could swear noises were louder. The creak of the door shutting, of clothes rustling, resounded in his ears. And the expressions! Every glance between Draker and his partner twanged with meaning. Could they see the truth in his eyes? In the twitch of his hands, the exaggerated rise and fall of his chest? Darren spread his fingers upon the table, then brought them together, fearing they looked too stiff. He could barely control his breathing. He was on the edge and the chasm ran deep.

"Can we get you some coffee?" Draker indicated his own cup. It looked black, bitter, like Darren's soul. His stomach turned over.

"No thanks."

Draker's partner, Les Kelly, dragged a chair to the table, on Darren's right. He leaned forward, lacing his fingers on top of the worn wood, his narrow shoulders military straight. Kelly wasn't a tall man but his presence screamed authority. Darren glanced distractedly at the man's hands, wondering at his own. At what they'd done.

"What's happening with my house?" He forced the words to be chopped, forceful, like those of the Darren Welk he used to know. *The* Darren Welk of Salinas Valley, who could fill an employee with fear with a mere glance.

Draker cleared his throat in a brief staccato. "Don't worry, your house will be fine."

Darren met the man's eyes. They were brown and deep-set, unfathomable. "Which means . . ."

The Monterey County sheriff's detective shrugged. "Look, I'm sure we can get this all cleared up quickly. That's why we brought you down here. But before we can talk, I just need to tell you that you have the right to remain silent. Any statement you make may be used against you in a court of law. . . ."

Darren stared at the detective's wide face, his skin pebbling. He could hardly believe what was happening. "I watch those crime shows, too," he managed when Draker finished. He tried to laugh but it sounded more like a choke. He inhaled deeply, forced himself to lean back in his chair.

Draker's lips curved at his little joke. A knowing smile, Darren thought. He pressed his heels against the floor, resisting the urge to check Kelly's reaction. Shifty eyes he didn't need.

"Okay," Draker said. "We need you to tell us about the blouse."

Darren closed his eyes. The white blouse with gold buttons. Long-sleeved, expensive silk. She'd worn it out to dinner before they ended up on the beach. When Draker had pulled it from beneath the newly planted bush, clods of dirt clung to it like bugs. Darren had nearly retched at the sight. Brett had hovered nearby, his face turning pasty white, chest heaving with ragged breaths. *"No, Dad—"*

Darren steeled himself, the panic in his son's voice still echoing in his mind. "Shawna cut her head."

"After you hit her, right?"

Darren gave him a hard look. He could feel Les Kelly watching him intently. "I told you, I'd never hit her before. She just got me mad, that was all. And I was drunk. I didn't even hit her that hard. But she stumbled and fell. Her forehead hit a piece of metal or something in the sand. She got up right away. It wasn't a very big cut, but you know how a head can bleed."

"Right. So the blood got on her blouse?"

"Look at what you've done! How dare you!" Her scream of rage echoed through his alcohol-laden brain. *"Hit me again and I'll have you in jail!"*

Darren vaguely remembered her fumbling with the buttons. "Yeah. That's when she took it off."

"Right there on the beach?"

Darren shrugged. "It was one o'clock in the morning. Nobody else was around. The Browards had already left. Shawna saw she was getting blood on it and took it down to the water to wash it. She didn't like messes; you can ask anyone that."

The detective stared at him. "Why didn't she have a jacket?" Draker asked. "Even for an unseasonably warm night, this is still February."

"She got hot sitting near the fire and took it off. I guess Tracey brought it home."

Draker nodded knowingly and Darren's heart skipped a beat. Shawna's daughter had been spouting her mouth in the past two days to anybody who'd listen.

"So. When did the Browards leave?"

"I don't know exactly. I told you, I was drunk." Darren caught Les Kelly's slow blink. So the man was weary of hearing that, was he? Too bad; it happened to be true.

"Mr. Welk"—Draker leaned forward—"what did you do when Shawna went to wash the blouse?"

Darren's insides stilled. He forced himself to look Draker in the eye as he tried to remember.

The iciness of the water on his ankles. Shawna whirling on him in a fury. "What are you going to do now, Mr. Do-Anything-I-Please? Drown me?" His utter disgust with her, the fire in his belly, his fist pulled back ...

"I was *drunk.* I passed out on the sand by the fire. Next thing I knew, Tracey was kicking me awake, screaming that her mother was gone."

"You don't remember anything?"

"No."

Draker surveyed him unblinkingly. "Where do you think your wife is, Mr. Welk?"

Darren's gaze raked the ceiling. "How should I know? Probably ran off with some boyfriend. She had 'em all along, you know."

"Mm." The detective rubbed his chin. "She was a very pretty woman."

Words formed on Darren's tongue but he made no comment. A moment passed while the two men surveyed each other.

Les Kelly shifted in his chair. "You saying she just ran off into the dark without her blouse?"

"I told you she had a jacket."

"You said Tracey brought the jacket home."

"Well, who knows? Maybe she didn't. Why don't you ask her?"

"We did," Kelly said. "She brought it home."

"Don't you think," Draker pressed, "that if your wife was going to run off, she'd at least have put the blouse back on?"

Darren's nerves tingled. "Look, I don't know, okay? I don't know! The blouse was wet and cold and still had blood on it. She wouldn't have wanted to put it back on."

"Okay, Mr. Welk." Draker held up a hand. "All right. But I'm still curious. Why did you bring the blouse home and bury it?"

Darren's brain scrambled for an answer. A thought, a meaning, some memory that made sense. "Look," he said slowly, "I know it sounds crazy. I brought the blouse home, thinking I'd get it cleaned. Thinking that when Shawna showed up, she'd be happy to see I'd taken care of it. I figured it would smooth things over, you know.

But by the time I got home, I was mad all over again. Mad that she'd taken off. And I had that one bush in the backyard that the gardeners hadn't yet planted, and I thought, *I'll show her. I'll stick that blouse where she won't ever find it. Serves her right.*"

Les Kelly spread his hands, palms up. "Why didn't you tell us this when we first asked you?"

"I was . . . embarrassed. Sounds like such a juvenile thing to do."

Draker massaged his bottom lip with a forefinger. "Your wife is missing, and you lie to detectives because you're embarrassed?"

His words hung in the claustrophobic air. Darren couldn't respond.

"Perhaps we should talk to your son again," Draker suggested casually. "Maybe he'll remember some things you don't."

"No!" His response was too quick, and Darren tried to lighten his tone. "What would a twenty-two-year-old know?"

"Well." Draker eased back in his chair, folding his arms. "Doesn't matter. We'll know more when our folks finish searching your house."

Apprehension pinged across Darren's shoulders. He sat very still.

"You did ask about that." Draker raised his eyebrows. "Sorry, we should have answered your question sooner. While you waited in our car to come down here, I froze your house. Meaning it's now under our control; no one comes in or goes out without our okay. We'll have a search warrant in a few hours. Then the criminalist will go over every square inch of your place, right down to the shower drains. Of course, that's only part of the investigation. They'll also search your car and rope off the beach where you were that night. They'll look for anything unusual that could point to where your wife could have gone. Anything washed up on shore, things like that."

Darren's thoughts spun.

Tracey slapping him—"*What have you done to my mom?!*" *Stumbling across the beach, holding his aching head. Blood drops on the sand.*

Draker was staring at him. So was Kelly. He could feel their gazes snake through his head. "Something washed up on shore?" he feigned. "Just because Shawna's missing?"

The detective's smile chilled. "Are you aware, Mr. Welk," he said slowly, "that both you and I have referred to Mrs. Welk in the past tense?"

"When did I do that?" Darren challenged. "I'd have no reason."

"Your wife washed her blouse because she *didn't* like messes?"

Darren's body drained cold. And in that worst possible moment, Brett's voice, tight with anxiety, filtered through the battered door.

PART 1 | TROUBLE

*Do not be far from me,
for trouble is near
and there is no one to help.*

Psalm 22:11

MONDAY, AUGUST 5

ONE

Stan Breckshire's right shoulder throbbed. The pain crept up his neck to the base of his skull and all the way down to his fingers. Great. His pinched nerve was cheerleading another touchdown, and the game hadn't even begun. Rah, rah, pretrial stress; let's give Stan another mess!

In the prosecutor's seat behind the counsel table, Stan held his arm out from his side, rotating it at the elbow. Then rubbed the pressure point in his neck. Not even through with jury selection yet, and just look at him. Today's panel of potential jurors had been the lousiest he'd ever seen, and apparently the worst was yet to come in the search for the second and final alternate.

The courtroom door opened behind Stan. He resisted the urge to look back, although both defense attorneys did so. With such pleasant faces, he might add. Stan worked to keep his own expression as pleasant as possible. He was well aware of the twelve jury members and first alternate already seated in the jury box, watching the attorneys' moves with morbid curiosity.

"Come on in, folks," Judge Carol Chanson greeted the last two stragglers as a bailiff led them in. "I know it's been a long day for you.

If you'll have a seat at the end of the first row in the jury box, I'll explain how we might need you."

Stan's eyes darted to the two people taking their seats. One very impatient-looking man. And a knockout of a woman in her mid-thirties. Shoulder-length, cinnamon-colored hair and matching eyes. Clear skin and a trim figure, well fitted into an expensive-looking green silk shirt and off-white, belted pants. She fairly oozed grace and intelligence. Stan's heart sank.

Chelsea Adams looked even worse than he'd imagined.

Quickly he shuffled papers before him. Anything to keep from staring at her. He wondered if T. C., as he privately called lead defense attorney Terrance Clyde, or his sidekick, Erica Salvador, had any hint of who this woman was. As fate would have it, the defense shared the same sinking boat with Stan—they'd used the last of their preemptory challenges allotted for alternates. Stan almost smirked. Nice little irony to their demanding a change of venue. Monterey County had its share of eccentrics, but it would have had to work mighty hard to spit out a sample the likes of this woman.

Knowing T. C., he'd probably used one of the minions on his fat payroll to run a check on the names of summoned people as soon as the attorneys received their lists that morning. All by his lone-some, Stan had wheedled help from a gum-snapping secretary in the district attorney's office. With rolling eyes, she'd finally agreed to check his list against the criminal clerk's records, finding out which people had previously served on a jury. But of course that's not how he'd heard the stuff on Chelsea Adams. Rather it was the I-know-something-you-don't-know look on the face of some deputy D.A. he'd run into during break just fifteen minutes ago. Someone in county records had noticed an infamous name on the list and had said something to her coworker, who'd said something to someone else, who'd run into said deputy D.A. during lunch hour.

As in every county, gossip was alive and well within the court-house walls. Stan had heard an earful and reentered the courtroom with rising panic.

Stan rubbed his arm, wincing. So what? At the very worst, the woman would only be second and final alternate. *If* she got past his questioning at all, which she wouldn't.

Judge Chanson slid on her gold-rimmed reading glasses and, for the benefit of the newly arrived, began to read the complaint against the defendant. That in *The People vs. Welk*, Darren Wayne Welk was charged with second-degree murder under Penal Code Section 187, yada, yada. Stan forced his eyes to the judge, barely hearing her words. Not that he needed to. He'd heard them at least two dozen times since that morning, every time a new batch of potential jurors had entered the courtroom.

"Okay." Judge Chanson exchanged one paper for another, her glasses still perched on her nose. The ends were attached to a purple chain around her ample neck. Her salt-and-pepper hair was cut short, leaving nothing to frame her double chin. "First we have Greg Seecham. Mr. Breckshire?"

You're my boy, Greg, thought Stan as he pushed back from the table, automatically pulling his tie. He hustled to the podium that faced the jury, making eye contact with Mr. Seecham. "Good afternoon." The guy looked almost too good to be true. A yuppie white businessman, every prosecutor's dream. Brown hair perfectly coifed; the drawn, beleaguered face of stressful success; and a designer suit—right down to the magenta power tie. Stan knew that yuppies tended to fear crime, be fiercely protective of their property, and usually hadn't suffered enough to be sympathetic to some defendant. Unfortunately, the man also brimmed with impatience, obviously not happy at missing a full day at the office. Stan opened his mouth to begin questioning, hoping against hope that Seecham wouldn't claim work hardship.

"Your Honor, I have a real problem with staying." Seecham addressed the judge as if Stan weren't there. "Since I received my summons, things have now changed at my start-up software company, and I'm the only one there who can ..."

Uh-uh, too late for a sob story. It was the end of the day and everyone was tired. Besides, these two were it for the panel. No one wanted to wait for another group to be called.

"Let's talk about this, Mr. Seecham," Stan pushed in before the judge could reply. "Court usually ends around five o'clock, and this case is only expected to take about two weeks. Can you manage to work in the evenings just for that long?"

"No way; that's not enough time!" the man replied, as if the mere thought were ludicrous.

"Well, is there a coworker who can fill in for you?"

"*No.* As I said, I'm the only one who knows how to run the place."

"And the staff can't do without you for just a few days? Surely you have a cell phone. You could check in during breaks."

Seecham's face compressed. "I can't run the office from a courtroom. We're right in the middle of some very important projects, and I *have* to be there all day."

"Could you possibly—"

"Mr. Seecham," Judge Chanson cut in, her tone betraying impatience. She leaned forward, puffing herself out over her cherry wood desk as if to intimidate Mr. Irreplaceable with her very size. "I know this is a difficult time for you. But jury duty is what it says—a duty that should be fulfilled if at all possible."

"I understand that, but for me it *isn't* possible. Not at this time." Greg Seecham began ticking off manicured fingers like a scolding young parent. "First of all, we've run into problems with the software program we were supposed to launch last week. Every day we take to fix those problems, we lose an estimated $267,000. Second, another program . . ."

Stan Breckshire hung on to the podium, right arm throbbing, as Greg Seecham fired every shot from his company's heavy artillery. The man started quoting numbers right and left—amounts of dollars his company would lose on this project and that one. All with multiple zeros. And of course they weren't just *his* dollars; they were the *investors'* dollars, blather, blather. His boy or not, Stan wanted to wrap his hands around the man's starch-collared neck and choke him silly.

"All right, Mr. Seecham," the judge intoned, pulling off her glasses, "we get the picture." She sat back in her large black leather chair with a sigh. "Mr. Clyde, anything you want to add here?"

"Well, Your Honor," T. C. said without rising, his baritone voice oozing empathy, "I think we should let Mr. Seecham go. Clearly, he has a work hardship issue that simply can't be overcome."

Well, thought Stan, there was his answer. T. C. hadn't a clue who Chelsea Adams was.

"I'm not so convinced of that." The judge fingered the chain on her glasses, eyeing Greg Seecham. "A company of this apparent size is certainly maintained by more than one person. I think—"

"I don't even see why this defendant *needs* a trial," Seecham growled suddenly, casting a purposeful glance at the jurors down his row. "He's obviously guilty."

"Your Honor!" T. C. protested, half-rising from his seat. He shook his gray, craggy head at the judge as if to say, "What more do you need?"

Judge Chanson narrowed hard eyes at Seecham. Her wide jaw set and her chest swelled with air. Stan cringed. Seecham's gig was obvious enough, but Stan knew the judge couldn't give him a chance for further prejudicial statements in the presence of the jury. Even if the other members were giving him looks of pure derision. Seecham stared back at the judge with a spit in the Constitution's eye. Stan could have punched the guy. He hoped Greg Seecham's software company bit the dust. And gagged on it.

Judge Chanson arched back in her chair, still staring daggers. "You are excused, Mr. Seecham." Her words were clipped. Seecham darted from his seat, slithered past the knees of Chelsea Adams, and made for the door. Judge Chanson lodged her glasses on her nose just so and busied herself with papers, her eyes flicking up to aim one last knife at Mr. Yuppie's fast departing back.

The courtroom door closed. The judge took a cleansing breath. "All right," she announced tiredly, then checked her list. "Chelsea Adams."

Stan Breckshire's heart fell to his toes. Greg Seecham's trail still slimed the courtroom floor, and now he needed to convince Judge Chanson to excuse the last juror for cause.

No problem, Stan rallied himself. He'd produce enough cause, all right.

"Good afternoon, Ms. Adams." Stan bobbed his head, lips pulling back for a brief moment. The faces of his peers back in Monterey County flashed like neon before him. He could just imagine their head-shaking upon hearing he'd let this babe on his jury. Could just hear his nemesis Harry Kent blabbing it up, feigned sympathy on his face and a jingle in his step. And Stan wouldn't be around to defend himself.

Well, no matter, because he wasn't about to let that happen. No way, no how. Whatever it took, Stan Breckshire was going to get the religious lunatic named Chelsea Adams out of his jury box.

TWO

Chelsea sat straight-backed in the padded jury chair, keenly aware of her surroundings. Every color, every scent, seemed to flood her senses. She at least was glad they were in a different courtroom, and even on a different floor, from last year. That one would have held far too many memories. This courtroom, 2H, was on the second floor, while the Trent Park case had taken place on the fourth.

Darren Welk ... second-degree murder.

The judge's voice still whirled in Chelsea's head. A case not even from her county, and of all people *she* was sitting in the jury box.

"Good afternoon, Ms. Adams." The attorney standing before her looked to be in his mid-thirties, slight in build and short. His nose was large and hooked, his eyes small and dark. Chelsea braced herself as she watched him move with quick, nervous motions. She was sure he'd recognized her name. It was in the hunch of his shoulders, the unnecessary shuffle of his papers. Wariness crept through her.

"Good afternoon," she replied. She kept her voice level, casting a glance at the judge. The woman was studying her a little too intently.

"My name is Stan Breckshire." The prosecuting attorney bobbed his head again. "As you heard some minutes ago, I'm from Monterey

County. This case has been moved here to the San Mateo County courts in what we call a change of venue. Let me first ask you, do you know anyone involved in this case?"

"I don't think so."

"Recognize anyone in the courtroom?"

Chelsea allowed her gaze to drift once more to the faces she'd noticed upon entering. Behind Stan Breckshire sat two sophisticated-looking defense attorneys, a gray-haired man who was probably in his early sixties and a young Hispanic woman. On the far side of the room two sheriffs, one male and one female, hunched on opposite sides of a battered desk, looking bored. A court reporter sat below the judge's raised platform at the top center of the room, repeating every word into the large, cupped microphone of her machine. Chelsea knew that the large computer monitor before the judge would immediately display her record of the proceedings. Another woman—the courtroom clerk—occupied a second desk near the judge, also with a computer.

"No," Chelsea replied.

"Okay. How about this case? Have you heard about it?"

"Yes, some. I've read about it in the newspaper and have seen some segments on the news." Her voice seemed so loud. Did she sound too forceful? Nervous?

"I see. Have these news stories led you to form an opinion as to the defendant's guilt or innocence?"

"No, not at all." Chelsea realized the words were too quick, springing truthfully from her past experiences. Hardly the words that would see her excused.

The attorney thumbed the corner of his notes. "You say that with some assurance."

Heat prickled Chelsea's scalp. "Yes. I mean, guilt or innocence is something that has to be proved in court. I really couldn't know just from the media."

"So you haven't heard anything in the reports that would prejudice you in any way regarding the guilt or innocence of this defendant?"

Chelsea shook her head. "No."

"Okay." The prosecutor paused, as if pondering his next question. His thumb picked up speed, riffling his papers in earnest. Irritation poked at Chelsea. Why couldn't he just come out with it? Get this foreboding discussion over with so she finally could be excused. She'd waited all day in the jury room, when she could have spent precious time with her husband, Paul, before he left on his business trip to England. And she still wanted to get some errands done before picking up her niece at the airport after her flight from Kansas. Kerra's arrival time was approaching all too soon.

"Ms. Adams," Breckshire said, obviously feigning ignorance, "have you ever been involved in a criminal trial before?"

Chelsea took a deep breath. Here it came. "Yes."

The attorney's face remained impassive. "Would you tell me about it, please?"

"I'll try." Chelsea hesitated, forming her words carefully. "I know it's hard for people to understand. It's hard for *me* to understand. But sometimes I'm able to 'see' things in my mind. The best words for describing this are probably 'seeing a vision.'"

The attorney nodded, urging her on.

"Last summer I had a vision about a murder. I didn't know who had been murdered or when, but I became sure it had happened in Trent Park in Haverlon. After a lot of deliberating, I went to the police. I really didn't want to get involved, but I just felt I *had* to, because the knowledge of what I'd . . . 'seen' was so clear and real to me. The police didn't believe me at first, because they hadn't even heard anyone was missing. It's kind of a long story, but I ended up discovering the body of a young woman in Trent Park. This was the woman I'd seen being murdered in the vision. Months later when the defendant was brought to trial, I was a witness for the prosecution. But only because I found the body, not because of the vision I'd had. That was not considered evidence in the trial and couldn't be mentioned."

Chelsea could feel the eyes of every person in the jury box pressing upon her. And she could almost hear their thoughts, their formulating impressions. Could well imagine the conversations around their dinner tables that evening. *"You won't believe who almost got on our jury today. Remember all the news stories about that woman who . . ."* She swallowed hard.

Stan Breckshire pulled at his tie, his chin scrunched and neck extended. Then reassembled his face into a mask of empathy. "That's quite amazing. Really amazing. And what do you believe is the source of these 'visions,' as you call them?"

Chelsea looked him straight in the eye. "God."

Stan Breckshire's head cocked, eyebrows rising. "God."

"Yes."

"I see." He scratched rapidly under his left ear. "Why would God . . . do this?"

Chelsea managed a tiny smile. "Mr. Breckshire, I don't know. That is, I know in the general sense. If God gives certain knowledge to one of his followers, he surely must have good reason. There's some kind of outcome he wants to see. Probably he's working in answer to someone who's praying out there. But why *me?* I've asked that many times."

The attorney's hands pressed together, a forefinger beating time on each side of his chin. "Okay. Well. Let me just ask you some more questions about this particular case last year." He pulled his fingers abruptly away. "There were other extenuating circumstances regarding your involvement, isn't that true?"

Chelsea's insides grew still. This was the part she'd dreaded all day as she waited hour after hour in the jury room to be called. But it was also the part that would get her out of the courtroom. Paul had made his expectations very clear while packing for his trip that morning. "Do us both a favor," he'd said, "and get yourself excused in a hurry." Chelsea had understood his fears. He was still very protective of her, after all that had happened.

"Yes," she replied, "there were."

The prosecutor leaned his forearms against the podium. "Let's talk about that for a moment."

The "moment" stretched into many. First Stan Breckshire grilled her; then Terrance Clyde grilled her. They went over every aspect of last year's Trent Park case, every thought Chelsea had entertained, every action she had taken. In the beginning the two attorneys were respectful, nodding in understanding, masking their disbelief. Chelsea had learned enough about attorney tactics to know they both were doing everything they could to get her off the jury. No doubt she seemed far too unpredictable to be appealing to either side. Why didn't they just use a challenge and kick her off? As their questioning continued, the attorneys became more forceful, more cunning. Forty-five minutes passed. Every muscle in Chelsea's back grew rigid. Her hands grew clammy and her throat dry. As if the attorneys' attitudes weren't difficult enough, Chelsea could feel the growing animosity of the jury. She was a troublemaker, taking their precious time, making them all sit there while she proselytized about her "religion." The more she was forced to explain about her visions and following God's leading, the more their judgment against her seemed to blanket her shoulders, weigh her down.

Why are you allowing this, God? she prayed silently even as she continued answering carefully, deliberately. *Why should your words fall on such hollow ears?*

Perspiration dampened her upper lip as Terrance Clyde gathered his notes from the podium. Surely her face was flushed. Chelsea stole a look at the clock. Four forty-five. Kerra would be arriving at the airport in an hour. Chelsea would need to allow herself plenty of time to reach the airport, commuter traffic on 101 being so slow. No way did she want to miss being on time. The poor girl had not been able to recover from the tragedy she'd been through, and Chelsea had practically begged her to come for a rest. She needed her Aunt Chelsea to be waiting for her with open arms.

"No more questions, Your Honor," Mr. Clyde announced.

"Okay." The judge turned to the prosecutor. "Mr. Breckshire, anything further?"

"Yes, yes, just a few more questions." Stan Breckshire rose, agitation showing in his step.

Chelsea searched within herself for the last remnants of energy as she watched him hurry to the podium. *God, please give me an honest answer that can get me out of this trial!* She couldn't in good conscience pull a trick like that of the man before her, but surely there was *something* she could say. Grief-weary Kerra desperately needed her attention for the next two weeks.

"So, Ms. Adams"—Stan Breckshire rapped a finger against the podium—"let me ask you an important question. As a result of the events in the trial last year, do you now have a moral conviction about sitting in judgment of anyone?"

Chelsea wished for all the world that she could truthfully say yes. "No, I don't."

"Well, would you find making a decision as to guilt or innocence difficult?"

"Sure, it would be difficult. I couldn't do it lightly."

"Yes, yes, but would you find it *too* difficult to make after your experiences?"

Would she? Maybe so; maybe she'd never be able to make such a decision. The tempting excuse cavorted in Chelsea's mind. Mentally she grasped for it, sought to rationalize such an answer. But she knew it was not the truth. She fought to keep the disappointment from her voice. "It wouldn't be too difficult, no. I would just weigh all the facts, taking all the time necessary to do that. And then I'd make a decision."

The prosecutor eyed her. Chelsea resisted checking the clock again. Time was ticking by.

"Would you feel comfortable finding a defendant guilty?" the attorney pressed. "Would you be able to look him in the eye and say he's guilty?"

"Yes, if I believed so."

A jury member behind her coughed. Another one sighed. She wanted to turn around and apologize, say she didn't like this any more than they did.

Stan Breckshire grasped both sides of the podium. "How do you feel now about the police? Would you lean toward helping them? Or do you think you'd need to give every break to the defendant?"

Chelsea hesitated. She so wanted to give the man the answer he sought. Kerra *needed* her; what was she doing? "I would neither lean toward helping the police nor lean toward the defendant. I'd just have to follow my own conscience."

"Ms. Adams." The prosecutor hunched over the podium like a teacher toward a recalcitrant pupil. "How many of your 'visions' have you had since that trial last year?"

Chelsea blinked. "I'm not sure. Ten, maybe."

"So you have almost one a month, perhaps?"

"Well, I . . . You can't really time them like that, but I guess on average that's about right."

"Any more having to do with crimes?"

"No."

"What did they have to do with?"

Her chest tensed at the memories. "Different things. For the most part they're about people's hurts, perhaps something that happened in their past. God shows me how to pray for these people."

"So again, they show you things that you couldn't possibly know any other way?"

"Yes."

"Okay. And how long has it been since you've had a vision now?"

Sudden understanding of where he was headed washed over Chelsea. She watched Stan Breckshire's fingers drum the podium. Behind him the lead defense attorney watched her without blinking. His assistant sat forward with an elbow on the table and two fingers dug into her cheek.

"It's been about six weeks, I'd say."

"Six weeks." Stan Breckshire's chin jutted out and back. "Then aren't you about due for another one?"

Chelsea suppressed a nervous laugh. "I have no idea. God tends to do things in his own time."

The attorney sniffed. "Still, six weeks certainly fits the pattern, wouldn't you agree?"

"Well, not really. There is no pattern."

His gaze hardened. "Ms. Adams, stick with me for a moment. Let's just say that during the course of this trial, you were to have another vision. And let's further say the vision was about the trial itself, perhaps leading you to think you knew information not given in court. Now. Once you were in deliberation, *would you tell others on the jury about your vision?*"

"No."

He drew back in overt surprise. "Why not?"

"Because any visions I have are between me and God."

"But wait a minute; you've told others about them before, right?" His words were pointed, precise. "You certainly told police about your vision of the murder last year."

"Yes."

"Then why wouldn't you tell this jury if you had a vision that you believed added information that should be used in deciding guilt or innocence in this case?"

Chelsea shook her head. "It's just not something I would do. It's a completely different circumstance to tell the police about a murder in the first place than to say something when I'm on a jury. A jury has to decide on evidence."

"Well, if it comes from God, isn't that evidence enough?"

"It's not evidence as provided in court. The evidence that a judge instructs a jury to rely upon."

Stan Breckshire leveled beady eyes at her. "So you would not tell anyone."

"No. I would not."

He raised his hands as if in deep quandary. "Then why would God send you a vision about the trial at all, if there's nothing you could do with it?"

Chelsea stared at him, momentarily befuddled. "Who said he would?"

"Who said he wouldn't?" the attorney shot back. "You yourself indicated that you can't control these visions."

"I . . . That's true."

"So who's to say your 'God' wouldn't send you one about this case? You certainly claimed he sent you one about last year's trial."

Chelsea flinched at his sarcasm. "I don't claim to know what God will or will not do, sir," she said quietly.

"But what if you *did* have what you call a 'vision' about this case?" His voice grew louder. "Would what you 'saw' affect your decision in any way?"

How to answer such a question? Chelsea breathed a prayer for the right words. "As I said, the way I understand it, the jury hears evidence in a trial, and they must listen to the judge's instructions as to how to weigh that evidence as they deliberate. I would follow those instructions."

"But"—the attorney pressed his forefinger against the podium—"what *if* God told you to do something different from what the judge told you? Who would you obey?"

There was the clincher. Everyone in the courtroom knew it. Jury members on the front row openly leaned forward to ogle Chelsea, awaiting her answer. She could feel the sets of eyes behind her, watching. The whole room seemed to hang on her reply.

Kerra's desperate needs pulled at Chelsea's heart. Wasn't this question God's means of allowing her to be with her niece? And of giving her a way to get herself excused, as Paul wanted? For how could she not answer that she would obey God above all else? Wasn't that the truth?

And yet for some reason Chelsea sensed this was not what she should say.

God, help! What do you want of me?

She opened her mouth and words flowed of their own accord. "The Bible tells us to obey the government. I can only tell you that if I were on this jury, I would listen to the judge's instructions and follow them as I reviewed the evidence brought out within this courtroom."

The prosecutor's thin lips pressed as he leaned halfway over the podium. "Do you *want* to be on this jury?" he demanded.

Chelsea smiled wearily. "No. Believe me."

"You sure?"

Frustration tightened her throat. "Sir, there are other places I'd rather be right now. If I may suggest, since you don't want me on this jury, can't you just send me home?"

A gleam appeared in his eye. "Do you want to go home?"

"I sure do."

He turned to the judge in sheer desperation.

She spread her hands and shrugged.

"She wants to go home, Your Honor." He sounded almost petulant.

"So do I, Mr. Breckshire." Her tone was dry. "It's after five o'clock."

He sighed. "Fine. We can resume this questioning tomorrow, if you like."

The judge gave him a look. "What I'd *like*, Mr. Breckshire, is to seat this jury. Let's finish with Ms. Adams today, shall we? If she is excused, we'll have to call an entire new panel." She considered Chelsea with a weary expression. "Ms. Adams, you've undergone considerable questioning today, and I'm sure you're tired, as we all are. It's already past time for court to recess, so I'm going to just ask you a few final questions, okay?"

Chelsea nodded, holding her breath. *Please, Lord, let this be it.*

"All right then. As you have gathered, this court's main concern rests upon your ability and willingness to be fair and impartial. I'd like to conclude all the questions by asking you this: If circumstances led to your deliberating in this case, could you consider the evidence entered into this trial—and *only* the evidence entered into this trial? Could you do this *regardless* of what you may believe God told you privately, through a vision or any other means?"

Air escaped Chelsea in a thin stream. She closed her eyes a moment before answering. How ironic that all the hard lessons she'd learned from last year's trial would lead her to this moment. "Yes, I can." Her voice held unmistakable defeat.

Judge Chanson sat back in her leather chair, raising her eyebrows at the two defense attorneys. They bent their heads together, whispering, then pulled apart. "Nothing further from us, Your Honor."

A thought rose in Chelsea's mind. A last grasping-at-straws attempt to be excused. "Your Honor?" she said timidly. "Is there such a thing as family issues getting in the way of someone serving? My niece flies in today to visit for a few weeks. If I'm on a jury all day, what will she do? No one else is at home, and this trip has been planned for a long time."

Judge Chanson inclined her head, thinking. Chelsea felt a swell of hope.

"I understand your concern," the judge said at length. "The problem is, I was just about to deny hardship to Mr. Seecham before you. Now you are asking me to grant you the same thing. At this point in time, we are simply too under the gun to seat this jury. So I'm going to deny your request."

Chelsea dropped her eyes, then nodded miserably.

"Mr. Breckshire?" Judge Chanson said. "Satisfied?" Her tone indicated what she would have him say.

"Just one more question, Your Honor."

She considered him, then waved a tired hand in the air.

He turned back to Chelsea. "Ms. Adams, after all my questioning of you today, how can you be impartial to the prosecution in this case?"

To her surprise, Chelsea's lips curved upward slightly. The poor man seemed so deflated. As if she were really anything to fear. "Your questioning today will not prejudice me one way or the other. I know you're doing your duty." She added quietly, "As I have to do mine."

The prosecutor's head bobbed once. Clearly, there was nothing more he could do. "I thank you for that recognition." He smiled briefly, showing teeth. Chelsea decided she liked his frown better. "That's it," he announced. "Nothing further, Your Honor."

The judge plopped her hands on the armrests of her chair. "Well, Ms. Adams, we thank you for your sincere answers. I'm asking you to stay now as second alternate." She picked up papers before her and glanced at the clock. "Okay, we know it's late. Just a minute longer for the rest of you, and we'll swear you in. And then we'll expect to see you back here tomorrow morning at nine o'clock."

The finality of the words stunned Chelsea. She could hardly grasp what had just happened. What in the world was she going to do with Kerra now? And how was she ever going to tell Paul?

THREE

The baby cried.

Yolanda did not hear the baby's wails with her ears. Her heart heard them and wept, then shared them with her head, where they echoed and reechoed among all the sounds of the little house in which she lived.

La chiquita was hungry. If she was not fed soon, her cries would rise, grow more angry. Like the long-ago cries of Yolanda's own baby when she had no milk to feed her. Those cries had pierced Yolanda's heart, even as these imagined ones pierced it now.

The front door squeaked open. Rogelio was finally home. Yolanda wiped her eyes. Surely her grandson was tired of seeing her cry.

"Hi, Mama Yolanda." He entered the dingy kitchen, his T-shirt stained with dirt, and leaned down to kiss her cheek as she sat at the wooden table. The smell of grass and sweat hung from him, mixing with the scent of *mole* chicken simmering on the stove.

"*Mijo.*" She raised twisted fingers to pat his shoulder, forcing a smile. He looked at her and saw the wetness in her eyes. She knew because he drew back just a little, his own eyes darkening. Yolanda pressed her fingers into his skin, nodding that she was fine. She could feel his guilt, and she loved him too much to add to it. He was already weighted enough from the death of his mother and his responsibilities as man of the house. Life had aged Rogelio beyond his twenty years.

Yolanda's tired gaze took in the face she knew so well—the narrow cheeks and deep-set eyes, the perfect white teeth against skin turned dark from the sun. A black smudge ran along his jaw, and she wiped it automatically, feeling the smoothness of his skin. "You've been working very hard." She spoke to him in Spanish—the only language she knew well. She hadn't needed English in the thirty-seven years she'd worked in the fields. If only she knew it now.

"Same as always," he said with a shrug, squeezing her hand lightly before pulling away. He turned toward the stove and opened the skillet lid, sniffing. "Smells good."

"For you, *mijo*. Your favorite." She placed both hands on the table and pushed herself out of her seat. "I must check the rice."

As she reached the stove, the baby cried again.

She stopped, eyes closing, her hand hanging above the pan.

"What's the matter?"

Her head filled with so many scenes that she couldn't speak. What was the matter, he'd asked. Praise *Dios,* much in her life was good. She thanked God for bringing her and her husband out of Mexico to California years ago and for providing food for her baby, the only one she was to have. She thanked God that her beloved Jorge had died in his sleep last year before the pain from cancer became too great.

But dear Jesus, her Rosa. How much pain could an old woman's heart take? Her beautiful daughter, only thirty-nine, dead last year, just ten months after Jorge's death. Then Yolanda had lost her great-grandchild. Why such punishment for her years of faith?

"Grandmother?"

Yolanda's eyes opened. "It's nothing, just a pain in my back." She lifted the lid on the rice. It was done. Turning off the burner, she shuffled back to the table and dropped into her chair. The newspaper she'd bought at the store lay folded at the far edge of the table, the picture of Señor Darren Welk hidden from view. A sigh puffed from Yolanda's lips as she reached for it, her ample stomach pressing against the table's worn wood.

She did not need to see Rogelio to feel his tensing. She could read her grandson so well, ever since he was a little *niño* bouncing on her knees. She pulled the paper toward her, unfolded it, and held it up, pointing to the man's picture. It had been taken when he was still Mr. Big Man of the Valley. He was pointing out across a wide lettuce field on his ranch, deep creases around his eyes and along each side of his mouth. His square jaw was firmly set, his thinning hair sticking up in an apparent breeze. He had the look of a man in charge. Well, he wasn't in charge anymore.

Rogelio's deep brown eyes moved from the picture to her face. Then his gaze fell to the scarred linoleum floor, his eyebrows pulling together.

"*Mijo*," Yolanda said gently, "please. Read it for me."

Rogelio studied her face, his lips pressing at the corners, a sign she had upset him.

She held out the paper and he took it, rounding his shoulders in reluctance. He was still such a child, her Rogelio. How to explain to him the feeling God had placed inside her to pray for this trial? Every day she prayed—for what, she did not know. For justice? Ay, surely God could do that without her. And what did it matter to her anyway? Still, Yolanda was drawn to the trial.

Rogelio took a deep breath. "It says, 'Jury Selection for Salad King Today.'"

Yolanda fixed her eyes on his face, sucking her gold front tooth.

"'Redwood City,'" he translated into Spanish. "'Darren Welk's trial for second-degree murder begins today with jury selection, which sources close to the case say could take one to two days. The trial itself is expected to take up to two weeks. The panel of those summoned is comprised of 150 people.

"'Neither Deputy District Attorney Stan Breckshire nor Defense Attorney Terrance Clyde would comment on the trial, citing the gag order issued by Judge Carol Chanson.

"'The case was moved to San Mateo County after a Salinas judge declared a change of venue due to the large amount of publicity it has generated in Monterey County. Darren Welk allegedly . . .'" Rogelio lowered the paper. "You know the rest."

Yolanda nodded.

The baby cried. An ache welled in Yolanda's chest and instant tears pricked her eyes.

"Grandmother." Rogelio eased into a chair and leaned forward, his fingers intertwined between his legs. He swallowed and Yolanda could see the tightness in his throat. "You need something new to do. Why don't you learn English? I'll teach you. Or I'll find a class for you and drive you. Or how about visiting Mexico; wouldn't you like that? I could get another job, earn the money to send you. You could see your brothers and sisters, all the family you haven't seen in years . . ."

Dear Jesus, thought Yolanda, how heavy was his guilt. She did not mean to be such a burden.

"*Corazon.*" She smiled sadly. "I am an old woman. I do not care to learn new things; I only do what I know. I love to cook for you and keep this house. I love to see you become more and more of a man every day. And God takes care of me. You do not need to worry about your grandmother."

He twisted his mouth, his gaze dropping. Finally he nodded.

"*Mi madre,*" Yolanda said, pushing lightness into her tone, "look at those hands of yours. Did you leave any soil in the gardens you worked in today? Go clean up, Rogelio, so I can feed you without holding my nose."

Rogelio smiled, obviously relieved to fall into their usual teasing. He pushed back his chair and rose, shaking his head. "*Porque Dios medio una aguelita mandona?*" Why did God give me such a bossy grandmother?

He left the room, his footsteps sounding in the narrow hallway toward the house's one bathroom. In the sudden stillness of the kitchen, Yolanda pushed herself to her feet and turned purposefully to the stove. Soon it would be time to eat. Supper at their little table was Yolanda's favorite time of the day. She turned down the burner beneath the chicken, then busied herself setting the table, humming a Spanish tune under her breath so she would not hear the baby cry.

AFTER SUPPER ROGELIO STOOD in the street, waxing the hood of his old Chevy with hard strokes, his grandmother's *mole* chicken still warm in his belly. The next-door neighbor's children laughed and hooted in their front yard, a scruffy brown dog barking at their heels. Bits and pieces of conversation and music filtered from the various run-down houses lining their narrow street on the east side of Salinas.

"Hi, Rogelio!" the little girl next door called. Rogelio raised his left hand in greeting while his right hand kept buffing, his lips slipping in and out of the expected smile.

His grandmother's mournful face filled his head, and he buffed harder. How was he ever going to convince her that he'd done the right thing?

Maybe when he convinced himself.

The thought ragged at him and he made a face. He *had* done the right thing. How could they have afforded to raise a baby? Rogelio had quit high school to work full-time when his mother's heart condition forced her to bed. Now, one and a half years later, his meager earnings barely covered the bills for him and his grandmother.

Rogelio gathered the rag and stuck it in the tin for more wax, then resumed rubbing, his face a mask of concentration. Sweat trickled down his neck, and he swiped it away with the back of his free hand. The baby would be seven months old now. To Rogelio, seven months was plenty of time for his grandmother to adjust. But she hadn't. Every day she mourned. Sure, she tried to hide it, but Rogelio knew his grandmother as well as he knew every inch of this car he'd worked so hard to buy. In the past half year it seemed she had resigned herself to mere existence. She visited with neighbors less. She sighed more, looked out the window more. She'd been like this after his mother's death, even worse. But hope of the baby had brought new life to her lined, worn face. Until he'd trashed that hope.

Rogelio squatted down, spreading wax along the side of his car. For the millionth time he wondered why he'd done it, then wondered what choice he'd had. Five thousand dollars was a lot of money, almost four months' take-home pay. Most of that money was still sitting in the bank. He felt good knowing it was there. It would pay for medicine if his grandmother took sick, would help pay bills.

Trouble was, the money also made him feel terrible. Rogelio tried to stuff the truth down deep inside him, but it kept pushing its way up like the weeds he cut in people's lawns. He'd nearly killed his grandmother with disappointment. In the back of Rogelio's mind screamed the knowledge that somehow they would have gotten by. Somehow he'd have found a way to pay for the baby too, even if it meant getting a second job. But a baby had seemed so much to handle, and the money had looked so good. And he'd had little time to make the decision. At least that's what Kristin claimed. Now he wondered if that was really the case. She'd been so anxious, a strange light gleaming in her eyes, as if she had far more at stake than he.

Rogelio's hand banged against his car bumper, and he dropped the rag onto the dirty street. He snatched it up, muttering under his breath, and shook it fiercely. Then examined it, picking off tiny bits of debris. He flicked them off, his muscles tense, then resumed waxing harder than ever. Only his grip on the bumper kept him on balance.

He'd rarely seen Kristin in the last six months. Thoughts of her made his heart want to crack in two. Couldn't figure out whether he loved her as always or hated her for convincing him to go for the money. He'd driven past her house a thousand times, his foot wavering between gas pedal and brake. Gas pedal always won. He didn't know what to say to her, and somehow the thought of facing her made him ashamed. As if *she* didn't have as much or more to be ashamed of.

No, she had less. Her mom hadn't wanted a thing to do with the baby. His grandmother had.

For the next ten minutes Rogelio rubbed and rubbed, until his arm was sore and his face felt flushed. He watched the wax smear, then buff out, wishing he could do the same with all his problems. Wipe at 'em and watch 'em disappear. Moving on his haunches along the side of the beige Chevy, he told himself his grandmother would get over it. She'd forget the baby and so would he. Maybe in another seven months, maybe in a year, maybe, maybe, maybe—

Rogelio flung the rag to the ground. He sat down hard on the street, elbows hitting his bent knees, fists at his temples. Laughter drifted from the house two doors down, and the sound dragged anger up his throat. Life was going on around him, people laughing, people moving on. And he was *stuck*. He might as well admit it. Stuck watching his grandmother mourn because of what he'd done. Stuck trying to deny the regret that ate at his insides like bugs on a leaf. For seven long months he'd been stuck.

Suddenly he'd had enough. He could not keep living like this. He'd survived the death of his mother, hadn't he? Found a way to take care of his grandmother. Then, couldn't he take care of this too? Yes, he told himself, he could. He *would*. He'd make his grandmother happy once again and rid himself of the terrible weight he carried around inside. That was a promise, and Rogelio Sanchez did not go back on his word.

Somehow, some way, he was going to get that baby back.

FOUR

Kerra hugged the edge of the sofa, feet tucked beneath her. From an armchair, Chelsea watched her gingerly lift a mug of steaming tea and blow on it. The girl looked worn, fragile, despite her smooth tan skin and shining blond hair. Kerra had not taken well to news of the trial. Who could blame her? Regret weighted Chelsea's shoulders like a damp wool blanket. Why hadn't she managed to get off that jury?

"So." Kerra set her mug down on a cut-glass coaster. "You haven't told me how the boys are. Must be a lot quieter without them."

Chelsea found a smile. "I'll say. I'm used to constant ruckus. This is quite different for me."

"Where's the church camp?"

"Down in the Santa Cruz mountains. They should have a great time. And they won't be back for another two and a half weeks." Chelsea eyed her niece ruefully. "Which is why I thought it would be such a perfect time for you to visit."

Kerra drew circles on the sofa arm with a finger. "It's okay, Aunt Chelsea. Really. We'll think of something." Her eyes roved the floor. "Maybe . . . maybe I'll go with you."

"Go with me?" Chelsea raised her eyebrows. "That's the last thing I would have thought of."

Kerra shrugged. "Well, I'll sleep on it. I don't know what else—"

The phone rang.

"Oh." Chelsea's back tensed as she glanced at her watch. It was almost eleven. "That's probably Paul." She pushed out of her armchair, mentally preparing herself for the conversation, and forced her legs toward the kitchen.

Paul had never traveled overseas on business before, and he and Chelsea did not relish being apart for so long. If Kerra hadn't been scheduled to visit, Chelsea would have jumped at the chance to go. In hindsight, leaving the country certainly would have kept her from jury duty. Their family did not need any more publicity; last year's events had inundated them with it. Paul loved Chelsea fiercely, but he wasn't a Christian and didn't understand the spiritual gift of visions that God had chosen to give her.

Chelsea took a deep breath and picked up the cordless phone. "Hello?"

"Hi, babe." Paul's weary voice sounded so close, it was hard to believe he was thousands of miles away.

"Hi. Was your flight okay?" Chelsea walked into the library and shut the door.

"Everything was fine. Now I'm ready for bed, but the day's beginning here. I'll try to sleep for a few hours."

"Good." Chelsea perched on the edge of a leather chair, vainly searching for something more to say.

"You there?"

"Yes. Sorry."

"Did Kerra arrive? How does she look?"

"Pretty worn." Again she flailed for words.

"What's the matter?" Paul asked. "You don't sound very talkative."

Chelsea's eyes closed. This was not going to be easy. "I have something to tell you." Her fingers tightened on the phone. "They put me on the jury."

The silence was deafening. Chelsea pictured her handsome blond husband sitting on the edge of a hotel bed, a sick expression on his face.

"They *what!* Why didn't you get off?" His tone mixed accusation and fear.

Steeling herself, Chelsea told him. Including the worst part—that it was the murder case they'd heard about on the news.

"I can't believe this," he breathed. "Why didn't you do what I told you?"

"Paul, I couldn't."

"Of course you could! All you had to do was tell them about the Trent Park case."

"Believe me, I told them everything." Chelsea's tone held an edge. "For an *hour* I told them. It didn't do any good."

Paul puffed out air. "Then you should have found another reason. All you needed to do was say you couldn't be impartial."

Frustration rose within Chelsea. "Why would I say that? It's not true."

"Doesn't matter whether it's true or not; the point was to get yourself excused."

"What do you want me to do, Paul, *lie?*" Her voice was rising. "You know I can't do that."

"Of course not, Chelsea. But how can you possibly be a normal person on a jury after last year?"

The words pierced. Paul was right—her being on this jury made no sense. Surely God had a reason for it, but that's the last thing Paul would want to hear. "I don't know." Tears bit Chelsea's eyes. "I even asked them to send me home. And still . . ."

Silence.

"Oh, Chelsea, I'm sorry," Paul said finally, his voice flat, tired. "I'm just scared, that's all. I don't want you to go through anything as awful as you did last year. And now I'm not even there to keep an eye on you."

"I know, I know. I'm sorry."

Paul sighed. "Look, I need to go. Do one thing for us, okay? Keep a low profile. No crazy God stuff. Just do your duty like everyone else. I'll check in with you tomorrow night. And remember how much I love you."

"I love you, too."

At the sound of the dial tone, Chelsea dropped her head into her hands and prayed. *God, why have you placed me on this jury?*

Suddenly something clunked into place inside her, like machinery locking into gear. She knew the sensation well—the sign of an oncoming vision of particular evil. Most of the time Chelsea felt no physical symptoms when a vision came. But once in a while, as with the Trent Park case last year . . .

Chelsea pressed her head back against the chair and stared straight ahead, muscles tensing. A piece of knowledge, implacable, unquestionable, shot through her mind: this vision had to do with the trial.

No, she screamed silently, *don't tell me anything, God! I don't want to know; I can't know!*

The edges of her sight began to blur like water at the stir of a finger. On the right, the curtained window shimmered; on the left, the bookcase. The wavering expanded, moved into the center, shimmering over the edge of the bookcase, a painting on the wall, until everything disappeared.

Darkness.

Silence.

Then sound filtered into the darkness and the shimmering retreated. Undulating back, wider, a new picture filling the center of her sight. A man seated in a leather chair, staring into the distance, cigarette smoke drifting from his nostrils. His hair was shiny black, like a crow's wings, his eyes dark, narrowed. He brought a cigarette to his hard mouth, a raised scar jagging between his thumb and index finger. He inhaled deeply, held the smoke. Chelsea could almost feel it burning her own lungs. One thick eyebrow raised slightly and satisfaction flicked across his face. Chelsea's stomach knotted. His thought was hurtful, evil. Dread coursed through her veins.

Quickly the picture melted, leaving darkness once more. Bits of color shimmered until the painting reappeared, the undulation flowing wider, over the bookcase, the window.

Chelsea's mouth hung open as she dragged in air. Tears stung her eyes. Her imagination ran wild with fears of what the vision could mean. For the moment she couldn't even pray. She could only silently plead, *No, no, not again. I can't live through this again....*

PART 2 | DECEIT

The heart is deceitful above all things
and beyond cure.
Who can understand it?

Jeremiah 17:9

TUESDAY, AUGUST 6

FIVE

Sitting at the kitchen table, Chelsea sipped her pungent coffee and stole glances at Kerra's face. Her niece stood at the sliding glass doors of the kitchen, gazing out into the backyard, which was abundant with flowers and an expanse of green lawn. Kerra seemed to chew her bite of bagel forever before swallowing, as if the very act of eating taxed her.

"You have such a beautiful yard," she said, sighing. "All so pretty and green."

"Glad you like it." Chelsea paused. "Sure you don't want to just stay here today?"

Kerra turned to consider her plate. "Do you really not want me to go; is that why you keep asking?"

The man's face from the vision flashed into Chelsea's head. Carefully she set down her mug with both hands. "Kerra, as you know, I've been involved in a murder trial before, and they're no fun. After all, they're about—"

"Death?" Kerra raised her light blue eyes with a hint of defiance that could not cover her pain.

Chelsea fingered the handle of her mug. "It may be too much for you, Kerra. I just want you to be sure."

"What'll be 'too much' for me, Aunt Chelsea, is sitting here by myself all day with nothing to do but *think*."

Her accusing tone stung. Chelsea's gaze fell to the table. Another sigh escaped Kerra, and she flopped herself back in her chair.

"I'm sorry. Really. I thought I got all this out of my system last night."

"No, *I'm* sorry." Chelsea's voice was soft. "Believe me, if I could have done anything . . ."

"I know, I know. You would have." Kerra's eyes closed, as if her continued harshness surprised her. When they reopened, she forced a tiny smile. "Look. I want to go, okay? I can at least be near you. We can be together during breaks and at lunch. And maybe we can leave right from there at the end of the day and go into San Francisco. Besides, it really will give me something else to think about. You don't know how crazy my head gets when all I can do is remember and feel sorry and . . . think."

Chelsea laid a hand on her niece's arm. "No, I don't know, completely. But I do know what thoughts can do. I had a hard time last year with all that happened, and my own head wanted to drive me crazy."

Silence. Chelsea sensed that Kerra was trying her best to equate Chelsea's experiences with her own loss—and failing. Her niece was right, of course. Chelsea's nightmare had not been permanent, while Kerra's was.

"Well." Chelsea withdrew her hand. "We'd better get going. Court's at nine o'clock." She stood to clear her dishes. "And Kerra?" She waited until she held her niece's gaze. "I am glad you're going with me. Very glad. You'll bring a ray of sunshine into that room, as far as I'm concerned."

Kerra made a face as she picked up the last of her bagel. "Yeah, right. Some sunshine."

Twenty minutes later they were approaching the courthouse. The entrance to 400 County Center in Redwood City sported numerous security guards and a metal detector. Chelsea and Kerra placed their purses in plastic bins, then stepped through the scanner. They rode up the escalator to the second floor and found a seat on one of the long benches that lined the expansive hall back-to-back. Attorneys with briefcases milled and chattered while the mix of jurors and witnesses sat silently, watching with curious gazes. Chelsea's eyes locked momentarily with a young Japanese man standing near one of the pillars. She remembered him from the jury box the day before. He looked at her almost derisively, then turned his eyes away.

ENERGY ZIPPED AND CRACKLED from Stan Breckshire's head to his toes. He perched in his chair behind the prosecution table, one heel tapping as he waited for the judge to enter. To his left at the defense table sat T. C., Mr. Dapper Dan himself, in a dark blue suit and silk tie. The man was so laid back, every movement like a languid river. T. C.'s helpmeet, Erica Salvador, a thirtysomething single woman who'd been his partner for the past seven years, reflected the man's grace, her left elbow resting lightly on the table, two French-manicured fingernails demurely beneath her chin.

The door leading to the hallway behind the courtroom opened. Down that hallway lay jury deliberation rooms and judges' chambers. Sidney Portensic, the heavyset bailiff spilling over his wooden chair at the far left of the courtroom, lazily pushed himself back from his desk. "All rise," he announced in his gravel voice as Judge Carol Chanson made her entrance. Stan stood and sat back down, the proper puppet. Whoa, the adrenaline rush! Before he knew it, his left heel was busy keeping time with his right. He picked up the notes to his opening argument, leafing through them with deliberate ease, hoping the calm movement would convince his metabolic rate to slow. No such luck. The jury pulled at his eyes, but he focused on the judge as she positioned her computer keyboard just so and generally settled herself like a hen over eggs. Behind him all whispering had stopped. Stan could imagine the reporters' poised pens, the craning necks of the lookie-loos as they waited for the show to begin.

Anticipation prickled. Nothing in this world, he thought, absolutely nothing, sawed his nerves like a murder trial. The judge, the attorneys, the jury, the defendant, the crowd. This courtroom. For the next couple of weeks this would be his cosmos, the mini-world of "being in trial." The Dow could fold, gas prices shoot through the roof, countries bomb each other to smithereens, but for the next two weeks Stan Breckshire would hardly notice. Trials had the strangest way of collapsing the world into small, adjoining pieces, like parts in a Lego set. Pieces of evidence, pieces of sidebar arguments and jury responses and wins and losses. They built upon each other to form a tower that to the outside world may look like pick-up sticks but to him loomed like Babel.

And this wasn't just any trial. This was a prosecutor's worst nightmare—a murder without a body. Or it could be a prosecutor's best dream, *if* he won the case. The first thing on Stan's plate was to prove *corpus delicti*—that "the alleged victim met death by a criminal agency." Normally, this wasn't so difficult. But without a body, proving *corpus delicti* could be difficult indeed. He had to convince the jury to a "moral certainty" that Shawna Welk had been murdered. And that the "criminal agency" was none other than her husband, Darren Welk.

Stan itched to get started. Shawna Welk's body may never have been found, but she was calling from her watery grave, pointing to the truth. With all the evidence, he had little doubt in his mind that he'd help the jury hear her cry for justice.

"All right." Judge Chanson swept her gaze over the jury, attorneys, and onlookers before landing momentarily on the defendant. "Good morning, everyone. Let's get some housekeeping out of the way, shall we? First"—she turned to the jurors—"since speaking with you yesterday, I have decided to do something I don't usually do. In most cases, jurors wait outside in the hall like everyone else while court is not in session. But because of the media's interest in this case, and since it's already been through one change of venue, I'm going to be a little more cautious. From now on I've opened up the deliberation room in which you members of the jury will meet each morning and be able to take your breaks. There are two bathrooms in there for your use. During lunch you can go where you please, but of course remember that for the duration of this trial you are under admonishment to speak to no one about the case. When we take our first break, your bailiff will show you the deliberation room and how to access the hallway that leads to it. All right?"

The jurors nodded as one.

"Okay. Now let's turn to our other items, and then we can get down to business."

Stan flopped his papers back onto the table, a forefinger riffling one corner of the stack. His heels picked up speed.

" ... WHAT DARREN WELK did not know," Stan Breckshire declared, "was that in the corner of that little interrogation room and hidden from view, a video camera was running."

Chelsea maintained a passive expression as she sat in the prosecutor's line of fire. Stan Breckshire paced in staccato steps before the jury box, abruptly turning, his arms jerking now left, now right. His dark suit hung a little large on his shoulders, and his red-flecked tie was slightly askew. His forehead collapsed in lines of fitful concentration, his hand raking his coarse dark hair until it stuck out like stiff feathers.

"Understand," the prosecutor continued, "a hidden video camera is common procedure." He pulled up to the rail separating him from the jury box, his right palm bouncing off the wood. "You will see this tape. You will see firsthand how Darren Welk"—he half-turned his body to indicate the defendant—"looks and acts as he tells the detectives what he 'remembers' about that night. How he hit his wife. How she fell in the sand and cut her head. You will see"—Breckshire's face screwed into a cynical expression—"how he happened to remember everything that could be verified by his friends, Lonnie and Todd Broward. And then, amazingly, how his memory stops just about the time these friends leave. How it doesn't resume again until his stepdaughter, Tracey Wilagher, arrives at the beach, panic-stricken because her mother is missing." Stan Breckshire paused to allow his insinuations to sink in. "And you'll hear Darren Welk confess that he buried his wife's bloody blouse."

Chelsea felt her own face pulling at the mental picture of a man burying a bloodied blouse in the middle of the night. Her eyes wandered to Darren Welk, who sat unmoving except for his hands. One large fist knotted into his other palm, then slid away, the fingers opening to cover the other hand, now fisted. Then slid again. Back and forth. Back and forth. Chelsea watched those fingers, feeling their force. Could this man be capable of killing his wife? Chelsea gazed at his face. Darren Welk was fairly handsome in a weary and rugged sort of way, with a wide, square jaw and gray brown hair. His skin seemed to hold a permanent tan, even after almost six months in jail. Chelsea guessed he would be even more brown if he still worked the fields. His face was deeply lined. Something about the man looked implacable, hard.

" . . . you will hear Lonnie Broward's testimony," the prosecutor continued. "You will hear that the last time she saw the deceased, Shawna Welk and the defendant were fighting. . . ."

Chelsea's gaze drifted to Kerra, then to a man sitting in the center of the second row. She froze. *Milt Waking.* That awful reporter from Channel Seven who'd broken the story about her last year, who'd spread her name across television screens. How could she have failed to spot him until now? He was staring at her, watching her every move.

Her heart tripped over itself. She tore her eyes away, forcing herself to keep calm. First the vision last night, now this. *God, I need your strength and guidance!*

In her peripheral vision she saw Milt Waking slip out of his seat and hurry from the courtroom.

"I DON'T CARE *WHAT* you have planned, Ron; you have to make room for me on the noon news!" Milt snapped into his cell phone. "We'll scoop the other stations. Both the other television reporters here are new; they don't know who she is yet."

"Are you sure she's the same woman?" The news director's voice grated in his ear.

"Of course I'm sure! I've been watching her all morning, and then when she got a look at me, you should have seen her face! She recognized me, all right."

"I just can't believe it's her. How on earth would she end up as an alternate on the jury?"

"Who knows? But I certainly aim to find out."

Silence. Then, "I couldn't let you say her name, Milt. That would be going too far."

"I don't need to say her name; it's not even important. Every viewer in the Bay Area will know exactly who I'm talking about. And they'll be as surprised as you. Remember your own line, Ron: 'Curiosity means viewers.' Come on, for heaven's sake; you know I need this!"

Milt had enjoyed a real coup last year with his exclusive on the Trent Park events. But in television you were only as popular as the last minute. His luck had seemed to run out since then, fate placing him again and again in one Bay Area town while some unexpected story broke miles away. Milt's ratings had slipped. He'd even been called in for a "serious word" with Ron.

"Yeah, but, Milt, you can't be wrong. Heads would roll, starting with mine."

"I'm not wrong!" He exhaled loudly. "Put me on the noon news, Ron. And write a head-spinning trailer for the evening edition. I'll know more by then."

Milt snapped off the phone and snatched up his briefcase, which carried his state-of-the-art computer with wireless Internet hookup. Then he paused, working to catch his breath. Only when he'd recovered his cool and collected image did he return to the courtroom.

SIX

"Where's the body?"

Brett Welk swallowed and his dry throat clicked. The sandwich he'd eaten for lunch sat heavily in his stomach. Terrance Clyde, his father's defense attorney, stood before the jury box, hands spread in a shrug of elegant puzzlement. The question seemed to swirl through the courtroom's claustrophobic air, funneling into Brett's ears to storm through his head. His lungs felt thick, clouded.

How would he ever survive this trial?

The stepmother he'd never managed to accept, referred to as a body. His father, sitting woodenly in the defendant's chair. Brett closed his smarting eyes, then self-consciously blinked them open. He glanced left, right. Who was watching him? Which reporter's story would speak tomorrow of the grief-stricken son hearing the sordid details of his father's crime? Brett's face heated at the thought. He flexed his jaw, forced himself to stare at the attorney.

Terrance Clyde glided his hand toward the prosecution table. "You have heard the prosecution's opening remarks. Quite a dramatic, forceful beginning, I must admit. I imagine that the scenes

Mr. Breckshire has painted in your heads are quite vivid. Shocking, even. And of course it is Mr. Breckshire's job to continue painting those scenes in your heads throughout this trial. What *I* will ask is that you be suspicious and cautious of the picture he is presenting. You see, when it comes right down to it, the prosecution has very little proof. Much of his story hinges on a blouse. And a supposed confession of burying it."

The attorney said the word *confession* as if it held not the slightest weight. Brett cringed. *He* knew the weight of the word and it was heavier than lead. His shoulders nearly crushed beneath it.

"Dad, *why?*" he'd whispered that February afternoon as he faced his father in the tiny visiting room of the Salinas County jail. Brett had hulked toward the glass that separated them, his arms as stiff as his heart. He remembered how he'd heard the pulse beating in his head as he pressed the telephone into his ear. His father's explanation about the blouse echoed through his mind like an avalanche through a canyon. His father, a man he'd barely recognized, had sunk into his battered wooden chair on the other side of the glass, a hand over his forehead. A long moment passed before he spoke into his receiver, his words distant and frail.

"I didn't mean to hit her."

So many words went through Brett's head at once. He couldn't speak.

His father's forehead wrinkled, the grooves down the sides of his mouth deepening. He looked exhausted, old. "I was drunk and she got me mad...."

The words cut through Brett like a knife. His muscles turned watery. Words fell from his lips in a guttural fury. "Dad, why did you tell them you buried the blouse? That's just going to give them more ammunition against you!" He threw out his hands in despair, head tilting back as he breathed hard at the ceiling. Shock and anger and guilt raged through him in a confusing, nauseating flood. He opened his mouth and a low moan slipped out, resonating through his stretched vocal cords. Like a wounded puppet's, his head dropped back down.

"It'll be all right, Brett. It'll be all right." His dad leaned toward the glass. "*Listen* to me. They can't keep me in here; that's what Terrance says. They don't have enough evidence. We'll get through this. We *have* to. We're all we've got right now."

Brett's head shook back and forth, back and forth, his breaths coming in ragged puffs. The pain of the last four years welled within him. "You shouldn't have married her in the first place, Dad; I *told* you that. She was selfish and greedy." His lips pulled back as he locked eyes with his father. "And why did you have to drink so much? Why did you have to run around with all your girlfriends in front of Shawna like you were spitting in her face? Now all that's going to come back and haunt you. They'll use it as an excuse for you wanting your wife out of the way! Why didn't you listen to me when I told you not to marry her?"

How could you try to replace my real mother after her death, the mother I loved so much? The unspoken words hung in his throat. Brett glared at his father and watched the man's head draw back, hurt sinking his eyes into his head.

"Brett, don't," his dad rasped. "You have to help me now. I need you."

Brett's anger vaporized. He sucked in a breath, chest heaving. He'd waited all his life to hear those words from his father—always capable, in control. Now here they were, on this day, in this godforsaken room. The irony nearly squeezed his heart shut.

Brett held up a palm against any further words. He couldn't take any more. His father was in trouble, his father needed him, and all he was doing was blubbering about his own pain. Suddenly the walls closed in. Brett raked a hand across his chest, pulling his shirt away from his skin. "This place is awful; we have to get out of here. I'm going to get Terrance, tell him to get you out right now!"

"Brett!" His father pressed a hand to the glass. "Terrance is already doing all he can. I'll be home before you know it."

Before you know it . . .

"Let me say that again." Terrance Clyde's resonant voice boomed through Brett's memories. Brett blinked, forced himself to focus.

"Because it's the most important thing you'll hear during this trial." The attorney leaned on the railing of the jury box, eyeing the jurors with fatherly wisdom. "The 'evidence' the prosecution will present to you cannot surmount the high standard of reasonable doubt."

A reporter on Brett's left cleared her throat as she wrote. Brett stared at her hands for a moment, then let his eyes wander. So many people filled the row in front of him. He'd come in late enough to know that the rows behind him were just as filled. Many of the people he could see were obviously not reporters. Who were these people? Was this their idea of entertainment, watching his family laid bare? Somewhere behind Brett sat Shawna's older sister, Lynn, who'd traveled from her home in Michigan for the trial. The first sight of her had disgusted Brett. So heavily made up. Such lewd clothes and rough manner. She even made Shawna look good. Lynn had come to watch his father "fry for the death of my sister," as she'd put it, eyes narrowed in hatred. Brett could practically feel her vengeance at his back.

"And so you will see, ladies and gentlemen," Terrance Clyde concluded, "that this case is built upon nothing but circumstantial evidence. Evidence that can't possibly add up to the high standard that must be met in order for you to consider a guilty verdict."

With all his heart Brett hoped that was true. His dad couldn't be convicted; he simply *couldn't*. Brett couldn't imagine how his father, who so loved the outdoors, would ever survive years in jail. The last six months had been bad enough. Or how he himself would survive without his father. Fortunately, they had their foreman, Rudy, to take over main duties for the ranch. But nobody could run it like his dad. There was only one Salad King.

Terrance Clyde thanked the jury and sat down. The judge rapped her gavel, recessing court for a fifteen-minute afternoon break. All around Brett people rose, gathering notebooks, purses, murmuring to one another. On the row in front of him, a young figure stood slowly, glancing behind her at the milling bodies. Brett caught a glimpse of a beautiful, high-cheeked face framed by blond hair. The cut of her jaw was both chiseled and dainty, her lips full.

Her eyes caught his and hung there before sliding away. Something about her looked healthy and frail at the same time. Brett watched the hesitation of her movements, felt a lostness wafting from her to him.

From the corner of his eye Brett caught sight of his father being escorted toward a back courtroom door by a bailiff. Thoughts of the young woman fell away as he watched, hoping his father would give him a glance. Just before disappearing through the door, his father looked back and nodded at him. Brett forced a grim smile. He turned toward the courtroom exit, wondering what to do with himself for the next quarter hour.

SEVEN

In the hall, Stan Breckshire broke up his tête-à-tête with Lynn Trudy. Nutty woman. She was constantly cornering him with questions and suggestions. Darren Welk wasn't going to get away with the murder of her sister, no sir. They'd discussed his opening remarks, the various jurors. Stan tried to convince her he *did* know what he was doing. He'd already begun watching the jurors, taking in their reactions, he told her. Who took notes and who didn't? Who seemed more emotional? Lynn agreed that the Japanese college student, Tak Nagakura, was a stoic one. His face never seemed to move. He looked like a spindly spider next to B. B., the overweight, brown-haired bartender, a woman who practically oohed and aahed with every statement. And that English teacher, Hesta Naples. Lynn rolled her eyes. Hesta sat straight-backed, her lips in a prim line, dark hair slicked into a severe bun. Stan told Lynn how he pictured Hesta's house, a game he played in reading jurors. It would be immaculate, with silverware and underwear perfectly stacked. The latter was probably chain mail.

Lynn had emitted a dark laugh till she choked.

Stan neared the courtroom door, jerking his neck. His pinched nerve throbbed. In just a minute court would resume.

"Stan Breckshire?" a voice sounded on his left. "Milt Waking, Channel Seven news." The man held out his hand and Stan shook it. The guy was Mr. Television, all right, down to the thick dark hair and chiseled jaw.

"You know I can't comment about the case," he said.

Waking acted as if he hadn't heard. His gray eyes pierced. "How nervous are you, knowing Chelsea Adams is in the courtroom?"

Stan blinked.

"Surely you know her background."

Stan tilted his head in a "So what?"

"I hear you tried pretty hard to get her off yesterday."

"Really. I don't recall your being present."

Waking shrugged. "I have my sources."

"Then go ask your 'sources' how I feel." Stan darted into the courtroom.

He banged down his briefcase on the table. What a jerk. Not a word about his opening statement. Just, "How do you feel about Chelsea Adams?"

Stan's hands stilled. Before lunch he'd noticed Waking yakking into the camera. Had he mentioned Chelsea Adams? Stan cringed. What would all his colleagues back home think?

So? He tossed files out of his briefcase. He'd known this. Keeping reporters' mouths shut was like telling a skunk not to spray. It didn't matter. In the end winning was all that mattered.

KERRA SLID INTO HER SEAT and glanced around. Reporters, clustered up front, were settling, pulling out their notepads. Spectators sat mostly in groups of twos or threes. One sat alone—the young man she'd noticed when court broke for recess. He was solidly built, with brown hair cut very short. He caught her eye. She smiled briefly, then looked away, wondering. He looked like a young version of the defendant.

She sighed, wishing they'd had a longer break. And she wished that chatty old woman juror, Irene Bracken, hadn't horned in on her lunch with Aunt Chelsea. All the same, given the circumstances, Kerra was glad she'd come today. At least she had something to do. And she had to admit, the case was interesting in a morbid way.

"All rise," the bailiff intoned. The judge swept in.

The prosecution's first witness was a black-haired woman named Lonnie Broward, a close friend of Shawna Welk. Kerra could see that she was nervous. Lonnie and her husband, Todd, had gone out to dinner with the Welks on February fifteenth, the night Shawna disappeared.

"We met at Croft's Restaurant in Moss Landing," Lonnie Broward informed the court. She spoke stiffly, her eyes fixed on the prosecutor.

"Was this dinner something you had planned in advance?" Stan Breckshire asked.

"Yes. The four of us usually got together about once a month."

"How well did you know the Welks?"

"We were their closest friends. In fact, Todd and I were with Darren the night he met Shawna at the restaurant where she used to work—the Villager in Monterey. She was our waitress."

"I see." Breckshire jerked his right shoulder. "So you were actually friends with Darren Welk *first*."

"Yes."

He nodded as if the answer held great import. "I'd like you to re-create for us that Friday evening of February fifteenth. Let's start with you and the Welks at dinner. How did the evening go?"

Lonnie Broward took a deep breath. Kerra could feel the emotion welling from the woman. "Everything was fine," she began, "until Darren caught sight of someone across the restaurant...."

As the prosecutor coaxed details, the defense attorney often interrupting with objections, Lonnie Broward's story slowly unfolded.

DARREN WAS DRUNK. *Laughing in his deep-throated way, fingers wrapped around his third after-dinner drink. Todd had cracked some male-oriented joke. Shawna shook her head at Lonnie. Shawna looked* great as always in a white silk blouse, navy jacket, and matching slacks. Her hair had recently been bleached to a brassier shade of blond. She'd told Lonnie on the phone just that afternoon that she was ready for a celebration. Another successful adoption had been completed, the baby placed in the long-awaiting arms of a childless couple. "That's what I live for," Shawna had said.

Darren's laughter cut short, surprise dulling his face. Shawna saw the look. She scanned the bar across the dimly lit room and her eyes stopped. Lonnie followed her gaze to a long-legged twenty-something in a short skirt and plunging neckline. The woman blinked slowly, almost snidely, at Shawna, then arched her eyebrows and looked away. Shawna's cheek muscles flexed, her eyes hardening. She could turn from one emotion to another faster than anyone Lonnie had ever known.

"Another one of your little bimbos, Darren?" Shawna's words fell like chipped ice.

Darren waved a callused hand. "Oh, don't start, Shawna." He sounded bored. "I've never seen her before."

"Don't give me any of your 'Don't start, Shawna.' I know that look on a woman's face."

"Well, I can't help it if perfect strangers find me outrageously attractive. You did, too, as I remember." He leered at his wife.

Shawna glared pure venom. "And I married you," she hissed. "As I remember."

"Hey, knock it off, you two," Todd cut in.

Shawna sipped her liqueur in silence, hand shaking. Lonnie could hardly blame her. Darren made little secret of his running around. Still, Lonnie didn't want to witness another fight between the Welks; she'd seen enough of those already, especially when Darren was drunk. For a solidly built man, he sure couldn't seem to hold his liquor.

Animosity swirled between the Welks while they all finished their drinks. Darren ordered another. Lonnie just wanted to go home.

As they left the restaurant, Darren suggested they stop by the beach. Lonnie hesitated. "Why not?" Todd responded heartily, trying to break the tension. "This night's too great to waste. Ever seen it this warm in February?"

"I've got heels on," Lonnie protested.

"So take 'em off," Darren said, fishing in his pocket for his car keys. "We'll meet you at Breaker Beach. Nobody'll be there. We'll build a fire." He fumbled his car door open with the air of a man in charge. Darren Welk said they were going to the beach, so it must be so.

"What's the point?" Lonnie pressed. "You and Shawna haven't spoken a word to each other in the last twenty minutes."

"Well, tha's better than screamin' at each other, isn't it?" Darren placed a hand on Lonnie's back and pushed. "Get in your car. We'll meet you there."

Shawna rolled her eyes in weary submission. "I'm driving, Darren," Lonnie heard her say as the Browards headed for their car.

"No, you're not," Darren shot back. Before getting into his car, he ambled over to a stand of free local newspapers near the restaurant door and took out a few.

"She's trapped," Lonnie told Todd as they followed the Welks' car up Highway 1. "She's got no money; no way can she divorce him. With the prenuptial agreement, she wouldn't get a penny."

"Trapped, nothing; she's got a great life. Look at the house she lives in. Where'd she and Tracey live when she was just a waitress? And where would she have gotten the money to open her adoption agency?"

Lonnie folded her arms. "If they start one of their out-and-out fights, we're leaving, you hear?"

"Fine. But you know them—they could be cooing like lovebirds by the time we get there."

They passed the turnoffs to various beaches. About three miles past Zmudowski State Beach, the Welks' car turned left onto a narrow road. The Browards followed. The road undulated through strawberry and artichoke fields spread under the canopy of night. The heady, wild scent of eucalyptus trees filtered through Lonnie's barely open window; she could see their white bark peeling in smooth rivulets down their large trunks. After about a mile the road turned into a dirt lane bordered by more trees. The Welks' car rolled to where the road ended at sand. Todd Broward pulled in behind and parked. The narrow beach was on their left. Large black boulders framed the beach's near side, starting at the end of the lane and stretching into the surf. The far side of the beach ended in a rocky cliff. Darren lumbered into the trees near the road and picked up loose firewood. Todd would start the fire with his cigarette lighter.

The smell of salt water hung in the air, fresh and clean. The sand near the water looked undisturbed and perfect, apparently blown smooth by wind earlier in the day. Now the air was calm. Lonnie held Todd's hand as they navigated the sand, the surge-hiss of the ocean captivating. Lonnie was beginning to feel glad they'd come.

The mood soon shattered. Shawna was clearly in no mood to play the cooing lovebird. As the two couples sat on logs in front of a crackling fire, Darren downing four beers pulled from a six-pack in the trunk of his car, all she could do was peck at him. The drunker he got, the more he started to peck back. Before long they were pacing in the sand, waving their arms and yelling at each other. Well, Shawna paced; Darren lurched. His anger turned black, vicious. Lonnie grew frightened.

"Come on, Shawna, we're leaving." Lonnie plucked at her friend's sleeve. "We'll take you home."

Shawna wrenched away, eyes fixed on Darren, her mouth in a thin line. "I'm staying right here. We're going to have this out, once and for all."

"Tha's right, she's not goin' anywhere," Darren drawled, flames from the fire playing across his reddened cheeks. He hulked against the inky sky, flexing his fingers.

Lonnie caught her breath. She'd never known Darren to hit Shawna before, but she felt something new in the air. Something pulsing, like the tide against the beach. "Come on, Shawna," she pleaded. "Go with us."

It was no use. Todd pulled Lonnie away, saying the Welks were both adults. He never imagined Darren would hurt Shawna. They'd have their fight; then Shawna would drive Darren home. . . .

LONNIE BROWARD SWALLOWED and closed her eyes. The courtroom fell silent. Despite all the interruptions from the defense, Kerra had found Lonnie's testimony painfully riveting. She could practically reach out and touch the woman's guilt over surviving that night while her friend had died. Kerra rubbed her arms, suddenly chilled. She understood Lonnie's suffering all too well.

"Mrs. Broward?" Stan Breckshire prodded. "You were telling us the last thing you saw?"

"Yes." Lonnie took a deep breath. "As I slid into our car, I heard Shawna screaming and Darren screaming back. I couldn't understand their words. And then we started to drive away. I looked back and saw Darren lumbering toward her. I could just barely make them out in the firelight. Then they were out of sight." Lonnie's eyes filled with tears, her voice faltering. "That's the last time I saw Shawna Welk."

EIGHT

"'That's the last time I saw Shawna Welk,'" Darren mocked in a singsong voice. His words sloshed bitterness and angst against the separating glass in the dreary room that the Redwood City jail reserved for meetings between prisoner and attorney. The room was vented so they did not need to use telephones. Darren planted himself wide-legged in his chair, square jaw set, eyes hard.

Terrance Clyde sat back in silence, hands clasped over his waist. Darren's foul language and roaring anger intimidated him not in the least. He'd seen it all before. Best to let the client blow off steam.

"Why didn't you tear that woman apart on the stand?" Darren's fingers rent the air in vivid illustration. He pushed out of his chair and paced, muttering under his breath. "One day of court, and I already can't take any more. Have to sit there like a head of lettuce while my 'friends' betray me." He smacked the wall.

"She didn't say you were a killer, Darren." Terrance's voice was mild.

"She might as well have!"

"Lonnie is a prosecution witness; what do you expect? You knew this was coming, Darren; we've talked about it for weeks now. Relax. I did all I could with her testimony."

"Relax?" Darren drew to a halt, snorting. "*You* are telling *me* to relax? I'm the one who's cooped up in this ratty place while my crops rot! Where have you been since February? Sleeping in your own bed. Taking your sweet time preparing this case!"

Terrance cast him a knowing look. "Darren. You know very well I rushed to prepare this case. Most attorneys would have taken far longer."

"Well, you didn't rush enough!"

Terrance refused to take the bait. He eased back his shoulders, sending pops down his tired spine. Air in the tiny room was stale. He was glad he'd left his suit coat in his car.

Darren Welk was proving to be every bit the difficult client Terrance had expected. Terrance had practiced law in Salinas for a long time, and although he hadn't known Darren personally, he had certainly known his reputation—as both the most successful rancher in the area and the most outspoken. As a free man in his own fields, Darren Welk might well have been king. When he barked orders, employees jumped. So did his colleagues. But as a jailed murder suspect, he was told when to eat, when to sleep, when to wake up. His whole world as he had known it, everything he'd taken for granted, had been turned inside out. Anger, despair, and terror would inevitably haunt him in vicious cycles. Terrance had known, as Darren's attorney, that he would become both the man's lifeline and his punching bag.

"Well?" Darren threw himself into his chair. "Aren't you going to say anything?"

The attorney regarded him in silence. This meeting would come to order when he had control.

"Come on, Terrance!"

"Are you through yet?"

"Yes, I'm through," Darren spat. He pressed back in his seat with crossed arms, waiting in fury.

"All right. I'll tell you what I've already told you. And you're not going to like it any more than you did the first time. Tomorrow's going to be worse. Tracey is most likely to be a very sympathetic witness—"

"That little twit," Darren snarled.

Terrance pressed his teeth together and waited.

"Yeah, yeah, okay, go on." Darren swiped a hand through the air.

"She lost her mother, Darren." The attorney spoke as if addressing a slow child. "I can't very well 'tear her apart' visibly, as you would have me do. It'll only make the jury dislike us. However, I will poke holes in her testimony. And I'll milk the money issue all I can upon cross-examination. I'm betting Breckshire brings it up. He'll figure it's better for him to do that than for me to do it, so the jury won't think he was trying to hide it."

"The money's all she wants anyway." Darren's eyes remained slits.

Terrance didn't bother to argue. He knew the facts behind the large life insurance policy Shawna had managed to carry, with her daughter as full beneficiary. Darren had insisted that Shawna sign a prenuptial agreement, and she'd readily agreed, with one *quid pro quo*. Apparently the lack of trust had worked both ways. She was willing to leave the marriage without a penny, but if something were to happen to her while she was married to Darren, she wanted her daughter taken care of. Shawna evidently had been afraid that Darren might cast Tracey out on the street. She'd insisted that Darren pay for the policy.

"So what are the 'holes' you're gonna poke?" Darren demanded.

"Our arguments haven't changed, Darren. One, Shawna's not dead. Two, even if she is, someone else killed her."

"Yeah, well, no question she's dead, so who are you gonna come up with that did it? Especially after Lonnie's testimony."

Terrance repressed a wince. Darren had just broken one of the attorney's cardinal rules—not that it was the first time. Terrance did not care to openly speak with Darren Welk about any certainty of a fact they were going to argue against. For all the rhetoric about the open relationship between attorney and client, often the most important things remained unsaid. This delicately danced *pas de deux* began in the very first meeting. An attorney would pose careful questions to his client—where he was at the time of the crime, what he thought happened—while artfully sidestepping the main issue of guilt or innocence. The attorney could not put words in the client's mouth that might be a lie. Yet he had to lead the client to make statements that could support arguments of innocence.

A defense attorney's main goal was not to seek the truth. It was to defend his client.

"Darren," Terrance said, his voice firm, "you hired me to handle your case. Now shut up and let me handle it. I don't have to 'come up with' anyone in particular. All I need to do is raise the issue that there are others who *could* have done it. We've discussed this a dozen times."

Darren opened his mouth in obvious retort, then clamped it shut. He groaned a sigh, dropped his head in one hand. "Terrance," he mumbled, "I don't think I can stand this. I just want to get home to my son."

Terrance focused on the dusty floor, feeling a mixture of sympathy and judgment. No matter what crime a defendant may have committed, ties to remaining loved ones often ran deep.

He pushed back his chair. "Get a good night's sleep, Darren," he said quietly. "You did well in court today. You'll have to pull it off again tomorrow."

Darren's head came up. He stuck a thumbnail against his teeth and gazed unfocused at the wall. "I just want to be with my son."

Terrance regarded him in silence, then left the room.

NINE

Rogelio revved his car down the street, back muscles sagging from the day's work. The sun glinted off the hood of his Chevy, polished like glass the previous night. Rogelio took pride in his car. He was lucky to have it. Just as he was lucky to have a job and a roof over his head. Mama Yolanda had drilled gratitude into Rogelio since he was small. "God has given you many blessings," he could hear her say. "This house, your mom, this country you live in. Be thankful."

A familiar pang shot through Rogelio's heart. He *was* thankful. Even now. But how he wished he could still be thankful for his mom's presence. Her death had left an ache inside him that nothing seemed to fill. Grief had grown to be such a part of him, as familiar and attached as an arm or a leg. Losing Kristin had only added to the pain. But losing Kristin had been his fault. He was the one who'd dumped her because of his own guilt.

In ten minutes Rogelio was on the other side of town, waiting at the stoplight he knew so well. A right turn, two blocks, and he would be at Kristin's house. He wiped a trickle of sweat from his head. Scratched his ear, leaned an arm out the window, trying to tell himself he was okay, in control.

Rogelio prayed she would be home. Then prayed she wouldn't.

As he neared Kristin's house, his eyes landed on a new black convertible Mustang in her driveway. His heart fell. Who owned *that?* Some rich new boyfriend? Rogelio pulled up to the curb and stared at it, wondering if he should just drive away. He'd never said a word to his grandmother; she would never know. But Rogelio would. He'd made a promise to himself. He was not going to back out now.

So what if she has some new dude? he told himself as he slid out of his car. It wasn't like he wanted her back.

He expected Kristin's front door to be open, letting air through the screen to cool the house. But the door was closed. So were the windows. He heard the sound of an air conditioner.

The front door pulled back and Kristin stepped out. Rogelio halted in his tracks, heart shaking.

"Hi," she said. Looking so incredibly Kristin. Her white blond hair was a little shorter, now cut to her shoulders, her light skin smooth and creamy against a blue T-shirt and jean shorts. Her feet were bare. She gave him a tentative smile. "I saw you drive up."

Rogelio nodded, searching for words. Her sudden presence jumbled all meaning from his head. He glanced at the Mustang. "Whose car?"

Kristin hesitated. "Mine."

His eyes bugged. *"Yours?"*

She surveyed him. "Why did you come, Rogelio?"

Hearing his name on her lips sent darts through his chest. "I . . . I wanted to talk to you."

Her light green eyes wouldn't lift from his. "Okay. Want to come inside? It's cooler in there. My mom's not home."

Rogelio nodded. Wordlessly he followed her into the small living room, a blast of air-conditioning surrounding him. "Nice refrigeration." He pointed his chin at the unit in a side window.

"Yeah."

Kristin sat on a yellow-flowered couch. It was new. So was the matching armchair across from it. And the television was larger than Rogelio remembered. A voice deep inside him whispered unwanted suspicions, and he pushed them away. He eased onto the opposite end of the couch.

"How'd you get that car?" he asked, trying to sound as if it didn't matter.

An unreadable expression flitted across her face. "My dad. He's got a new job. And he always said he wanted to buy me a car when I graduated from high school."

"A car, yeah, but that's some ride!"

She shrugged. "Well, he's working at a dealership. He could get it for less money, you know?"

Rogelio looked into her eyes and knew she was lying. Her father was a loser. The man hardly ever talked to either her or her mom. And never paid any child support. "And the air conditioner and furniture?"

Kristin tensed. "Why all the questions, Rogelio? What is it to you?"

What's the baby to you, Rogelio? The words filtered through his memory—the words she'd used to persuade him to sign the paper.

"Nothing, Kristin," he said.

They stared at each other, defensiveness hanging between them. Then she rolled her eyes. "Oh, let's not fight. We haven't seen each other in too long. I'm glad to see you. Really." She looked at him playfully, as if she were trying to tease him out of his suspicions. Funny thing, but it worked.

"I'm glad to see you, too." He stretched his arm across the back of the couch. She reached out and grazed his fingers.

Her expression softened. "I've missed you."

Rogelio could only nod. He placed his fingers over hers.

"Tell me what you've been doing," she said.

Not much to tell. He still worked for the gardening company and sometimes picked up odd jobs on weekends. He couldn't save any money, every penny going toward bills. He and Mama Yolanda still visited the graves of his mother and grandfather every Sunday after Mass. He occasionally hung out with some of his old friends. But mostly he stayed home at night, watching Spanish television stations with his grandmother. He felt sorry for her; she was alone so much. Her few friends were with their own families in the evenings. When he went out, she was left by herself.

"How about you?" He rubbed her fingers.

"Well, I graduated from high school. Wish you'd been there."

Rogelio felt bad. "Me too."

"And I'm just kind of hanging out this summer."

"You're not working?"

She lifted a shoulder. "No. But I—"

"What about insurance for the car?"

"It's paid for." She didn't miss a beat. "For the next two years."

Rogelio absorbed that fact. "So what are your plans?"

"I think I might move. I want to get out of Salinas. There's nothing here for me, you know?"

Rogelio's insides stilled. There were so many things he wanted to say.

Kristin seemed to sense that she'd hurt him. She blinked away her words. "Tell me why you came."

He almost backed down. Saying the words would put his plans into action. He ought to just lie to her the way she was lying to him. He pulled his hand from hers. "I want to get the baby back for my grandmother."

Kristin's face paled. She stared at him as if he'd gone mad.

"You won't have to do anything," he assured her. "Except sign custody of the baby over to me and Mama Yolanda."

"I can't do that." Her eyes were wide. "And you can't, either. We made our decision, Rogelio. The baby belongs to someone else; there's nothing we can do."

"Well, I've changed my mind. And I want her back."

"You *can't*, don't you see?" Her gaze raked the wall. "It's legal; it's done. You can't just go get a baby once it belongs to someone else."

"Not 'it,' Kristin—she. The baby's a girl, not a thing."

Her breathing grew shallow. "I know she's a girl," she said tightly. "I birthed her. What did *you* do?"

Rogelio tilted his head back. "Kristin, we don't have to fight about this. I'm just telling you I'm going to fix what we did. Mama Yolanda cries over Roselita every day."

"You can't, Rogelio." Kristin scrambled to her feet. "An adoption isn't something you can 'fix'!"

"Oh, yeah?" Rogelio pushed himself off the couch. "Isn't that what you did?"

Her mouth tightened. "What's that supposed to mean?"

He let his eyes wander over the couch, the chair and television set, the air conditioner. "Who *really* paid for all this, Kristin? And the car? And insurance?"

Anger made her throat splotchy-red. "I don't have to listen to this. Go home, Rogelio!" She flung her arm toward the door. Rogelio caught her by the wrist.

"I'll go," he said, his voice low. "But first you've got to tell me what you know about the adoption. What really happened."

"I'm not telling you anything." Her eyes filled with tears. "You signed the papers. If you want to blame someone, blame yourself."

"I *do* blame myself, Kristin." His grip tightened. "That's why I'm going to fix it. Now tell me. Who adopted the baby?"

Her mouth fell open. "How could I possibly know that? It wasn't that kind of adoption. I don't know them and they don't know us!"

Rogelio's eyes narrowed. "You don't know."

"No! Now let go of me."

He held on. "Then you're going to help me find out. We'll go to the adoption agency."

"What adoption agency? Shawna Welk is *dead*, remember? There's no agency left." A tear spilled on Kristin's cheek.

"You've got to know something."

"I don't, really." Her voice shook. "Please let this go, Rogelio. You don't know how hard it's been for me. I don't need you bringing it back in my face. I just want to get on with my life."

For a moment Rogelio felt sorry for her; then it melted away. "I can tell how hard it's been. Must be mighty tough driving that car."

She shook her head. "I just got it. I had to wait all this time. *Please,* Rogelio."

"What do you mean, 'wait'?" He pulled at her wrist.

Realization whisked across her face. "Nothing. I just—"

"What do you mean?"

"Nothing!" she cried, yanking away her arm. "You'd better get out of here, or I'm calling the police!"

He turned away, disgust filling his throat. "No, you won't, Kristin. Because if you do, I'll have to tell them how you sold your own baby."

"You sold her, too," she sobbed. Rogelio jerked back to her.

"I got five thousand dollars, Kristin," he breathed. "How much did *you* get? Forty thousand? Fifty?"

"Get out of here, Rogelio!" She pushed his chest. "I don't ever want to see you again!"

"Listen to me." He shoved his face close to hers. "I'm getting our baby back. And you're going to help me. After that you don't ever need to see me—or her—again. You got that? You'll be hearing from me, Kristin."

He spun around and slammed through the door. As he jumped down the porch steps, he heard her rising wail.

WEDNESDAY, AUGUST 7

TEN

Rain pounds the windshield of Dave's car. Kerra senses the motion of driving, feels the familiar fabric of the seat beneath her.

From nowhere a high-sided truck leaps into view, its brake lights reflecting blood red through the rain. The truck swerves left into their lane as its back tire bursts and flaps in the wind. "Dave!" Kerra feels the scream rip her throat as he throws on his brakes, veering his Acura to the right.

Something jolts inside Kerra, and the picture transforms into cruel slow motion. . . .

Her hands rising to her mouth, her hair floating around her face, sticking to her tongue. Dave's head slowly turning, his eyes drifting too late behind him to check for traffic, his head turning back. The squeal of tires against wet pavement, sounding on and on like a stuck record as their car merges onto that record, revolving, revolving, the world spinning, the tree, its bark shiny with rain, disappearing, cycling closer, disappearing, cycling closer. Nausea rising in Kerra's stomach . . .

Then a distant horn blares and weeps, ramming the scene into warp speed. The tree rushes at them. Dave yanks the wheel harder to the right, and the tree jumps left. The smash deafens the world and every-thing in it. It splinters and grinds and tears and shatters. The left front of the car dissolves. A ragged branch explodes through the windshield and crunches Dave's shoulder. His head snaps back; his eyes glaze. The steering wheel crumples toward him, buries itself in his stomach. Dave's jaw sags. Blood, dark and thick, bubbles over his bottom teeth.

Somebody screams. Kerra feels the gush of air through her own mouth.

Dave lifts dazed eyes to her.

The scene freezes, just for a moment. A moment hanging in the air, fuzzed at the edges, like a paused frame on a home video. Kerra's eyes lock onto Dave's, reading their pain, their utter disbelief, their hope-lessness. Shock immobilizes her. She wants to reach for him but can-not. She gazes deeply into his eyes—and she knows. They remain fixed, and she sees life ebbing from them, as a wave would pull back from shore. The wave recedes . . . recedes . . . recedes . . . then is gone. The eyes settle, flatten, like sand once the water has passed. The lids slowly droop shut.

Kerra cries out. She reaches for him, the man who has become her world, who would be her husband. "Dave! Dave!" Her cries sear her throat, the world blurring. She grasps his head, her fingers sinking into his thick dark hair, her arms shaking him, shaking him. She lets go and his head sinks to his chest. She grabs it again, shaking it, sobbing his name, pleading to God to save him, save him, save him. . . .

Kerra's body jerked and her eyes flew open. For a moment her mind scrambled to catch up with itself.

Morning light. The guest room at Aunt Chelsea's.

A dream. It seemed so real.

But then, it *was*.

Kerra breathed raggedly as tears spilled from the corners of her eyes. *When* would she get over Dave's death? When would she be able to move on?

She turned on her side, fingers grasping her pillow. Her gaze fell upon the digital clock. She'd have to pull herself together soon so she could go with Aunt Chelsea to the trial again. No way did she want to stay home, not after the dream. She'd have nothing to do but think.

FORTY MINUTES LATER KERRA was still trying to clear her head as she walked down her aunt's long driveway to retrieve the newspaper from its box. She was curious to see how reports of the trial compared with what she had witnessed. She'd had no time to watch the news the previous evening. She and Aunt Chelsea had gone straight from the courthouse to sightsee in San Francisco.

"Don't tell me what you read," Aunt Chelsea had said as she stepped onto the porch. "I'm not supposed to hear anything about the trial."

Too hard a rule, Kerra thought. She couldn't imagine following it, if she were in Aunt Chelsea's shoes.

She reached the box and pulled out the paper. Opened it to the front page. She read the large headline ... and her breath snagged in her throat.

"Visions" Woman from Trent Park Murder on Welk's Jury

Kerra scurried back into the kitchen. Aunt Chelsea took one look at her face and stilled. "What is it?" Fear flattened her mouth. "No, don't tell me."

"Aunt Chelsea, I have to."

"No, you don't!"

"You're in the paper!" Kerra blurted. "Not your name but all about who you are—how you were involved in the Trent Park case."

Aunt Chelsea's eyes closed. She gripped the counter, breathing hard. Kerra froze, not sure what to do. Not sure what it all would mean.

A long moment passed. Finally resolve crossed Aunt Chelsea's face. "It's okay, Kerra. I knew it would happen. I was hoping it wouldn't, but ..." She brought a hand to her forehead. Straightened. "You'd better not go today. More people will come out of curiosity, and they'll all be watching me. I don't want you involved in it."

Indignation bounced up Kerra's spine. This was just too much. Life wasn't fair—not for her, and now not for Aunt Chelsea. She smacked the paper down on the tile counter. "Oh yes, I am going! I'm going because I need to—both for me *and* you!"

"There's nothing you can do for me, Kerra."

"Well, if nothing else, you'll know I'm out there!" Kerra focused her fury on her aunt, a fist at her hip. "I'm not going to let you be there alone. And I'm not staying here alone."

Aunt Chelsea regarded her wearily. Kerra could practically read her thoughts. All right, so she was spewing out her passion again. Kerra always felt deeply, fully. What's more, she'd never learned how to hide it. And she wouldn't back down once she'd made up her mind.

Air puffed through Aunt Chelsea's lips. "You know what makes this even worse? I can't act like I know, because I'm not supposed to."

Inexplicably Kerra's anger drained away. She rubbed her aunt's arm. "It'll be all right. I'll be there."

"But you just can't. The reporters will be all over you."

"We'll go in separately," Kerra declared. "No one will know I'm with you."

"No, Kerra."

"You can't stop me."

"Yes, I can."

Kerra's face hardened to stone. "I'm going. I won't talk to reporters. But I—am—going."

Her aunt's shoulders sagged. She raised a hand in futility. "I can't believe I'm letting you do this."

ELEVEN

Milt Waking ruled. Yesterday's scoop about Chelsea Adams had practically turned the media upside down. Other stations had heard his noon story and scrambled to come up with their own. Then newspapers picked it up. Some of the print reporters may have recognized Chelsea Adams themselves, but Milt was willing to bet most of them owed their stories to him.

And hadn't a crowd turned out to watch the proceedings this fine day.

Milt greeted his colleagues with the charming smile and slightly raised eyebrow that he'd made famous in his five years at Channel Seven News. As a mass communications major at the University of California, Berkeley, he'd literally practiced that smile in the mirror, lacing it with just enough warmth. Somehow during those practice sessions the slightly raised eyebrow had become part of his expression. Milt thought it lent him a sense of sincerity.

He smoothed his hair, patted down his tie. He hung back as a couple of newspaper reporters and the gal from Channel Five claimed their seats among those reserved for the media. Milt's seat would be carefully chosen. He wanted at least an over-the-shoulder view of certain people, namely Brett Welk and Shawna's flamboyant sister, motorcycle mama Lynn Trudy. Trouble was, they wouldn't be sitting together. Milt hoped they didn't place themselves as far apart as their loyalties would have it.

A moment later Brett Welk entered the courtroom. He was dressed in khaki pants and a red Tommy Hilfiger shirt, coming down the aisle as if attending a funeral. Milt sidled next to a row of seats to let him pass. He caught the young man's eye and nodded. Brett gave him the once-over, then nodded back. Something about the young man's brown eyes captivated Milt. They were deep-set and watchful, dark brows practically jamming together. Brett's shoulders slumped but his chin led him down the aisle. Deeply tanned muscles bulged beneath his shirtsleeves, his arms held away from his sides. Milt watched as Brett slowed at the second row, then slid toward the middle, his large hands clasping empty chairs in front of him. He lowered himself into a center seat, resting his hands on his thighs. His jaw flexed as he stared straight ahead.

One down, one to go. Milt eased toward the back wall to wait for Lynn Trudy. He didn't have to wait long. A small flurry of activity out in the hall aroused his attention, and he leaned around to peek out the door. The sister of the deceased was holding court, four or five reporters pressing around her, scribbling down her vehemence against the defendant.

"Darren Welk had better be convicted for what he did to my sister," she declared, "or everybody in this state's going to have to deal with *me*."

Milt suppressed a satisfied smile. This gal was obviously enjoying the limelight. He caught a peek at flashing green eyes under heavy mascara. When he'd first seen her yesterday, he knew he had to get this lady on camera. Everything about her bristled, right down to her short, blue black spiked hair. Her lips flamed red, as did the long fingernails that stabbed the air as she vented. Over her rolling hills of flesh she wore a tightly fitted blue shell top with equally tight white pants.

Milt wondered if her long fingernails got in the way when she was riding her Harley.

Yesterday he'd cornered her for her "essentials," as he liked to call them. She lived in Flint, Michigan, and worked as a salesperson in a store that catered to motorcycle riders, offering leather gear and all the accoutrements a biker's little heart might desire.

"Ms. Trudy," a reporter jumped in. "What do you think about Chelsea Adams being an alternate on the jury? Are you concerned that her so-called visions from God may interfere with the proceedings?"

"Well, she won't be deliberating as an alternate, right?" She looked to the reporter for confirmation. "But even if she was," she added with defiance, "as far as I'm concerned, she can have all the visions she wants. *God* knows who killed my sister!"

What a quote. Milt whipped out his notebook and wrote it down. *Later, babe,* he thought, *and I'll catch you on camera.* He'd get some exclusive stuff from her then. He didn't doubt for a moment that she'd hesitate to run her mouth some more. Having your name in the paper was one thing; being on TV was something else.

The laconic Brett Welk was another story. Milt wondered what he thought about the morning papers. He strode down the aisle and crossed over to stand directly in front of Brett. "Lynn Trudy's out there talking to everyone about the visions gal on the jury," he declared. "How do *you* feel about this woman?"

Brett frowned at him. *Yes!* thought Milt. He'd caught the guy by surprise. "You haven't seen the papers?" Milt asked.

No response. But Brett's eyes questioned.

Swiftly Milt told him about Chelsea Adams. "I was the first to cover the story last year," he added. "I know all about her."

"She for real?" Brett blurted.

"Apparently so."

Brett's gaze drifted to the empty jury box. Milt moved in for the kill.

"Are you worried she'll see the truth about your stepmother's murder?"

Brett's eyes flew back to Milt, trailing fear. Then his expression fell into a poker-faced mask. "Get out of here," he snarled.

Milt shrugged as he turned on his heel. At least he'd gotten something. The words for his next segment began running through his head. *Brett Welk, son of the defendant, seemed shocked to learn . . .*

Lynn Trudy and her entourage bowled into the courtroom. Milt stepped aside and waited. Lynn propelled herself into the third row, awkwardly scooting past the knees of two elderly spectators and a young blond woman before plopping into a seat. Eschewing the reporters' seats, Milt claimed a chair in the fourth row, where he could keep an eye on both Brett and Lynn. He pulled out his pad and pen as Darren Welk was escorted to his seat beside Terrance Clyde. The jury filed in.

Milt watched Lynn examine each of the jurors as if they were specimens under glass.

His eyes fell on Chelsea Adams. *Well now, Ms. Adams, what kind of day shall we have today?* He wondered if she knew about the news reports. Far more important, would she have a vision about this trial? The Trent Park case had proved that this woman possessed remarkable skills, however incomprehensible they were.

One thing was puzzling. Judge Chanson could have kicked Chelsea Adams out of the courtroom during *voir dire.* Yet for some reason she hadn't. Milt shook his head. If he were a God-fearing man, he'd say it was a miracle Chelsea Adams was sitting in the jury box.

"All rise," the bailiff intoned. Judge Carol Chanson bustled in, her reading glasses resting on her ample chest.

"Good morning," she addressed the jury, a swift smile curving her pale lips. They murmured back a greeting. "Good morning, counsel." She nodded at Stan Breckshire and the defense team. Terrance Clyde's grayed head bowed gracefully while Stan's dipped and jerked like a hyperactive schoolboy's. "Good morning," Erica Salvador murmured.

Judge Chanson busied herself with her computer, positioning the mouse just so. "Okay." She turned to the prosecution table. "Ready with your first witness for the day?"

"Yes, Your Honor." Stan Breckshire sprang to his feet. "The people call Tracey Wilagher."

Milt watched the young woman approach the witness stand with the discomfited awareness that all eyes were upon her. Tracey was short, as apparently her mother had been, and very slender. Her hair was a light brown, layered and with fashionable bangs cut at various lengths. Not too bad-looking. She wore a sleeveless green dress that exposed bony shoulders and a graceful neck. Milt pondered the outfit. Was she trying to make herself appear wispy, vulnerable?

Stan Breckshire massaged his right arm. Pacing before the witness box, he asked questions about the background she and her mother shared. Her mother, formerly Shawna Wilagher, had married Darren Welk four years ago, when Tracey was sixteen. Shawna had been thirty-seven. Tracey had rarely seen her biological father, although they kept in contact. The father she'd known as a child had been the man whom Shawna had married when Tracey was seven. He and Shawna divorced six years later.

"How did you feel about your mother's marriage to Darren Welk?" Breckshire asked.

Tracey raised a knobby shoulder. "It was something she wanted to do. She really loved him." Her expression sickened, as if she couldn't believe such a thing could ever have been true. She lowered her gaze to her fingers, laced and fidgeting.

"Did you get along with Mr. Welk?"

Tracey's eyes wandered toward the defendant, then swung away. "Sometimes."

"What do you mean by 'sometimes'?"

"I basically stayed out of his way. He had his work; I had school. And then I started working after school. So we didn't see each other too much. Plus it was a big house, you know?"

Breckshire nodded. "Where did you work?"

"When Mom opened her adoption agency, she paid me to help answer the phones and do books."

"I see. Were you the only person who worked with your mom in the adoption agency?"

"No. Janet Cline was there. She was Mom's partner. I just helped out where I could."

"Did you like working there?"

"Yes." Tracey managed a smile. "For the same reasons my mom did. We loved seeing couples matched with babies. It made people so happy."

Tracey's words curled at the edges. She blinked rapidly.

Breckshire paused. His next statement was in the *sotto voce* of lawyerly empathy. "Tracey, I need to talk to you about the night your mother was killed."

"Objection," Terrance Clyde's voice boomed. "There is no basis in fact for that statement."

Breckshire swiveled a hawkeyed stare at the defense attorney, then shook his head.

"Sustained." Judge Chanson's face was impassive. "Continue, Mr. Breckshire."

The prosecutor pursed his lips with a look of rabid apology. "Tracey. I need to talk to you about the night your mother . . . disappeared." He emphasized the word as if it were utter nonsense. "Are you ready to do that?"

Tracey seemed to shrivel in her dress. "Yes."

"Okay. How did you first hear that something was amiss?"

"I got a phone call," she said quietly. "About one forty-five in the morning."

Milt Waking's pen scrawled as Tracey Wilagher told her story. . . .

TRACEY WAS SOUND ASLEEP *in her large bedroom. She'd come down with the flu three days before and had finally given up and crawled into bed after twenty-four hours of suffering through fever. She'd hardly been out of her room since then except to eat and go to the bathroom.*

The ringing phone jangled through her head like a distant warning bell. Slowly she opened her eyes. Her room glowed with the bluish tint from the "flying windows" on her computer's screen saver. The jeans and sweater she'd worn two days ago draped over the padded chair in front of her desk. She fumbled an arm to answer the phone.

"Tracey, you've got to help me." Her mother's voice sounded tense. "Darren's drunk and I'm afraid. I need you to come get me."

"What?" The words swirled in Tracey's head.

"We're at Breaker Beach. Darren's drunk and roaring mad. The Browards are gone and I'm scared. I'm afraid he's going to hurt me."

"Hurt you?" Fear chased away the thickness in Tracey's brain. "Where is he right now?"

"He's stumbling around the fire, cursing and breathing his own smoke. I'm up here by the car."

"Well, get out of there. Take the car and come home. We'll worry about him later."

"I can't. Darren has the keys. I tell you, he's roaring mad. I don't dare ask him for them."

Tracey struggled to compute. "But it'll take me twenty-five minutes to get there."

"I know." She breathed hard into the phone. "Darren's drunk enough; I hope he'll pass out soon. If he does, maybe I can get his keys. You come on and get me. Keep your cell phone on. If I can get the keys, I'll call you and let you know."

Tracey ran a warm hand over her face and swallowed. Her throat still hurt. "Okay. I'll move as fast as I can. But I'm still kind of shaky."

"Oh, I'm sorry, I forgot. You're sick!"

"That's okay. I'll come. Just be careful. Call me soon, okay? Once I'm on the way, call me and let me know you're all right."

"I will. I'll just stay up here by the car until you come. Hurry."

Tracey tried to hurry, but her legs and arms shook from fear as well as flu while she dressed. She'd seen her stepfather drunk before and it was not a pretty sight. He turned mean, illogical. Even Brett steered clear of Darren Welk when he drank. As far as Tracey knew, Darren had never yet physically hurt her mother. But there was always a first time.

Dizziness washed over Tracey more than once as she fumbled for her keys and purse. On the stairs she sat down hard, closing her eyes until the woozy feeling passed. Her car was parked out front. She slipped through the front door without seeing Brett. She assumed he was in bed and his car in the garage, but she gave him barely a thought. She was too concerned for her mother.

Tracey knew the location of Breaker Beach. She hoped she could roll in quietly, pick up her mom, and back out in a hurry, never laying eyes on her stepfather.

Turning right out of the long driveway, Tracey headed up Cooper Road and onto Nashua, crossing over Highway 1 where it temporarily turned inland. Nashua turned into Molera Road, which cut a corner and crossed Highway 1 again, nearer to the ocean. Tracey turned north on the highway.

Fifteen minutes passed. Tracey's body felt heavy and dull. Uneasiness settled at the back of her neck. Her mom hadn't called yet. She checked her cell phone, reassuring herself that she had a signal. Another five minutes passed. Still no call. Tracey bit her lip, fighting the urge to call her mom's cell phone. Probably wasn't a good idea. What if her stepfather heard the ringing? What would he think? Tracey drove on, slumped close to the wheel, her labored breathing loud in her ears. The turnoff was about five miles up. She passed no one on the road. By this time it was 2:30 a.m. She turned left onto the winding road that would take her to Breaker Beach and eased her way around its dark curves. Her eyes cruised the night, expecting that her mother had walked out a ways to meet her. But she saw no one. When Darren Welk's car came into view ahead, she immediately stopped, cutting her own car's lights and engine.

Her heart drummed hard, beating pain through her head as she clicked open her door and slipped into the night air. The sliver of a moon did little to light her way as she took a few hesitant steps, gazing toward the beach. Down toward the water a fire flickered, casting light on a form sprawled in the sand. Tracey stared at the still form, heart clutching. It had to be Darren, passed out. Tracey cast her eyes right and left. "Mom?" she whispered into the darkness. "Where are you?"

No response.

Her knees trembled. She swallowed hard, wincing at the pain in her throat. Where could her mother be? The last thing she wanted was to waken Darren Welk. "Mom," she whispered louder, muscles tense. Still no answer.

Tracey's next memories jumbled into a near-mindless sequence. She found herself stumbling around the top of the beach, calling her mother's name louder and louder, the rising flood of fear within her sweeping away all caution. Her chest grew heavy, her knees jellied. Then she was raking open the doors of Darren Welk's car, searching the front seat, the back. On the floor of the front seat she saw her mother's small evening purse. A horrifying, black thought mushroomed in her brain, and she fumbled for the latch to pop open the trunk. Tears scalding her eyes, she stumbled to the back of the car, swaying with relief when she saw the trunk was empty.

Finally she could stand it no more. She made her way back to her car and drove forward as far as she could, stopping at an angle so her headlights washed the length of the beach. The figure of Darren Welk lit up but still did not move. Tracey lurched out of her car, searching the beach up and down, forcing her fogged brain to process. "Mom!" she called. "Mom, please, where are you?"

The sizzle-hiss of waves upon land was the only sound.

Something on the sand caught her eye. Something glistening darkly, not far from the fire's embers. A block of ice fell into Tracey's stomach as she stared. She forced her leaden legs forward. As she neared the glistening dot, she saw others like it. She stopped above them, unwilling to bend down and add undeniable senses to the terrifying shadows ghosting her mind. Slowly she reached out a trembling finger and touched the disfigured surface of the sand. Granules stuck to her skin. She raised her finger, turned it toward the car's headlights. The granules were dark red.

With a cry she flecked them off her finger and shuffled backward, eyes widening as she noticed more and more drops of what looked like blood. She tried to convince herself they belonged to Darren Welk but knew it wasn't true. The man breathed heavily in his drunken stupor, one beefy hand on his chest, the other flung out wide. She saw no injuries on him. Tracey scanned to his right and saw her mother's jacket draped over a nearby log, and her pair of low-heeled shoes. A cell phone lay in the sand. She dragged herself over and picked up the jacket, inspecting every side, air jagging in and out of her mouth. No blood.

Tracey let it drop. Her eyes grazed the sand near the water, windblown smooth except for three places.

The footprints fairly leaped out at her.

Tracey's next memory placed her beside a trail of kicked-up sand leading into the ocean. It ended in a half print of a bare foot, the heel defined in wet sand, the rest smudged away. Surely it was her mother's. Another larger trail headed into the ocean as well, leaving a partial shoe print in the wet sand. A second partial shoe print pointed back out of the water. With her eyes Tracey followed that print to a trail of churned sand leading away from the ocean. It became impossible to follow once it hit sand that had been walked upon many times. Still, its beginning led toward the fire, where Darren Welk slept. The truth hit her like a brick.

Three trails in and out of the ocean, not four. No bare footprint left the water.

"Mom!" Tracey screamed at the dark tide under the black sky. Surely her mom hadn't gone swimming. A large sign near the dirt lane forbade it; the currents were far too dangerous. Even the area of water on the right that was partly sheltered by the curving line of boulders was not protected enough to be safe. And just before Tracey had gotten sick, hadn't she heard that someone had been attacked by a shark not far from there? If her mom had been bleeding . . .

Tracey emitted a sob. In desperation she shuffled toward Darren Welk. Only when she reached his side did she notice that his shoes and the pant legs around his ankles were wet. Fresh fear for her mother made her forget herself. She kicked him with all her might.

"Wake up! Wake up!" She kicked him again. "What have you done to my mother? Where is she?"

Her stepfather coughed and hacked and snorted, then drew himself into a sitting position, incensed. "What're you kickin' me for, you brat? Get outta here."

Tracey screamed accusations, pointing to the blood, sweeping her hands around the empty beach. Darren Welk lurched to his feet and lumbered around, calling, "Shawna! Hey, Shawna!" There was no reply.

"I don't know where she is," he insisted over and over. "When I passed out she was ... she was here." He turned in a full circle, arms lifting.

"Where did the blood come from?" Tracey rasped. Her legs quaked and her chest was molten lead.

Sudden awareness shuttered his face. "She fell."

"She fell? In the sand?"

Fury and fright sucked up Tracey's veins, trailed by denial. Surely her mother was all right. Maybe she called a friend, someone who could come get her more quickly. Maybe she'd called the Browards. Maybe the bare footprint leading into the water belonged to someone else. Tracey had to get home; that's what she had to do. She had to get away from this beach, this man, this place of darkness and blood and—

She could not allow herself to finish the thought. The next thing Tracey knew, she was back in her car, ignoring the bellows of Darren Welk. She'd brought her mother's jacket, shoes, and cell phone with her, flinging them onto the front seat. She turned her car around, then surged forward, tires spinning. At some point along the way home she thought to snatch up her cell phone, flicking on the overhead light to see if the message icon was visible. It wasn't. By the time Tracey jerked up to the front of the Welks' home, she'd convinced herself that she'd find her mother inside. The surety of her coming relief swelled her lungs with anger. How could her mom have done that to her? How could the woman have frightened her so?

Tracey stumbled up the stairs toward the master bedroom, words of relieved accusation coiled and ready to spring from her tongue. But the room was empty. Tracey banged through the door of the guest room, her own bedroom, then to every bathroom, all to no avail. Finally she fell against the wall and wept until she sank to the floor. Brett emerged from his room, clad only in pajama bottoms, demanding to know what was happening. The story hiccupped from Tracey's mouth. Brett's eyes grew wide, his face pasty.

And then Darren Welk appeared, heavy-lidded and swaying, miraculously having managed to drive himself home. Tracey accosted him once more while Darren denied any knowledge of her mother's *fate.* Brett scurried downstairs and returned about ten minutes later, visibly shaken. He towered over Tracey, shoving a finger in her face. "Shut up!" he demanded. "Shut up and I'll help you. But we have to think."

He forcibly pushed his father into the master bedroom. "You're going to bed," Tracey heard him say. "I'll handle this."

Tracey slumped against the wall of the hallway, unable to move, her mind a whirlwind of terrorizing visions. As she waited for Brett to return, her body grew numb. Amazingly, then she grew sleepy. All the emotions, all the expending of energy, had gotten the best of her. A milky stupor puddled in her brain, oozing thickly through her arteries. She wiped her forehead, and her hand came away wet with sweat.

Brett emerged from the master bedroom, breathing hard.

"Is he—"

"I've put him in bed. I'm not sure he'll stay." He surveyed her. "You need to go to bed, too. You look awful."

"I can't." She fought to rouse herself. "I have to find Mom. He's done something to her—"

"He hasn't done anything. I'll figure this out. You sleep awhile."

"We should call the police."

Brett winced. "They couldn't do anything yet anyway. She's barely been gone any time at all. Go to bed. I'll drive back to the beach. Maybe she's shown up by now."

Tracey had no reason to trust his words. There was no love lost between them. Brett had openly resented her and her mom since the day they'd moved in. But at that moment a look of compassion flitted across his face. The look in itself was frightening, for Tracey could only imagine the reasons behind it. But she simply could do no more. She wasn't even sure she could drag herself to bed. She held out a reluctant, heavy arm. Brett pulled her up. She closed the door of her room and fell onto her bed.

When she awoke, the clock read 9:30 a.m. The doors to Brett's room and the master bedroom were closed. She eased open the door to the master bedroom and saw Darren Welk sprawled and snoring. Her mother wasn't with him. Doggedly, unwilling to face the truth, Tracey *looked for her mother in the wing of the house where the adoption agency offices were located, then drove back to Breaker Beach. By the time she arrived home, Brett was up. It was around noon. He said he'd driven to the beach after she went to bed but had found nothing. Nor had there been any phone calls from her mother. That's when she called the police. They referred her to the Monterey County sheriff's department, which had jurisdiction over Breaker Beach....*

MILT WAKING WROTE FURIOUSLY. Breckshire had done a masterful job in extracting Tracey's story, despite the defense's attempts to squelch it. Milt could visualize everything she had said.

Stan Breckshire looked as if he'd been through the wringer. His tie hung askew, his hair sticking out from constantly raking his hands through it. He leaned against the prosecution table, fingers nervously drumming the wood.

"Miss Wilagher." He pushed off from the table, and his thumb began rubbing his fingertips with anticipation. "I'm sorry for the question, but I have to ask it. Is there any chance your mother may have just chosen to disappear? And leave you?"

Tracey shook her head, tears welling in her eyes. "No. *Never.* We were very close. She'd never leave me. And besides that, she had the adoption agency. She would not choose to walk away from that." Tracey's forehead crinkled and her mouth turned to mush. She inhaled a ragged breath. "I miss her very much." The last word turned high-pitched. Tracey covered her face. Milt barely heard the muffled, "I'm sorry."

"That's quite all right; take your time." Breckshire jerked a tissue from a box on the witness stand and waved it before her. "Here."

"Thank you."

He waited until she had gathered herself. "Miss Wilagher, before I let you go, I need to ask you one more thing. I know it's a sensitive subject but it can't be helped. Did your mom leave a will?"

Tracey held the tissue to her nose. "Yes."

"Did she leave anything of value to you?"

"Yes."

"Please tell us what that was."

With trembling chin, Tracey related the gut-wrenching day on which she'd met with Randy Atworth, her mother's attorney, to hear the reading of Shawna Welk's will. Even though Shawna's body had not been found, once Darren Welk had been arrested for her murder and the forensic evidence pointed to her death, Mr. Atworth had deemed it appropriate that the will be read. Tracey had been amazed to learn that her mother carried a two-million-dollar life insurance policy, payable in full to her. At the time that the policy had been instated—four years ago—the will ordered that if the money were paid out while Tracey was still a minor, it would be held in trust until she was eighteen. Tracey had turned twenty a month ago.

"Have you now received that money?"

Tracey shrugged. "No."

"Why is that?"

She looked at her lap. "The insurance company can't issue the money without a death warrant. And without a . . . a body, evidently a death warrant can't be issued for many years."

"Unless one thing happens, is that correct?"

She nodded, her jaw working. "A death warrant can be issued by the judge as soon as the murderer is convicted. I guess"—her voice grew bitter—"my mom's not dead until a court says she's dead." She swallowed hard. "Tell that to my heart."

Breckshire managed to still his entire body while he and the courtroom watched Tracey cry. "Do you care about the money?" he asked quietly.

Another shrug. "I care about it so I can get out of Salinas and try to start a new life."

"Where are you living right now?"

"In a little apartment. I moved out of Darren Welk's house long ago. I . . . I couldn't stand to stay there."

Breckshire nodded. "Where do you get the income to pay for your apartment?"

Tracey sniffed. "When Mom's adoption agency closed, I lost my job. Now I'm working full-time at Halding's Dress Shop, but it's barely enough to live on my own. I did get some money through the sale of the agency's equipment and furniture, and that's helped. But I don't have enough money to leave Salinas. Besides, I felt like I should stay until I saw justice done for my mother."

"Two million dollars is a lot of money. Where will you go?"

"Far away from Salinas, I can tell you that." Tracey looked at Breckshire almost defiantly. "I just want to go someplace where I can try to forget. Someplace so different that there's nothing there to remind me of these past few months." Fresh tears pooled in her eyes.

The prosecutor rubbed the back of his head. "Thank you, Miss Wilagher. I'm sorry I had to ask all these questions." He threw an accusing look toward the defense table, as if it were their fault. Then turned to Judge Chanson. "Your Honor, I'm through."

"All right then." Judge Chanson checked the clock. "Let's take a fifteen-minute break before we begin cross-examination."

Milt slid his pen into his pocket. Two million dollars for a mother. Wow. Quite a recompense. He stood thinking, plans for his television report churning merrily through his head. He'd use Dottie's rendering of Tracey on the stand. Dottie was the better of the two courtroom artists present. He figured she'd caught the girl crying. Milt absentmindedly patted his hair. He could already hear his voice-over. *"The grief-stricken daughter of Shawna Welk broke down on the stand today as . . ."*

Ah yes. This was going to be a good day. And cross-examination hadn't even begun.

TWELVE

"Oh, Chelsea," sang a birdlike voice.

Chelsea turned as the small hand patted her back. Seventy-year-old Irene Bracken beamed a smile that spoke of secrets and anticipation, brown eyes twinkling behind their thick glasses. "It's so *interesting,* isn't it."

Chelsea's eyes flicked across the deliberation room. Becka—known as B. B.—was filling a small paper cup at the water station, barking a deep-throated laugh over some comment Sylvia Caster had made. Sylvia looked to be in her late fifties, a rather hefty woman with short dark hair and no makeup. Latonia, a black woman about Chelsea's age, stood talking to an elderly and stooped Hispanic man named Victor Chavarria. Latonia's perfectly arched eyebrows lifted as she spoke, her red-nailed fingers laced and held at the waist of her navy business suit. None of these jurors was paying any attention to Chelsea and Irene. But Tak had no doubt heard Irene's remark. He sat at the long table looking over his notes, yet something about the tilt of his head told Chelsea he was all judgmental ears. Tak was the juror she'd seen yesterday morning in the hallway. When she'd later introduced herself to him, he'd been cold as ice.

Chelsea looked back to Irene and saw the truth in her eyes. Irene had read the morning paper. How many of the other jurors knew what the media were saying?

"We'd better talk about something else, okay?"

Tak's head remained bent over his notes. He turned a page.

"Oh yes, of course." Irene's hand fluttered. "I know we shouldn't talk about the trial. Well, let me tell you what happened last night. Have you ever seen that television program . . ."

Chelsea only half-listened to Irene's chatter. Break would be over soon, and she wanted to sneak a peek into the lobby, make sure Kerra was all right. She didn't know how to cut Irene short. She stole a look at the round-faced clock on the wall.

Irene stopped in midsentence. "Oh dear, am I keeping you from something?"

"There's just a small matter I wanted to take care of before break is over." She touched Irene's arm. "Would it be all right if you told me the rest of the story later?"

"Of course, of course." Irene's face was pure radiance. "You go on now. Maybe I could join you for lunch again today."

Chelsea hesitated. Kerra would not be happy. Still, Irene was such a sweet woman. How could anyone say no to her? "Sure. Love to have you."

She hurried through the passageway that led to the main hall and opened the door. Cautiously she stuck her head out. She spotted Kerra almost immediately, near one of the long benches in the middle. Kerra was talking to a young man, the one Chelsea had noticed sitting by himself in the courtroom. The one who looked, in both build and facial features, like a young Darren Welk.

A pang of apprehension struck Chelsea. Could this be the defendant's son? She watched them talking for a moment. Kerra's expression was guarded, one hand absently fiddling with the purse slung over her shoulder. The young man stood stiffly, muscular arms dangling with discomfort, as if they wished for a task. Kerra said something and the young man raised his chin in a nod. They exchanged more words.

Chelsea closed the door and leaned against the wall. She shouldn't have let Kerra come. Her niece was so vulnerable. She didn't need to get mixed up with people who most likely were carrying their own emotional baggage.

Reluctantly Chelsea returned to the jury room.

"Well, there you are." Sidney Portensic, the bailiff, who easily weighed three hundred pounds, shook his meaty head at her in mock reprimand. "Thought we were going to have to start court without you."

Chelsea hitched her shoulders. "Oh, sorry."

"That's all right, ma'am, that's all right. Just get yourself in line now; time to hear more e-vi-dence." He rolled out the last word as if it were honey on his tongue. Sidney stood back and counted heads silently, a thick finger poking the air. "All right, all the ducks are in a row. Follow me, ladies and gentlemen." With a good-natured crook of a finger over his shoulder, he led his jury members into the courtroom.

KERRA SHOT BRETT A TIGHT smile as they took their seats in the courtroom. Her heart went out to him. Not that he'd said much, but hearing his name was enough. Brett Welk, the son of a man accused of killing his wife. What kind of nightmare would that be? Kerra wondered where Brett's real mother was. Even if the woman hated her ex-husband, she should be here to support her son. Kerra also wondered if Brett thought his father was guilty.

She watched as the jury filed in. Aunt Chelsea glanced at her with a concerned expression. Kerra gave her an encouraging smile.

The courtroom quickly filled. Milling reporters scurried back to their chairs, pulling out notebooks. The woman with the spiked blue black hair trudged to her seat with a scowl. Down front two artists, a man and a woman, reassembled their drawing pads on their laps. As Kerra had left the courthouse yesterday, she'd seen their drawings of the attorneys, judge, and defendant taped to the walls so television news crews could film them. "I have to admit," she'd told her aunt as they headed up Highway 101 toward San Francisco, "this trial stuff is kind of interesting."

Aunt Chelsea had raised her eyebrows. "Can't wait to hear what your parents say. You come visit me to relax and I take you to a murder trial."

"Actually," Kerra had replied, "I came here to get my mind off things." She'd looked out the window, turning her head to watch a set of black, round buildings sporting the name Oracle glide by. "And this has managed to work. At least for now."

The morning's dream filtered through her thoughts. Today was not proving as easy.

"All rise." The pitted voice of the bailiff yanked Kerra back to the present. She pushed to her feet as the judge plodded in, black-robed and all business. Kerra watched the woman sink into her chair with a small sigh, then tent her stubby fingers. The courtroom rustled as all resumed their seats.

"All right." Judge Chanson raised her eyebrows. "I believe we're ready for cross-examination, Mr. Clyde?"

"Thank you, Your Honor." The defense attorney rose, inclining his head with the courtliness of an aging prince. He glided around the table and stood in front of it, his tall frame erect and fitted into an expensive-looking suit. "Miss Wilagher, I'd just like to ask you a few follow-up questions, based on the information you've already given to my colleague. These are only to clarify, you understand. Are you ready to continue?"

"Yes." Tracey licked her thin lips, regarding him warily.

"Fine. First I want to go over the time with you. Now, as I remember, you said the phone rang about one forty-five a.m. Is that right?"

"Yes."

"And then you say you reached the beach around when?"

Tracey thought a moment. "I'm not sure exactly. Probably about two thirty-five."

"I see." Terrance Clyde considered his shoes. "And yet the drive from the house to Breaker Beach is only about twenty-five minutes."

"Yes, but I had to pull myself out of bed and get dressed. I wasn't moving very fast, even though I tried to hurry."

"Did you go anywhere else first? Make a stop on the way?"

Tracey looked taken aback. "No."

"And when you left the house, you say you did not see Brett Welk or his car?"

"No."

"Was he home?"

"I think so."

"How do you know?"

Tracey's lips parted but she made no reply.

"Since you didn't see him."

She rubbed a thumb across the desk. "I guess I can't say for sure."

"When you returned to the house, did you ask Brett if he'd been there when you left?"

Kerra stole a glance at Brett. It must be so hard, sitting there and hearing people talk about you. She could read nothing from his expression.

"No," Tracey replied. "I was thinking of other things."

"Okay." The attorney smiled kindly. "Getting back to the beach. You said you saw, in the wet sand, a footprint that you believed to be your mother's, correct?"

"Yes."

"Could you explain more about where it was?"

"Um . . ." Tracey hesitated. "It was on the wet part where the sand is packed—you know, once the tide begins to go out."

"I see." Terrance Clyde nodded. "Did you say you saw an entire footprint?"

She thought a moment, her expression tense. "No. It was half of one, the rest smudged out."

"Okay. Now. What time did you leave the beach?"

"I don't know. Around three o'clock."

"So you think you stayed there about twenty-five minutes?"

"I think so."

"And you arrived home at what time?"

"Probably about three twenty-five. I know I was driving faster then."

"Then when you went back to bed, it was what time?"

"That I remember for sure. I remember looking at my clock radio just before my eyes closed. It was four o'clock."

Terrance Clyde picked up a tablet of paper from the defense table and flipped through a few pages. "Now, when you went to bed, you didn't hear a thing until you awoke around nine thirty, is that right?"

"Yes."

"So you have no idea what happened around the home in those five and one-half hours."

"No, I don't."

"You didn't hear or see Darren or Brett Welk during that time and cannot state *from firsthand observation* what they were doing?"

Tracey hesitated. "Well, Brett told me the next day that he'd been out to the beach to look around and hadn't seen anything."

"I'm not asking what he told you. I want to know if you personally observed Brett's movements between the hours of four and nine thirty a.m."

Kerra glanced again at Brett. He stared at the defense attorney's back with a face of iron.

"No," Tracey answered. "I did not."

Terrance Clyde slid the tablet of paper back onto the table. "And when you got up Saturday morning, you say you went out again to look for your mother. Why didn't you call the police right away?"

Tracey Wilagher dropped her eyes. "I just couldn't," she said in a small voice. "It's hard to explain, but calling the police would be like admitting something was really wrong. And I just couldn't face that. I had to look one more time. I *had* to."

The attorney regarded her dolefully, the slightest narrow of his eyes suggesting doubt. Kerra surveyed Tracey but could see no hint of deceit.

"By the way, how did you feel that day? Were you as sick?"

"I think," Tracey said, frowning, "I was better. I guess I just had too much on my mind to pay much attention."

"I see." Terrance Clyde thought a moment. "You mentioned you brought home your mother's jacket, shoes, and cell phone. What did you do with them once you got home?"

Tracey sucked her upper lip into her teeth. "I just left them in my car. I think the detectives ended up taking them."

Delicately Terrance Clyde led Tracey through a discussion about her relationship with her mother. She'd claimed they were very close. But that couldn't mean they had never fought, could it? Hadn't they in fact had numerous screaming matches? Tracey admitted they had, but that was just due to her being a teenager plus trying to adjust to a new home. And what about the home? the attorney prompted. Was Tracey glad her mother had married Darren Welk? After all, he had plenty of money, and she and her mother had little. It must have been quite a dream for them, moving into such a house.

Little by little the attorney elicited information about the Welks' household. Kerra listened to the growing intrigue with the fascinated disbelief of a newcomer to a soap opera. Darren and Shawna apparently fell hard for each other and were married within four months of meeting. Although happy for her mom, Tracey couldn't seem to trust Darren Welk. She didn't like his drinking, and she didn't like the way he threw his weight around as the so-called Salad King of Salinas. What's more, Brett Welk didn't appear to care for either Shawna or Tracey in the least, acting constantly resentful of their presence in the house. Shawna tried to get along with Brett, Tracey insisted, but he just didn't seem to want to be friends. Then, within the first year of marriage, Shawna began to hear reports that Darren was cheating on her. One time she actually caught him with someone else. Shawna grew unhappy, furious at Darren for his affairs and for his drinking. She wanted something of her own to do, something to make her life worth living. That's when she opened the adoption agency.

"So the adoption agency was more for *herself* than to help others," Terrance Clyde commented.

The prosecutor objected. Stan Breckshire hunched over his table as though ready to spring across it at any moment. Judge Chanson sustained.

"Okay. Miss Wilagher," Terrance Clyde said, pressing his palms together, "I have some final questions about the life insurance monies, and then you'll be able to get out of here. All right?" He waited for her nod. "You say you were not aware of this insurance policy until you met with Mr. Atworth?"

"Yes."

"Hm. I thought you said you and your mother were quite close."

"We were."

"Then why would she not tell you of such an important policy?"

"Objection," the prosecutor interjected. "Calls for speculation."

"Sustained."

Terrance Clyde gazed upward with a slight frown, as if searching the heavens for an answer to the question. He lowered his eyes with an "Oh well" expression, then focused intently on Tracey.

"Miss Wilagher, why would your mother—"

"Objection. Calls for speculation!" Stan Breckshire barked.

The defense attorney turned a perturbed look on the judge. "Your Honor," he protested, his voice smooth as butter, "I haven't even asked the question yet."

"It was obvious where you were headed." The prosecutor pressed fingers into the table.

"Gentlemen!" Judge Chanson's tone sharpened. "I'll thank you to hold your comments while I rule on an objection." She glared at them both. "Now. Mr. Clyde. Would you like to continue asking the question?" Her inflection bespoke of the futility in doing so. Kerra glanced from the judge to both attorneys, then to her aunt Chelsea, who seemed unaffected with the whole thing. The reporters throughout the courtroom sat with pens poised, waiting. They all seemed to expect this kind of interaction. It was all so new to Kerra. She couldn't quite figure out who to root for.

"Well, let me put it another way, for my colleague's sake." Terrance Clyde lifted a hand vaguely in the prosecutor's direction. Stan rolled his eyes.

"From talking to Mr. Atworth," the defense attorney said carefully, "what is your understanding of the reason for this insurance policy?"

Tracey's hands fidgeted. She slid them into her lap. "The policy was there to insure that I'd be taken care of just in case anything happened to her. It was there because she loved me so much."

"I understand." The attorney nodded his head sagely. "It was there so you would be cared for. Tell me this, Miss Wilagher: will you be better off or worse off once this money is in your possession?"

Tracey looked puzzled. "I don't understand."

"Well, you mentioned previously that you looked forward to receiving this money so you could afford to leave Salinas, correct?"

"Yes."

"So do you feel you will be better off or worse off once you have the money?"

Tracey lifted a thin shoulder. "Better off, I guess."

"Certainly." Terrance Clyde inclined his head. "Anyone with two million dollars would be better off, don't you agree?"

"I suppose so."

"Is that a yes?"

Tracey thought a moment. "Yes," she replied softly.

"Your mother would be happy knowing you're so well taken care of—"

"Objection!" Stan Breckshire half-rose in his seat. "Who's testifying here?"

The defense attorney lifted his arms in frustration. "Really, Your Honor—"

"Sidebar, both of you," the judge commanded. Her face stern, she pushed back her chair and marched down to meet the two attorneys near the front, the court reporter following. Kerra watched the prosecutor's hands jab the air while he ranted. Terrance Clyde stood back, shaking his head. Judge Chanson pointed a finger at the prosecutor, apparently cutting him off in midsentence. Kerra's eyes remained glued to the trio. Why all the arguing; what was so important?

A sudden impatience to witness the outcome of the trial rose within her. Kerra was immediately ashamed of herself. How leering of her to watch true human drama unfold for the sake of her own morbid curiosity. Since Dave's accident she had purposefully never slowed to view a wreck she happened to pass while driving. The thought of drinking in someone else's tragedy had disgusted her. Yet here she was, watching another kind of tragedy and basking in her own fascination.

The judge uttered a final proclamation and whisked her hand toward the attorneys as if to push them back into their respective places. She bustled back to her black leather chair and placed both elbows on the gleaming wood before her, hands firmly clasped. "All right. Mr. Clyde. Did you have any *other* questions for this witness?"

Terrance Clyde slowly scratched his chin, turning to focus accusingly on the prosecutor. Kerra let her eyes rove over the jury. Most of them had followed the defense attorney's gaze. Kerra could see his unanswered questions reflected in their own eyes. Before she knew it, she was staring at the prosecutor herself.

What was he trying to hide?

When court recessed for lunch, Kerra rose, eyes drifting to Brett Welk as he pulled slowly to his feet and hung over the seat in front of him, absently staring. She hesitated, again ashamed of her crackling interest in what had transpired. He was obviously upset. She wished she could say something, but had no idea what. Reluctantly she slipped into the aisle and headed toward the door.

THIRTEEN

Brett sighed his way out of the courtroom, ambivalence weighting his shoulders. If only he could testify, part of him cried. If only he could tell everyone what a whiner Tracey Wilagher was. Slinking about the house—*his* house—as if she were the biggest victim in the world. Helping Shawna redecorate rooms that Brett's own mother had lovingly designed. That may have been years ago, but Brett could well remember his mom laying fabric samples against the carpet, running her delicate fingers over the textures. "Which one do you like best, Brett?" she had asked. Brett, with the blithe attitude of a fourteen-year-old, had shrugged profoundly. "I don't know that stuff, Mom; you decide."

The memory radiated heat into his throat. If only he could hear such a question from his mother now. If only he could just *be* with her, hang out with her. If only he could do even the most feminine of tasks with her—help her choose wallpaper, hang drapes.

The other part of Brett was glad he wasn't testifying. Facing an opposing lawyer on the stand had to make you feel like a duck gliding onto open water in hunting season. And besides, he'd have made a lousy witness, just as Terrance Clyde had said. Brett's animosity toward Tracey and her mother would have shown through. He'd lost a mother, yes, but so had she, the attorney had pointed out. The jurors would be sure to wonder at his lack of empathy. What's worse, Brett thought, they might even sense the real truth that he couldn't state aloud. He was glad Shawna Welk was gone. Oh, he never would have chosen for her to go the way she did. In fact, given the present circumstances, he'd choose to have her back again, just so his father could be home running the ranch. Still, he would not miss Shawna Welk.

Brett stuck his hands in his pockets, wondering what to do for lunch. His eyes cruised the hallway, taking in the reporters, the attorneys, the folks who'd come to watch. Anger rose within him as he spotted the reporter who'd cornered him that morning about the strange juror. *"Are you worried she'll see the truth?"* Brett shuddered.

A blaze of red caught his eye, and instinctively he turned his head toward it, blinking, his breath catching. It was only the jacket worn by the television reporter from Channel Four. Still, the fleck of color propelled him back to that moment when he'd first seen Shawna's blouse stained with blood. Brett swallowed, turning away. That moment would haunt him for as long as he lived.

Brett took a deep breath, stilling himself. At times like this he had to focus, bring himself to the present. Get through the next minute. That's what life had become lately—enduring one minute at a time.

He leaned an arm against the wall. A newspaper reporter sidled over toward him. Brett waved a hand. "I'm not talking to anybody." Amazingly, she eased away.

Brett rode the escalator to the first floor and left the courthouse. Rounding the corner of the building, he caught sight of Kerra, perched on a bench as if waiting for someone. He wondered who that might be. And what she was doing at a murder trial in the first place. She wore navy pants and a light blue top that reflected the translucent color of her eyes. Her hands rested on the edge of the bench, her face serious, as if she were contemplating the end of the world. *Lost* was the word for her, Brett thought for the second time that day. It was in the way she held her body, in the way she'd talked with him during break, as if her mind had been only half present. Brett knew that feeling well enough. He gazed at Kerra, then with the mindless movement of a milkweed seed on the wind, drifted toward her.

When he caught her attention, she gave him a sad smile. "Hi."

"Hi. You waiting for someone?"

"Yes." She tilted her head at him, offering no further explanation.

"Oh. Well. I'd better go get some lunch." He turned to leave.

"No," she said, surprising him, and from the look on her face, herself as well. "You don't have to go just because of that. Why don't you wait with me until she comes?"

She. The word pleased him more than he would have expected.

He gestured, "Why not?" then slid onto the bench. Leaning forward, he clasped his hands between his legs. An awkward moment passed as he struggled for something to say.

"Are you okay?"

Her hesitant words flickered in his chest. It had been a long time since any female had seemed to care a whit about him. He bounced his laced fingers. "Yeah. Thanks for asking."

"Sure." She paused. "I didn't know if I should, but I just feel . . ."

He looked at her, seeing the embarrassment in her eyes. She'd almost said the word. *Sorry.* Brett leaned back, trying to appear at ease. "So what brings you to this trial?"

Kerra hesitated. "I'm visiting my aunt. She ended up having to be here. I figured I might as well come along. I didn't know what else to do with myself."

"Is she the court reporter?"

"No, actually—" She inhaled quickly. "She's an alternate on the jury."

Brett took a moment to process the news. There were only two alternates, and one was a man. His eyes bugged at her.

"Believe me, she didn't *want* to be," Kerra blurted, then looked horrified. "Oh, I'm sorry, I didn't mean it that way. I mean, I know your dad needs a jury." Her words dangled. She blinked, as if amazed at her own stupidity.

"That's okay." Brett forced calm into his voice. "I'm sure it's no fun sitting up there, either."

Kerra's glance shot right through him. She fingered her purse. "Do you think we shouldn't be talking?"

Oh no, Brett thought. "I don't see why not. Your aunt's not supposed to talk to anybody about the trial, including you, so—"

"Oh, she's not," Kerra interjected. "She wouldn't do that."

"Well then?" Brett raised a shoulder.

Kerra nodded slowly, then considered the sidewalk.

Brett searched for a way to keep the conversation going. "Are you in college?"

"I just graduated in June."

"Oh. What are you going to do next?"

Pain danced across her face. "I'm supposed to start teaching math this fall in a junior high back home in Kansas. I've committed to a year."

"Doesn't sound like you're too excited about it."

"I guess I'm not."

Brett wanted to ask why but decided not to press.

"There's Aunt Chelsea," Kerra said suddenly.

Chelsea. Yes, that was the name Milt Waking had told him.

"Oh, great. She's with that chatty Irene Bracken again. I bet that woman's invited herself to lunch for the second time in a row."

Brett's mouth opened before his brain had a chance to stop it. "Well, don't go with them. Go with me."

She swung a surprised look at him. What a blunder he'd made. "I mean, if you want to."

"Well." She seemed nonplussed. "Let me see what's happening." Kerra rose and met the two jury members out of earshot. The aunt stared at Brett. He looked away, feigning indifference. A moment later Kerra returned.

"Guess what," she said, as if not quite believing her own words. "Irene's all geared up to go with Aunt Chelsea. The woman seems to have latched on to her. I don't think Irene will care a bit if I'm not along. So I guess you're stuck with me."

Brett pulled to his feet, both awkward and pleased. "What about your aunt? She didn't seem too happy."

"Well, she isn't." Kerra laughed at her own candidness. "But she won't have time to think, with Irene talking her head off."

"Okay. If you're sure. Uh . . . Most people walk down Broadway. But I found a coffee shop yesterday across the tracks. It's only a few blocks."

She smiled at him, and warmth spread across his shoulders. "Let's go."

"So. WHY DON'T YOU want to start your teaching job?"

Shaded by a large green umbrella, Kerra sat across from Brett at a glass-topped table outside the coffee shop, toying with a French fry. Brett had placed himself in full sun, barely squinting, as if he were born to the outdoors. One arm was hitched over the back of his chair, his body at an angle toward her. His deep-set eyes regarded her steadily.

"It's not that I don't want the job; it's just that I don't know how I can manage it. I'll have six classes a day and well over one hundred students. I'll have to teach them, keep order in the classroom. I'll have to *think*."

His eyebrows knit. "Isn't that what teaching is all about?"

"Yes, but I just don't know if I'm up to it." Anxiety rose in Kerra at the very thought. She'd done nothing since graduating but hang around her parents' house, mourning. June twenty-second had been a nightmare. She'd mourned so deeply that day and all the days surrounding it, not to mention the entire year before, that she'd become used to the weight of it. Grief had become a familiar wrap, the blanket she spread upon herself by night and the cloak she donned by day. Sometimes she felt as if the grief were stitched to her. Shedding it would pull off a part of herself.

"You want to tell me why?"

Brett's voice sounded so kind. His concern, and her thoughts of his own pain, pushed aside Kerra's reticence to talk. She laid the French fry down, eased her plate away. "Forty-six days ago, June twenty-second, was supposed to be my wedding day. My fiancé, Dave, and I had set the date early last year when we got engaged. Then in May of last year he was killed in a car accident. I was with him. I wasn't hurt much. But I watched him die."

Brett leaned forward in his chair, eyes piercing hers as he struggled for words. Kerra could see the rise and fall of his chest. "I'm sorry. I had no idea."

Kerra fiddled with the edge of her plate. "Well. I should hardly be telling my troubles to you. Seems like you've got a few of your own."

"Yeah."

They were silent for a moment. Kerra was dying to know if he'd read the morning papers, but didn't know how to ask. What would he think if he knew that the "visions woman" was her aunt?

"Tell me about where you live," she prompted. "How far away is it?"

"About an hour and twenty minutes with no traffic," he said. "Salinas is in Monterey County. It's a farming area in a valley." His face softened. "Absolutely beautiful place."

"And your family owns a farm?"

"Actually, it's called a ranch. Three hundred acres. It's one of the most productive ranches around. We grow lettuce, broccoli, cauliflower, celery, spinach, mushrooms, artichokes. You name it." Brett's pride was evident.

"So your dad is pretty well known there?"

"Yeah. He's very respected for his business skills. In fact, Dad's called the Salad King. You know those prepackaged salads that are in all the grocery stores now? Dad was one of the main inventors. He's also one of the main inventors of the precut broccoli and cauliflower and other vegetables. When the ready-to-go products hit stores, sales went way up. Even sales of the stuff we already sold a ton of, like lettuce."

Dozens of questions swirled in Kerra's mind. "Are you running the ranch right now?"

"We have a foreman. I've been helping him. I'll go back this weekend to check on things."

"Oh." Kerra couldn't think of anything else to say. She took a drink of water.

"Tell me about your aunt," Brett said.

Uh-oh. She set down her glass with care. "What about her?"

"She's the one the papers talked about, right? She had a vision about a murder last year?"

Kerra could hear no accusation in his voice. Just curiosity. And perhaps uneasiness.

"She's a wonderful person. So supportive after Dave was killed. She kept calling me again and again. She invited me here, hoping she could help me get over things."

"No wonder she didn't want to end up sitting in a courtroom."

Kerra nodded, warmed that he would be so empathetic, given his circumstances. "You don't have to worry about her, Brett, if that's what you're thinking. She's really just like anyone else. Most of the time anyway."

"She sounds very religious."

"No, not religious; she's a Christian." The words popped out before Kerra had time to think. *Terrific.* She really didn't want to get into a discussion about God.

He frowned. "What's the difference?"

Oh, great; try getting out of this one. She shifted in her chair. "Well, the way I've heard it explained is that religion is any sort of belief system that man invents to try to reach God. Christianity is God reaching out to man. Through Christ."

His chin puckered. "Do you believe that? About God reaching out to man?"

Sure, for all the good it had done her. "Yes."

Brett nodded slowly, as if the concept were brand-new to him. Then suddenly he glanced at his watch. "It's almost one. We need to be getting back."

Kerra scraped back her chair, relieved. "Thank you so much for paying for my lunch."

"You're welcome. Hope your aunt didn't mind."

Kerra made a face. She may feel protective of her aunt Chelsea, but the woman could hardly tell her what to do. "I *am* an adult." Slinging her purse over her shoulder, she fell in step with Brett toward the courthouse.

"Hey, Rogelio, come with us for lunch, man."

Rogelio wiped the sweat off his face and shook his head. "Can't. I've got some stuff to do."

"What you got to do now?" Carlos asked.

"He's got responsibilities you know nothing about." Their boss, Chester, a man in his forties with six kids, waved a dirty hand at Carlos. "Leave him be."

The two of them drove off in Chester's dusty truck as Rogelio slid into his hot Chevy and headed for a small park around the corner. He didn't have anything to do; he just wanted time to think.

Rolling up to the curb by the park, he grabbed his lunch box. He walked a short distance, then heaved himself on the ground by a tree. Scooting back to lean against the trunk, Rogelio closed his eyes for a five-minute siesta. Vague red images moved across the insides of his lids. Kristin yelling at him to get out. Mama Yolanda clutching a baby's sleeper to her eyes and crying. His hand trembling over a document, then suddenly, fiercely, signing.

"Relinquishment," the document was headed in bold capital letters. "I do hereby relinquish and surrender ..." The words were branded into his brain. When Kristin had handed him the paper, all the information had already been filled in for him—his name, the date, the Welk Adoption Agency name and address.

All, that is, except his signature.

"I'm making a copy of this, Kristin," he'd declared after signing it. Self-loathing already churned in his chest.

"Just give it to me now." Her arm had shot out to grab it.

He'd whisked the paper out of her reach. "No! I'm going to make a copy of it." His voice had turned acid. "At least I should have some proof. Just in case I don't see the money."

"You'll get your money, I told you! As soon as you give me that paper, I can get it."

Rogelio squeezed his eyes against the memory. Part of him thanked God in heaven that he'd taken the time to make a copy. Without it he would have no clue where to look for his baby. But the other part of him cringed at the guilt it caused. All that time he'd taken to make the copy, he could have changed his mind. He could have torn up that paper at any time.

Instead he'd torn up his grandmother's heart.

FOURTEEN

Chelsea settled into her jury chair, worrying about Kerra. What could she possibly have to talk about with Brett Welk? Chelsea didn't trust him. He seemed as tightly wound as a ball of string. Something about those eyes, the way he held himself. He looked too much like his father. Chelsea couldn't help but think of the strength of Darren Welk's genes running through his son. Did Brett have the same kind of temper?

Besides, the whole idea left her with a strange feeling. The niece of a juror having lunch with the son of the defendant. There may not exactly be a law on the books against it, but it just didn't sit right.

"All rise."

Chelsea watched the judge take her seat.

The prosecutor first called a witness from the service company for Shawna Welk's cell phone. The woman identified the phone bill that covered Shawna's calls in February. In support of Tracey's testimony, the bill included a record of the call Shawna had placed to Tracey's private line at the exact time of 1:47 a.m. No other calls were made around that time. Stan Breckshire logged the phone bill with the court clerk.

The prosecutor's next witness was Ralph Petsky of the Monterey County sheriff's department. Petsky, a ruddy-faced man with a flat, wide forehead, testified that he had taken the call when Tracey Wilagher reported that her mother was missing.

Erica Salvador drew herself up in her chair at the defense table, a pen poised over a yellow writing tablet. She stared at the witness, arched eyebrows raised, as if she were mentally dressing down an anticipated foe. Chelsea wondered if she would be cross-examining. Next to her, Terrance Clyde eased back in his chair, one arm stretched out, knuckles lightly bouncing off the table.

"What did you do after you talked to Miss Wilagher?" Stan Breckshire asked.

"I went out to the Welks' house to take down all the information."

"But you did not end up investigating the entire case yourself, is that correct?"

"Yes sir. Once my report was done and we saw what we were possibly dealing with, the decision was made to bring in detectives Draker and Kelly. They are the ones who investigated the scene at Breaker Beach."

"Okay." Stan raised a hand. "We're getting ahead of ourselves; let's back up. So you initially went to the Welks' house. What kinds of questions did you ask the members of the Welk family?"

"With a missing person, it's typical that we ask lots of questions. We ask if the person has been involved in drugs or drinking, for example. Could Mrs. Welk have gone somewhere with a friend or boyfriend? And I asked Mr. Welk at length about fighting with his wife, since Tracey Welk had reported in her phone call that this was the case."

"May I approach?" Stan Breckshire asked the judge.

"Go ahead."

The prosecutor picked up a document from his table and slipped it in front of Deputy Detective Petsky. He perused it, then looked up.

"Sir, would you please tell me what this document is?"

"It's the written report of my initial interviews with the Welk family."

According to Petsky's notes, Darren Welk had been cooperative as he answered questions. Welk admitted that he and Shawna had been fighting, but claimed he was quite drunk at the time and did not remember much of what happened that night.

Directly in front of her, Chelsea could see the first alternate's arm moving as he took notes. The man on her right was writing as well. Chelsea had chosen merely to listen. Had that been a mistake?

Stan Breckshire asked Petsky to turn to page three and read the second paragraph.

"Okay." He flipped the pages. "'Mr. Welk said that after the Browards left, he and Mrs. Welk were involved in a further altercation, which continued to involve words only. The alcohol in his system then made him groggy, and he lay in the sand by the fire and fell asleep. When he awoke, Shawna's daughter, Tracey, was kicking him, demanding to know where her mother was.'"

"'Involve words only'? What does that mean?"

"That according to Mr. Welk, they were arguing, that's all."

"He didn't mention hitting her?" Stan sounded amazed.

"No."

"Didn't mention blood?"

"No sir."

The prosecutor shook his head.

For the next half hour Stan Breckshire went over the report with Deputy Detective Petsky, sometimes line by line. Finally he logged the report with the court clerk and turned the witness over for cross-examination.

Erica Salvador pushed back her chair with a determined air. Her high heels clicked as she strode to stand before the witness, two documents dangling from her hand. Erica's suit was ice blue—fitting, thought Chelsea, for the coolness that seemed to swirl around her shoulders. Even in heels, she couldn't be over five feet two. Erica blinked slowly, considering the witness. He shifted in his seat. Stan

Breckshire hovered over the prosecution table like a hawk, right leg madly jiggling.

"Detective Petsky." Erica's voice was smooth as silk. "You testified that Mr. Welk was cooperative when you came to his house, correct?"

"Yes."

"Were Brett and Tracey also cooperative?"

"Yes." The man held himself very still, as if expecting Erica to pounce.

"And according to your report, Mr. Welk said he couldn't remember events of that night because he'd had a lot to drink."

He stared at her a moment before answering. "That's right."

"Did you believe him when he said he couldn't remember?"

"Objection!" Stan cried. "Irrelevant."

Judge Chanson flicked her eyes at the prosecutor without moving her head. "Sustained."

Erica didn't flinch. "Detective, have you ever forgotten something because you've been drunk?"

"Objection. Irrelevant!" Stan's face flushed.

"Sustained."

The defense attorney glanced at the jury with half-lidded eyes. Her meaning was clear to Chelsea. *I know something about this man.*

"Permission to approach the witness?" she asked as she tossed one of the documents before Stan.

He flicked through it, then shoved back his chair. "Your Honor, sidebar, please!"

Judge Chanson and all three attorneys met beside the judge's bench. Chelsea watched as the court reporter picked up her machinery and stood nearby, talking into her cupped recording device. Erica folded her arms and tipped her head disdainfully as Stan jabbed the air with spread fingers. Judge Chanson pointed a pudgy finger at the two attorneys, and they both simmered down as she addressed them. With a dismissive motion of her hand, she sent them back to their places. Stan took his seat like a missile ready to fire. Erica lay the document before Deputy Detective Petsky with the utmost tenderness. Her voice was hardened sugar. "Would you please tell us what this document is?"

With reluctant eyes he glanced over the papers, then raised his head with an expression of feigned boredom. "It's a report of a three-day suspension of duties. It's dated over *six years* ago."

Erica ignored the emphasis. "And what was the suspension for?"

"Being drunk and disorderly."

The attorney allowed his answer to hang in the air. "'Drunk and disorderly.' I see." She ran her tongue along her top teeth. "Would you kindly turn to page two and read the paragraph at the bottom?"

With a protesting shake of his head, he flipped a page and read. "'When asked about details of his physical altercation with Buster Lakeland, Deputy Detective Petsky replied that the alcohol he had consumed made it impossible to remember much of the events.'"

Erica nodded. "Were you telling the truth when you made that statement?"

"Yes."

"So you understand firsthand, do you not, that a large amount of alcohol in someone's system can render that person unable to remember well?"

"Objection. Leading the witness!" The words rat-a-tatted from Stan Breckshire's mouth.

Judge Chanson rubbed her neck with a finger. "Overruled."

"Yes," replied Petsky.

"Uh-huh. So when Mr. Welk told you he couldn't remember events of the night in question, I assume you believed him?"

"Objection, Your Honor!" Stan's voice rose with indignation.

"Sustained." Judge Chanson leaned forward and glared at the defense attorney. "Ms. Salvador, I warned you."

Erica raised her hand in a gesture of apology that didn't fool Chelsea one bit. "I am so sorry, Your Honor; I just got carried away. I have no further questions."

She clicked high heels back to her seat with a knowing smile.

Stan Breckshire sprang to his feet. "Deputy Detective Petsky, do you still drink?"

"No sir," the man replied with firm pride. "Not at all since that incident."

"Not had another suspension?"

"No. And I don't plan to."

"Good, good." Stan tapped his chin with a forefinger. "Tell me, in the past six years which kind of evidence have you discovered to be more reliable: information someone tells you or proven facts?"

"No question there. Proven facts."

"Is it a common occurrence for a discrepancy to exist between the two?"

"Yes sir." Petsky shrugged. "Happens far more than we'd like."

"I'll bet it makes your job of discovering the truth a whole lot harder."

"Objection." Erica looked disgusted. "Leading the witness."

"Sustained." Judge Chanson gave Stan a look. "Try asking a question, counsel."

Stan rephrased, but Chelsea read his implication clearly: Darren Welk's claim that he did not remember what had happened that night on Breaker Beach would be far overshadowed by the "proven facts."

She wondered what those facts might be.

TRACEY DROPPED HER CAR keys onto her kitchen table, fighting back a nervous burst of tears. She was done. Through with her testimony. She'd nearly worried herself sick about it, wondering how she would sound. Wondering if the prosecutor could really protect her, as he'd promised. Tracey had known that the attorney for the disgusting Darren Welk would try to catch her in a lie. Her stomach had churned at the thought that she might make a mistake. But Stan Breckshire told her she'd done well.

Just a few more days, she told herself. *A few more days and the trial will finally be over.*

She sank into a kitchen chair and placed a hand over her eyes. She would not cry. Goodness knows she'd cried enough. As day after day dragged on, she didn't know how she could stand it anymore.

Sometimes she thought she would go crazy. All she could do now was hang on and wait—alone. What she wouldn't give to have someone beside her, caring for her, helping her through this. But she had no one.

The clock on the wall ticked softly as she rubbed her temples. After a moment she eased back her head, rolling it from side to side. Then she pushed away from her chair. Fetching a soda, she headed for her computer, set up on a square folding table in the living room of her apartment.

As her computer booted up, Tracey impatiently waited, hoping for some email—her one lifeline. She certainly couldn't talk to anyone in Salinas. Soon after that night on Breaker Beach, she'd gotten burned by two "friends" who'd run their mouths to snoopy reporters. After that Tracey had abandoned all her local friends. A chat room freak, she had turned to a few faceless people she'd "met" on-line who lived in other countries. Now she emailed them regularly. She could talk of her loneliness without her mom, about her desire to leave.

Tracey logged on to her server and checked for new mail.

Bananas4U@starmail.net

She sighed in relief. A message from Maria in Brazil. She tapped her mouse button and began to read.

Tracey,
    Hi, how are you? It's so hot here. But the beaches are lovely.
    Did you testify at the trial today? How did it go?

Tracey clicked the reply button and began to type.

Dear Maria,
    You wouldn't believe how much I miss my mom. . . .

FIFTEEN

"Good afternoon, Detective." Stan Breckshire caught himself patting his palms in anticipation. Abruptly he pulled them to his sides. Detective Douglas Draker's six-foot-two frame filled the witness stand with an air of familiarity. He rested his forearms easily on the desk, hands lightly clasped.

Step by step Stan led Detective Draker through testimony about the crime scene investigation that Draker and his partner launched when they first visited Breaker Beach Sunday afternoon. As Tracey Welk had indicated, there were indeed in the sand red drops that appeared to be blood. The detectives took samples. Due to Darren Welk's insistence that Shawna had fallen and cut her forehead on a piece of metal or something in the sand, the detectives searched for such an object but did not find it.

As for the half footprints in wet sand that Tracey had spoken of, nothing remained. The tide had come in again since the early-morning hours, washing away any potential evidence.

The detectives sealed off the beach as a crime scene, even though they could not be certain a crime had been committed. As Detective

Draker put it, at that point things looked "more than a little suspicious." The stained sand was sent to the county forensic lab. Upon returning to their offices, the detectives had a rather heated discussion with their superiors over whether or not they should obtain a warrant to search Darren Welk's car. Politics came into play, the detective reluctantly admitted. Darren Welk was a powerful man in Salinas.

Sunday evening came and went. On Monday morning the local paper carried the news of Shawna Welk's disappearance. Then the Salinas police station received a serendipitous phone call. A man said that he'd been working as a security guard in Brothers Memorial Cemetery around 4:20 a.m. and had witnessed something. Stan did not pursue what that something was. The man who had called would have to testify to that himself.

The call gave the detectives reason for a very limited search warrant. They would be searching only around a newly planted bush in the Welks' backyard.

Stan asked about the defendant's actions when the detectives arrived at his door, warrant in hand.

"I should tell you that we chose not to show the warrant immediately," Detective Draker explained. "We wanted to gain Darren Welk's cooperation if we could. He had cooperated up to that point, and we felt it would be easier for all involved if we could get him to continue to do so."

"And did he cooperate?"

"Yes sir, he did."

Stan stole a glance at the defense attorneys. T. C., who would be cross-examining, leaned back in his typical position, bouncing a hand slowly and silently against the table. Erica Salvador was bent over her writing tablet, pen flying furiously.

"By the way, who was in the house at the time, other than the defendant?" Stan asked.

"No one at first. But just as we were leaving, Brett came home."

"Okay. We'll get back to that. What did the defendant tell you about planting the bush?"

"Objection. Hearsay," T. C.'s voice boomed.

Judge Chanson considered, absently rubbing her double chin.

"Your Honor," Stan jumped in, "I'm not offering this for the truth of the matter but merely to show the defendant's—"

Judge Chanson waved a hand at him. "Overruled. But be careful, Mr. Breckshire."

"Thank you." Stan felt a wave of satisfaction. The jury would not be impressed with the defense's attempt to cover up the detective's answer. "Go ahead, please."

"He said the gardeners planted it," the detective replied tersely.

Stan let the words hang in the air. The stereo sound of reporters' scratching pens was music to his ears. "The *gardeners?*"

"Yes sir. He said they were supposed to plant the whole row of bushes along the driveway the previous Friday. He'd come in from work and had showered to go out to dinner and hadn't stopped to check the backyard. Still, he assumed that all the bushes had been planted at that time."

With a shocked expression Stan pursued details. Detective Draker testified that he asked the defendant three times about the bush, and each time the defendant told him the same story. Finally the detective told Darren Welk that his story just didn't stack up with their information.

Stan began to pace, blood flowing warmly in his veins. "How did Mr. Welk respond?"

"Your Honor, I *must* object to this entire line of questioning; it's all hearsay." Terrance Clyde's deep voice implied the obviousness of the prosecutor's errant ways. He unfolded his frame and stood in one smooth movement, hands spread. "We have no way of knowing Darren Welk's understanding of such questions at that time or whether—"

"I think he was sober by then, Terrance," Stan commented. Someone behind him snickered.

"*Mr.* Breckshire!" Judge Chanson turned a livid eye on him.

"Sorry, Your Honor." Stan pretended to check his notes so she wouldn't see the smirk on his face.

"See to it that you mean it." The judge sat back with a huff and blinked. "Now, Mr. Clyde, I'm going to allow the questioning. But I assure you I'll give you plenty of leeway on cross-examination." She sent another searing look at Stan before turning to the witness. "You may answer the question."

"Mr. Welk responded that our information was wrong," Draker answered. "We talked some more, but he wouldn't change his story. So I finally said we'd like to dig up the bush."

"Did Mr. Welk comply?"

Draker shook his head. "No. According to him, the bush was expensive and would be harmed if we dug it up. When we could not get him to comply, we showed the warrant. My partner went to our car to get two shovels and evidence bags, and we began to dig."

"And what did you find?" Stan began to pace again.

The detective's expression remained neutral. "Underneath the bush we found a woman's white silk blouse."

A collective breath sucked through the courtroom.

"Really," Stan responded. "Was there anything unusual about the blouse? That is, other than the fact that it was underneath a bush."

A titter ran through the onlookers. Stan glanced at the jury. B. B. the bartender giggled, then caught herself. A small *tsk* puffed from the lips of Mike Bariston, the black man sitting next to Chelsea Adams.

"Well, it was very dirty, as you would expect," Draker said. "But we did notice, down the front, numerous stains which appeared to be blood that had been partially washed away. Also, the blouse was wet."

"What did you do with the blouse?"

"We put it through our standard procedure, placing it in a paper bag, labeling it. From there it would go to the county lab to be examined."

"For?" Breckshire prompted.

"For one, to see if we could possibly get any prints off it. Although because of the dirt and since it was fabric, we couldn't count on that. And of course to check to see if those stains were indeed blood, and if so what type. Further, since it was wet, to examine it for possible traces of salt water, which obviously could have come from the ocean."

Stan Breckshire ducked his head in a few quick nods. With a meaningful glance at the jury, he plucked a sealed paper bag from his table and carefully began to open it. The courtroom fell silent except for the rustling of the bag. When the top was open, the prosecutor picked up a pair of clear latex gloves and slowly, painstakingly pulled them on. From the corner of his vision Stan saw Erica Salvador close her eyes in an "Oh brother" expression. *Let her make faces,* he thought. He dangled a gloved hand above the bag, took an audible breath, then reached inside. He pulled out a filthy blouse and turned to the judge. "May I approach?" At her nod he carried the blouse gingerly to the witness stand and spread it before the detective.

"Is this the blouse you found?"

The detective eyed the blouse solemnly. "Yes sir, it is."

"And the partially washed stains that appeared to be blood are where?"

The detective pointed without touching the blouse. "Here around the front buttons and a little to the left."

"Thank you." Breckshire picked up the blouse again as if it were a bomb about to explode. He displayed its stained front to the jury, stepping slowly down the line. Hesta Naples cast it a prim look while Tak Nagakura's expression never changed. B. B.'s eyes widened. Henry Slatus, the hang-jowled black man in the back row with a flashy diamond ring on his pinkie, strained to see around Hesta. Chelsea Adams clearly tensed. His display complete, Stan returned the blouse to the bag and officially logged it with the court clerk.

"Now, Detective Draker," he said, rocking on his heels, two fingers thrumming against his chin, "what was the defendant's explanation, if any, when you and your partner uncovered the blouse?"

"He didn't talk, sir."

"Didn't talk."

"No sir."

"He just said nothing?" Breckshire's eyebrows rose. "No explanation, no reason for why the blouse would be there?"

"No sir."

The prosecutor turned a lingering look of accusation on Darren Welk. The moment stretched.

"Mr. Breckshire, since you're apparently thinking," Judge Chanson broke in dryly, "perhaps this would be a good time to take a fifteen-minute break."

CHELSEA WAS WASHING HER hands in the bathroom when the impression hit. It wasn't a vision, nothing seen or heard. But deep within her the voice of God resonated, a voice that she had come to know well. Imparting to her one intense command.

Pray for all the people associated with this case.

Chelsea withdrew her fingers from under the tap. Turned off the water. She waited for God to say anything else, perhaps something more definitive, but nothing more came.

Absently she dried her hands. *Yes, Lord, I'll pray. Anything specific?*

Again she waited but received no further impression.

A knock sounded on the door. "Be right out!"

Chelsea didn't want to keep the person waiting. As she unlocked the door, silent prayers for the jurors began to flow through her mind. She would begin with Irene, juror number one, and go down the line. Then, during those waiting moments in the courtroom, she would pray for others—the attorneys, the judge, reporters, witnesses.

She sensed there was something more here, that in time God might lead her to pray more specifically and perhaps for certain people. She sensed too a heightened alertness within her. That she was entering a time in which prayer and careful listening to God's further leading would be particularly important.

God, please help me hear you. She opened the door. *You know I can't do this alone.*

SIXTEEN

Stan Breckshire ogled the lookie-loos returning to their seats, vaguely wondering how many would stick out the entire trial. He was beginning to memorize their faces. There was the couple probably in their seventies, she carrying a bag in which she could hide a soda six-pack, and he sporting a striped bow tie, of all things. A threesome of older women were settling themselves dead center in the second row, whispering furiously. Amazingly, all three of them had long, straggly gray hair. They reminded Stan of the Three Fates from Greek mythology—the old crones who decided how long each mortal would live. Stan caught snatches of the words *blouse* and *blood* and "that handsome defense attorney." He sniffed, turning his attention elsewhere. A fine-looking young blond sat on the end, all by herself. A wiry man with a half-bald head, looked about in his forties, also sat alone, arms crossed, rocking with a "Let's get on with the show" expression.

The jury filed in. Stan took his seat, foot jiggling. He jerked his neck to the left. The discomfort in his arm was a tad less today. Probably because of all the pain relievers he'd downed.

A few minutes later, with Detective Draker back on the stand, Stan launched into details of his investigation after the blouse had been found. The detective sat just as he had before, with the same amount of emotion on his face—nil. Mr. Personality.

Discovery of the blouse, the detective intoned, prompted them to take the defendant down to the sheriff's department in Salinas for immediate questioning. Darren Welk could have requested a lawyer to meet him there but did not do so. Brett arrived home just as they were leaving, and his father quickly explained what had happened. Brett's face, according to the detective, turned a sickly white. He followed his father out to the detectives' vehicle, demanding to know what they were going to do. When they pulled away, Detective Draker said, Brett stood on the sidewalk looking after them with a dazed expression.

While Detective Draker and his partner questioned the defendant at the station, their colleagues were busy obtaining a search warrant for the defendant's house and car. The house was immediately "frozen," or sealed off. No evidence of foul play was discovered in the house. On the floor of the passenger side in Darren Welk's car they found a woman's purse. And far back underneath the left rear seat, numerous grains of sand were discovered. These were also sent to the lab to be compared with grains of sand taken from Breaker Beach.

Stan stopped pacing and scratched his head. "Could these grains of sand possibly have come from Darren Welk's shoes?"

"The evidence doesn't support that." The detective's face remained deadpan. "Sand granules were discovered in the floor of the driver's area. This would be expected, since we know that the defendant drove home from the beach. However, the sand under the backseat was different. First of all, who could have tracked it in? More importantly, it was too far back under the seat to have come off someone's shoes."

"What were your thoughts about how it could have gotten there?"

"Objection. Calls for speculation."

"Sustained."

Stan moved on. "What further investigation did you conduct at the beach, if any?"

They had to move as quickly as they could, the detective replied, as the beach was a constantly changing environment. The sheriff's department launched a full-scale search for the body. They examined nearby beach and rock areas to see if the body had washed up onshore, and they sent out divers to check around rock formations underwater. They also contacted the Coast Guard.

"Why the divers?" Stan asked. "Wouldn't a body always wash ashore?"

"Not necessarily. Many times a body can be pulled out to sea, especially if it floats rather than sinks. This particular beach is known for its strong currents. And of course the tide would have continued to go out Saturday morning. This combination could easily have sucked a body out of the beach area. As a result, the body could have gotten caught between rocks somewhere underneath the surface. In time, with decomposition of a body, it will likely loosen and float to the surface in whole or in part. But by this time it was only Tuesday afternoon, not even four days since Shawna Welk had last been seen."

Stan stole a long glance at his jury. Candy Lowe, the fresh-faced young pregnant woman in the back row, looked a little green. Chelsea Adams's eyes were closed.

"Was there anything else of interest about this particular beach?"

"Not the beach itself but the nearby area. Just about a week earlier a man had been attacked by a shark."

"Oh, lawsy, the shark got her," a woman breathed.

Judge Chanson shot a testy glance in the direction of the three gray-haired Fates. Immediate silence. Stan worked to keep his mouth straight.

"Keep moving, Mr. Breckshire," the judge intoned.

"Yes, Your Honor." His knuckles kneaded his palm. "Did you find any other possible pieces of evidence during your search of the beach on that Tuesday?"

"No."

"And after that?"

"Yes, two more things. We sealed off Breaker Beach to the public in order to watch for anything washing up on shore. During that time we searched the beach daily to see if anything appeared. Finally, on Saturday, two items did wash in with the tide on Breaker Beach. The first item was a piece of torn navy blue fabric. The second was a tooth that looked to be human."

The courtroom rustled. Stan hoped for another rise out of the Three Fates but none came. Oh, the power of a judge's evil eye. He checked the jury. They were hanging on the detective's every word.

The courthouse clock read almost 5:00 p.m. "Your Honor," he offered with an air of innocence, "I think this would be a good place to stop."

THE COURTHOUSE HALLWAY WAS a beehive as Kerra made her way toward the escalator. Camera crews readied themselves, and reporters called questions to anyone who might answer. Spectators gaped at the action. Several reporters crowded around that black-haired lady with the spiked butch haircut. Suddenly the hallway lit up as a television crew's lights went on. A camera aimed in the lady's direction. She squinted, then continued her animated diatribe.

Kerra felt a presence at her side. She turned to see Brett, who watched the woman with obvious distaste. "Who is she?" Kerra asked.

"Lynn Trudy. Shawna's sister."

The line of demarcation became clear. The sister out for justice. The son hoping for mercy. Kerra felt a welling of renewed sorrow for Brett. "It must be so hard." Even as she said the words, they felt shallow, trite.

His eyes remained on Lynn Trudy, half-focused. "The whole thing's pretty surreal. You work hard, do well, make some money. Provide the country with needed products and lots of people with jobs. The town respects you, but beyond that nobody pays much attention. Then you're accused of a murder. And suddenly anyone around you is noteworthy. Everybody wants to talk to them; everybody's their instant friend."

Kerra didn't know how to respond. Brett blinked, then turned his deep-set gaze on her. "Sorry. Didn't mean to ramble."

Kerra glanced back to Lynn Trudy. A reporter was asking her a question. "How come they don't try to talk to you?"

"Oh, they have. I just never say anything, so they finally gave up. Doesn't stop them from filming me coming and going, however. Great background shots for the evening news." His voice was tinged with bitterness.

She shook her head, unable to imagine how it felt to walk in Brett's shoes. In the next moment she spotted Aunt Chelsea emerging from the door that led to the hallway behind the courtrooms. Her aunt looked around, spotted her, and headed for the escalator with purpose. Kerra crimped her mouth. "I have to go."

"You going sightseeing again tonight?"

Kerra felt almost guilty. "Yes. What will you do?"

Brett shrugged. "Visit Dad for a while. After that not much. But I'd better get out of here while the vultures' attention is turned on a willing victim." He gestured toward the reporters. "See ya 'round."

Kerra shot a glance at Brett's retreating back. A television camera swung around, aiming at his profile as he stepped onto the escalator.

SEVENTEEN

Rogelio drove through his neighborhood, mouth dry. He thought he'd been nervous last evening, going to see Kristin. This evening his hands didn't even want to turn the wheel in the right direction. The moment he'd hit the end of his street, he'd had to fight the urge to head the wrong way, looking for friends, acquaintances, anyone who'd give him an excuse for hanging out. It would be so easy just to whittle the time away. He could begin his mission just as well tomorrow when he had more courage.

How he wished he had Kristin beside him! She'd cut out another piece of his heart yesterday. What would she do if he got Roselita back? *When* he got Roselita back. Would she care? Would she want to see the little girl? How would Rogelio ever tell his growing daughter that her own mother didn't want her?

Surely that would not happen. Rogelio knew Kristin. She wasn't selfish and uncaring. She'd just gotten into something over her head. Something he now had to fix.

He drove through east Salinas, heading toward John Street, which would cross the freeway serving as a barrier between his neighborhood and the nicer areas of town. The streets were lined with old cars, sometimes three or four to a house due to the large extended Hispanic families. During the day the cars were gone, many of their owners working the fields of the ranches surrounding Salinas. If Rogelio hadn't been introduced to his boss just when the man needed another pair of hands, he'd probably be working the fields himself. Maybe even the fields of the Welks' ranch. He'd been glad to avoid that backbreaking labor—yet look where his gardening work for the Welks had gotten him.

For the thousandth time Rogelio cursed the day that Kristin, then eight months pregnant, had picked him up after a full day's work on the Welks' sprawling property. Kristin had needed his car to get to a doctor's appointment, and Rogelio had let her take it for the afternoon. Around five o'clock she drove up the Welks' impressive driveway and pulled herself awkwardly out of the car, staring openmouthed at the large house. A light rain was falling through the chilly air, but Kristin didn't seem to mind. "One thing about being pregnant: you don't get cold," she'd told Rogelio. He saw her from a distance and pushed away from his weeding long enough to walk over. "I'm not quite done yet," he told her, flexing his back after hours of bending. "We've got about another half hour of work. Why don't you sit in the car, get out of the rain."

She looked disappointed. "That's a long time to wait."

"I have to finish."

Kristin put a hand on her spreading hip and gazed at the Welks' house. "I want to live in a place like this someday, Rogelio."

Her wistful words pierced him. "Don't we all," he mumbled as he turned away, self-defensiveness edging his tone.

Rogelio returned to his work. Kristin leaned against the car and looked at the house, oblivious to the drizzle. Crouching next to Chester, Rogelio yanked at weeds too hard and brought away a section of a spreading ground plant. "Hey, watch what you're doing," Chester growled. Rogelio clamped down on his emotions and paid attention to his work.

A few minutes later Rogelio looked up to see Shawna Welk's car easing to a stop behind Kristin. Mrs. Welk got out and they began talking. Kristin pointed at him, and Mrs. Welk gave him the once-over. Rogelio's eyes flicked back and forth between his work and the two women. What could they possibly have to say to one another? Kristin standing in the rain with her long-sleeved denim maternity shirt over a pair of jeans she'd worn just about every day for the last two months, and Mrs. Welk holding a newspaper over her perfectly combed hair, red high heels matching her red business suit. Rogelio felt a stab of embarrassment for Kristin. She would probably gush over the house. Mrs. Welk couldn't help but look down on her. Rogelio pressed his lips together, his fingers scraping through the flower beds. Then he sat back on his haunches, hands stilling. Mrs. Welk was escorting Kristin into the house.

Looking back on that moment, Rogelio had to admit that deep inside he'd known. He knew Shawna Welk ran an adoption agency from offices in the west wing of the house. He knew because he'd mowed the lawn right under the Welk Adoption Agency sign, had seen the couples and the pregnant women come and go. But at the time, Rogelio chose to dwell on the fact that Kristin and Shawna Welk had gone in the front door, not the side entrance to the offices. Mrs. Welk was just being kind, showing Kristin the house, he told himself. Getting her out of the rain.

By the time he finished, wet and sweaty and tired, Kristin was exiting the Welks' front door by herself. "Why'd she take you inside?" he demanded as they drove away.

Kristin shrugged. "I said I liked the house. She offered to show it to me. That's all." She looked out her window, as if she'd suddenly found the flat, familiar ranch lands of Salinas very interesting.

Remembering the purposeful turn of Kristin's head, Rogelio berated himself for not listening to his gut and asking more questions. Hadn't she been tucking something in the pocket of her jeans when she left the Welks' house? A phone number maybe?

Why, Rogelio wondered for the hundredth time, had Shawna Welk wanted Kristin's baby so much?

Rogelio turned left onto California. Soon he was cruising down Hawthorne, nervously checking street numbers. Eleven thirty-four.

There it was—a pale blue stucco with a rounded front window. Multicolored cyclamen bordered the small porch on either side.

He pulled up to the curb and shut off the engine. Reached for the piece of paper in the glove compartment, then sat frozen, staring at its typed and handwritten words.

> I/We, the _father_ of _Roselita Nicole,_ a minor _female_ child, born _January 3, 2002_ in _Salinas, California,_ do hereby relinquish and surrender said child for adoption to _Welk Adoption Agency_. . . . It is my/our intention that the agency place the child for adoption with _____ . . . . I/We fully understand that when this relinquishment is filed with the headquarters office of the Adoptions Branch of the California Department of Social Services by said agency, all my/our rights to the custody, services, and earnings of said minor child, and any responsibility for the care and support of said minor child, will be terminated.

Terminated.

Rogelio's signature was underneath.

A few things about the document puzzled Rogelio. There were lines for the signatures of two witnesses who apparently were supposed to watch him sign the document. But no one had done that and the lines remained blank. At the bottom the form included a line for the "authorized agency official," presumably Shawna Welk, to sign. That was blank, too.

Rogelio smoothed the document in his lap and prayed that something on it was wrong. Wrong enough that someone would listen to him.

JANET CLINE SPRAWLED IN her recliner before the television, half-dozing through _Wheel of Fortune._ Her shoes lay on the carpet, her stocking feet pointing at opposite corners of her blue and yellow living room. Janet's hands lay folded across her belly. Every once in a while her heavy eyelids slid up, allowing glimpses of the turning letters.

Her stomach growled. Janet shifted in her chair. She really ought to drag herself into the kitchen and make some dinner. But she was so tired. She'd been up almost the entire night, coaching a seventeen-year-old through her first delivery. Janet had held the girl's hand, massaged her, comforted and encouraged her. When dawn finally broke, the girl was in the final stages of labor. The baby, a boy, was born at 8:21. The poor girl lay back on her pillow and sobbed as the baby was handed to her. Janet stood aside, allowing the young mother the time she needed to hold her baby and say good-bye. No matter how firm a birth mother's decision, no matter how much she liked the adoptive couple, giving up her baby was like giving away part of herself. Janet had only one word to describe these mothers— *courageous*. As a mother of two adopted children, Janet could only begin to imagine the pain birth mothers must feel, even as they held fast to their decision to do what was best for the baby.

The doorbell rang. With a sigh Janet eased down the footrest of her recliner and pushed to her feet. Running fingers through her short gray hair, she plodded to the entryway. The bell rang again. "Yes, yes," she mumbled, "I'm coming."

A young, wiry Hispanic man stood on her porch, fingers tightly clasped. His black hair was slicked back neatly. He wore a navy blue T-shirt tucked into jeans that were clean but frayed. A breeze sauntered across the porch, and Janet caught a whiff of spring-scented men's soap. At first Janet thought he must be selling something, but he carried nothing in his tensed hands. Then she looked at his face and saw an all-too-familiar sight. His dark eyes held a mixture of pain, fright, and purpose, like crushed coal gathered and pressed into new form.

"May I help you?" She worked to push aside her tiredness.

He swallowed. "Are you Janet Cline?"

"I am."

He nodded once, as if to urge himself on. He opened his mouth again and words blurted forth. "I need to talk to you about a baby."

The statement was of no surprise to Janet. His girlfriend was probably pregnant. She wondered if the girl knew what he was doing. "I would be very happy to talk to you. However, my office is downtown. Would you like to call tomorrow during business hours to set up an appointment? I can give you a card."

"No, please." He tilted his head. "I work all day. This is the only chance I have. It won't take long. I just need some information."

Janet glanced beyond him to his car, an old Chevy, buffed and shined. This young man clearly took pride in what was his. Her eyes rested again on his face. An aura of resilience and desperate hope hovered about his narrow cheeks. "What's your name?" she asked.

"Rogelio Sanchez." He looked at her expectantly.

Something about him made her step back, open the door wider. "Come on in. But understand I can only give you a few minutes."

She led him to the living room couch, picked up the remote, and switched off the television. She sat opposite him in her recliner, with her feet on the floor. Automatically she donned her business persona, a mixture of empathy and calm experience. "Okay. What can I do for you?"

He took a deep breath, eyes raking the carpet. "I have this paper." He pulled a piece of paper out of the front pocket of his jeans and unfolded it. "I signed it seven months ago but it was a big mistake." He held it out to her.

Janet held his gaze for a moment before accepting it. If this was about an adoption already completed, there was nothing she could do. She read the familiar title of the document—one she'd signed many times in the last two and a half years. Then her eyes ran down the words and signature and her heart stilled. She stared at the name and address of the Welk Adoption Agency, then at Rogelio's signature. A moment passed before she could think of what to ask first.

"You signed this?"

He nodded.

"And the adoption was handled by Shawna Welk?"

"Yes."

She frowned at the document, willing it to divulge its meaning. "Who was the mother?"

"Kristin Bockner."

Janet mouthed the name silently. She'd never heard it before. "And the baby was born in January."

"Yes."

She stared at him, mind dimly turning like an engine that couldn't start. "You'd better tell me your story from the beginning."

Janet's limbs slackened as she heard his tale. His baby adopted at the last minute. A payment of five thousand dollars to him, and evidently much more to the mother. As Rogelio spoke, Janet fought to keep her face impassive, even as her heart thudded dully against her chest. Dozens of thoughts entangled her mind. How could Shawna have done this? *Why* had she done it? She and Janet had run a successful, reputable agency. They'd placed twelve babies their first year of business, twenty-six the second year. Why would Shawna suddenly pay for a baby?

Janet lay the paper on her lap and gazed out her front window, trying to make sense of it all. If this boy's story were true and this piece of paper were real, what might this do to her reputation? She'd spent the last months building up her own adoption agency after Shawna was killed. How could she prove she'd had nothing to do with such illegal proceedings?

What's more, the timing only made matters worse. Darren Welk was now on trial for Shawna's murder. The jury needed to identify with Shawna, mourn her untimely death, so they would seek punishment for her killer. This was not the time for Shawna's memory to be tainted.

There had to be an explanation for this.

Janet blinked her thoughts back to the young man poised nervously on the edge of her couch, hands fisted against his legs. "Shouldn't those witness lines be filled in?" he ventured. "And the name of the people who adopted the baby?"

Janet lifted her hand from the offending paper. "Rogelio, if what you're telling me is true, there are numerous problems here. Every state has adoption laws that must be followed exactly. A birth couple doesn't have to know the name of the adoptive couple. But one of the laws in California is that a birth mother and father must meet with an LCSW—a licensed clinical social worker—twice. I was the LCSW for the Welk Adoption Agency. Mrs. Shawna Welk was the director, but she was not a trained social worker. That's why she teamed up with me when she opened the agency. The only other way to handle adoptions is to use an attorney." She paused. "Did you ever see an attorney?"

"No." His eyes remained fixed on her. Janet saw the hope swirling over his features and winced. "So I was supposed to meet with you twice?" he pressed.

"Yes. And when you signed this document, I and two witnesses were to be present."

He gripped his hands. "So the adoption wasn't legal."

She inhaled deeply, wrestling with the answer. "This piece of paper is not legal. But I'll need to check the file and see if other papers make it so."

"But how could there be any other papers? I didn't sign anything else, and I never—"

Janet held up a palm. "I hear you. But I'll have to see the file."

He pressed his lips together and glanced away, clearly upset that she wouldn't simply accept his word. "How long will that take?"

"A couple of days. The file is at social services in Sacramento. All the files from the agency were sent there when it was closed."

"Sacramento? How will you get it?"

"I know people in the social services office. I had to deal with them quite a bit in sending all the Welk agency files to them. I can call someone tomorrow and ask her to look at the file, just tell me what's there. Then if necessary she can send me copies of documents."

"Okay." He straightened his shoulders. "I'll come back tomorrow evening and see what you found out."

"No, call my office." She scooted forward in her chair. "You have to understand, this is after my work hours."

Rogelio rose as she did. His lanky frame was a good six inches taller. "I can't; I work all day at gardening. Unless I call you during my lunch hour. That means you'd have to find something out in the morning." He gazed down at her, resolve in his expression.

"I'll try, but I have lots of other work to do." Janet hoped her words sounded more firm than her legs felt as she walked him into the hall. There had to be a way out of this. As she pulled open the door, for sheer argument's sake she asked, "Rogelio, if you work all day, who would raise your baby?"

"My grandmother will help." Contrition laced his voice. "She wanted to care for the baby all along. Kristin had said she could, and she was so excited. It was all she had to look forward to after my mom died. But then Kristin said she could give me all this money . . ." He averted his eyes, a tangible cloud of guilt descending over him. When he turned back to Janet, lines etched his forehead. "I have to get the baby back for my grandmother. She cries every day."

Janet's palm grew damp against the door handle. She understood the importance of extended family in Hispanic culture. It was an emphasis she found sorely lacking in so many white American families. She imagined her own grief if her daughter were to snatch a baby from her grandmotherly arms in such a way. Then she thought of the adoptive parents of Rogelio's baby. Talk about snatching a baby out of a mother's arms. If this adoption truly were illegal, Janet would find herself in the midst of a battle to take a seven-month-old child away from the only parents she had ever known.

"And Kristin? Would she be a part of the baby's life at all?"

Pain crossed Rogelio's face. He traced a fingertip down the wood paneling of her door, considering his answer. "I want us to be a family." His eyes cut to Janet, as if his own words surprised him. His mouth opened again, then closed abruptly.

Making no comment, Janet ushered him out to the porch. She watched Rogelio move down her sidewalk with lean agility, then fled into the house. Closing the door, she sagged against it, exhaustion trailing unknown fears down her limbs. "Shawna," she moaned, "what have you done?"

EIGHTEEN

"Hi, Dad," Brett mouthed.

Through the glass in the visitors' room, his father smiled ruefully. They both picked up their phones.

"How's the ranch?" Darren Welk asked.

Brett focused on his dad's large, powerful hands. Some things never changed. How often had they discussed the same thing at their own kitchen table? Seemed as if most of his life their relationship had been played out in details about the ranch. Fields, crops, transplants, harvesting, packaging. When would they ever learn to *talk?*

"Things are going okay; I called Rudy just before I came here. Field six is almost done with harvesting. We got those holes patched in the irrigation in field four. The only main problem now is that Rudy heard Chef Mate's messing with their prices again."

Darren Welk's fist hit the table in frustration. "How many times do we have to put up with this? Delgadia's nothing but a cheat!"

Enrico Delgadia was the owner of Chef Mate, the most successful prepackaging company in Salinas. As crops were harvested, they were immediately sent to Chef Mate for packaging and shipping to stores in the form of ready-to-eat salads and vegetables. Delgadia wasn't a convicted felon but it wasn't for lack of trying. He'd been charged with numerous illegal activities over the past few years— money laundering, tax evasion, price fixing—and had somehow managed to weasel out of them every time. Brett agreed with his dad; you couldn't trust Delgadia. All the same, Chef Mate was the packaging company with the highest efficiency and best distribution, so like many other Salinas ranchers, the Welks put up with its owner.

"Don't get all riled up yet; Rudy's not through talking things over with him."

Darren's face was hard. "You tell Rudy not to agree to anything until he gets through to me."

"Yeah, okay, Dad; you know he'll call you."

Darren gripped the telephone. "How's a man supposed to run a ranch from jail, huh? What do they want to do, *break* me?"

Brett's throat tightened. Silently he watched his father, feeling the familiar kaleidoscope of emotions in his gut. Fear, loneliness, bitterness, guilt. Sometimes he thought the ambivalence would crush him. How to love a father, want to reach out to him, while images of one night's crime crawled like roaches through your mind? If only they could talk about it. Sometimes Brett was hit by the inanity of it all—both of them knowing bits of the truth but saying nothing.

"Never mind," his father growled, "I've got other things to think about now." He raked fingers through his hair. "I could have strangled that Tracey today. Skinny little money-grubbing—"

"Dad, stop. You don't do yourself any favors by looking angry all the time."

"I'm *not* angry all the time! I've sat like stone in that courtroom for two days now, not showing one emotion on my face! Don't you tell me what to do, boy."

Brett flopped back in his chair and regarded his father in utter weariness. His throat clenched once more. Amazing, this sudden weakness within himself. He hadn't cried since he was a kid. His father had taught him that crying was for sissies.

And he wasn't about to cry now.

"I gotta go, Dad," Brett said quietly.

The frown lines in Darren Welk's face flattened. He rubbed his forehead. "Yeah, yeah, I know. Can't stand to be in here for long."

Brett made no comment.

"What're you gonna do the rest of the evening?"

He shrugged. "I don't know. Get something to eat. Watch some TV in the hotel room. Try to sleep."

His father snorted. "You make it sound not much better than life in here. Don't be so down in the mouth, Brett; at least you're a free man."

This was freedom?

Three hours later Brett sprawled on the hard mattress of his hotel bed, eyes fixed mindlessly on the television. The dregs of fast-food burritos lay heavily in his stomach. His whole body seemed weighted, his head thick. Disjointed scenes filtered through his head. His parents together, so long ago. Working alongside his dad on the ranch. The nightmare of his life ever since February. The trial.

Kerra.

Her face wafted into his thoughts like the scent of spring rain. Those blue eyes against smooth, tanned skin, the lines of her jaw. Brett smiled to himself. She had a way of tilting her head to look at him sideways when she talked. And when he talked, she listened, her gaze fixed on him with concern and ... something else. Compassion. Understanding.

Selfishly Brett hoped that old lady latched on to Kerra's aunt again tomorrow. Maybe Kerra would go to lunch with him again.

CHELSEA AND KERRA DUG into shrimp appetizers at their outside table in Sausalito, overlooking the bay. The evening had remained warm. Sailboats lazily floated near Angel Island and around Alcatraz.

"Kerra," Chelsea ventured, "may I ask how you're doing spiritually? The last time we talked about it ... well, you didn't want to talk about it."

Kerra ran her thumb and fingers up and down her water glass. "Sure, you can ask. That's pretty much why I came here in the first place. Well, that and to rest. I had my hopes up, probably more than I should have, that somehow I'd go back home and be able to face life. Like this would be a clean break for me, you know?" Her eyes drifted to the bay. "Guess that's a lot to expect."

Prayers for wisdom sifted through Chelsea's mind. Answers for another's grief usually sounded so trite. "I don't know if there is such a thing as a clean break after what you've been through. But I do know that God can heal, as long as you'll let him. He can use time, other people, and circumstances. I'm just not sure how open you are to him right now."

Chelsea was well aware that a streak of stubborn independence ran through Kerra. It had often played itself out in the form of rebelliousness before she'd become a Christian. With non-Christian parents, Kerra had never had any sort of spiritual training until Chelsea had begun talking to her about Jesus. Chelsea had only been a Christian for two years herself, and when she'd made the decision to follow Christ, her priorities had changed significantly. Excitement about her newfound faith had bubbled into most of her conversations, and when they'd talked on the phone, Kerra obviously had been captivated with what she'd had to say. After a few months Chelsea had prayed with her over the phone to accept Christ. Kerra's excitement had equaled Chelsea's. Until two months later when Dave was killed.

"I'm open to anything that's going to make life worth living again." Kerra's tone was etched with weariness. She eased a lock of blond hair behind her ear and stared at her plate. "I'm tired of the why questions. I just want to move on. It's been over a year, for goodness' sake." She raised her blue eyes to Chelsea. "You know what I want?" she asked almost defiantly. "I want to love again."

The words hung over their table. For no reason at all Chelsea pictured Kerra talking to Brett Welk, her beautiful young face full of compassion. Chelsea tried to sweep the thought aside, but it clung to the corners of her mind like a cobweb out of reach. For the first time she realized the depth of her niece's vulnerability.

Kerra's face veiled as if she couldn't believe she'd uttered such heresy. She looked away. Chelsea's lips curved sadly. "Of course you do, Kerra. Of course you do."

Their entrees arrived. Chelsea wanted to continue the conversation without pushing. Instead of focusing on Kerra, she talked about the many times that God had come through for her in the last two years—even when she'd stared helplessly into the eyes of a killer. "One thing God taught me during those times, Kerra," Chelsea said. "He taught me that he's always with me, no matter what happens. His purpose *will* be accomplished. As the Bible says, he's our dread champion. He's a whole lot bigger than the circumstances here on earth."

Kerra screwed up her face. "Huh?"

"It's from Jeremiah 20:11. 'The Lord is with me like a dread champion.' Jeremiah said it after he'd been beaten and put into stocks for speaking God's word. He knew God would continue to watch over him and in time would subdue his enemies." Chelsea searched for words to explain what the name meant to her personally. "God is our champion, Kerra, our provider and protector. He is also fearsome, awesome, striking dread in the hearts of his enemies. He is to be both loved and revered. He works his will through situations in which many times all we can see is the mess. We have to keep our eyes on him and trust him."

Kerra listened intently, her lips parted. A crumb of sourdough bread rested on her cheek. Chelsea reached out to wipe it away. Her niece smiled self-consciously, brushing a finger across her lips in case there were more. "Aunt Chelsea," she declared, "you ought to be a preacher."

Chelsea rolled her eyes. "No thanks. A wife, mother, and aunt will do just fine, thank you very much."

"Don't forget jury member," Kerra teased, wagging a finger.

"Ha, ha." That was the one thing Chelsea wished she could forget.

IRENE BRACKEN HUMMED a little tune as she negotiated the turn into her narrow driveway. The rosebushes climbing the fence on her left hung pink and red against the worn wood, a proud display of her gardening abilities. She turned off the engine and smiled at the flowers. She could remember planting those fledgling rosebushes with Bill as if it were yesterday.

Irene slid out of her car. She checked the mailbox, looking as always for the familiar handwriting of her daughter in Arizona. Her son never wrote. Males just had a thing against writing, Irene had learned. She'd never once known her husband to send a letter to his own mother.

Nothing in the mail except a few bills and plenty of junk. Irene sighed. So much for a bit of company.

In her small entryway Irene set her purse and keys on the long table against the right wall. Automatically she looked at the picture hanging above the table—a large photo of her and Bill on their thirtieth wedding anniversary. Their heads were bent together, their hands clasped. Their daughter had said they'd posed like teenagers. Well, thought Irene, they'd felt like kids. Married three decades and more excited about each other than ever.

Irene headed into the kitchen and laid the mail on the counter. For the next half hour she puttered about, mixing a casserole of rice and chicken and sliding it into the oven, opening the mail, all the while talking to her cats. Her supper baking, she plopped herself before the television in the family room and flipped to Channel Seven. "A revealing day in court in the so-called Salad King case," the lovely female anchor read. "That story and others coming up." Irene settled back against the cushion, only half-watching the commercials. She sure liked that Asian gal on the news. Such shiny black hair.

Irene knew she wasn't supposed to see any media coverage of the trial, whether in the newspapers or on TV. But she just couldn't help it. Besides, who would know?

A few minutes later the story about the trial filled the screen. Irene watched in fascination, her bottom lip dropping as she concentrated. Milt Waking was standing by that awful-looking spiky-haired woman in the courthouse hall. He pointed a microphone at the woman's bright red mouth. He asked a question, and the camera zoomed in to show tears standing in eyes heavy with mascara. "I can't begin to tell you what it's like for me to hear testimony like that," she said. "That my sister, the sister I loved so much, is reduced to . . ." Her voice broke and she lay two fingers against her lips. Irene thought her dark red nail polish looked like dried blood. "That she's reduced to a few pieces of clothing and a tooth." The woman's eyes focused past the reporter as she blinked back tears. "I have to go; I'm too upset. That's all I want to say right now."

"Oh, *look!*" Irene threw out a hand. "There I am!" She watched herself walk toward the long set of stairs. "Oh my." Did she really look like that? Like such an old woman, moving so carefully, as if she didn't trust her own legs.

When the news was over, Irene flicked off the television and sat motionless on the couch. She felt thrilled at being on television, despite her appearance. Surely at least one of her friends had seen it and would call. Irene frowned at the black telephone sitting on the end table, willing it to ring.

It didn't.

After a time her casserole was finished baking. Irene dished some onto a plate, poured a glass of ice water, and took both back to the family room to watch TV. She ate slowly, as was her habit, savoring the spices. Just when she was about to take the last bite, the phone rang. "Oh!" She placed the fork on her plate with a clatter. Then took a breath to calm herself before picking up the receiver. "Hello," she said with anticipation, wondering which friend it might be.

"I have a message for you."

She blinked and drew back her head. Whoever was calling had a serious case of laryngitis. "Yes?"

"Listen very carefully," the voice rasped. "Vote not guilty for Darren Welk. *Not guilty.* Do you understand?"

Irene's mouth opened, then closed. Her hand tightened on the phone. "I don't—who is this?"

"Vote . . . not . . . guilty." The gritty words sandpapered her ear. "Or you'll be sorry."

Click.

Irene stared unseeing at the carpet, her mind trying to land on one coherent thought. The dial tone sounded loudly. She slammed down the phone, fingers still clutching the receiver.

A dam broke in her mind, questions and fears pouring. Somebody knew her phone number. Who? Did the caller also know where she lived?

Irene's head jerked as she sent a frightened gaze through her front window. Was someone out there watching? She saw no one in the street, no unusual car. Irene trembled. She should get up and close the curtains. Then get out of the house. But what if the caller was waiting for her to go outside to her car?

"Oh," Irene said, gasping. She sank into the couch, ducking her head. What was she to *do?*

She had to move.

Before she knew it, her hand was dialing the phone. The receiver shook in her ear as she waited for her friend Rachel to answer.

"Hello."

"I—" No more words came. Air gushed from Irene's mouth.

"Hello?" Rachel sounded impatient.

"It's me," she croaked. "Irene."

"Irene? What's the matter?"

"Is Tom there?" Irene's heart hammered against her chest. She threw a wild look out the window.

"Of course he's here; where else would the old man be?"

"Tell him to come over right now and get me. *Right now,* you hear?" Tears bit Irene's eyes. Her body melted into the couch. "I need to stay at your place tonight."

"Irene, what—"

"Just come! *Now!*" Irene smashed down the phone.

Thursday, August 8

NINETEEN

From the moment she rushed into the jury room, Chelsea knew something was wrong. At first she thought it was her own anxiety over arriving so late with Kerra. Traffic had been particularly slow, and with every red stoplight she'd felt her muscles tense. She didn't want to think about the entire court being held up just because of her. She already felt uncomfortable enough around certain members of the jury. No need to heighten the hostility emanating from Tak, or the distrust from prim and proper Hesta. And more than once Chelsea had caught a piercing glance from Antonio, the short, muscular man who worked in construction.

In the jury room B. B. slouched in a chair, tapping one long pink fingernail against the table. Mike Bariston leaned a shoulder against the wall, arms folded, surveying the floor with his buggy eyes. Sylvia Caster caught Chelsea's gaze and raised her eyebrows almost expectantly. Chelsea drew in a long breath, willing her metabolism to slow. "What's going on?"

"Something, that's what," Henry Slatus answered before Sylvia could open her mouth. He spread pudgy arms, the large diamond ring on his right hand sparkling against his black skin. "Irene ran in a few minutes ago like a mouse chased by a cat. Went right up to Sidney and whispered something in his ear. I swear she was shivering. Next thing we know, he was ushering her out."

Chelsea felt her face go slack. "Is she okay?"

"Don't know." Henry studied her. "You've had lunch with her, haven't you? Did it seem like something was wrong?"

"No, not at all." Chelsea glanced at Sylvia. Clay Alton, the first alternate, sauntered over. He towered above all of them, tilting his head to observe the group from the corner of his eye like some waiting vulture. Gloria Nuevo, a Hispanic woman in her thirties with sleek, chin-length hair, turned from the water cooler, a small cup in her hand. "Candy's not here, either."

"I saw Candy." Victor Chavarria's stooped frame moved behind Sylvia. "She and I were the first ones here. She was jittery, too. Said she needed to talk to Sidney."

Two jurors asking for Sidney Portensic. Chelsea's eyes locked with Clay's.

"So now what?" B. B. asked in her smoky voice.

Clay shrugged. But his bushy eyebrows jumped with obvious anticipation. "We wait."

MILT WAKING PROWLED the courthouse lobby, once again checking his silver Rolex watch. Nine twenty. He drew to a stop near a bench, arms crossed and fingers drumming against his properly exercised biceps. His watchful eyes swept the large hall. Everyone involved in other cases had long since disappeared into their respective courtrooms. Lynn Trudy revved across the way, avidly conjecturing with reporters as to what was going on. The Three Fates perched on a bench, jabbering. It hadn't taken long for the nickname Stan Breckshire had given them to circulate among trial watchers. Lynn Trudy had repeated it to just about everybody.

The sleek-haired reporter from Channel Four popped open a tiny cell phone and began to dial. *That's right,* Milt willed silently, *get bored and leave.* Milt knew enough to stay. Delays happened for a reason. It could be as simple as the judge getting caught in traffic. Or it could be something far more interesting.

Milt's eyes rested on Brett Welk, sitting at the end of one of the long center benches. He leaned forward, hands locked between his knees, eyes fixed on the floor. The knockout young blond appeared, coming from the direction of the bathroom. She slowed, as if not quite sure what to do. Milt watched her catch sight of Brett. She hesitated. Then eased over to him and sat down. He looked up at her and smiled.

Smiled. First time Milt had seen that. Brett straightened, leaning ever so slightly toward the blond, a bit of body language of which Milt doubted he was even conscious. The blond smiled back and said something to him. She looked at Brett with intensity as he answered, as though searching beneath the surface for the truth. Then she began talking, her expression animated. Milt cocked an ear. He heard the words *Golden Gate Bridge* and *Alcatraz*. She sounded like a tourist. Milt pondered that. A tourist at a murder trial?

Brett listened to the blond talk, a softened look on his typically serious face. One hand rested on his knee, the other on the bench between them, practically touching her. Milt didn't need his practiced reporter's eye to see the effervescing attraction.

Very interesting.

STAN STOOD BEFORE Judge Chanson's cherry wood desk, one heel bouncing against the dark carpet. His shoulder wasn't bothering him yet, but he knew he wouldn't have to wait long. Stress was already gathering like a bowling ball, ready to roll down every nerve ending that dared exist between his neck and thumb. Naturally, T. C. was the epitome of cool, which only caused Stan to jitter all the more. The defense attorney's mane of hair lay with perfection as always. Stan was beginning to wonder if the man slept in a hair net. Sitting up. A court reporter huddled, repeating every word into her machine. Jed Trutenning, a tall, heavyset detective with the Redwood City police department, stood wide-legged and formidable, scratching notes in a handheld pad.

"I haven't a *clue* who did this," Erica Salvador declared. Indignation rose from her narrow shoulders like heat from asphalt. She stood with hands on hips, lips pursed, her orange lipstick matching the color of her suit. "This is just too much. All the grief of having a change of venue for our client, and some nutcase butts in from Salinas."

"Who's to say he's from Salinas?" Judge Chanson growled. "For that matter, who's to say it was even a he? Ms. Bracken and Ms. Lowe clearly couldn't tell." She heaved a sigh, shifting in her seat. "Okay." She smacked her hands on the arms of her chair like a general summoning the troops. "Now we get to see if we still have a trial, ladies and gentlemen." She put on her reading glasses, shuffled papers on the desk with a businesslike air. "Let's see, Irene Bracken was juror number one. Juror number two is . . ." She ran a finger down a page.

"Hesta Naples," Stan interjected.

"Yes. Hesta Naples." She looked to the detective, sliding off her glasses. "Okay, Jed. Tell Sidney to bring in Ms. Naples."

For the next two hours they questioned the jurors one at a time. Stan's nerves frayed a little more with each person. One more reported telephone contact and they'd run out of jurors. A mistrial would be declared. That would be even worse than having Chelsea Adams end up on his jury. Finally they faced the final answer with Ms. Adams. No, she said, she had not been contacted and neither Irene nor Candy had told her anything.

The jury was intact. Clay Alton had already replaced Irene Bracken as juror number one. Now Judge Chanson moved Ms. Adams to serve as juror number ten. Ms. Adams looked stunned to hear she would be deliberating.

Well, thought Stan. Apparently, God wasn't telling Ms. Adams very much these days, or she'd have seen it coming.

A thought hit him as Sidney Portensic ushered Chelsea Adams out the door. "You don't think somebody did this just to get Chelsea Adams on the jury, do you?" he burst.

Judge Chanson looked at him askance. "Huh?"

"You know, after the all news stories about her—"

"If I may so remind you, I do not read or listen to the news when I'm in trial!"

"Of course, of course," Stan said, backpedaling. "I'm just saying that if her presence as an alternate made good headlines, imagine how it will be now that she's on the jury."

The judge's cheeks blanched. "I am not interested in what the media has to say, *is that clear?*"

Stan held up both palms in a gesture of surrender.

Judge Chanson snatched her pen off the desk and tapped it furiously. They all waited for her to settle. "You know what I'm going to have to do now," she declared.

Oh yes, they all knew. But no one had wanted to say it. The jury would be anything but happy, and no one wanted an unhappy jury.

"Why didn't you tell each of them when you questioned them?" Stan demanded.

The judge glared at him. "And what would that have accomplished? I didn't even know if we still *had* a jury." She pointed a finger. "I'm going a step at a time here, understand? This is still my trial. No matter what's happened, I do not plan to lose control of my own courtroom."

Stan ducked his head. "Sorry, Your Honor. Just a little upset, that's all." He began pacing.

Judge Chanson's finger turned from Stan to Detective Trutenning. "Jed, I want you to find whoever did this. And do it quick!"

"Good afternoon, ladies and gents." Sidney Portensic bustled into the jury room. "And I do mean afternoon." He made a point of looking at his watch. "For those of you having too much fun to notice."

"Yeah, yeah, Sidney," Victor murmured. "Lots of fun."

"Okay, listen up; here's what coming up next in this here circus." He cringed at the tired chuckles. "Oops, perhaps I shouldn't have put it that way." He drew himself up like a ringmaster addressing his audience. "Now for your entertainment—before we get you some lunch, that is—you all get to see the judge together in the courtroom. No onlookers, no reporters, just you and the judge. And the attorneys, of course. What would the courtroom be without attorneys?" He let his eyes sail toward the ceiling.

"Quieter," Sylvia Caster declared.

"Okay, I want my ducks in a row." Sidney shooed them with his wide hands. "Line up, please."

Gloria Neuvo looked none too happy as she motioned Chelsea to take the emptied place in line behind her. Raising her shoulders in apology, Chelsea slid into place. Juror number ten. She could not believe this was happening. The thought of deliberating with this group filled her with discomfort. *Did you plan this all along, Lord? Is this what you wanted?*

Sidney stood beside the line, his head bobbing up and down on his thick neck as he checked each juror. "Okay. Let's head 'em up and move 'em out."

Chelsea filed with the others down the hall, worries of Kerra filling her head. Had she been with Brett Welk all morning as they waited for news? Chelsea was afraid she knew the answer too well. Brett was the only other person Kerra had talked to. *Dear God, please protect Kerra.*

The air in the courtroom seemed thick and full of portent, as if dark thunderheads were gathering. Judge Chanson and the attorneys watched the jurors take their seats in silence. Stan Breckshire perched on the edge of his chair behind the prosecution table, a bouncing foot pushing his whole body into motion.

"Well, folks," Judge Chanson began, "we're back together, with a few changes. We welcome Mr. Alton and Ms. Adams onto the jury." Her brief smile was overshadowed by the seriousness of her tone. "Now that it's clear we still have twelve members for the jury, we face the next obstacle. We can't afford to lose one more of you. Therefore"—she leaned forward—"I find myself in the position of having to take extreme precautions to protect the proceedings of this trial. Even though the trial is only two days under way, much money, time, and energy has already been spent on the change of venue and all the pretrial hearings. So until this trial and your deliberations are concluded, I'm going to have to sequester you."

Gloria gasped softly. Chelsea's stomach wrenched. *God, no!* She could not possibly be sequestered. Absolutely no way.

"Obviously, this is a surprise. If there is anyone who unequivocally cannot be sequestered, this is the time to say so. But remember"—the judge raised a hand—"that the loss of just one of you means a mistrial. So even though I might empathize with your situation, I will not easily be persuaded to allow any of you to go at this time." She shifted in her chair. "Now I imagine some of you have questions."

Chelsea sat frozen as questions and answers ping-ponged back and forth. Where would they sleep? Where would they eat? What about their clothes? In Chelsea's first thoughts none of that mattered. *How can you let me be separated from Kerra, God?* she raged. *After you made it so clear that I should bring her here for spiritual help? What's she going to do now, hang around with Brett Welk?*

And what about Paul? What if he can't call me? Surely, Lord, you're not going to let me be cut off from everyone!

Chelsea rested her forehead on her fingers and closed her eyes. Landing on this jury had been a bad dream to start with. Now it was turning into a nightmare.

TWELVE FORTY-FIVE. Kerra glanced up to see Stan Breckshire hustle out the courtroom door. Within seconds Lynn Trudy had cornered him, hair and blood red fingernails spiking the air as she demanded to know what was going on. Stan gripped her elbow and pulled her aside, where they spoke animatedly.

A moment later Terrance Clyde glided from the courtroom, Erica Salvador's heels clacking at his side. Brett pulled to his feet, mumbling, "Finally." Kerra watched him make a beeline for the attorneys. Milt Waking snapped to attention, along with the cadre of newspaper reporters. The other television reporters had long since packed it in.

Kerra watched the defense attorney talk to Brett, his spread hands and calming expression like that of a parent breaking bad news to a child. Brett's shoulders slumped.

Like a flash fire, the news spread through the courthouse hallway. The air crackled as reporters surrounded the attorneys, launching futile questions. Milt Waking's cameraman jockeyed for position, lights flaring. The attorneys backed into the courtroom and disappeared, leaving the media to feast upon Lynn Trudy and Brett. Channel Seven's camera whirred in Brett's whitened face.

Kerra found her way to a far wall and leaned against it, mind scrambling. What would happen to Aunt Chelsea? How would they see each other? Realizations licked at Kerra like flames. She couldn't be with Aunt Chelsea at all. She might as well go home. Tears pricked her eyes.

"I said no comment!" Brett's voice, thick with emotion, reverberated in her ears. Furiously he pushed through reporters. Remorse pinched Kerra's nerves. How could she be thinking only of herself?

"Brett!" Before she knew it, she was scurrying toward him, reaching out a hand. "Come on, let's get out of here!"

Brett gripped her hand, aiming a sizzling look over his shoulders at the reporters. Fueled by adrenaline, they hustled down the courthouse escalator, across the first-floor hall, and out the doors, not stopping until they'd rounded the corner of the building. There they sank onto a bench, breathing hard, blinking in the warm sun and trying to collect their wits.

TWENTY

Janet Cline sighed as she returned to her office after ushering the childless couple out the door. Her chest felt like lead. She hadn't slept well the previous night, thanks to the visit from Rogelio Sanchez.

Why am I so unhinged? she asked herself for the dozenth time. There had to be an explanation. Perhaps Rogelio's girlfriend had begun proceedings with the Welk agency but had dropped them and moved to another. Perhaps she'd lied to him about his being the father.

The fax machine on her desk clicked. Janet dropped into her chair and stared at it, hoping it was the fax from Sacramento. Paper began feeding through the machine. Janet's back muscles tensed. The top of the fax scrolled into view. She saw the familiar social services logo and drew in a hard breath. She leaned forward, ready to snatch the paper. As it continued to scroll, she ran her eyes over the handwritten note.

Hi, Janet. Here's the document you wanted. Let me know if I can do anything else for you.

Pat

Janet pulled the first sheet out and waited for the second. The top of the relinquishment form rolled up. One hand hovering over the machine, she read the typed and handwritten language on the official document.

I/We, the _father_ of _Roselita Nicole,_ a minor _female_ child . . .

She held her breath and prayed to see the name and address of some other agency. To no avail. "Welk Adoption Agency" practically leaped off the page. Briefly she closed her eyes.

All right. So she and Shawna had handled the adoption. Then Rogelio couldn't be the father. Some other young man's signature would be on that form—some name she would recognize.

The legalese scrolled into view. Below it would be the name of the father.

Please, God, let it be somebody else.

Rogelio Sanchez

Air seeped from Janet's throat. She stared blankly at the name, trying to absorb the news. Suddenly a vivid memory spun through her head. Shawna snapping up straight and yanking a key from a square gray lockbox when Janet had unexpectedly entered her office. She'd looked flushed, like a child caught with her hand in the cookie jar. Janet hadn't given it much thought. Now she wondered.

What had been in that box?

Slowly Janet slid the paper from the machine. She checked the lines for the required signatures of two witnesses—lines that had been empty on Rogelio's copy. They were filled. Tracey Wilagher and Shawna Welk. Janet dropped her gaze further to the "authorized agency official" line, and her heart stumbled.

Her own forged signature stared back at her.

TWENTY-ONE

This is a fine how-do-you-do, Stan Breckshire ragged to himself as he tried to swallow the last bite of a turkey sandwich. He'd eaten at the deli counter, standing up. Couldn't restrain his energy enough to sit.

As he walked briskly back to the courthouse, he wondered how his twelve were doing in the jury room. Heaven knew they'd better get used to those four walls, because they were going to be seeing a lot of them. Lunch would be brought in from now on. Escorted trips to and from the courtroom. Escorted trips to some nearby hotel, probably as sterile and cold as his own. Only one or two immediate family members would be allowed to call.

Nearly two o'clock. Court would be resuming. Finally. It seemed like days ago that Stan had questioned Detective Draker. The man had been cooling his heels all day as he waited to continue his testimony. *Great,* thought Stan as he bounced up the courthouse steps. A ticked-off witness, a ticked-off jury, and no doubt about it, a ticked-off judge.

Just great.

By two thirty Stan was once again ensconced in questioning the detective. Everybody had reconvened, one big unhappy family—except for the extra-large flock of reporters. Stan wondered where they all had come from. Some soundless cry had summoned them from all corners of the wind. Now they perched in their seats like beady-eyed seagulls picking just-hatched turtles off a beach.

Something else swirled in the courtroom. Suspicion. Stan saw it played out in the probing eyes of the spectators and jurors, the glare of the judge, the stone face of Darren Welk. Somebody had contacted the jury—somebody with a lot to gain or lose. Was that person in the courtroom? Stan knew that the major players in the case, like Lynn Trudy, Tracey Wilagher, and Brett Welk, would be among the first questioned, regardless of whether they were rooting for the prosecution or the defense. And hopefully Trutenning would question reporters too. Calls from the jail were taped, so Darren Welk couldn't have managed the deed. Nor could he have known the phone numbers of the two jurors. But he certainly had the dough to pay someone.

Was he that stupid?

"Now, Detective Draker," Stan said, bringing his thoughts in line as he paced in front of his table, "you told us yesterday that on the Saturday after the disappearance of Shawna Welk, two items washed up on the beach—a piece of navy blue fabric and a tooth. Would you tell us what you discovered about these two items? Perhaps the fabric first."

Detective Draker's expression was as flat as always. "The fabric was ripped and looked as if it had come from the bottom of a pant leg. Tracey Wilagher identified the fabric as belonging to the suit her mother had worn the night of February fifteenth."

Stan nodded. "Did you verify this information?"

"Yes. Miss Wilagher had brought her mother's jacket home with her from the beach. We were able to match the piece of fabric to the jacket."

Stan turned to the prosecution table and pulled forward a large paper bag. Opening it, he extracted the piece of fabric and the jacket and spread them carefully before the detective. "Can you identify these items?"

The detective examined them carefully, almost grimly. "Yes. This is the piece of fabric that washed up onshore, and the matching jacket."

"Thank you." Stan gathered the items and held them out for the jury to see. Slowly he walked the length of the jury box. The new juror number one, Clay Alton, perused the items at length, then jotted in his notes. Stan slid a glance to Chelsea Adams. Her expression was impassive as she considered the clothing. Her hands lay folded in her lap. No notebook.

His display done, Stan returned the clothes to their bag and logged them with the clerk.

"Now, Detective. What about the tooth? You said it appeared to be human?"

"Yes. We took it to Dr. Richard Cooper, Mrs. Welk's dentist, and asked him to determine if the tooth belonged to Shawna Welk."

IT WAS EVERYTHING CHELSEA could do to keep her eyes from straying to Kerra as the afternoon's testimony dragged on. Sequestered only four hours, and already Chelsea's fears were coming to pass.

Kerra and Brett were sitting together.

Chelsea had given up trying to convince herself that it didn't matter. Trouble was brewing; she could smell it. A young woman ready to "love again" thrown together with a lonely young man.

Lord, please protect Kerra. You know she needs to draw back to you. I claim in your name, Jesus, that this relationship won't lead her further astray.

How Chelsea wished her Christian mentor, Gladys, were around to help her pray for Kerra and the trial. But Gladys was on a three-state tour with her group of "motorcycle grannies." Chelsea also longed to talk to Marian Turnbow, the dear friend she'd made during the Trent Park case. But Marian and her new husband, Pat, were still on their long honeymoon in Europe.

Dear God, appoint someone to cover me in prayer. You know how much I need it.

Chelsea drew in a deep breath. She needed to keep her mind focused as Terrance Clyde cross-examined Detective Draker. Brett and Kerra continued to pull at her eyes. But she would not look. She would not allow her dismay to show. Chelsea knew Kerra well enough to realize that her concern would be seen as overprotection. Raising a barrier between herself and Kerra would be the worst thing she could do. The only communication they would have now would be by telephone, and Chelsea needed her niece to listen.

Only four hours had passed. And the weekend was coming. That would be a lot of empty time. Chelsea needed to get Kerra on a plane back home—now.

THE JURY ROOM BUSTLED with activity. Court was over for the day, and Chelsea knew that she and the other jurors would soon be escorted to a bus that would take them to their as-yet-undisclosed hotel. Once in their individual rooms, they'd be allowed to call family members and instruct them what to pack. Suitcases were to be brought to the hotel lobby and disbursed from there. Dinner would be brought to jurors in their rooms. Once in a while, Sidney told them, they'd be escorted as a group out to dinner.

One detail after another had to be dealt with. Some of the jurors lived alone. Who would pack for them? Friends had to be called to the courthouse to be given a key to these jurors' homes. Victor Chavarria had planned to stop by a twenty-four-hour pharmacy after court and drop off a prescription for his heart pills. His wife would need to come get the prescription, now tucked in his pocket. Mike Bariston was supposed to pick up his four-year-old son from day care. He wasn't sure if his wife could make it from work in time if he waited to call her from the hotel. Could he call now? Sylvia Caster had a meeting that evening. She needed to call to say she couldn't attend.

Sidney managed to deal with them all, never losing his good cheer. Chelsea felt sorry for him as he tried to keep everyone straight.

She waited until things had finally calmed down, then pulled him aside to speak with him.

"Sidney, I have no one to call at home, either," she said. "My husband's out of the country. However, my niece is visiting and has been watching the trial. She's no doubt in the hall right now, wondering what to do. She has no way to get home; I have the car keys. I need to see her now."

The whites of Sidney's eyes grew large as he drew back to study her. "Your niece is watching the trial?"

Chelsea hesitated. "Yes. But we certainly haven't been talking about the proceedings. Do you think it's wrong that she's here?"

"I really don't know." Sidney thought a moment. "Do the judge and attorneys know your niece is out there?"

"I doubt it. What would they do anyway?"

"Not sure." He gave her a grin. "Let me go find your niece. You'll have to meet her outside the door here in a hurry, okay? What does she look like?"

Chelsea told him. Then prayed hard as he disappeared to find Kerra. *Please, God, help me convince her to go home.*

BRETT PUSHED OUT the courthouse door, thoughts cycling between hope and fury. He was headed straight for his hotel room, where he'd take a shower before going out. For the rest of the evening he wanted nothing to do with reporters, attorneys, onlookers, even his father.

"Brett Welk!"

He scudded to a stop, snapped his head around. "What?"

A large man with steel gray eyes approached, dripping authority. "Afternoon. I'm Jed Trutenning, detective with the Redwood City police department." He held out a hand.

Brett shook it reluctantly. What now?

"I'm investigating the jury tampering that occurred last night," Trutenning said. "Just need to ask you a few questions."

Brett looked heavenward in disgust. "What do you want to talk to *me* for? I don't know anything about it."

"It's routine; I have to talk to everyone connected with the case." Trutenning shifted his considerable weight. "The best way to catch the perpetrator is to cross the innocent ones off our list."

Brett blew out air. "I've got to be somewhere; can't we do this another time?"

"Afraid not. I've got to get moving. You want us to get to the bottom of this, don't you?" He gave Brett a piercing look.

"Yeah, sure. Whatever." Brett's shoulders slumped. "But better make it quick. I'm not missing my appointment."

CHELSEA AND KERRA FACED each other outside the jury room, Sidney respectfully waiting at a distance. Chelsea handed Kerra the keys to the car and told her she'd be calling with instructions about what to pack.

Kerra hesitated. "Okay. What time will you call?"

"I don't know; as soon as I can. Why?"

A shrug. "No reason."

Chelsea eyed her, not bothering to mask the distrust on her face.

Kerra looked perturbed. "Okay, so I may be going out for a quick dinner, that's all. But I'll do everything you need first, don't worry. I'm going to miss you. I was so upset when I heard the news! But I've gotten hold of myself now. At least it's good I'll be around to feed your fish and water the plants."

"Kerra," Chelsea replied, "there's no point in your staying. About the time the trial's over, you'll be scheduled to fly home."

"I know, but I'm not leaving." Kerra fiddled with the handle of her purse. "What's to go back to anyway? I can sit around here as well as at my parents' house. Besides, like I said, I can take care of your place. And just by being in court every day, I'll support you. Plus you said we can talk at night, right?"

Desperately Chelsea sought the right words. "Kerra, what are you going to do the whole time, especially on the weekend? You don't even know anyone else here."

Kerra's eyes flickered. "I'll be fine. Really."

They stared at each other, unspoken words almost tangible between them. Kerra blinked first. "Look, I'd better go to the house. I'll be waiting for your call."

They hugged each other. "I'll be praying for you," Chelsea said, defeat in her voice. "You take care of yourself. And be careful."

Chelsea leaned against the wall as she watched Sidney lead her niece away. If Kerra had been as upset at the news as she'd claimed, she certainly had recovered in a hurry.

MILT WAKING HOVERED NEAR the door leading to the hall behind courtroom 2H, thoughts churning. Moments ago he'd seen the blond babe that had been hanging around Brett Welk disappear through it, ushered by the bailiff. And he'd overheard the bailiff's explanation: "Your aunt needs to see you." With the inevitable back-stage chaos of sequestering the jury, Milt could only imagine one reason for such a statement. One jaw-dropping reason.

The blond's aunt was one of the twelve.

His mind raced through the possibilities and came up with few. There weren't that many white women on the jury. He pictured the thin-lipped, severe-looking juror number two; juror number seven, about the same age, with short dark hair; and the younger, rather chubby woman with the straight brown hair who sat in seat five. And of course Chelsea Adams.

No way. Too good to be true.

Footsteps sounded behind the door. Milt gathered himself for the gamble. He'd slam her with a question, see if she squirmed.

The door opened. The blond slipped through, car keys clutched in her hand.

He pounced. "Did your aunt have any visions about this happening? She is Chelsea Adams, right?"

The blond jumped. Her face drained white. Milt couldn't believe it. He'd hit pay dirt!

"I'm not . . . I don't want to talk to you," she stammered, turning away.

"Please, wait." He laid a hand on her arm, voice coated with sincerity. She darted frightened eyes to his face. He thought quickly. "I just want to tell you to be careful. You're visiting here, aren't you?"

Her lips parted. "How did you know that?"

"I heard you talking about sight-seeing. But look, my concern is that you're now left on your own while your aunt's sequestered, and—"

"What's that to you?" she snapped, drawing away from his touch.

How ridiculously easy this was. Milt zigzagged worry lines into his forehead. "Sorry. I shouldn't have bothered you. But I was hoping . . . Would you have dinner with me tonight?"

She gazed at him in utter disbelief. Then blinked in defiance. "Sorry, I'm busy."

He sighed. "I knew it. Brett Welk beat me to it."

She drew back, mouth tightening. The glare she gave him could have frosted ice. "I have nothing to say to you. *Ever.*"

Milt smiled to himself as he watched her stalk away on shaky legs.

TWENTY-TWO

Mama Yolanda sat on the worn couch in her living room, eyes closed, head bent. The windows were open, and a hot breeze filtered through the screens, flicking at a page of an open Spanish magazine lying on the coffee table. The soft crackle of the paper mixed with the shouts and laughter of neighborhood children, but Yolanda barely heard the noises as she prayed.

The feelings had grown in strength today. Strong enough to drown out the sounds in her head, the sounds of the baby crying. Something was wrong with the trial. Yolanda had no idea what. She only knew that she was to pray. Still, she did not know why God was calling her. But surely he had a reason. Yolanda's faith, honed over years of hardship, was simple: Give your heart to Jesus, then trust him enough to do what he says.

A car chugged up to the curb and cut its motor. Yolanda only half-registered the sound. A moment later the door opened, then closed. Yolanda's lips ceased moving. Rogelio was home.

"Hi, Mama Yolanda." He wiped sweat from his brow as he dragged himself to stand before her. He looked so tired. "What are you doing, dozing?" He spoke to her in Spanish.

"What do you think I am, an old woman?" She clucked her tongue. "I was praying."

Remorse flicked across his dirty face. Ay, did her grandson think she prayed about nothing but the baby? An urge to ease his pain filled her chest. "I was praying for the trial of Darren Welk."

A frown. "Why?"

Yolanda sighed. "I am not sure, *mijo*. God knows."

He regarded her silently, processing.

"When God wants to do something special on this earth," she said, "he calls people to pray."

"But why you? About the trial, I mean?"

Something in his tone. What was it? Yolanda sucked her gold tooth, considering him. It was almost as if he knew something.

But that was impossible.

She flicked a hand. "So many questions. And I have yet to hear, 'What's for supper?'"

His shoulders relaxed. "What *is* for supper?" He lifted his nose and sniffed.

Unfortunately, there was nothing to smell. She'd been praying so hard, she'd forgotten to start cooking.

ROGELIO WONDERED AT HIS grandmother's words as he drove toward Janet Cline's house. The amazing thing was, Mama Yolanda did not know that the Welk Adoption Agency was responsible for taking her own great-grandchild away. Had she guessed?

He parked in front of the woman's house, turned off the motor, and took a deep breath. He was ready to face whatever she told him. If she stopped helping him, he would do what he had to—even go to authorities with his story. But he cringed at the thought. The rift between him and Kristin was already bad enough.

Kristin.

Rogelio's heart sagged with grief. He dropped his head back against the car seat and closed his eyes. He *would* get Kristin back. Just as he would get their baby back.

"When God wants to do something special on this earth, he calls people to pray."

Rogelio exhaled audibly. The car was so hot. As he slipped the keys from the ignition, he offered his own prayer. *God, please. If you do this for me, I'll do whatever you want.*

He got out of the car and shut the door. As he forced himself to saunter up Janet Cline's sidewalk, he fervently hoped God would accept a bargain.

THROUGH THE SHEER CURTAINS, Janet watched Rogelio approach the door, dread in her veins. She could not tell him everything she now knew. Once she'd seen the smoking gun of that first fax, she'd called her friend in Sacramento and asked that the other signed documents be sent, including the ones from the adoptive parents. She'd nearly dropped the papers when she read their names.

No wonder Shawna hadn't told her about this adoption. Janet never would have accepted this couple. The question was, why had Shawna? Surely she knew the man's reputation as well as anyone who read the Salinas papers. The *Californian* had certainly run enough stories about all the charges he'd faced. He'd always managed to squirm out of them, but that only spoke more loudly of his guilt, as far as Janet was concerned. The man evidently had friends in high places.

What was she going to do?

Could she convince Rogelio to drop the whole idea? Leave his baby with the adoptive parents? Janet bit the inside of her cheek. Could she have that on her conscience? What kind of future might the little girl have with a father like that?

Yet how to set this matter straight quietly? Unquestionably, the media would pick up on it, obsessed as they already were with the other events surrounding the Welks' lives. It would be just one more titillating detail for the public to feast upon. And she, Janet Cline, would be thrust into the spotlight. That was what she feared most. She didn't trust the adoptive father. What might he do if he heard his baby was about to be taken away?

The doorbell rang. Janet propelled herself to answer it.

"Okay," she began slowly after she and Rogelio had seated themselves in her living room. "I've seen the papers, and it seems there is a problem with the adoption."

Rogelio leaned forward on her couch, long arms dangling between his knees. At her statement his face lit up. Janet's heart sank. "What do we do now? How soon can I get the baby?"

Janet searched for words. "I don't think we should pursue this."

Surprise contorted his face. "Why?"

What to say? He could end up going to the police, telling them she'd refused to help. "I don't think it would be safe. For either of us."

"Why?"

As its jaws opened before her, Janet realized the trap she'd set for herself. Mentally she flung about for a way out, landing in the formal speech of a social worker. "First, the reputation of the adoptive father suggests that he's not likely to accept his child being taken away from him after so many months." She shook her head. "What father or mother would? Second, these parents are the only ones the baby has ever known. It would be very upsetting to the child to remove her from the home now."

"Who is the father?" Rogelio demanded.

Janet braced herself. "I'm not going to tell you that."

"You *have* to tell me! If the adoption's not legal, you have to make it right!"

"Rogelio"—Janet leaned forward, intensity in her voice—"you're not hearing me. This man's not going to give up easily; he'll fight. And it may not be pretty. I can't allow you to go banging on his door. What if he hurt you?"

"*Hurt* me?" Rogelio shoved to his feet, lips whitening. "I don't care what he tries; I can take care of myself. Besides, if he's so bad, why should I leave my baby with him?"

Janet traced a pattern on her skirt with a fingertip. She hated herself for what she was about to say. "You may not worry about your own safety. But what about your grandmother? She is older, less able to defend herself."

Rogelio's anger undulated over her. "A man can take care of his own family! I want my baby back, especially after what you have told me. And I'll get her, with or without your help!"

Weariness weighted Janet to the chair. "What can you do if I don't help you? These records are closed. You cannot find out the name of the adoptive parents."

"I'll go to the police, that's what I'll do! I'll tell them everything."

"Think about it, Rogelio." Her words fell rapidly, twisting the truth to save her hide. Even as she spoke, Janet felt sick. "What kind of trouble will you place yourself in if you tell the police? You sold a baby. What about your girlfriend? Kristin was given a lot of money. How is she going to feel about you after you turn her in to the police?"

Rogelio swallowed, anger crumbling into obvious confusion. He stared at her, breathing hard. Seconds ticked by. "Will you help me or not?"

Janet squeezed her eyes shut. "I don't know."

"Fine." He headed for the hall. Janet hurried after him.

"Wait—"

"I'll give you until tomorrow to decide." He pointed an accusing finger at her. "You say the problem is me, Kristin, my grandmother. No, Mrs. Cline, the problem is you. I *will* get Roselita Nicole back, for my grandmother's sake. You won't stop me."

He strode into the entryway and yanked open the door. It slammed on his way out.

TWENTY-THREE

Kerra pulled the large wheeled suitcase up to the reception desk of the Welthing Hotel in San Carlos. In it was enough clothing for her aunt Chelsea to wear to trial through the end of the following week. Kerra had found herself scanning pages in Aunt Chelsea's Bible as she packed it. The Bible sure had been used a lot. Verses were underlined, notes carefully written in the margins. Kerra had closed the Bible reverently, hands lingering on the textured leather cover. How did it feel, she'd wondered, to know God as well as Aunt Chelsea did?

Within minutes the transaction at the reception desk was complete. The suitcase would soon be delivered to the appropriate room. Kerra exited the hotel, reading a short note Aunt Chelsea had left for her at the desk.

Please call Paul in London and give him the number of this hotel. You and he have been approved to call me. Also, please phone me yourself sometime this evening. Take care.

Kerra folded the note and slid it into her purse, then checked her watch. In ten minutes she was to meet Brett for dinner at Max's in

Redwood City. Her skin fairly tingled at the thought, despite her anxiety over the encounter with that awful reporter. She did not know how that man knew. But she told herself she didn't care. She just wanted to think about tonight.

Something had happened that afternoon between her and Brett. Holding hands as they ran from reporters, breathlessly flinging themselves on the bench—those actions, fueled by shared surprise and fear, had linked them together within this bizarre chain of events. They'd sat on that bench for over an hour, ignoring the beating sun, saying nothing in one moment, venting their frustration the next. By the time they returned to the courthouse, their dinner date had been set.

Entering the crowded restaurant, Kerra put her name on the waiting list, then stood aside, watching the door.

Ten minutes passed. Fifteen. The host called Kerra's name, and she had to let others go ahead of her. Twenty minutes. Her legs grew tired from standing. Kerra leaned against a wall, doubts filling her. Should she give up and leave? Maybe this wasn't the right thing to do anyway. Wasn't she being terribly unfaithful to Dave's memory?

Of course she was. How could she even think of doing this?

She pushed away from the wall to go. Then in whisked Brett, eyes darting, his face a mask of concern. "I'm sorry! I'm just so glad you're still here." He caught her hand, drawing quick breaths.

Her heart melted at his touch, her doubts tumbling away. "It's okay. I wouldn't leave."

Brett's eyes searched hers, as if he wondered whether she was telling the truth. "Let's get our table and I'll tell you what happened."

As soon as they were settled, Brett related his interview with Detective Trutenning.

"What did you tell him?" Kerra asked, amazed. How could they even think Brett had anything to do with the phone calls?

"Nothing, except I didn't do it." Brett took a drink of water. "How would I know those jurors' phone numbers? I don't even know their names."

Kerra tilted her head. "How would anybody know?"

He shrugged. "Someone with access to records, maybe. Someone who at least knows how the system works. And evidently someone who wants my dad found innocent. Although it's not too hard to think of a whole list of such people. Do you know how many we employ on the ranch? Someone may figure that if my dad were convicted, we'd have to sell the place, even though that's not true. Still, how would someone in Salinas know those numbers?" He lapsed into silence. Then shook his head. "But I don't want to talk about the trial anymore," he declared. "I've had enough of it." He pushed aside his water glass and slid his hands across the table to cover hers. "I want to talk about you."

"I want to talk about you."

Kerra's throat constricted as Dave's face rose in her thoughts. The same words, at another table, another restaurant, so long ago. Dave had urged her out of her shell, eventually made her fall in love.

Brett watched her intently. For a moment she thought she'd pull back in sudden vulnerability, and they'd fall into the quicksand of trivial chatter. Perhaps that was best. Perhaps this should go no further.

"Earth to Kerra." Brett squeezed her hand. She couldn't help but be drawn toward him.

The guilt rose again. She pushed it down. What was wrong with being attracted to Brett? She'd loved Dave, but Dave was dead. He'd died a year and a half ago. Now here was Brett, holding her hands. Waiting.

Willfully Kerra blinked away the memory of Dave. She gave Brett a wan smile. "What would you like to know?"

"Okay, so I may be going out for a quick dinner."

Right, Chelsea thought as she unpacked her suitcase. A quick dinner. Nothing to trouble her head about. Her niece, who'd apparently left God far behind, was only going out for "a quick dinner" with the son of a man accused of murder. And there wasn't anything Chelsea could do about it. Not tonight. Nor tomorrow or the next day, should this new friendship continue to grow. And why shouldn't it, with no sensible person around to stop it?

Is this what you brought Kerra here for, God? Chelsea railed. *Just to separate me from her when she needs me badly—now more than ever?*

Chelsea jerked her Bible out of the suitcase and tossed it on the bed. Then stood staring at it. She really ought to pick it up, read some. Perhaps she'd find some comfort.

She swung away and hung up clothes instead. At the moment she was too mad for comfort.

When all her clothes were put away, toiletries placed on the bathroom counter, the suitcase stored in a closet, Chelsea paced at the foot of the bed, wishing for some other task to channel her energies. A commentary of her disappointments ran like a broken tape through her head. She simply could not understand what God was trying to do. Why, why, *why* had he allowed her to be sequestered? Some thanks this was for her obedience.

For another fifteen minutes Chelsea fretted and fumed. Then finally, in sheer desperation, she parked herself on the bed and reached for her Bible.

Where to read?

She didn't want to read *at all.*

Chelsea closed her eyes, tiredly asking God what to do. After a moment the book of Daniel came to mind. She'd always found it both fascinating and comforting, particularly because of Daniel's ability to serve God in such a pagan place as the palace of the Babylonian king. Sighing, Chelsea stacked two pillows against the wall, leaned against them, and opened her Bible to Daniel.

She read for a while, hoping that the words would calm her spirit, but no verse in particular caught her eye. Then at chapter 9, verse 3 seemed to leap off the page.

So I gave my attention to the Lord God to seek Him by prayer and supplications.

Chelsea read the verse again, then lay the Bible on her lap, allowing her gaze to drift across the room as she pondered. There Daniel was, she realized, in the king's court, removed from his own people the Israelites. Given earthly power by the Babylonian king and used as a channel for God's power. Daniel had accomplished some amazing things with God's help—discerning dreams and God's handwriting on the wall, surviving the lions' den. But in this situation of seeking the Israelites' freedom from captivity, the only power Daniel could wield was through prayer.

Chelsea rested her head against the pillows.

... seek him by prayer and supplications ...

The phrase resounded within her. She knew God had called her to pray for individuals involved in the trial. But she felt he was trying to tell her more. Chelsea prayed now for further understanding, asking God to help her push aside her anger and disappointment. Slowly then, as she sat waiting, listening, impressions began to fill her mind. The sense that God had chosen her for a particular purpose in this trial. That he needed her obedience, regardless of her emotions. Maybe he would send her visions. Maybe at times she would need to *do* something. Other times all she would be able to do was pray. She needed to keep her eyes on God every moment, as she'd learned through the Trent Park case last year. God would lead her. Even in moments when she felt very blind.

As this understanding seeped through Chelsea, it did not bring comfort. She merely felt all the more frightened. She was no Daniel. She was just a mom who lived in California with two rowdy boys and a non-Christian husband. She could make mistakes so easily—she'd made them before. How was she going to do this?

"Help me, Lord," she begged aloud. "Help me be faithful. I want to do whatever you ask of me. I want to know when I should act and when I should pray. I want you to accomplish your will through my obedience."

Tears pricked her eyes. "But right now, Lord, I still feel pretty mad about the whole thing. Plus lonely and scared, both for me and for Kerra. I just want to run and hide, and take my niece with me. *Please*, God, protect her. Please."

KERRA RETURNED TO THE house just before eleven, heart shimmering over her evening with Brett. They had talked a long time. Mostly she had talked of losing Dave. And a funny thing had happened. The more she spoke of her past grief, the more she realized just how much she longed to put it behind her. She not only wanted to love again; she needed it. She needed to connect with *life* again.

Brett had said little of himself, although he had told her of his mother's death and how much he missed her. With unspoken agreement, they had avoided any discussion of Shawna and his father.

It was late now but Kerra knew she should call her aunt. Then she wanted to watch the news. As she dialed the hotel number, she tried to force down her excitement. Aunt Chelsea had a knack for picking up vocal nuances.

Their conversation was brief. Aunt Chelsea sounded tired, distracted, plus she asked too many questions. Kerra remained vague about how she'd spent her evening, although she sensed that her aunt already knew. Promising to call again tomorrow night, she hung up the phone with relief.

Hurrying into the family room, she flicked on the television to Channel Seven. Commercials. She went into the kitchen for a glass of water and returned. She told herself she was simply curious about the media coverage. What would the station have to say about the jury being sequestered? But deep within, a little warning niggled in her stomach. What if her own defensive anger at the reporter had given her and Brett away?

Kerra stood before the television, shifting impatiently from foot to foot. The news anchorwoman flashed on the screen. "Tonight we have extensive coverage on the Salad King trial," she announced, "as the case faced a major shake-up this morning." Kerra's eyes remained glued to the set as the anchorwoman told of the juror phone contacts and sequestration. "And Channel Seven has obtained inside information about the trial that only further complicates this already fascinating case. Here is Milt Waking's exclusive report, filmed at the end of today's court session, to give you all the details."

Kerra's insides gelled. Milt Waking's disgusting, handsome face filled the screen. Her fingers gripped the glass, her eyes narrowing as she listened to his report about the sequestering. He played up the fact that her aunt Chelsea, "the visions woman from the Trent Park case last year," was now one of the twelve who would be deliberating. "And in further stunning news," he continued, "I have learned that the visiting niece of this woman has been attending the trial and has struck up a friendship with Brett Welk, the defendant's son. An inside source has confirmed that the two are having dinner together tonight...."

Kerra choked out a cry. The glass of water slipped from her hand.

FRIDAY, AUGUST 9

TWENTY-FOUR

Stan Breckshire fumed his way toward the judge's chambers, the morning newspaper clutched in his hand. Media report or not, Judge Carol Chanson was going to hear about this. Maybe the woman would finally admit she never should have allowed that fanatic Chelsea Adams on the jury in the first place. Look at all the trouble Ms. Adams was causing! Stan drew up short in front of the door and banged with his knuckles. Only problem was, it was too late for the judge's admission. Now all she could do would be to call a mistrial, and Stan certainly didn't want that.

"Who *is* it?" Judge Chanson's voice griped from behind the door. She opened it, scowling.

"We need to talk," he declared. "Summon Terrance and Erica."

Her features darkened further. "I'll thank you not to take that tone of voice with me, counsel." Her eyes fell on the newspaper. "What is it now; you know I can't look at that."

"You *have* to look at it."

She drew herself up, neck mottling. "Mr. Breckshire, if—"

"The niece of our favorite juror, Chelsea Adams, has been attending the trial since day one," he spouted. "And now she's going out with Brett Welk!"

Myriad expressions crossed Judge Chanson's face. She blinked rapidly, eyes dancing from Stan to the newspaper and back. Finally she drew in a deep breath, hefty shoulders rising. "Find defense counsel and bring them here immediately." She swung the door shut.

Five minutes later they were all assembled in the judge's chambers. The court reporter stood nearby, machine ready. Judge Chanson had donned her robe. No doubt, Stan crabbed to himself, to remind them all that she was in charge. If that's what she could call it.

The judge eyed all three of them as if they were recalcitrant pupils. She turned to Terrance Clyde. "I suppose you know why we're here."

T. C. was all pomp and circumspection. "Yes, Your Honor. I saw the paper. Apparently, the print media has picked up the story from one of the—"

"I don't care about who's saying what." The words kicked across her massive desk like pebbles under an impatient foot. "I want to know if you knew about this relationship."

"Of course not!" T. C. exclaimed as air puffed from Erica's offended mouth. Erica threw an icy glance at Stan. "I didn't even know the niece was in the courtroom," T. C. added.

Judge Chanson considered them both. "Who is she anyway?"

T. C. raised a shoulder. "Not sure, but from her description I'd guess she's that young, pretty blond."

"Not that it matters." The judge waved a dismissive hand. "I've checked my records as to who was allowed to call Ms. Adams after the jury was sequestered. A husband is listed, who's apparently overseas on a business trip. Also listed is Kerra Fraye, a visiting niece."

"Well, there you go," Stan said snidely.

Judge Chanson shot daggers at him. He stuck a hand in his hair and rubbed.

"All right. I'll have to get to the bottom of this. Then I'll decide what to do. Mr. Breckshire"—she aimed laser eyes—"any other thoughts at this time? That are worth sharing?"

Erica snorted. Stan's fingers curled at the sound. The judge glared at her. Erica recovered, managing a delicate cough.

Stan could think of a dozen things, all better left unsaid. "No, Your Honor."

"Fine then." A look of regal command settled upon the judge's features. "Mr. Clyde, may I prevail upon you to find Sidney and ask him to bring Ms. Adams to my chambers? The rest of us shall wait."

A LUMP SAT IN Chelsea's chest as she entered the deliberation room. She'd slept intermittently the previous night, her mind swirling with thoughts of Kerra and the trial.

Oh, Lord, I know you've called me to pray. But I'm tired this morning, and I still can't help being frightened for Kerra. She sounded so distant when she phoned last night. Please draw her to you. Protect her.

"Good morning, good morning." Sidney Portensic bustled cheerily into the room.

"Morning, Sydney," B. B. and Gloria replied in stereo as others voiced their greetings. Hesta gave him the nod of a queen to a serf.

Sydney's face remained all grins. "I trust you all had a good sleep on the county's dollar."

"Oh, the best." Clay's hand slid to his lower back, his face feigning severe pain.

Sydney laughed good-naturedly, then quickly turned all business. "Ms. Adams"—he turned to Chelsea, his voice low—"may I speak with you for a moment?"

Kerra. Anxiety singed the back of her neck. "Of course."

He ushered her into the hallway and shut the door. "The judge wants to see you."

Chelsea stared at him, seeing the concern on his face. "Why?"

"Guess you'll find out soon enough." His features creased into an empathetic smile. "Come on."

When Chelsea entered the judge's chambers, the judge, attorneys, and court reporter all were there. Apprehension skidded around her stomach.

Judge Chanson came right to the point. "Ms. Adams, it has come to my attention that your niece is attending this trial. This perhaps is the niece you mentioned during *voir dire?*"

All three attorneys stared at Chelsea. She felt like a schoolgirl called before an accusing principal. "Yes. She's visiting from Kansas."

"Have you discussed this trial at all?"

"Of course not." Indignation fueled the need to explain. "We'd planned to spend these two weeks together, as I told you. She's been through a tragedy and I wanted to help her. Then when I ended up on this jury, what else was she supposed to do?"

"Apparently, she's found something," Stan Breckshire burst.

"Counsel!" Judge Chanson smacked her desk. Steam fairly rolled off her shoulders. She turned back to Chelsea. "The media are reporting that your niece has been spending time with Brett Welk, the defendant's son. That they had dinner together last night. As you can imagine, this is most disturbing news."

Chelsea fought for a breath. She could find no words to say.

"I must ask you again if you have talked with your niece about the trial."

Her indignation seeped into anger. As if she'd encouraged any of this. "I told you, *no.*"

"I see that she is on your list of callers. Did she phone last night?"

"Yes. Finally. It was nearly eleven. I asked where she'd been and she wouldn't tell me."

For another ten minutes Judge Chanson and the attorneys questioned Chelsea. Did she approve of this relationship? Would it affect her ability to deliberate fairly? Even as Chelsea told herself to remain calm, she could not keep the anger from her voice. Any "relationship" Kerra had with Brett Welk was completely her niece's own doing, and Chelsea was not about to accept the blame.

Finally Judge Chanson leaned her forearms on her desk. "All right. I appreciate your candor, Ms. Adams. Now there is only one thing I can do to save these proceedings. I will have to remove Miss Fraye's name from your contact list. That way, regardless of what she chooses to do, no one will be able to question your veracity in deliberating. Understood?"

Chelsea's throat locked. *God, you can't allow this!* Complete separation from Kerra at a time when her niece's rebellious nature was rearing its ugly head. Chelsea knew her niece all too well. With the entire court frowning upon her friendship with Brett Welk, Kerra was bound to stick to him like glue.

KERRA MEEKLY FOLLOWED the heavy bailiff down the narrow hall. Her ankles shook as they approached the judge's chambers. What was going to happen? Surely this had something to do with Brett. The mere thought of the judge trying to run her life filled her with both fear and indignation. And poor Brett. He was already beside himself with the media reports. When the bailiff had sidled up to her outside the courtroom, saying the judge wanted to see her, Brett's face had paled.

That horrid Milt Waking had watched her every move.

"Just go right on in; they're waiting for you." The bailiff smiled broadly as he swung open the intimidating door.

They?

Kerra forced herself through the doorway. Five heads turned to stare at her. The judge, all three attorneys, and the court reporter. Her stomach turned over.

"Come in, Miss Fraye." Judge Chanson beckoned Kerra to stand before her. The attorneys parted to give her room. Kerra had a fleeting thought of the Israelites in the middle of the boiling Red Sea.

Judge Chanson loomed larger than life in her black robe, one arm resting on her expansive desk. She cleared her throat and considered Kerra. A ground-swallowing earthquake would have been most welcome at that moment. "Miss Fraye, it has come to the court's attention that you are the niece of juror Chelsea Adams and that further you have, ah, begun a friendship with Brett Welk. I assume this is true?"

Kerra could only nod.

"I see." The judge fingered the purple chain around her neck, looking grim. "We have already spoken to your aunt about this matter, so she is aware of what I must do. I cannot tell you not to come to court, Miss Fraye, as this is a public trial. But I am concerned that you would have any contact with your aunt, given this unusual situation. So I am taking your name off her list of callers. You will not be able to speak to your aunt until the verdict has been given and your aunt is released from this court. Understood?"

"Yes," Kerra squeaked.

Judge Chanson gave her a probing look. "I hope you also understand why I must take this measure. Surely you can imagine that your continued communication with your aunt would bring into question her ability to deliberate fairly."

"It shouldn't," Kerra blurted, then drew back, amazed at her audacity. Well, so what? This was ridiculous. Aunt Chelsea had done nothing wrong and neither had she. Defensiveness kicked through her like a sudden dust storm. These people couldn't begin to know the extent of her grief since Dave's death. They couldn't begin to know what it felt like to be attracted to someone again, to feel alive again. What was she supposed to do, turn her back on this chance?

Everyone was staring at her. Kerra felt Erica Salvador's eyes giving her once-, second-, and third-overs.

"What I mean is," she declared, "I have never talked with Aunt Chelsea about what's happened in the courtroom. I'm sure she told you that. And she is the most honest person you'll ever meet. You're lucky to have her on your jury."

"I'm sure, I'm sure," Terrance Clyde soothed.

"Well," the judge said after a moment, "my decision stands. This is to protect your aunt just as much as the rest of us. It will ensure that her honesty cannot be questioned."

Kerra focused unseeingly on the sleeve of the judge's robe. The woman was right. This *was* for Aunt Chelsea's protection. Suddenly a burden Kerra hadn't allowed herself to admit lifted from her shoulders. She wouldn't have to call Aunt Chelsea every night. She wouldn't have to worry about her aunt's probing questions.

She was free to do anything she wanted.

TWENTY-FIVE

For the second day in a row, court was late getting started, this time thanks solely to herself and Kerra. Chelsea sank into her jury seat wearily. She was half glad she couldn't read the papers. The media was sure to get wind of the judge's decision to cut her contact with Kerra. Chelsea shook her head. This was all her fault. She never, *ever* should have let Kerra come to the trial.

As if on some twisted cue, Kerra and Brett entered the courtroom at that moment. They sat side by side.

Kerra's eyes drifted to the jury box. Chelsea gave her a wan smile. Kerra nodded back, brows knit. Her expression mixed apology, determination, and . . . something else.

Anticipation.

Chelsea turned her eyes away. *Lord, I know you want me here, but I never should have allowed Kerra to come. You've promised me that you'll take care of her while I do what you've called me to do. Please keep your promise!*

Stan Breckshire called his first witness of the day—Victor Mendoza. He looked to be in his mid-fifties, his perfectly straight back betraying his discomfort at having to testify. With one last prayer Chelsea pushed aside her worries about Kerra so she could concentrate. Under questioning, Victor Mendoza admitted that he and his family had run the Mexican border into America when he was four years old. As an adult, he had become an American citizen. He told the court how loyal he was to the country that had taken him from poverty, offered him a good life.

Carefully then the prosecutor elicited every detail about how Victor Mendoza had seen Darren Welk planting a bush in his backyard at 4:20 a.m. on the night Shawna Welk was killed. How when he had realized the information might be relevant, he'd called police, fulfilling his duty as a citizen.

Victor's testimony filled in a missing puzzle piece for Chelsea. No wonder the detectives had come to the Welks' house with a search warrant to dig up the bush.

An hour later Stan Breckshire turned him over to the defense for cross-examination.

Terrance Clyde rose in one easy motion. Victor Mendoza shifted in the witness chair, as though gathering himself for an unwanted confrontation. He raised his chin with an air of forthrightness and watched the defense attorney approach.

"Good morning." Terrance Clyde smiled briefly. Victor Mendoza gave a wary nod. "I have just a few questions for you. You estimated you were about seventy feet from the person you saw digging, correct?"

"Yes."

"And it was dark with little moonlight."

"That is true."

"Further that the lantern that cast the long shadow was on the ground directly behind the digger."

"Yes."

Terrance Clyde brought a hand to his chin, thinking. Someone coughed. "So in other words, this figure that you saw was backlit?"

Victor Mendoza considered the word. "You could say that, yes."

"Would you say the light was brighter around the person's feet or face?"

"His feet and legs. Since the lantern was on the ground."

"Sure." The attorney inhaled slowly, frowning at the carpet. "Then how did you see the person's face?"

"As I said, I didn't completely see his face. But I saw his build and height and enough of his features to recognize him as Darren Welk."

"Did the fact that this digger was in Darren Welk's backyard help you reach that decision?"

"I am not sure."

"If you had seen that figure at the same distance, lit the exact same way at night at any other location, say near your own house, would you have recognized the person as Darren Welk?"

Victor Mendoza fingered the starched collar of his shirt. "I do not know, sir. I can't answer the question, since that is not what happened."

Chelsea liked that honest answer. She found Mr. Mendoza very believable.

"All right." Terrance Clyde almost shrugged. "Let's try this." He sauntered to his table and picked up an envelope. "May I approach?" he asked Judge Chanson.

Stan Breckshire pushed to his feet, requesting to see what was in the envelope. A short sidebar ensued, Stan arguing about the contents. Apparently, he lost. Sidebar over, Terrance Clyde approached the witness and showed him a photo. "Recognize this person?"

Victor Mendoza bent over the photo, a finger tracing its edge. "Yes. It's Darren Welk, very much as I saw him that night."

"Where was this picture taken?"

"In his backyard. About where I saw him digging."

"Would you say this photo was taken from about the same distance as that from which you saw the digger?"

"Yes, I think so."

Pulling back the photo, the attorney handed Victor Mendoza another. "Recognize this man?"

Again Victor surveyed the photo with care. A minute passed. He bent closer. Chelsea looked from him to the defense attorney. Terrance Clyde stood with absolute composure, as if merely waiting for a bus. Finally Victor Mendoza's head came up. "I cannot be sure who this is."

A nod. "Where was this picture taken?"

"I don't know. Looks like a house but I don't recognize it."

"All right." The attorney took back the photo, replaced it with a third. "Do you recognize this person?"

The witness's head bent a third time. "Yes. This is Darren Welk, again as I saw him that night."

"And the photo was taken where?"

"In his backyard. About where I saw him."

"Fine. Thank you." Terrance Clyde now spread the three photos in front of Victor. "Just to be sure, you said this one and this one"— he pointed to the first and third—"are of Darren Welk, and you can't be certain of the identity of the middle one. Correct?"

Victor rechecked each one in turn. "Yes."

"Would you please pick up the middle one, the one you don't recognize, and read the writing on the back?"

Victor's eyes lifted to the attorney, a new awareness glimmering. His jaw shifted as he surveyed Terrance Clyde with distrust. The atmosphere of the courtroom tensed. Chelsea noticed Milt Waking's hand poised above his notepad. Suddenly the reporter's gaze cut to hers, as if he'd felt her looking at him. She glanced away and her eyes fell on Brett. He sat bolt upright and still.

Too still.

A warning bell sounded in Chelsea's head. She tore her attention away from him and turned back to Victor Mendoza.

With obvious reluctance Victor picked up the middle photo, turned it over. "Bud Howershack." Confusion and relief flicked across his face.

"Do you know Bud Howershack, one of the assistants in my office?"

"No."

"No wonder you didn't recognize him," Terrance Clyde said lightly.

An anxious titter ran through the courtroom.

"All right, how about photo one."

Victor swallowed and picked up the first picture. "Darren Welk."

"As you said," the attorney commented. "Now. Photo three. The one you also recognized as Darren Welk."

In that instant Chelsea knew what was coming.

Victor's chin shifted one way, then another.

"Mr. Mendoza?"

With an almost defiant flick of his wrist, he turned over the photo.

"Brett Welk."

The three gray-haired women in the second row gasped. Every juror's head swiveled toward Brett, like those of spectators at a tennis match. His face drained. Chelsea saw the rise and fall of his chest. Kerra looked at him in shock, then turned a disgusted glare upon the defense attorney.

By the time Terrance Clyde was through with Victor Mendoza, the poor man was practically stammering. He'd had to admit that indeed the fact that the digger was in Darren Welk's backyard had helped lead to his identification.

Stan Breckshire could barely contain himself at the prosecution table and tried with much animation to redeem his witness during rebuttal. But the damage had been done. Victor Mendoza could not possibly be certain who he saw digging that night.

Chelsea could not push her fears away. Had he seen Brett Welk?

EARS BURNING, BRETT WAITED. He'd told an anxious Kerra she was on her own for lunch; he had things to attend to. When the courtroom cleared, he accosted Terrance Clyde as the attorney placed papers in his briefcase. "What are you trying to do to me?" he demanded.

Terrance exchanged a knowing glance with Erica. She picked up a stack of folders and exited the premises.

"I'm trying to save your father's hide." He slid a document into his case.

Brett grabbed the sleeve of the attorney's expensive jacket. "You don't have to sacrifice me to do that!"

"Let go of me," Terrance said evenly.

Brett could have punched the man. He gripped the suit. Then jerked his fingers away.

"Thank you." Terrance adjusted his jacket, considering Brett with a cool-as-a-cucumber expression. "Now. Do you want your dad found innocent . . . or don't you?"

"You know I do."

"Then leave me to my business."

"It's not just your business; it's mine too! I've got to live out there." He flung out an arm. "You know how the reporters are going to hound me now?"

"Don't talk to reporters, Brett."

"What do you think I am, *stupid?*" He swung away in frustration, then swung back. "Besides, I don't have to say a word. All they have to do is quote what they heard from you! If I'd known you were going to use that picture this way, I'd never have posed for it." He glared at the attorney, breathing hard. "Is this what my father wanted you to do?"

Terrance's mouth firmed and Brett knew he'd hit a sore point. "I don't have to talk to you about my client," Terrance said. "But I'll tell you one thing. Contrary to what you might think, my job is not to make either you or your father happy. My job is to do whatever I must so the jury will find him innocent. Reasonable doubt, Brett—that's what it's all about."

Brett racked his brain for a comeback. The ground was shifting beneath his feet, and he wasn't quite sure where to jump.

"Now if you'll excuse me, I'd like to get some lunch."

Without another word Terrance lifted his briefcase from the table and glided toward the door.

JUDGE CHANSON RESTED an elbow on the large desk in her chambers, two fingers dug into her temple. Her lunch wasn't sitting well in her stomach, and her head hurt. "Tell me something good," she said with a grimace.

Detective Jed Trutenning's mouth pulled upward. "Not much to tell. We're still working on it."

She cast him a weary look. Couldn't *anything* go right with this case? This wasn't a trial, for heaven's sake; this was a circus. "What have you got?"

"Our interviews with interested parties haven't told us much. But we've discovered the phone the calls came from."

"Well, that's something."

"Phone booth on El Camino. That's how we traced it down. We'll stake it out in the evenings, asking anyone who shows up if they happened to use it on the night of Wednesday, August seventh. If we get real lucky, we'll find a witness who can identify the caller."

"You'd have to be very lucky indeed," the judge said dryly.

Jed shrugged. "Right now it's our best shot. I'll keep you informed."

"All right. Thanks."

"No problem." The detective slipped out of her office with barely a sound. Judge Chanson leaned back tiredly in her chair and massaged her forehead.

When court resumed after lunch, Chelsea sat ready with a new pen and pad of paper, courtesy of Sidney. She'd realized she should be taking notes. If God wanted to use her in some special way during deliberation, she'd better at least be fully prepared.

Stan Breckshire called criminalist Bill Jaworski to the stand. Jaworski's massive frame filled the witness chair, elbows spilling over its sides. His jowls hung like folds of pie dough, and his striped tie barely covered his stomach.

Chelsea's pen flew as the criminalist explained his investigative work on the bloodstained blouse. Using charts to illustrate, Jaworski first detailed the process by which he determined that the blood belonged to Shawna Welk.

First, samples of blood from the blouse were compared with blood samples taken from Tracey Wilagher and her birth father, who had agreed to cooperate. "A child's DNA is fifty percent from the mother and fifty percent from the father," Jaworski explained. Once Tracey's DNA bands from her father were determined, he compared her DNA with samples of blood taken from the blouse. He found bands that matched. "You can see the match from Tracey here"—he used a long pointer to indicate the band on his chart—"and from Shawna Welk here." He moved the pointer over.

"Seeing the match between these two, we moved to the next step, which was to compare blood from the blouse with a sample taken from Lynn Trudy, Shawna Welk's sister. This is because siblings also will have matching bands." He slid a chart from behind the first and placed it in front. "This chart shows the comparison of Lynn Trudy's blood with that taken from the blouse. Once again we had a clear match on certain bands." He indicated them. "Together these tests demonstrate conclusively that the blood from the blouse is from Shawna Welk."

The blood issue covered, Jaworski next explained how he had tested the grains of sand found on the blouse, using a large scanning electron microscope. He had compared this sand with grains he had taken from Breaker Beach. The results indicated a clear match. Then he'd compared sand found underneath the backseat of Darren Welk's car with grains picked from the blouse. Granted, the blouse still wore plenty of dirt from being buried, but the grains of sand had been easy to spot because of differing color and texture. Again, as the charts illustrated, the match was conclusive.

By the time Bill Jaworski left the stand, Chelsea had no doubt that the buried blouse had been stained with Shawna Welk's blood. And that the blouse had been transported to the Welks' house while lying underneath the backseat of Darren Welk's car.

Maybe Victor Mendoza had been right all along, Chelsea thought as court broke for the day. He *had* seen Darren Welk burying that blouse. At the moment, as she watched Kerra leave with Brett, she desperately wanted to believe that the defendant's son was completely innocent.

TWENTY-SIX

Another newspaper. Rogelio spotted it on the kitchen table as soon as he came in from work. He ignored it. The enticing smell of supper drifted from the oven, making his stomach rumble.

His grandmother was wearing one of her better housedresses. And her newest pair of sandals. "You going somewhere, Mama Yolanda?"

She picked up two pot holders. "Consuelo invited me over to watch some movies after supper. I said I would go. She will come get me soon, okay?"

"Sure."

She pulled a small glass pan covered with foil out of the oven and set it on the stove.

Kristin's face flashed before Rogelio. He tried to picture her in this kitchen, Roselita in her arms, talking with Mama Yolanda. But he could not. Those two were from such different worlds. Even if he could bring Roselita home, why should he think Kristin would want to be a part of their lives? And what about Mama Yolanda? Would his grandmother be able to forgive Kristin for what she'd done?

Rogelio's gaze fell to the floor. Suddenly the odds against accomplishing all his heart's desires seemed overwhelming.

He wandered to the table. "Want me to read to you about the trial?"

She waved an arthritic hand. "It makes no difference now; I'll see a paper at Consuelo's."

They had barely finished eating when Consuelo arrived. Rogelio shooed Mama Yolanda out the door, glad to see her going somewhere. He washed the dishes, the unusual silence hovering about his shoulders. What would he be doing if a baby were with him? How did you leave a small child alone long enough to wash a dish? He wasn't even sure what babies could do at seven months. Did they just lie there? Could they crawl? Walk? Did they talk?

What did he know about being a father?

Rogelio's hands slowed under the running water. For a moment he almost hoped Janet Cline would refuse to help him. Then he could let this foolish thought go. Thank God he hadn't told Mama Yolanda. He still could change his mind.

But could he leave his daughter in the home of a man who was potentially violent? Could he stand to let Kristin, the mother of his baby, go?

Firmly Rogelio turned off the water and placed the dishes on the counter. They could air-dry. He had a call to make.

He looked up Janet Cline's number and dialed it on the handset of the cordless phone, pacing the kitchen as her line rang. "It's Rogelio," he said when she answered. "Are you going to help me?"

She sighed. "Yes, I'll help you." Her words sounded flat, weary. "I don't see that I have a choice."

Rogelio's eyes closed. He didn't know whether to feel relieved or scared. "What do we do?"

"One thing first." Her tone told him she had practiced the words. "I want to wait until the trial is over."

"Why? What does the trial have to do with me?"

"Nothing. But if I go to the authorities about this now, because of all the media coverage of the trial, the word is sure to get out. And even though this has nothing to do with Shawna's murder, I'm afraid somehow it would complicate things. I want Darren Welk found guilty, you understand?"

Rogelio's lips tightened. "How long is the trial supposed to take?"

"Only about another week, I think."

"I can't wait that long."

"Yes, you can! One week, Rogelio. Long enough to see that man found guilty."

"Why should I do it?" Rogelio's voice rose. "Why should I care? Mama Yolanda's waited long enough as it is."

"Hear me: I will *not* help you this week," Janet shot back. "I won't have Shawna's reputation sullied at the very time she's supposed to be given justice!"

Rogelio grabbed the countertop, fingertips whitening. He hunched over to rest his forehead against a cabinet. He could hear Janet breathing into the phone. "I don't need you, you know," he said tightly. "I can just go to the police right now, tonight."

"Don't do it, Rogelio. The first thing they'd do is haul in your girlfriend to find out what she knows."

"That's going to happen anyway." His stomach churned. How Kristin would hate him.

"You don't understand how this works; I won't be going to the police. This is a matter for social services and the courts. Even once we get started, the process will take time."

"Now you want more time!" Rogelio hit the cabinet with his fist. "How long is all this going to take?"

"I don't know. Weeks. Months. I haven't exactly done this before."

Fear flushed through Rogelio's veins. "But in the meantime that man could hide Roselita, couldn't he? What will he do if he knows we're trying to take her away?"

"Rogelio." Janet spoke slowly, as if talking to a child. "He will hire the best lawyers. He will fight this all the way. It will drag through the courts. And knowing this man, it will most likely get very, very ugly. He'll find out whatever he can about you and Kristin. And he'll use the fact that you accepted money for your baby. He'll try to convince the judge that you and your grandmother wouldn't be fit parents. You're too young and she's too old. Is she an American citizen?"

"Yes. She and my grandfather became citizens soon after they were married."

"How about education; did she finish high school?"

"No."

"Does she speak much English?"

Rogelio hesitated. "No."

Silence.

"He will tear you and your grandmother apart in court." Janet's words had softened. "Are you willing to put her through that?"

Rogelio fell into a kitchen chair. Put a hand over his eyes. How naive he'd been. How stupid. To think he could get Roselita back quietly, just surprise Mama Yolanda one day and place the baby in her arms. Now he would have to tell her. She would be willing to fight, of that he was sure. She'd certainly fought through hardships before. But what if they did everything they could and still lost? How much more would she grieve?

Surely they wouldn't lose. They were in the right.

Rogelio straightened. "We will do what we have to do to get our baby." Janet started to speak but he cut her off. "I will wait until after the trial on one condition. Tell me the name of the man who adopted her."

"No, Rogelio. I don't want you contacting him on your own. That's the worst thing you could do."

"I won't bother him; I told you I'd wait."

"Then why do you want to know?"

Anger surged through him. He gripped the phone. "Why shouldn't I want to know? He's got my baby!"

They argued and argued but Rogelio would not budge. Finally, reluctantly, Janet told him the name. He did not recognize it.

"Okay," he said wearily. "I will call you as soon as the trial is over."

Rogelio hit the off button and the line disconnected. Plastic clicked against wood as he rested the handset on the table. He sat unmoving for a long time, hand still on the telephone, imagining what he was going to tell Kristin. A child's playful shout outside blinked him back to the present. He shifted in his chair, and his eyes fell on the folded newspaper at the edge of the table. He reached for it, flipped it open. The article was front-page news.

Jury Sequestered in Welk Trial

Rogelio drew back his head in surprise. Swiftly he read the story. Read it a second time.

He folded the paper and picked it up, as if weighing its worth. Thoughts began to form in his mind like swirling mist. One little sentence to certain key people, and look at all the commotion it had caused. The result had been immediate and sure. Rogelio unfolded the paper again and gazed at the article. The key to his own problem lay here. If he could just come up with a plan.

He lay the newspaper down, absently thumbing its edges, and stared out the kitchen window, thinking.

THE PHONE RANG SHRILLY in the silent hotel room. Chelsea jumped. Pushing aside her dinner plate, she reached for it across the small table. "Hello?"

"Hi, darlin'; how are you?"

Warm sweetness filled her at the sound of the voice. She gripped the receiver. "Oh, Paul, it's so good to hear you."

"Kerra called and told me what happened. What terrible timing for her visit."

"She called? When? Just now?"

"No, it was yesterday. Why, what's wrong?"

Chelsea could have kicked herself. She did not want to tell Paul what was happening with Kerra. What could he do? Besides, he wasn't happy with her for being on the jury in the first place. She didn't want to admit that he was right. That because of her, Kerra was falling in with the wrong person, someone who would only lead her further away from God.

Not that Paul would understand that part.

"Nothing's wrong," she said. "I just haven't heard from her tonight, that's all."

"I don't understand why she's staying. She was rather vague about her reasons when I asked."

"You know Kerra." Chelsea worked to keep her tone light. "She's going to do what she's going to do." She fiddled with the phone cord. "So how's everything going there?"

Paul talked for about five minutes, telling her how well the office and fledgling projects were coming together. Chelsea closed her eyes and listened to the music of his words. If only he were sitting in their family room at home. With their boys. They were all so far away. And she felt so alone.

She hung up the phone, not knowing whether she felt better or worse. Restlessly she walked about the room, then flung herself on the bed.

Suddenly black spots began to crowd the sides of her sight. The room dimmed. Chelsea focused on the flowers on the bedspread, frowning. The spots ate inward. The flowers dissolved.

She sucked in air. God was sending her another vision.

Oh, Lord, give me wisdom.

Her eyes pressed shut. The vision undulated into view. A man in a leather chair, smoking, staring with dark, narrowed eyes. Manipulation and greed etched his face, in the lines around his mouth, on his forehead. He took a long drag from the cigarette, held the smoke in his lungs, then exhaled slowly, evenly. A scar jagged between his thumb and forefinger.

Nausea and dread rose in Chelsea's stomach. It was the same man as before.

He turned his head toward her. Pierced her with his steel-cold eyes. Chelsea's heart tumbled over itself. The man turned back to the cigarette. Its curling smoke burned Chelsea's throat.

God, show me who this is.

His face shimmered, dissolved.

Once again blackness.

Chelsea's fingers slipped to the bedspread, balling the fabric against her palms. Her heart slowed with reluctance. After some time she opened her eyes. She lifted her gaze, saw only the hotel room.

She let out a deep breath, calming herself, reminding herself about what God had revealed to her last night. She was his servant. She'd been placed on the jury for a purpose. God was sending her these visions not to scare her but that his will might be accomplished.

Chelsea closed her eyes again and fervently began to pray.

TWENTY-SEVEN

Warm air flicked strands of Kerra's hair about her face. She laid her head back against the seat of Brett's convertible BMW, reveling in the sensation of wind and late-afternoon sun. Tree-dotted, rolling hills and groves of eucalyptus trees whizzed by. The terrain, so different from that of Kansas, the pulse of her emotions, and Brett's solid presence behind the wheel—all swirled together to bathe Kerra in tingling anticipation.

Brett glanced at her, smiling. "What do you think?"

"It's beautiful!"

Soon the hills surrendered to plowed, rich fields and molded themselves against the distant horizon. Fog blanketed them to the west. Kerra saw migrant workers leaving the fields to board white buses. Irrigation systems lay in rows across the fields, with pipes sticking up about every fifteen feet. The crops were so many different colors and heights. Kerra couldn't begin to imagine what they all were.

Brett took a Salinas exit off the freeway, staying on the outskirts of town. Five minutes later they rolled up to the Welks' large home of white wood and green shutters.

"Welcome to my place," Brett said, pride in his voice.

Kerra climbed out of the car, gazing openmouthed at the vast fields surrounding them, the fog-covered hills in the distance. Something inside her stirred, something both ancient and new. The land, the air, the sky, seeped into her pores, filling her with lightness, with life. Brett moved beside her and she looked at him, tongue-tied.

"I can tell you like it."

She nodded.

His mouth curved. Surprise flicked across his face, as if he couldn't quite believe she was with him. He raised his hand, traced a knuckle down her jaw. "I'm so glad you came."

She lay fingertips on his arm and squeezed. "Me too."

"Come on. I'll show you inside."

The house boasted a tiled, two-story entryway and a curved staircase. Brett led her through the spacious kitchen, the dining, living, and family rooms, all designed in shades of blue and cream. Kerra trailed her hand on the polished wood banister as they climbed the stairs. Five bedroom suites. And only one of them occupied. Kerra followed Brett into his room, heart clenching at the thought of his living in this huge house all by himself. His room was carpeted in plush navy. Kerra's eyes roved over a bookcase with numerous baseball trophies, a large desk scattered with papers.

"Sorry it's messy." Brett pulled up the cover on his unmade bed. "Would have fixed it up if I'd known you were coming."

She rolled her eyes as if to say, "How could either of us have guessed this?" Her gaze moved to Brett's dresser and landed on a photo of a dark-haired woman. She walked over to it slowly, picked it up. The woman had deep-set brown eyes and a kind mouth, lips turned up at the corners. "Your mom?"

"Yeah."

Kerra regarded the photo with reverence. "She's beautiful, Brett." Kerra raised her eyes to his. A tangible understanding flowed between then, connecting them. They both knew the depths of loss. Kerra could feel his loneliness in the pit of her being.

Carefully she replaced the picture.

They stood unmoving, awkwardly silent. For a fleeting moment the enormity of her choices stunned Kerra. First, that she'd adamantly refused to stay away from Brett during court just because the media were watching. "They already know, don't they?" she'd huffed to Brett when he suggested it. Second, that she'd accepted Brett's invitation for the weekend. A small voice had whispered that she hardly knew the man, that her aunt Chelsea, and probably God, would disapprove. But she'd whisked the voice aside with a toss of her head. Maybe God *did* approve. Maybe he'd brought her and Brett together. After all her grief, after all of his, didn't they both deserve some tenderness?

"Well." Brett turned away. "Let's go get our suitcases. I'll show you to your room."

The room had been Tracey's, Brett told her moments later as he set her suitcase on a high queen-size bed with a frothy beige coverlet. "But it looks a lot better with you in it."

He smiled but Kerra heard the underlying tone. "You didn't like her, did you. Or your stepmother."

Brett looked at the floor. "No."

There was so much they couldn't talk about. The strangeness of their situation constantly etched its way into their conversations and silences. Kerra felt a lopsidedness to their relationship that was unsettling. She longed to know as much about Brett as she had told him about herself, but didn't know how to ask. Somehow she sensed that all the roads of his past led to the trial. Clearly, that was one thing he did not want to discuss.

They went to dinner in a lovely seaside restaurant in Monterey, Kerra gazing at the surf as she formed safe questions in her mind. Slowly she was able to pull from Brett stories of growing up on the ranch, working alongside his father, his closeness to his mother. He even opened up enough to tell her of his yearning to have a closer relationship with his father. She fervently wished they could talk about the trial, but that remained a subject they couldn't broach. Brett wanted to be closer to his father, but Darren Welk certainly looked guilty. Did Brett believe that? Could he want his father found innocent, even if he knew the truth?

"Kerra. Where's your head?" Brett pushed aside his coffee cup and reached for her hand.

Her throat tightened. Her head was everywhere and nowhere. She still could hardly believe she was with him, that she was finally beginning to care for someone else. This wasn't wrong; it couldn't be. After all the horrible months, she needed this newness in her life. Dave would have wanted it for her.

She would not turn aside from Brett now, Kerra told herself decisively. She would not.

"My head's right here, Brett," she said. "Right here with you."

He smiled and her heart surged. They were silent for a moment.

"Mind if I ask you something?" he ventured.

She pressed his fingers. "Anything."

He hesitated, as if gathering his thoughts. "Remember when you told me the difference between religion and Christianity?"

Oh no, not this topic again. "Uh-huh."

"I've been wondering. If God reached out to man through Christ, like you said, then what are *we* supposed to do? I mean, I'm thinking about my trying to reach out to Dad. That's all well and good, but he's got to reach back, know what I mean? It takes two."

Kerra nodded slowly, her mind casting about for the merest of answers. Then the irony hit her. After she accepted Christ, she'd been so gung ho to talk to *anyone* about her faith. Now here she was, with someone she cared for, someone who needed all the divine help he could get, and her tongue didn't want to form the words. Didn't want to speak of the truths that deep in her heart she knew were right.

She gazed into Brett's questioning face, wavering between her own selfishness and his desire to know.

"I know what you mean," she said. "And you're right." She took a deep breath and plunged in. "God sent Jesus Christ, his Son, to die on the cross for our sins. That was his part. Our part is to accept Christ as our Savior. Ask him to forgive us of our sins, and turn our lives over to him. Then we can live every day having a direct relationship with God. Just as you want a closer relationship with your earthly father, God wants to be your heavenly Father." She tilted her head, looking at him from the corner of her eye.

His brow furrowed. "Is that what you did?"

She nodded.

Silence hung between them. Kerra could not find a word to fill it. Brett reached up and grazed her cheek with his finger. "Well. That must be one of the things that makes you so special."

They left the restaurant hand in hand, Kerra practically trembling. Before unlocking the car, Brett pulled her close. She leaned against him, feeling the strength of his chest, his arms. He placed a hand beneath her chin and tilted back her head, drinking in the sight of her. "I can't believe I found you."

Kerra swallowed. Her breathing grew shallow. "Well," she said, vainly attempting lightness, "I'm glad you did."

His eyes fell to her mouth. Kerra's ankles shook. He lowered his face and kissed her, his lips like warm velvet. Kerra dug fingertips into his hair, her other hand slipping around his neck. All her anxieties melted away. For that long, pendant moment the world stood still. She felt only Brett, wanted only Brett. Not until a car turned into the parking lot, bathing them with headlights, did they pull apart.

She rested a hand on his knee as they drove back to his house. They sat for the next three hours on his family room couch, talking, kissing. Brett turned more lighthearted than she'd ever seen him. He even managed to laugh.

When Kerra slipped into her bed that night, she could still feel that first kiss on her lips. She closed her eyes and relived it. A sudden, fierce longing surged through her—the longing to nurture, to protect. Brett *needed* her. She was going to stick by him. And she hoped—oh, she hoped—this relationship would lead somewhere.

She could not be hurt again.

SATURDAY, AUGUST 10

TWENTY-EIGHT

Chelsea awoke in the middle of the night, her mind tangled with thoughts of the trial . . . Kerra . . . Brett. The digital clock on the night-stand read 3:20. For over an hour she fought to clear her head, but to no avail. Finally she turned on the reading light. She sat up in bed and pulled her Bible off the nightstand.

What is it, God?

She opened her Bible to the Psalms, seeking comfort, peace. She read various psalms of praise and of God's protection over his people. Of his majesty and mercy.

The LORD is my rock and my fortress and my deliverer,
  My God, my rock, in whom I take refuge;
My shield and the horn of my salvation, my stronghold.

A half hour later Chelsea still could not relax. She lay the Bible aside and began to pray.

First she prayed for Paul in England, for her sons at camp. Then she began to pray for Kerra. After that she moved on to the judge, the attorneys, the jurors, each by name. At first she prayed silently, then in a whisper. Before long she was speaking aloud. She prayed particularly for Tak Nagakura, who looked at her with hard, cold eyes. And for Hesta and Latonia and Gloria, all of whom treated her with indifference.

Then she began to think of Brett. She could not turn her mind away from him. Chelsea found herself praying for his salvation, his friendship with Kerra.

She prayed, listened for further guidance, prayed some more. Another name began crowding into her thoughts, slowly at first. Milt Waking. She pushed it aside. She was busy praying for Brett and Kerra. Besides, what did Milt Waking do other than air salacious news reports? Chelsea felt not one ounce of sympathy for the man.

She continued to pray for Brett. But the reporter's name grew stronger in her mind until she could no longer convince herself that this thought had not come from God.

All right, Lord. Her heart resisted even as she obeyed. *How should I pray for him?*

For some time she sat, eyes closed, waiting for understanding, asking God for sensitivity on her part to hear him. Twice she tried to move on to pray for someone else, but her spirit would not let her rest. *Milt Waking, Milt Waking.* In time she sensed a leading, initially vague, then growing clearer.

God had chosen specifically to work through Milt's actions during the trial.

Could that possibly be right?

Chelsea couldn't shake the thought. Nor could she help but react. *Oh, wonderful, Lord. Selfish, grandiose, non-Christian-if-there-ever-was-one Milt Waking. Couldn't you have chosen somebody else? Besides, what can he possibly do?*

Chelsea sighed. How she wished she could ignore this. Then she remembered the stories in the Bible about the Israelites' release from captivity. How, after Daniel prayed, God had chosen the pagan Babylonian king as his special servant to bring about these events. God was sovereign, he was reminding her. He would work through whomever he chose. She was not to question. She was to stay faithful and do her part—which would be key.

Yes, Lord, okay.

For a long time Chelsea prayed for Milt Waking and for those who would come into contact with him as the trial progressed. She prayed that God would work through the man whether he realized it or not. That Milt's actions, even those that might be wrong or selfish, would be used for God's glory.

By the time Chelsea felt she could stop praying, the clock read 5:45. She hoped to get a few more hours' rest. She turned out the light and lay down.

As sleep overtook her, she sensed God calling her to fast for the day and to continue praying. Terrific. She couldn't fast without the whole jury knowing. She'd have to stay behind as they were taken out to dinner. *Oh boy, I wonder how they'll react to that.*

Her last waking thought was of Tak's hostile eyes.

TWENTY-NINE

Rogelio pulled his car in front of Kristin's house and shut off the engine. Her fancy Mustang was not in the driveway. He tapped the steering wheel, made hot by the Saturday afternoon sun. With a sigh he pulled himself out and climbed the three steps to her porch. Rang the doorbell. Her mother answered. All words froze in Rogelio's throat. He'd never known what to say to this woman after her daughter's pregnancy could no longer be hidden. Surely she blamed him.

"Is Kristin home?"

She stared at him. "She's out with friends."

Was it his imagination, or had she emphasized the word *friends?* In the past he would have turned away, but the insistent drumbeat of his mission urged him on. "Do you know where?"

"No."

They locked eyes. Rogelio felt his jaw harden. Fine. He'd find Kristin himself.

"Thanks." He strode back to his car, chin high. As he drove away, he glanced in the rearview mirror. Kristin's mom stood watching him, arms folded.

He searched Salinas for an hour, cruising by homes of Kristin's various friends, checking the movie theater parking lot. Finally he spotted her car, its top down, parked in front of a Seven-Eleven. He pulled into a space in the shade of the building and waited. Two minutes later she emerged, a slushie in her hand, with a girl he did not recognize. He got out of his car. "Kristin."

She spotted him and pulled to a halt. Her shoulders sagged, then raised with defiance. "I don't want to see you, Rogelio." With purpose she headed for her car. He sprang toward it and slapped a palm against the door.

"We have to talk, Kristin. It won't take long."

"No. Get away from my car." Her sea green eyes narrowed. The friend hung back, brows knitting with concern.

Kristin's coldness cut through Rogelio like a knife. He worked to keep his voice steady. "I'm not moving until you say you'll talk to me."

"Oh yeah? Fine then. Here I am; say what you have to say." She strutted within two feet of him, clunked the drink on the hood of her car, and tossed her head. A strand of white blond hair caught on the corner of her lips. Any effort to pull it away would have ruined her prideful pose. She didn't move.

An ache welled up in Rogelio's chest. Did she really think she fooled him, with her pink nails spread across her hips, her mouth in a taut line? He looked through her eyes, deep within her, and saw simmering pain and fear. With one finger he reached out and brushed the strand of hair away from her mouth. Her expression almost softened, then reassembled itself.

"What do you want?" she demanded.

His gaze roved to her friend. "You sure you want to talk right here?"

"I have nothing to hide."

He winced at her desperate lie. "Come on, Kristin," he urged with a sad smile, "just sit in my car with me for a minute, out of the sun."

She swallowed, fighting to retain her hardened mask. Clearly, his gentleness rattled her. "If I do, will you promise to leave me alone?" She sounded almost like a child.

"Kristin. Leaving you 'alone' is the last thing I'd do."

Her eyes closed, whether in resignation or at his meaning, he wasn't sure. She half-turned to her friend. "I'll be back in a minute, Tanya."

They sat in Rogelio's car, his heart doing an odd little dance. The tan of Kristin's skin, the lightness of her hair against the white seats, flooded him with memories. He longed for so many things at that moment, he hardly knew where to begin. "I've been looking into the adoption. I talked with Janet Cline, Shawna Welk's partner. It looks like the adoption wasn't legal, Kristin. Certain things were supposed to be done, and they weren't."

He watched the information play across her face. "What things?"

"We were both supposed to have meetings with Janet. And I was supposed to sign in front of witnesses." He paused. "Did you know that?"

She shook her head.

"Were there witnesses when you signed your paper?"

Kristin considered her lap, frowning. "Yeah. Shawna and her daughter, Tracey."

"Did you meet twice with Janet Cline? She said she doesn't know your name."

She stared at him, lips parted. "No."

Fresh hope unfolded in Rogelio's chest. He blew out air. "I'll have to go to court. Janet's going to help me. It won't be easy; she's already warned me. But I'm going to get Roselita back."

Kristin's shoulders drew inward, her hard pretense gone. "And you don't care what it'll do to me."

He leaned toward her. "Of course I do. More than you know."

"Then why are you doing it?" she blurted, tears seeping into her eyes. "What if you get me into trouble? No one but you and my mom knows where the money came from. I don't want my car taken away from me! And I don't want to see the baby again." Her words tumbled. "I *can't*. You don't know what it's like having a baby and then giving it up!"

"I'll raise her, Kristin, me and Mama Yolanda. You won't have to do a thing."

"I'll know where she *is*, don't you understand? Now I can't know; I'm separated from her! But if you raise her, how am I supposed to keep away?"

He lifted a hand. "Why do you have to keep away?"

"Because, Rogelio!" She shoved a palm into the car seat, chin trembling. "Because I just do!"

"*Why?*"

"I'm not ready to be a mother; I don't *want* to be a mother!" she cried. "I want to be with friends and have fun and go out! You've seen all the girls that have babies. What do they do? Stay stuck at home all the time."

"Kristin." He wrapped his fingers around her arm. "You wouldn't be stuck at home. Mama Yolanda's going to take care of her. But you'll be able to be a part of your own daughter's life. Wouldn't you want that?"

She said nothing, tears spilling onto her cheeks. Suddenly Rogelio understood her fear. You either were a mother or you weren't. A daughter's life wasn't something to play with.

"Oh, Kristin, come here." Sliding over, Rogelio put his arms around her and pulled her head to his chest. He stroked her hair while she shuddered and sniffed. Two cars pulled into the parking lot, the drivers casting them curious glances through his open windows. He paid them no heed. They disappeared into the Seven-Eleven, then emerged a few minutes later, bags in hand. Drove off. Still Kristin cried. Finally she raised her head. A new light illumined her eyes.

"Rogelio. Do you still love me?"

His heart turned over. How could he have stayed away from her so long? "Yes. Very much."

She eased away from him, sat up straight. Looked at him squarely. "I love you, too."

He pressed back against the seat, hands on his thighs. Why was he waiting for the other shoe to drop?

"I want to be with you. Let's stay together this time." She paused. "But I just can't do it if you're raising the baby."

Rogelio's stomach gelled. A moment passed before he could find a response. "Another bargain, Kristin?" The words were laced with shocked accusation. "Forget Roselita and I can have you?"

"She's in a good home. Shawna assured me—"

"She's *not* in a good home," Rogelio shot back. "The way Janet talked, the father's practically a criminal."

"I don't believe that!"

"Well, you'd better believe it!"

They glared at each other.

Kristin reached for him. "Please, Rogelio. Let's just go back to the way things were."

He pulled away. "Things can never be the way they were, Kristin. You had a baby. She was adopted—illegally. Now she's in trouble. She needs a good home. Mama Yolanda and I can give her that. Those are the facts. You can't change them—and you can't bargain your way out of them!"

Kristin drew herself up, defensiveness hardening her face. "I'm not trying to bargain my way out of anything; I'm just trying to talk some sense into you! But never mind, Rogelio. You've got a one-track brain. Fine then. Do whatever you want. Just leave me out of it. And out of your life!"

She yanked on the handle of his door and clambered out onto the hot pavement. Searing him with a final look, she stalked away.

Rogelio sat frozen in his seat, stunned. How had they gotten from hugging each other to this in a matter of minutes? He heard Kristin's angry voice command her friend, "Get in!" Her car doors slammed. The engine roared to life and she sped away.

MONDAY, AUGUST 12

THIRTY

In single file, Sidney Portensic's ducks followed him down the narrow hallway toward the courtroom. A cacophony of thoughts rang in Chelsea's head as she fell in behind Gloria. Not since awaiting the verdict in last year's trial had she experienced such a long weekend.

She had fasted on Saturday, as God had called her to do. Sunday she'd joined the others for dinner at a restaurant. Feeling drained and despondent, Chelsea sat near the end of the table, close to Mike, Gloria, and Latonia Purcell. The three of them chatted about work and their families. Down the table Henry loudly talked jazz with Clay. Hesta picked at her food. Tak sat silently at the other end of the table, emanating intellectual superiority. Although Chelsea tried to join in the conversations, those around her responded in chilled tones, as if viewing her absence the previous day as a slight to the entire group. Chelsea tried to tell herself she was being too sensitive, but she knew better. Truth was, she'd been laid bare before them during jury selection. And they hadn't liked what they'd seen.

Now as she entered the courtroom, Chelsea's eyes swept the long rows of seats. There was Kerra. Next to Brett. Leaning toward him and talking intimately. She looked up, caught Chelsea's eye, and smiled self-consciously. Chelsea's mouth curved upward for a moment, then slipped back into place. She didn't need to talk to Kerra to know who the girl had been with that weekend. The truth on her face was clear.

The prosecution's first witness for the day was Shawna Welk's dentist, Dr. Richard Cooper. Chelsea pulled out her paper and pen, heading a new page with his name. Using a projection screen, Dr. Cooper explained how he had compared X-rays of the tooth found on Breaker Beach with X-rays of the victim's teeth. Shawna's tooth number twenty-one, on the bottom left side, was unusual in that it contained two roots instead of one. Also, it had undergone an api-coectomy, or root canal, the filling showing up as a white spot. The tooth found on the beach matched this one exactly.

"I am absolutely positive that this tooth belonged to Shawna Welk," Dr. Cooper concluded. "Given these anomalies and the perfect match on every point, this tooth is as good as a fingerprint."

As good as a fingerprint, Chelsea wrote in her notes. Terrance Clyde stood up to cross-examine.

"WAIT, SIR; YOU'LL NEED to empty your pockets before going through the scanner."

"Oh. Okay." Nervously Rogelio did as he was told. The security guard pointed to the machine and he stepped through. On the other side he retrieved his wallet and keys. "Do you know which court the trial for Darren Welk is meeting in?" he asked the guard.

"Courtroom 2H. Up the escalator, down the hall, and on your left."

"Thanks."

Rogelio stepped onto the escalator, trying vainly to still his quivering heartbeat. Everything about the courthouse was new and overwhelming. How was he going to talk privately with the judge? What made him think the man would even see him? In desperation

Rogelio breathed a prayer—another bargain with God. He could not waste his time here. He'd begged a day off from his boss, saying he had personal matters to attend to. His grandmother thought he was at work.

On the second floor Rogelio followed the guard's directions to the courtroom. His hand trembled as he eased open the door and peeked inside. Trial was in session. Sucking air through his teeth, Rogelio closed the door. He couldn't just walk in, could he? Right in the middle of someone's testimony?

He paced slowly in the hall, checking his watch. Almost ten o'clock. How long would he have to wait? Surely they'd at least break for lunch. He would ask to see the judge then.

The courthouse door opened. Rogelio spun around. People began filing out, heading in various directions. Brett Welk appeared with a pretty blond at his side. His eyes happened to meet Rogelio's. "Hi," Brett mumbled as they passed; then he hesitated. "Do I know you?"

"Uh. Yeah." Rogelio swallowed nervously. "I worked as a gardener at your house."

Brett raised his chin in slow recognition. "Sure, that's right." He seemed distracted. "You coming to watch the trial?"

Rogelio looked from him to the blond. She was almost as pretty as Kristin. A dark-haired man in an expensive suit and carrying a briefcase sidled over, listening. She flinched away from him, distaste on her features. He didn't seem to care.

"No." Rogelio looked back to Brett. "That is . . . I need to see the judge."

"Oh." Brett aimed a searing glance at the dark-haired man. "Can't you ever quit spying on people?" Shaking his head in derision, he said, "Come on, Kerra." As they moved away, Brett looked back over his shoulder at Rogelio. "Don't trust that guy."

"I'm not so bad," the man said mildly. "At least I'm willing to help you. You said you needed to see the judge?"

Rogelio hesitated.

"Don't worry about them." The man tilted his head at Brett's retreating back. "At a trial everyone has enemies. I'm just here doing my job."

Rogelio didn't know who he could trust. But surely he could just ask this guy a question. "Okay, yeah. Do you know where I could find him?"

"Her."

"Huh?"

"The judge is a woman."

Rogelio's eyebrows rose. "Oh."

The man eyed him curiously. "Why do you want to see the judge?"

"I have some business."

"I see."

A man toting a television camera approached them. "Hey, Milt—"

"Give me a minute, Bill." He gestured his head with a dismissive air. The cameraman faded away. "I may be able to help you."

Rogelio regarded him. "Who are you?"

"Milt Waking, Channel Seven News. And you?"

A pause. "Rogelio Sanchez."

"Rogelio. Nice to meet you." He held out a well-groomed hand, smiling briefly. Rogelio hesitated, then shook it once.

"The judge is not an easy person to see," Milt said. "Especially when she's in the middle of a trial. Tell me, does your 'business' with her have anything to do with this case?"

"Why does that matter?"

Milt inclined his head. "Because if it does, she certainly won't see you. A judge can't talk to anyone about a case while it's going on, because it could mean hearing information that she doesn't hear in the courtroom, and that's not allowed. Judges aren't even supposed to read newspaper articles about a trial over which they're presiding."

Slowly the meaning of the words sank in. Rogelio could not imagine being defeated this easily. "It's not really about the trial itself," he hedged.

Milt peered at Rogelio. "Well, does it have to do with anyone involved in the case?"

Rogelio ran his tongue inside his bottom lip. He was afraid of saying too much. Especially to a reporter.

A light appeared in Milt's eyes. "I'm guessing by your silence that the answer is yes." His gaze roved the courthouse hallway. Rogelio wondered who—or what—he was looking for. Then Milt checked his watch. "We've only got a few minutes, so let me say this quickly. The judge won't see you, trust me on that. If you want to ask a bailiff, go ahead. But they'll want to know your business, and then when you tell them, they'll just say, 'Sorry.'" His hand slipped up and down his tie. "Fortunately, I know a lot of people. Tell you what. Trial's going to start again. Which means all of us are going to be tied up until noon. If you stick around, we can talk more then. I'll buy you lunch."

"Why would you do that?" Defensiveness crept into Rogelio's voice. Did this guy think he had no money to feed himself?

Milt waved a hand. "Okay, pay your own way then. My point is, that's all the time I can give you; take it or leave it. If you decide you can't trust me, you'll go home from here empty-handed." He raked another look around the hall, stopping to rest on a few chosen people. Rogelio followed his gaze.

With a start Rogelio realized who Milt was looking at. Other reporters. He was acting like a cat who'd caught a mouse and wanted it all for himself. This guy wasn't Mr. Helpful; this guy thought Rogelio could help *him*. Rogelio's mind sped up as he considered the possibilities. How could he use this? What should he do?

He needed to buy some time. He needed to think.

Rogelio leaned against the wall, folding his arms as if he were fully in charge of the situation. "Okay, I'll hang around. Maybe we'll talk at lunch." He hoped Milt couldn't see his legs tremble.

Milt nodded. "Suit yourself."

THIRTY-ONE

"The people call Dr. Theodore Gaston."

Stan rapped knuckles against the prosecution table as he waited for his witness to be sworn in. Dr. Gaston worked with the USGS— United States Geological Survey—and was an expert in tides and currents, particularly in Monterey Bay. The man was in his mid-forties but looked far younger, with a narrow, boyish face and thinning brown hair. Black-rimmed glasses only heightened his nerdy appearance. He stood tall and spindly as he raised slender fingers to take the oath, then settled into the witness chair like a gangly genius kid.

Stan yanked at his tie as he greeted the doctor, hot-to-trot to begin his specific questioning. But first he had to lead Dr. Gaston through *voir dire* to establish the man as an expert witness. This involved a necessary but boring discussion of the doctor's training and experience, including continued education, papers written, awards won, and on and on.

As expected, T. C. tried to poke holes in the man's stellar reputation. Had it really been five years since he'd taken any continuing education courses? And shouldn't an "expert" of his caliber have written for more scientific journals? Hogwash and more hogwash.

Back and forth the questioning went, from prosecution to defense, until both attorneys had exhausted themselves of points to be made. By the time Dr. Gaston was officially deemed an expert witness, an hour had passed. Stan hoped his jury was still awake.

"Now, Dr. Gaston." Stan pressed palms together and drummed his fingers. "What are the general characteristics of currents off Breaker Beach?"

Like the dentist, Dr. Gaston was prepared with various visual aids. Unfolding himself from the witness chair, he angled his way to stand before an easel with flip charts. The first was a depiction of the entire Monterey Bay and its beaches.

"Breaker Beach is right in the middle of the large Monterey Bay," he began in a reedy voice. "Here." He indicated with a long pointer. "Immediately below it is Zmudowski State Beach, and below that is Moss Landing State Beach. This entire area"—he moved the pointer up and down—"is known for its strong rip currents. Because of this, all water sports at these beaches are considered hazardous."

"Can you explain the specific hazards of a rip current?"

Dr. Gaston launched into an explanation, a man in his element. Rip currents created what was termed the Bernoulli effect, he said, their waters moving faster than surrounding water. The resulting force trapped a person in the middle of this rapidly moving stream. Experienced ocean swimmers knew not to fight a rip current if they found themselves caught in one. They allowed themselves to be carried out to sea until the velocity of the current diminished enough that they could swim parallel to the beach. Once they were completely out of the rip current, they could swim ashore.

"So rip currents can get the best of even a strong swimmer?" Stan prodded.

"Yes, if he fights it. The current can be so strong that the swimmer won't be able to pull out of it. He will waste all his strength fighting. Then once the current finally abates, sometimes far off-shore, he will lack the strength to swim back to the beach. Unless he is rescued, he will drown."

"And this is the condition of currents off Breaker Beach?"

Dr. Gaston adjusted his glasses with scholarly aplomb. "Absolutely."

Stan's eyes flicked to the courtroom clock. It would soon be noon. He did not want to be interrupted in the middle of key testimony about tides the night Shawna Welk was killed. "Your Honor," he said, looking to the judge, "this would be a good time to break for lunch."

IN THE JURY ROOM Chelsea ate her sandwich distractedly. She'd noticed a new face in the courtroom. A young Hispanic man. As she and the other jurors were filing out, she'd seen Milt Waking approach him.

Is this important, Lord? Do you want me to pray?

She received no definite answer. Still, she could not push that scene from her mind. The young man, obviously out of his element, and Milt, cool, slick as always. What would they possibly have to say to one another?

"What's the matter, Chelsea?" B. B.'s voice broke through her thoughts. "You look like you're in another world."

"Oh." She smiled. "I was just . . . thinking about the trial."

"Well, don't think too hard," B. B. said, laughing. "There's plenty of time for that yet." She pulled up a chair.

Chelsea's heart sank. She didn't want to be unfriendly. But she felt she should pray for that young man right now. And for Milt. God had called her to be diligent, to pray as seemed right. She couldn't expect a specific leading from the Lord every moment.

Can I do both, God? Can I talk to B. B. and pray at the same time?

Of course she could. Hadn't she been doing pretty much the same thing through much of the testimony? Asking God's blessing on the trial, Kerra, Brett, herself, even as she furiously took notes?

"So tell me what you do for fun when you're not stuck on a jury," Chelsea prompted B. B. And in the back of her mind she prayed,

Dear Lord, lead Milt's actions today. And be with that young man, whoever he is...

ROGELIO SAT OPPOSITE MILT in a corner booth of a small Italian restaurant near the courthouse. Rogelio wasn't used to eating pasta. He'd chosen soup and a salad, hoping his nervous stomach would allow him to eat. Milt didn't seem that hungry, either. He was picking at his tortellini, his mind clearly more on their lulling conversation. Rogelio still wasn't sure how much to tell him. He'd had little time to consider it. The testimony and atmosphere of the courtroom had interested him far more than he would have expected.

"Why is that guy's testimony such a big deal?" he asked, stalling for time. "All that talk about waves and tides."

"The prosecutor has to prove that Shawna Welk's body was swept out to sea," Milt explained.

"Well, yeah. Where else would it have gone?"

"Nowhere. But Welk's attorney doesn't have much to offer in the way of defense. The evidence is stacked against them. So he's got to make mountains out of molehills. The prosecutor knows that one of those molehills will be to suggest that if Shawna was killed at that beach, her body would have washed up on shore."

Rogelio could think of nothing to say. He ate his soup in silence.

Milt took a few more bites, carefully keeping a hand over his tie. "So. What did you want to talk to the judge about?"

Setting down his spoon, Rogelio stared at the white tablecloth. He still didn't have a clue what he should do. "First I have to know if you can help me."

"How can I promise to help you if I don't even know what you need?"

He had a point.

"Okay." Rogelio thought fast. "How about this to start? I need some information on a person. All I have is his name. I hear he's been in some trouble with the law, and I'd like to know exactly what. Could you find something out for me?"

"I'll see what I can do," Milt said, shrugging, "but I don't have time to be running around as long as I'm covering this case. What's the name?"

"Enrico Delgadia."

Milt shook his head, obviously not recognizing it. "Know where he lives?"

"Somewhere in the Salinas area, I guess."

"Mm. If he's been in trouble with the law, there may be some news articles about him. Let me fire up my laptop and check it out."

Hope surged through Rogelio. Could the guy possibly come up with answers this quickly?

Milt shoved plates and silverware aside and set up his computer. "This thing's got a wireless hookup. I'll plug the name into a search engine, see if we get lucky."

Rogelio didn't know what a wireless hookup was but did not ask. He watched the reporter's face as Milt typed quickly, then waited. Satisfaction creased Milt's features.

"Got a bunch of hits." His eyes flicked back and forth. He continued to read and click the computer for what seemed a long time, his reactions clear in the darkening knit of his brows. Tension stiffened Rogelio's legs. Finally he could stand it no longer.

"Tell me!"

Milt looked up. "Enrico Delgadia is the owner of Chef Mate in Salinas," he said. "A company that packages food products. You know it?"

Rogelio nodded, amazed. Chef Mate was huge, its buildings and green lawns spread along a road just outside Salinas. "What did he do?"

"Numerous things, according to these articles from the *Californian*. You don't read the Salinas newspapers?"

Rogelio shook his head.

"He's been charged with tax evasion twice, plus money laundering and price fixing. Sounds like he's been to court at least three times. Always found innocent. Know what he looks like? Here's a picture."

Milt turned the computer around and Rogelio leaned over the table. The news article showed a close-up of Delgadia, lips drawn back in anger. It was an evil face.

Milt pulled the computer back toward him. "This last article is particularly interesting. He'd been charged with running some kind of illegal gambling scheme, and the cops had a witness. Just before Delgadia was due in court, the witness 'disappeared.' Doesn't sound like the kind of guy you'd want to mess with."

Rogelio drew in a breath. "What happened?"

Milt read further. "They had to let him go. It mentions him walking away from the courthouse with his wife and newly adopted daughter."

"Roselita!" Rogelio moaned. He slumped back in his chair. He could not bear to think of his baby with such a man.

Milt eyed him. "Roselita?"

Oh no. Rogelio pressed his lips together.

The reporter continued staring. Rogelio could practically hear the wheels turning in his head. "Is Roselita the wife or the baby?"

"Baby." The word was barely audible.

"I see." Milt thought a moment. "Any chance," he said slowly, "she's your biological daughter?"

Rogelio couldn't hide the truth from his face.

Milt fell silent. "What's the connection to the trial?" he asked after a moment. "Was the adoption through Shawna Welk's agency?"

This guy was too smart. For a brash moment Rogelio considered walking out of the restaurant without looking back. But then— what?

"Yeah."

"When was it?"

"Seven months ago."

"Just before she was killed." Milt tapped his computer. "Why would an agency let someone like this guy adopt a baby?"

Rogelio gazed distractedly out the window. A Corvette rolled down the street, windows open, music blaring. Even in the restaurant he could feel the bass in his chest.

He thought of Janet's warning of a long, hard court battle. Of all the twisted accusations a man like Delgadia might throw out to win the fight. A fight in the courts was one thing; a fight with a man who apparently made people disappear was something else. Rogelio felt way in over his head. It wasn't just his safety. He had Kristin and Mama Yolanda to worry about.

Maybe he should forget the whole thing.

But how could he, knowing that his daughter would be raised by this ruthless man?

"*I know a lot of people.*" The reporter's words ran through his head.

"It wasn't legal," he said quietly.

"The adoption wasn't legal? Why?"

Rogelio sank fingers into the arm of his chair. What should he do? If he told his story to some reporter, would Kristin ever forgive him?

"Look, it's getting late." Milt sounded impatient. "You have something to tell me, you'd better do it now; I need to be back in court in fifteen minutes."

Rogelio felt as if he were jumping off an ocean cliff. He steeled himself. "Okay then. I'll tell you," he said. "But I . . . I want something in return. You have to promise that you won't tell anybody else until we agree what to do."

"Deal."

"It won't be in the news."

"Yes. Okay."

Solemnly Rogelio extended his hand over the table. Milt looked surprised, then shook it. When he tried to pull away, Rogelio held on firmly. "A man's word is his life." He gave Milt a piercing look. "If his word is no good, he is worth nothing."

The reporter held his gaze. "Agreed."

Rogelio's fingers slid away. Milt flexed his shoulders, adjusted his suit coat. "So go ahead."

Rogelio told him.

By the time he was through, Milt looked as if he'd been hit by lightning. His eyes cruised over the table as if searching for where to begin. "Do you realize what this means?" he said, gaping. "The defense would *kill* for this information. It would blow this case wide open."

All Rogelio could think of were his own problems. He gave Milt a blank look.

"It would bring a whole other person into the case," Milt explained rapidly. "A person with a real motive to want Shawna Welk dead. After all, dead people tell no tales. What's more, Delgadia's history suggests he's capable of knocking somebody off when it suits him."

The words streaked through Rogelio like wildfire. How could he not have realized? In that instant he understood the strength of Mama Yolanda's tie to the trial. No wonder God was calling her to pray. For a moment Rogelio marveled at that, amazed at what God had chosen to do, amazed that he would bother at all. Then worries crowded back into his head.

"I don't care about the trial." He pointed at Milt. "I told you so you could help me get Roselita back."

"But this is perfect." Milt pushed his computer aside and leaned toward Rogelio. "If the defense were to hear this information, they'd immediately subpoena Delgadia and Janet Cline, plus all the adoption papers. They'd requestion Tracey. If they could prove she went along with this, her testimony would be in tatters. And *she's* the prosecution's main witness."

"So?"

"So." Milt shook his head, as if astounded at Rogelio's ignorance. "Reporters watching the case would be all over your story. They'd be all over Delgadia. Everything would be out in the open, and he'd be watched like a hawk. Which means he couldn't pull anything underhanded."

"It didn't seem to stop him before," Rogelio commented.

"That was different. It was probably some sleazy witness with his own criminal history. Someone who could have been done in by lots of people. Delgadia could get away with it. But everyone would be watching out for you. Plus the adoption papers will prove you're telling the truth."

"What about Kristin? I don't want reporters bothering her, calling her a baby seller." Rogelio's gut churned. What had he done?

"It's all in the spin, Rogelio," Milt declared. "The defense would make Delgadia out to be a murder suspect, never mind that he was miles away from the beach that night. He'd be the bad guy. He already is. When I break the story, I'll tell how you and Kristin were lied to, taken advantage of. Just two young kids trying to do the best for their daughter. Besides, you were honorable enough to come forward with what you've discovered. The public would eat it up. They'd be outraged at Delgadia and Shawna Welk. Do you see?" Milt shook his head. "Delgadia wouldn't have time to form a plan against you. He'd be too busy defending himself!"

Rogelio stared at the floor, heart beating in his ears. He couldn't believe this was happening. "When would you report the story?"

Milt tapped two fingers together, frowning. "First I would need to get all the facts from you and verify them." His eyes fixed in the distance as he thought. Finally he nodded. "Okay." He pulled out his notebook, then his pen. "Let's go over all the information. Then we can talk strategy. I've got some ideas. . . ."

THIRTY-TWO

Dozens of eyes seemed to shoot lasers through Kerra as she and Brett resumed their seats after lunch. It was all thanks to the sound bite–hungry media, Kerra thought with a grimace. She and Brett had quickly become an official item, another fascination to ogle and whisper about as the trial unfolded.

Well, so what? She *was* with Brett. Let the people talk all they wanted.

Kerra had barely floated back to the ground after her two days in Salinas. One vignette after another still shimmered through her head. Sight-seeing with him in Carmel. A picnic dinner at the beach Saturday night, followed by a barefoot walk through the sand as the setting sun gleamed orange red over gentle waves. A drive through the ranch on Sunday, Brett pointing out the different crops. Brett had needed to spend some time with his foreman, catching up on the overall business of the ranch. Kerra had been prewarned and had taken a book along to read. But she never opened it. All she could do, as she lolled on the couch in the spacious family room, was think of Brett, relive her moments with Brett, *feel* Brett. Those two days were like a jewel suspended in time, worries of the trial temporarily pushed aside.

Reality had hit during the drive back to the Bay Area. When Kerra had slid into her bed in Aunt Chelsea's house Sunday night, she'd felt uniquely alone. Not the gut-wrenching aloneness that had claimed her ever since Dave's death but the aching desire of a heart newly awakened and trembling.

Kerra found the crowd at the courthouse that morning both unnerving and fortifying, if that made any sense. She didn't like the glances, the whispers, the reporters sidling up to her with questions she refused to answer. And now the cameras were filming her as well as Brett. But in an odd way, all those troubling ingredients pushed her closer to him. They'd been thrown into the same roiling stew pot, and all the stirring in the world would not keep her from him.

The jury filed in. Of their own accord Kerra's eyes fastened on Aunt Chelsea. Her aunt smiled and raised her eyebrows. The loving expression sent darts into Kerra's chest. She knew she was causing her aunt worry. If only Aunt Chelsea could realize that she felt better and more alive than she had in a long time.

"All rise." The bailiff's voice boomed through the courtroom. Judge Chanson settled into her chair and donned her glasses. Kerra cast a look at Brett. He reached over and squeezed her knee.

Dr. Gaston, definitely the nerdiest-looking man Kerra had ever seen, resumed his stance beside the easel and charts, pointer in hand. Stan Breckshire fussed with his notes at the prosecution table before skidding back his chair.

"All right, Dr. Gaston," the prosecutor said, scratching his jaw, "let's continue where we left off."

For the next hour Dr. Gaston's thin voice wafted over the courtroom as he displayed one depiction after another of current directions and speed off Breaker Beach. He also talked of wind speed, of how a body would float rather than sink and so was even more susceptible to being pushed out to sea. The testimony weighted the courtroom with its import. According to Dr. Gaston, the body of Shawna Welk would have been carried out to open ocean "unless some other presence in the water, such as a shark, interrupted the process."

Stan Breckshire paced as he questioned, snatching up his notes and throwing them back on the table, his forehead creased in concentration.

"Now." He halted abruptly, fingers drumming his chin. "Can you tell us about the tides on the night of February fifteenth and in the early-morning hours of February sixteenth?"

"Certainly." Dr. Gaston flipped a page on his chart. "Latitude and longitude for Breaker Beach are as follows: 36.8017 degrees north, 121.7900 degrees west. On the night of Friday, February fifteenth, the moon was at what we call the waxing crescent. This is the bare sliver we see as the moon begins a new cycle that will end in a full moon. High tide at Breaker Beach occurred at 1:02 a.m. on February sixteenth. The tide was at 4.20 feet. Low tide occurred at 6:45 a.m. and was at 1.88 feet."

"Okay. So in five hours and forty-three minutes, the tide receded . . ."—Stan Breckshire's lips moved silently; Kerra quickly calculated—"about two and one-third feet."

"That is correct."

"Which means, if you do the math, that in the space of an hour and a half, the tide would have receded approximately seven inches, is that right?"

"Yes."

"And when the tide recedes, what is the condition of the sand that was previously covered by water?"

"Well," Dr. Gaston said, pursing his lips, "it's smooth and packed. And wet."

"Yes, naturally." Stan Breckshire glanced at the jury, many of whom were taking notes.

Seven inches of wet sand. In that instant Kerra's mathematical brain put it all together. Tracey Wilagher's testimony of seeing half a footprint in the wet sand, the rest of it smudged away. The smudged part was where the water level would have been when Shawna left the print. The time of high tide, the time Tracey said she'd been at the beach—it all fit.

As the prosecutor continued his questions, a stillness settled in Kerra' stomach until she practically hummed with it. She fiddled with her pant leg; her neck tensed until it ached. She couldn't help boring a hole with her eyes into Darren Welk's one-quarter profile as he sat at the defense table. As always, he was still as stone, except for those flexing hands.

The strength in those hands.

Ever since the first day of trial, Kerra's mind had been filled with so many things. Her loss of Dave, her disappointment in Aunt Chelsea's being a juror, the initial fascination with the bustling and intriguing courtroom scene. Then Brett. She'd wondered about Darren Welk's guilt or innocence, had even on some rational level decided that he was guilty. But she'd held that knowledge away from her heart. The more her being had sung with the thrill of Brett, the more she'd cringed from that knowledge. Now it hit her full in the face.

Darren Welk had killed his wife on Breaker Beach. Her body had washed out to sea.

Kerra was falling in love with the son of a murderer.

WOULD THIS DAY'S TESTIMONY *never* end? The words dragged on and on for Brett, implications of the details sagging him in his chair. He surveyed the jury. Even with all the analysis and math, they seemed completely attentive. Tracey and Lonnie had enthralled them with personal, emotional stories. But these details were the facts, cold and clear, the evidence of tides and currents and inches of wet sand adding to the blood analyses, the tooth X-rays. His dad's claim of vague, drunken memories had been irreparably tossed aside, trampled underfoot by the weight of science.

Brett could hardly bear it. He was going to have to do something drastic to save his dad. He needed his father to come home.

Terrance Clyde cross-examined Dr. Gaston at length, but his answers did little to quell Brett's anxiety. Then, to make matters worse, the prosecutor called an expert on sharks. Eric Vanderling, who looked no older than thirty, was from the Pelagic Shark

Research Foundation in Santa Cruz. Brett groaned inwardly at what he knew would follow.

Vanderling talked about the three kinds of sharks that attacked people the most—tigers, bulls, and great whites. The great whites had attacked humans more times than had the other two types of sharks put together. Although shark attacks were extremely rare, the California coast around Monterey County, where Breaker Beach was located, seemed a prime spot. Great whites, the most lethal to humans, swam in the cooler waters off the California coast. They were known to eat seals voraciously in the Red Triangle—a hundred-mile area reaching from Bodega Bay to Santa Cruz.

On February 10, five days before Shawna Welk disappeared, a great white shark had attacked a man about a mile off Zmudowski State Beach.

Brett could feel Kerra's tension. Numerous times she shifted in her seat. When Vanderling showed enlarged photos of a great white's open mouth, she gasped quietly.

"Here we have an actual great white shark's tooth." Vanderling held it up as if it were treasure. "The tooth is about one and three-quarters inches long and razor sharp."

Carefully, milking the moment for all it was worth, Stan Breckshire held out his palm for the tooth, then eased over to the first juror, who stoically accepted it. The jurors passed it grimly, some of them gingerly touching fingers to the tip.

"Does the shark have similar upper and lower teeth?" Breckshire prompted. Brett clenched his jaw. Hadn't the point been made?

"Yes, it does." Vanderling pointed again to his photo. "In fact, a great white shark has multiple rows of teeth. If it happens to lose one, another moves forward to replace it."

"What about the power of the bite? Has it ever been measured?"

"It's very powerful. A great white can exert pressure of two thousand pounds per square inch."

Stan shook his head in horror. "Two thousand pounds as sharp as knives."

"Yes."

Brett stole a look at Kerra, then allowed his gaze to cruise the courtroom. Everyone was so horrifically fascinated. Shark's teeth formed a human's worst nightmare—being eaten alive.

At least Shawna had already been dead.

Or so he chose to believe.

He shuddered. Kerra flicked him a look of concern. Thankfully, the prosecutor was finally through with his questions.

Erica Salvador rose from her seat like a diminutive general come to calm the troops. She clicked her way around the table toward the jury box and thrust out a hand for the tooth. Juror number twelve obediently dropped it into her palm.

"Thank you." She swiveled to the court reporter's desk and tossed the tooth upon it. Then turned to face the witness with a deprecating stare.

"Mr. Vanderling, what were those statistics that you mentioned before the prosecutor's little sideshow? The one about how rare shark attacks are?"

Vanderling straightened with the expression of a chastised child. "Well, like I said, last year was an unusually high year for attacks. Ninety-four were reported."

"And in the year 2000?"

"Seventy-nine."

"And in 1999?"

Vanderling furrowed his eyebrows. "Fifty-eight."

"How about 1998?"

"Fifty-four."

"I see. And this is *worldwide*?"

"Yes."

"Would a person have just as much, if not more, chance of being struck by lightning?"

"Yes."

"Or dying by some freak accident?"

"Yes."

"How about being eaten by a bear?"

"Well, not in the ocean."

A nervous titter ran through the courtroom. Erica did not appear amused.

"Mr. Vanderling, is it not true that research indicates that these extremely rare attacks are in fact mistakes on the part of the shark?"

"That's what seems to be the case. Sharks are not out to get humans. They are wonderfully designed creatures who live in a habitat that humans like to enter. Sometimes we get in their way. As for the great white, we think the sharks mistake humans for seals, which are their favorite source of food."

"And do tell us, sir, what the great white shark does when he realizes his mistake?"

"They tend to spit out whatever they've bitten off."

"In other words, they don't *eat* an entire person."

"Usually not, no."

"Thank you, sir; that is all." Erica shot a look at the jury, as if to say, "The sky is not falling."

"Oh, one more thing." She turned back to Vanderling. "Were you at Breaker Beach the night of February 15?"

He looked surprised. "No."

"Do you have any idea what happened to Shawna Welk?"

"No."

"No proof or even the slightest bit of evidence that a great white shark, who doesn't like to bite humans, ate Mrs. Welk but somehow managed to miss one tooth?" The cynicism fairly dripped off her tongue.

"No, ma'am, I don't."

Erica let the answer hang in the air. Then she marched back to the defense table, stabbing Stan Breckshire with an outraged glance.

The courtroom rustled. Jury members sat back in their chairs. Reporters scribbled. Brett hoped against hope that Erica's disdain-filled tactics would work.

THIRTY-THREE

"The people call Eddie Hunt."

Chelsea watched Stan Breckshire eye the courtroom door with vindictive determination. The prosecutor was not adept at hiding his emotions. She could tell he was seething from the defense attorney's cross-examination of Mr. Vanderling.

The bailiff pulled the door open. Eddie Hunt, a craggy-faced young man with blond hair, stepped into the courtroom. Chelsea's heart immediately went out to him. Eddie slowly made his way down the aisle, favoring his right leg. Stan Breckshire fastened an empathetic look upon his face as Eddie took the oath, then seated himself awkwardly in the witness chair.

Chelsea headed a new piece of paper with his name.

Stan laced and unlaced his fingers. "Thank you for coming, Mr. Hunt," he said gravely. "I hope this will not be too difficult for you."

The young man nodded. "Sure, okay."

Eddie looked like such a sun-kissed California kid, Chelsea thought. He was probably only a decade older than her own son Michael.

"How old are you?" Stan asked, as if he'd read Chelsea's mind.

"Twenty-three."

"And what do you do?"

"I work at a store in Santa Cruz that sells surfing and scuba equipment."

"Do you take part in these activities yourself?"

Pain creased Eddie's face. "I used to surf. I hope someday I can do it again. Right now I don't even go in the ocean."

"Could you tell us why that is?" Stan asked.

"Yeah, sure."

Eddie seemed to gather himself. His eyes drifted beyond Stan. Chelsea's pen poised over her pad of paper. "It was on a Sunday earlier this year. February tenth. . . ."

EDDIE AND HIS BEST FRIEND, Ryan, had totally lucked out. Ryan's father had just bought a beautiful new forty-three-foot yacht, and he said they could use it for the evening. Ryan rustled up a couple of newly hired girls who worked with him at Mad Al's Restaurant. Getting them to say yes to the date wasn't too hard, considering the plush cruiser they were promised. If the rest of the crew hadn't had to work that dinner shift, Ryan and Eddie would have had three or four girls apiece.

The foursome eased out of the dock at Moss Landing at about four in the afternoon, Ryan at the helm. He'd grown up piloting his wealthy father's succession of crafts over the years and was not afraid of handling this one. It was a typical February day—chilly and overcast. Eddie wore his favorite jacket over a long-sleeved shirt and jeans. Jessica and Christy came bundled up to beat the band. Ryan laughed at them, asking them where did they think they were going, Canada? His jacket was no more than a light windbreaker.

They set out to sea about a couple of miles, then turned to cruise up Monterey Bay. When they reached Santa Cruz, they turned south again. Off Zmudowski State Beach, Ryan killed the motor and lowered the anchor.

They lounged in the cabin, each drinking a few beers, the extra-large pizza that Christy had brought keeping warm in the oven. Cutup

Ryan was in fine form, telling jokes, making the girls laugh until their stomachs hurt. Ryan was like that. People tended to flow toward him like a river to the sea. Eddie started to feel a bit left out. It was stupid, of course. Childish. Still, Christy was supposed to be his date, and all she seemed to be doing was laughing at Ryan's stories. What she needed was a little diversion.

"I think I'll go for a swim," Eddie announced, pushing to his feet with a determined look. "Anybody want to come?"

Christy ogled him. "Are you crazy? That water's freezing!"

"So? I'm used to it. I surf all year 'round, you know."

"Yeah, with a wet suit." Ryan gave him a look that said, "What are you doin', man?"

Eddie stared back in defiance. He wasn't about to back down now. Stupid, stupid.

"Wow, really?" Christy said. "You surf a lot?"

Eddie shrugged. "Yeah."

"I heard it's so hard to learn."

"Well, I've been at it a few years."

"Come on, Eddie, sit down," Ryan said. "We'll eat soon."

"Guess I need to work up an appetite then." The boat rocked gently as Eddie surveyed the blue gray water. He really didn't want to do this.

"You gonna swim in your clothes?" Ryan popped the top off another can of beer. "You go right ahead. I'll keep these two company." He grinned and raised his eyebrows. Christy giggled.

Eddie almost changed his mind, hearing that comment. If only he had.

"No way; I'm not sitting around in wet clothes." He unbuttoned his jacket and threw it on a cushioned bench. Took off his shirt. Christy's deep green eyes settled appreciatively on his muscles. Eddie pretended not to notice. Then nonchalantly he unzipped his jeans and slid them off.

"Woohoo!" Jessica called.

Christy dropped her jaw in surprise. Then she raised an eyebrow and grinned. "Take it off, take it all off," she chanted.

"Sorry, girls." Eddie snapped the waistband of his underwear. "These'll have to stay."

"Eddie, you're nuts." Ryan swigged his beer. "Go on then, freeze your tail off."

"I'll tell you what." Christy gave him a heat-soaked look through her chestnut bangs. "Just swim around the boat a few times, then come on back."

"I'll do that. But you all have to come out of the cabin," Eddie insisted. "If I'm going in that water, the least you can do is stand back there and watch."

Ryan rolled his eyes, then followed Eddie to the open end of the boat, girls in tow. Without a word Ryan unsnapped the bands holding up the ladder, then let it unfold into the water with a small splash. Eddie didn't wait to lose his nerve. He hopped on the first rung, then plunged into the water.

The cold hit him like a punch in the gut. He sank beneath the surface, then quickly kicked his way up again, flinging his head out of the water with a loud whoop.

"Go, Eddie!" Christy cheered as he began his first swim around, keeping close to the boat. Man, it was cold. He cut through the waves like a wolverine on speed and was soon back where he began. He stopped to tread water.

"One more!" Eddie grinned up at the girls. Christy gave him a sly wink.

It happened in the space of an instant. His right foot bumped something solid. Then a stinging pain hit him below the knee. He heard a muffled snap. The pain shot up his leg and through every nerve until his entire body pulsed with it. He listed sideways. He tried kicking his feet, but his right leg flopped strangely.

"A shark!" Christy shrieked. "Eddie!"

Then Jessica screamed and Ryan screamed. Eddie's own cries mixed with theirs until the whole world was screaming. The water ran blood red. Eddie flailed, sinking below the surface. He came up choking, yelling for help. Ryan leaped into the ocean, hooked an arm around Eddie's neck, and dragged him to the ladder.

The world faded to black.

CHELSEA'S EYES WERE CLOSED. She'd hardly taken one note. So vividly could she picture Eddie in the water, the blood, his terror. Just imagine if that were her own son....

"What was the extent of your injuries?" Stan prompted quietly.

Eddie sucked in a breath. "I lost my right leg below the knee."

A horrified sibilance whisked through the courtroom.

"Are you now walking with a prosthesis?"

"Yeah. I just got it a couple months ago. Still getting used to it." He forced a grin.

"I see." Stan rubbed his palms together. "Just one more thing, Eddie. You mentioned you haven't been in the ocean since this accident. Are you unable to surf with the prosthesis?"

A frown creased Eddie's forehead. "No, I could learn to do it, I suppose. It's just that . . ." He raised a self-conscious shoulder. "After what happened, I haven't been interested in going back in the ocean yet. I'll get there. But not this summer."

Stan nodded. "I understand, Eddie. I certainly understand." Grimly he turned to the defense table. "Your witness."

Erica didn't even bother to stand up. That wasn't right, Chelsea thought. How could the woman be so cold?

"Mr. Hunt," Erica said matter-of-factly, "I am sorry for your loss. Your story seems to indicate that the shark bit you just once, is that correct?"

"Yeah."

"And then what did it do?"

"Uh, Christy told me she saw it swimming away right afterward. That's when Ryan jumped in the water."

"So one experimental bite and then it left?"

Eddie considered Erica for a drawn-out moment, his face darkening. "Heck of an experiment, don't you think?" he said tightly.

"I didn't mean—"

"I lost my *leg*. I'd have bled to death if I'd been out there alone."

"Yes, Mr. Hunt; that did not sound as I intended it." Erica's face flushed and she bent low over her notes to hide it. Stan appeared pleased as punch.

Erica flicked busily through her notes. When she looked up, the flush on her cheeks had faded. "No more questions."

Court recessed for the day. As she stood to file out for another long evening, Chelsea saw the look Erica threw at Stan Breckshire. It could have withered stone.

THIRTY-FOUR

Standing on the San Mateo County Courthouse steps, Milt Waking wrapped up his live report, then beat feet toward his car.

"Where you going so fast? Have a hot date?" his cameraman called after him.

"Hot, hot!"

He could hear Bill's chuckles. "Go get her, Waking!"

At his car Milt took off his suit coat and laid it in the backseat. Checked his watch as he slid inside. Five fifty. It would take him about an hour and a half to reach Salinas. He snatched up his cell phone, drew from his pocket a piece of paper with a phone number, and punched it in. Amazing the difference an afternoon could bring, he thought as the phone began to ring. Under his tutorship, Rogelio Sanchez, gardener from Salinas, had returned home to play undercover detective.

"Hello."

"It's me. Did you get the address?"

"Yeah."

"Great. What is it?" He wrote it down as Rogelio told him. "She didn't see you?"

"No. I waited outside the dress shop, like you said. Followed her home, keeping a few cars back."

"Rogelio, I believe you're on the verge of a shining new career."

The kid gave a quiet snort. It was the first time Milt had heard him come anywhere near a laugh.

"Okay, I'm on my way. I'll call you after I've talked to her."

"You'd better, man."

Milt hung up, started his car with gusto, and took off for the freeway.

"GOD WANTS TO BE your heavenly Father." For the hundredth time Kerra's words echoed in Brett's mind as he followed the police officer toward the little room in which he was allowed to visit his dad. The words quickened his heart, brought to him a sense of hope he had not previously known. Still, even if Kerra was right, God was somewhere up there while Brett was stuck on earth with all its craziness. Right now he'd settle for a little more understanding from his real father.

Hey, God, if you're listening—

The policeman opened the door to the visiting room. "He's waiting for you. Fifteen minutes."

"Okay."

—help me with this father in front of me.

Brett stepped across the threshold. His father sat on the other side of the glass separation, hands on his thighs. They picked up their phones. "Hi, Dad."

"You've been mighty busy, I hear." Disapproval tinged Darren Welk's voice. "You haven't been to see me in five days."

So much for a happy greeting. The room smelled of dust, stale smoke, and despondence. Brett hated this room. He slumped in his chair wearily.

"You've sure managed to stir the waters." His dad considered him as if he were some kind of moron. "First those two phone calls to jurors T. C. thought he could sway our way. And now what's this about taking up with a juror's niece? Not just *any* juror, mind you, but that religious nut."

"She's not a religious nut." The words shot from Brett's mouth before he could stop them.

His father stared. "How do you know? You manage to talk to her too?"

Brett's gaze dropped to the floor. "Of course not. I just know because of the way Kerra talks about her."

"Kerra, is it? The blond girl you've been sitting with."

Protectiveness rose in Brett. He didn't like the sound of Kerra's name on his father's lips. "Yeah." Brett could say no more about her. How could he even begin? "And as for the phone calls—"

"I don't want to hear your flimsy explanations." His father swept out an impatient hand.

"Dad—"

"Forget it, Brett; it's done." He blew out air. "In the end maybe it's not such a bad thing. Now we've got your favorite aunt up there." He narrowed his eyes. "You think anything you planted in Kerra's head got through to the woman before their phone calls were cut?"

The words hit Brett's chest like darts. He gripped the phone. How could he have been so stupid not to realize the way his dad would view things?

"Well?"

"Kerra never talked to her aunt about the trial, Dad." His voice was low. "I knew that from the very beginning."

Silence.

"You mean to tell me your relationship with this gal has nothing to do with me?"

"It has *everything* to do with you!" Brett burst. "It has to do with your being in here while I'm out there. It has to do with going crazy day after day in that courtroom, listening to the testimony against you. It has to do with losing my mom and now you too. You just don't—" The words hooked in his throat. He fell back in his seat, breathing hard. Buffed a hand across his face.

His dad focused on the corner of the room. "I thought you were trying to help me," he said finally. "Didn't know this was all about you."

"Dad, I *do* want to help you." Desperation coated Brett's words. "Listen to what I came to say. First, we need to talk. Get everything out on the table, for once in our lives. Then I've got to tell the truth."

His father's eyes turned to stone. "No."

"No to what?"

"You're not telling the truth."

"I *have* to, Dad; it's the only way."

"*No.*"

Brett's chin flopped to his chest. "Dad, I can't keep on like this, especially after today. You're going to be convicted; don't you realize that?"

"And what would your telling the truth do, huh?" His father hunched toward the glass. "Nothing, that's what! Except give the reporters a new story."

"But how could the jurors convict you if—"

"*Think,* boy!" Darren Welk pulled himself up straight, anger widening his stocky shoulders. At the familiar sight Brett felt ten years old. "The evidence is all against *me.* It doesn't matter what you tell them. That beaky-nosed prosecutor will shout to the heavens that you're just trying to cover for me at the last minute. That since playing around with the juror's niece didn't work, you're now getting desperate."

"I am *not* playing around with Kerra!" Brett yelled.

"It doesn't matter what you're doing; that's what they'll say! It won't change a thing in the end, not *one thing!*" He glared at Brett. Finally air hissed out of his lungs. He dropped his shoulders, looking deflated and worn. "Except that you could be in here with me."

Sickness crept through Brett's veins. Was his father right? Could his relationship with Kerra have made it impossible to save his dad? His eyes closed at the thought.

"I'll stop seeing her," he said. The mere words filled his stomach with lead.

His father rubbed an eyebrow. "Won't help. It's too late." He raised his head and cast Brett a penetrating look. The anger in his face waned, and he regarded Brett as if seeing him for the first time.

"You care for this gal a lot." It wasn't a question.

Brett blinked at the thought. "Yeah."

"And you'd give her up? For me?"

He tried to speak but his throat was too thick. He nodded.

Darren Welk spread a hand upon the glass. "Well," he said gruffly. "You won't have to. Wouldn't do any good anyway."

Brett's eyes stung. "I can't stand this, Dad."

His father managed the barest of smiles. "We'll manage, Son. We always have."

BRETT PARKED IN A SPACE outside Max's Restaurant, got out, and slid inside Kerra's car.

"How did it go?" she asked.

"Fine." He focused out the windshield, feeling the weight of Kerra's gaze. Her unspoken questions swirled between them. After her public support she deserved a few answers. But what could he do? Even if he could tell her everything on his heart, his words would hardly put her at rest.

"Do you want to go in and eat?" he asked.

She looked away. "Not really. Someone could recognize us. I've had enough people staring at me for the day." Accusation tinged her tone.

"I'm sorry all the reporters are hounding you, Kerra. Maybe if you stopped sitting with me, they'd leave you alone."

"Is that what you want?"

"You know it isn't."

"Fine then." She pushed back in her seat, arms folded.

"So," he ventured after a moment, "where do you want to go?"

"I don't know." Her tone was clipped, irritated. "I can't take you to Aunt Chelsea's house, knowing that she wouldn't approve of that. I'm sure you can understand."

"Sure. I can respect that." He gathered his nerve. "Want to go to my hotel room?"

She gave him an exasperated look. "Oh, that would be just great. Imagine the news stories if someone were to spot us."

Tiredness washed through Brett. He knew this was hard for Kerra. It wasn't exactly a cakewalk for him, either. After the long day, after the visit with his father, he did not have the energy to shore her up.

"Kerra," he said quietly, "do you just not want to be with me tonight?"

She searched his face, her expression smoothing. "You know I want to be with you, Brett. I just don't know where we should go. And I just wish you would *talk* to me."

The words hit him in the chest. If only he could.

He reached for her hand. "How about this: I'll go inside and get some food to go. We'll drive up into the hills somewhere, see if we can find an out-of-the-way place to park. Nobody around to bother us. We'll try to forget the world's even happening. Okay?"

She read his thoughts all too well. Closing her eyes, she sighed in resignation. "Okay."

Twenty minutes later they were winding their way through forested hills on Skyline Boulevard, west of Redwood City. Brett pulled off at a vista point sign, and they trudged a short distance to a clearing overlooking the cities and the bay beyond. A large, flat rock provided the perfect picnic table. Brett set down the food.

"Looks like a great spot to me."

Kerra gazed at the view. "It is. Although I suppose someone else could come along at any time."

"Well, it's better than a public restaurant. Besides," he said, pulling her close, "we're supposed to forget about the world. Remember?"

THE JURY OPTED FOR individual room service that night. Chelsea was relieved to eat alone. Better to be cooped up in the same four walls of her hotel room than to share another uncomfortable meal with the others.

She couldn't decide what to order, distractions from the day filling her head. Finally she settled on soup and a salad. Soon after she placed her order, Paul called. She longed to spill her heart out to him about Kerra and the jury members but knew she could not. He was so far away. What could he possibly do about any of it but worry? Instead she urged him to tell her about his day. She drank in his words and his voice, imagining his touch. Wishing he were beside her. By the time she hung up the phone, she felt even more alone.

The food arrived. Chelsea could only pick at it. Worries descended upon her like a dark cloud. Try as she might, she could not chase them away. One negative question after another pounded, until her head felt like a whirling storm.

How was she going to do everything God expected of her? She didn't have the strength. She was already tired, and jury deliberations hadn't even begun. She pictured Tak's hard eyes and Hesta's chilled stares. The impatient expressions of Gloria and Latonia. Antonio's judging frown. What would it be like, stuck in a room with these people until they all agreed? How would they treat her if she disagreed with any of them?

And what was Kerra doing right now, and Brett? Were they together all the time? Did Brett have something to do with Shawna Welk's death? If so, dear God, what was going to happen to Kerra?

THIRTY-FIVE

It was almost seven thirty when Milt pulled into a visitor's parking space in the Valley Way apartment complex. Both buildings were grayed, needing fresh paint. Milt's eyes roved over the brown, sparse grass. Must be a far cry from Darren Welk's expensive digs, he thought. He got out of his car and put on his suit coat. Patted his tie, smoothed his hair. Took a moment to summon his charm. The mere thought of using it lifted one corner of his lips.

Tracey lived in number twenty-six. Fortunately, all the apartments had outside entrances. Rogelio would have been hard pressed to follow her down some long hallway.

He knocked on the door, rehearsing. He'd rehearsed his interweaving of fact and fiction during the entire drive.

A voice filtered through the door. "Who is it?"

"Milt Waking, Miss Wilagher, from Channel Seven News. I have to talk to you about your mother. It's important."

Silence. Milt could almost feel the girl's revulsion.

"I don't want to talk to any reporters."

"Miss Wilagher, I am not here as a reporter." He leaned forward, a hand on the doorpost. "My workday has ended; I could be home kicking my shoes off. But I've stumbled across some information that I knew you'd want to hear."

Milt heard a footstep. "What information?" The voice was closer.

"I can't talk to you through the door."

"How did you know where I live?" The words rang with suspicion.

"Miss Wilagher, are you going to let me in or not? If you don't hear this information from me, you could end up hearing it on the nightly news."

Another long pause. Milt closed his eyes and gritted his teeth, hoping against hope. Then he heard the sound of a bolt sliding back. Exhaling aloud, he pulled away from the threshold. Straightened himself as the door inched open. Tracey's thin face appeared in the crack. He smiled, pouring warmth into his eyes. "See? It's just me. No paper and pen. No camera." He pulled his eyebrows together in a look of concern.

She gazed at him, lips pressed. Milt watched her swallow. He stood absolutely still, afraid that the slightest movement would send her skittering. An interminable moment passed. Finally she stepped back, opening the door farther.

"Come on in. But only for a minute."

He slipped inside, looking around the living room of her apartment. A few pieces of cheap furniture, probably rented. A small television. No pictures on the walls, no knickknacks. A computer on a square folding table in one corner. It was on, displaying an unfinished email.

She saw his gaze, quickly crossed the room and switched off the monitor. "Okay, you're in." She crossed her arms, standing woodenly. "Now what is it?"

His presence clearly rattled her. Suddenly she seemed so small, her shoulders so narrow and frail. Loneliness and distrust hung about her like a fog. He felt a surprising pang of empathy, wondering what it must be like to have lost a mother in such a horrible way. Then it vanished.

"Could I sit down?" he ventured.

"You won't be staying that long."

"Okay."

He eased a few steps until he reached the back of her couch. Rested a hand upon it. "I was placed in a moral dilemma this afternoon, Miss Wilagher, due to some information I heard about your mother, and I realized that talking to you was the only right thing to do. I came as soon as I could."

The exaggerated rise and fall of Tracey's breathing bespoke her anxiety. She hugged her arms. Milt forged ahead.

"I now know that about a month before she was murdered, your mother sold a baby to Enrico Delgadia for a substantial amount of money. And that you signed as a witness to the adoption."

A gasp rattled through Tracey's lips. Her face blanched. "Where did you hear that? It's not true!"

Milt leaned over the couch, the picture of sincerity. "Please don't waste what little time we have denying this. I've seen the adoption papers. Believe me, I'm not here to make your life harder than it already is."

Her knees wobbled in shock, body tilting. Both hands flew out to steady herself against the folding table. The next thing Milt knew, he'd sped around the couch to her side and was bracing her underneath the elbows.

"No, don't touch me; get out of my house!" She flailed at him wildly, splayed fingers connecting with his chin. His head jerked back in surprise at the intensity of her reaction. For an instant he almost let her go. He hadn't counted on this kind of gamble. What was he doing? But if he left her now . . . He put his arms around her and pulled her to him.

"Let me go!" she sobbed into his shirt, writhing.

"Tracey, listen to me; I want to help you." He tightened his hold.

"No, you don't! You don't want to help me at all!" Her head tossed from side to side against his chest.

Milt hung on with rising panic. How on earth had this happened? The things she could accuse him of!

That very thought made him hold her all the more tightly. No way he could afford to fail at winning her over now. "Shh, it's okay," he soothed. "It's all right." He slid a hand to the back of her head, smoothing her hair. "It's all right."

After what seemed an eternity, Tracey's struggles began to lessen. Finally she seemed spent. She leaned against him, shaking like a leaf in the wind. She was still crying.

"Come on, let's get you to sit down." He gently led her to the couch and they sank upon it. He continued holding her, stroking her hair until all hiccuping subsided. She inched out a hand to clutch his sleeve, fingers trembling. He was struck again by her frailty. He found himself imagining her life, and his heart went out to her. Regardless of his reason for being there, comforting her at that moment felt almost . . . good.

Well, he thought, bringing his mind back to focus. All the more ammunition to make her feel she could trust him.

"Tracey. Can you listen to me now?"

His fingers sifted through her hair. After a moment she nodded. Her face remained buried in his shirt.

"Okay. I'll explain everything." He sighed. "First of all, I haven't told anybody what I know. Like I said, I came to you first. After watching how hard it was for you on the stand, I just really felt for you. But I'm putting my career on the line. Not to mention my conscience. I can't continue to keep quiet unless I'm sure all this wouldn't change things." He gazed down at the top of her head, feeling the flutter of her heart against his chest. "Obviously, the defense attorney doesn't know about all this. Do you realize what he could do with the information if he did?"

She stiffened. "What?"

Her response was perfect. "He's looking for any argument to convince the jury that someone other than Darren Welk could have killed your mother. This would make his day. He'd haul you into court and make you tell everything you know. Then he'd haul Delgadia in. And in his closing arguments he'd weave a tale about how Delgadia might have wanted your mother dead to silence her."

Tracey's fingers tightened on his arm. "You know that's not true."

"But I don't, Tracey," he said quietly. "That's just it."

She raised her head to look at him. Her deep brown eyes were red-rimmed. Hair lay flattened and stuck to her temple. "What do you mean?"

Milt brushed the hair off her face. "How can I know that with such a motive, Delgadia *didn't* kill your mother? Maybe he was looking for a chance; maybe he followed them to the beach that night. Do you see my problem? I can't sit on information if I think doing so would send an innocent man to jail. My conscience will force me to tell Terrance Clyde."

Her eyes widened in terror. "You can't do that! Please!" Fresh tears sprang to her eyes. "Believe me, it wouldn't make any difference; Enrico Delgadia didn't kill my mother."

"How do you know that for sure?"

"I just *do!*" The last word was almost a wail.

"Okay, okay." He cupped her chin. "I want to believe that. But I can't set everything straight in my mind unless I know all the facts."

She shook her head, tears spilling onto her cheeks. "I can't tell you anything. That's just it—I can't talk to *anybody* about *anything!*"

"Oh, Tracey." He urged her close again and let her cry. This girl was really on the edge. Tired and lonely, dying for some gentleness and a sympathetic ear. His gut stirred with excitement. He talked to her softly. Consoled her. Told her all the things he knew she needed to hear.

After some time she quieted, breathing irregularly in his arms. Milt felt her still. "Please," he said, "just explain things to me. So I can put this to rest. As long as you can do that, I promise you on my life that I'll never say a word to anyone."

She sat up, searching his face. "I don't know how I can believe you."

"You can. Just convince me it has nothing to do with your mother's death."

Her eyes closed in pain. "It doesn't."

"All right." He smiled at her, urging her on.

Tracey took a deep breath and focused on her lap. She seemed to gather herself, as if for a fatal leap. "Delgadia's wife couldn't have a baby. They'd tried for years. He came to my mom, saying they'd finally decided to adopt. His wife wanted kids so badly, she was about to have a nervous breakdown. Delgadia expected the moon. Mom said Enrico was used to throwing his weight around and getting his way. Apparently, he is Hispanic and his wife is white. A fair, green-eyed blond, my mom said. He insisted on a baby that would have that same mix so it wouldn't look obviously adopted. And he wanted it now. He said he'd pay lots. At first Mom told him to take a hike; she wasn't about to do anything illegal. But then . . ."

Tracey looked up at Milt. He took her hand and held it. She grasped onto him tightly.

"You'd have to understand how it was between Mom and Darren. He made the money and controlled every penny. Mom wanted more money to expand the agency, and he wasn't about to give it. Probably too busy spending it on his other women," she added bitterly. "Meanwhile Delgadia kept pushing her. And then she discovered a baby about to be born to parents of the same mixed race. Their coloring was perfect. She decided to do it. 'Just this once,' she told me. But then things started to go wrong. She got the birth mother to agree easily after offering her money. But the birth father was another matter. Plus Mom realized her business partner would never go for it. Still, once she'd told Delgadia she had a baby for him, she didn't dare back out. She made me forge Janet's name and sign as a witness on the father's relinquishment form—when I wasn't." Tracey inhaled raggedly. "And that's the whole story."

Milt rubbed her hand. "Did you ever meet Delgadia yourself? Or the real father and mother of the baby?"

"Only the mother. I watched her sign her paper."

"It must be so hard for you, knowing all this."

Tracey's mouth pulled. "Everything's hard for me. You don't know how much I miss my mom. You don't know how much I'd give if none of this had ever happened. I hate what's happened to my life. I *hate* it!" She melted against him and he hugged her. She held on to his shoulder, her breath warm against the base of his neck. "So." Her voice trembled. "That's why Delgadia never would have killed my mom. There was no reason why she'd ever tell what happened as long as she was alive. But a murder would just stir up questions. Which it did." She swallowed. "Then it landed on my head to keep everything quiet. I promised Delgadia I'd never say a word." Vehemence hardened her tone. "I don't want anything to stand in the way of Darren Welk getting what he deserves!"

"No, you're right." Milt's mind raced for any unanswered questions. "I don't, either." He massaged her back with his palm. "Delgadia should be shot for making your mom do this. How much did he pay for the baby?"

Tracey hesitated. "I don't know."

"Your mom didn't tell you?"

"No."

Milt pondered that. "What happened to the money?"

She raised her head. "I don't know that either. I don't even know if she'd been paid yet. She was killed so soon after . . ."

Her words faded. Weariness etched her face. Milt gazed at her, thinking how young she looked. Good grief, she was only twenty. Barely more than half his age.

He'd gotten what he wanted. He knew he really should go.

Tracey raised her eyes to his. Her look was forlorn. Vulnerable. It pulled at him. Before he knew it, his mouth was lowering toward hers. Her eyes closed.

He kissed her firmly and long, her heart scudding against his chest. She hung on to him like a drowning child clinging to a rock.

All part of his job, he rationalized as he got into his car ten minutes later, a satisfied smile on his face. He reached for his cell phone to call Rogelio.

All part of his job.

TUESDAY, AUGUST 13

THIRTY-SIX

Tracey's eyes blinked open to her blue gray walls. In the past few months she'd thought them dreary and ugly, a perfect complement to her life. But this morning the sun shone through the curtains, playing patterns of light and fascination. Had it ever done that before?

She stretched, exultance playing over her body, overcoming the fatigue. She'd barely slept all night. Over and over she'd remembered Milt's gentle comforting, his sympathetic eyes. Time and again she'd relived the moment when his lips met hers. Seven months of living her nightmare, of drawing further and further into herself like a lost, lone waif, and in the space of one hour things had changed. Finally someone had an inkling of her pain. Finally someone knew the truth—that months ago, even when she still had her mother, Tracey was being used. And he *cared*.

So what if he was a reporter. He was a man first. A man who was attracted to her, who had kissed her in a way that made her burst out of her entrapment like a butterfly from a cocoon. He hadn't come for a story. He'd come to set things straight in his own mind. And he'd fulfilled his promise. Nothing about the baby had been on the late-evening news.

After Milt left her apartment, Tracey had floated toward her computer like a balloon on a breeze. She couldn't wait to tell her story to her email friends. For once she could share not misery but wild happiness. Her fingers flew over the keys as she poured out her heart to Soraya and Kim and Regina. Of course she did not tell them everything. No mention of the baby or the information Milt had been checking. Only that he'd shown up at her door after seeing her testify. By the time she wrote Maria, her exuberance had gotten the best of her, splashing across the screen in exclamation points and capital letters. She even admitted that Milt had been checking a certain story and that under the circumstances she'd had no choice but to tell him the truth. But he'd PROMISED not to use it and he HADN'T. And after all she'd been forced to endure, after all these horrible months, wasn't Maria HAPPY for her!!!??

With another stretch Tracey checked the clock on her dresser. Eight fifteen. She had to be at the store at ten. She threw back the covers, grabbed her robe, and padded to the computer, anxious to read the happy responses from her friends.

Three messages popped up. Tracey smiled expectantly as she tapped the keys.

Wow, he sounds like a DREAM! Soraya wrote. *When are you going to see him again?*

Any chance I get, Tracey thought. Surely Milt would call. She'd given him her unlisted phone number.

Tracey, I'm SO HAPPY for you!! Regina crowed. *Wouldn't it be funny if, after all this time of planning to leave once the trial is over, you stayed right there? Sounds like this guy would be worth it.*

Tracey's gaze drifted to the bare wall above the computer screen. Regina was right. One evening with Milt and already Tracey didn't want to think of leaving him behind. She sighed as she tapped on Maria's post.

The vehement words shot right through her.

WHAT DO YOU THINK YOU'RE DOING??!!

He's a reporter, Tracey! You don't trust reporters, period, no matter WHAT *they tell you! All this guy wants is a story. You've fallen into his trap. I can't* BELIEVE *you've done this, after all these months of caution.* DON'T *see him again! Don't even* TALK *to him. Believe me, I'm telling you this for your own good!!*

Tracey wilted in her chair, tears springing to her eyes. It wasn't true. Milt's face had been so honest, so believable. Stunned disappointment twisted Tracey's stomach, followed by anger, both at herself and at the email. She should never have told all the details that she had. She should have expected this kind of reaction. Good grief, what was wrong with her? All her dreaming of Milt had downright fried her brain.

But so what? Tracey railed to herself. So she'd made a stupid mistake and told. Still, this email was entirely undeserved. Tracey tried to imagine a fun life on the beaches of Brazil, with friends and boyfriends. Contrast that with her own pitiful existence. How could *anybody* deny her this little bit of joy?

Mouth pressed in a tight line, Tracey banged out a reply.

Some "friend" you are. How would YOU *like to be living* MY *life? How would you like to be stuck here, testifying at the trial, grieving over your dead mother while everybody watches? If you can't write me back something nice—*DON'T WRITE AT ALL!

As Tracey typed the last sentence, independence surged through her, clear and cold. She reveled in the new sensation, basked in it as if it were the first spring sun after a long, dreary winter. Suddenly she didn't care about what *anybody* said, good or bad. All her life she'd been pushed around, doing what she was told. She was sick of being her mousy little self. She was sick, sick, sick of *everything.* For once in her life she was going to do what *she* wanted.

With a furious little smile Tracey clicked the send button.

THIRTY-SEVEN

After a surprisingly good night's sleep Chelsea felt better. The first person she sought upon entering the courtroom that morning was the young man she'd seen talking to Milt Waking. He wasn't there. Was that good or bad?

Chelsea reminded herself that she did not need to know the answer. She just needed to keep praying. As she watched the attorneys prepare for the day's proceedings, silently she talked to God.

Stan Breckshire was wearing a shocking orange tie with his brown suit. He scrabbled through pages of notes at the prosecution table, rubbing his right shoulder and stretching his neck from side to side. Darren Welk whispered with Terrance Clyde, Erica Salvador leaning over to listen.

The courtroom door opened. Sidney Portensic wheeled in a television set on a tall stand, a VCR on a shelf beneath it. Stan Breckshire scurried over to help him set it up.

The courtroom filled quickly. Reporters took their seats, Milt Waking's eyes gliding across the jury and landing on her. Chelsea did not immediately look away. What was he up to? For once she wished she could talk to him.

The TV set was ready. Stan eyed it with satisfaction, rubbing the side of his head until his hair stuck out. Chelsea suppressed a smile. Then he returned to his seat, perching like a hawk.

Court was called to order.

"Your Honor," Stan announced, "the prosecution calls Detective Les Kelly. And as part of his testimony, I will be showing the videotape of the defendant's interview on the morning of Monday, February 18, with Detectives Kelly and Draker."

"All right, Mr. Breckshire."

Detective Kelly took the oath in a reedy voice, his wiry frame held perfectly straight. Stan Breckshire asked him a few questions regarding the detectives' interview with the defendant, then quickly moved to the video. The judge fiddled with the chain of her glasses as the prosecutor started the VCR. Sidney turned down the courthouse lights. The television flipped on and Darren Welk's face filled the screen.

His expression leaped from the television like some feral animal caught in headlights. Chelsea's stomach immediately constricted. The onlookers sucked in a collective breath. Fear and defensiveness hardened Welk's eyes. The deep lines around his mouth and forehead pulled taut, then slackened, pulled taut, slackened, as if his conscience and his survival instinct wrestled for control. His hands spread stiffly on the table, then slid together, clasping with a desperately feigned casualness that made his fingertips tremble.

This, thought Chelsea, was a man with something to hide.

Detective Draker read him his rights. "I watch those crime shows, too," Welk joked. The words seemed to splatter the air around him. His thick chest rose as he dragged in a breath and pressed back against his chair.

He didn't deny hitting his wife. He didn't deny that the blood on the blouse came from a cut in her head. He remembered details such as Shawna Welk taking off the blouse and Tracey Wilagher kicking him awake later. Yet he claimed to remember nothing in between.

According to Darren Welk, his wife had probably run off with a boyfriend, somehow managing her complete disappearance from an out-of-the-way beach in the middle of the night.

Chelsea's eyes slid to Darren Welk, who sat stiff-backed at the defense table, fingers tightly laced. One thumb pressed into the other hand, wrinkling his sun-leathered skin. He eyed himself on the television screen as if he were his own worst enemy.

Yes, Chelsea thought, *you are.*

She glanced at Brett. He too sat stiffly. So like his father. His face was pale.

"Are you aware, Mr. Welk," the detective onscreen said, leaning forward, "that both you and I have referred to Mrs. Welk in the past tense?"

Darren Welk's reaction pulsed from the television through the courtroom. His face hardened like frozen soil. "When did I do that? I'd have no reason."

"Your wife washed her blouse because she *didn't* like messes?"

On camera Darren Welk's expression slackened, then worked to reassemble itself. Chelsea shot another glance at the defendant. He pulled his eyes away from the television and locked a firm-mouthed gaze onto the courtroom floor.

"Where's my dad?" a muffled voice from the video demanded off camera. "I want to see him *right now!* I want to talk to the detectives!"

The onscreen Darren Welk pressed back in his chair, eyes wide. "No!" He shot out a hand and grabbed the surprised detective's wrist. "You're not talking to my son. You've got your man." He stabbed his chest with a finger. "Leave Brett out of this."

The detective eyed him coldly. He picked the man's hand off his wrist as if it were a giant spider. "We've got our man?" He lowered his chin, staring at Welk. "Is that a confession, Mr. Welk?"

Darren Welk's mouth opened, then snapped shut. His gaze narrowed, darkened, his shoulders straightening. Suddenly he slammed a fist into the table. "I want to see a lawyer!"

His face froze on the screen, mouth in a snarl and teeth bared, eyebrows jammed together. Next to Chelsea, Gloria sucked in an audible breath. No one in the courtroom moved, all staring at the anger, the *hatred,* in that face. Chelsea's eyes moved back and forth between Darren Welk and his son. Brett sat in utter stillness, as if one move would make him explode. What *was* it? Chelsea's mind scurried for an answer. Everything about Darren Welk reeked of guilt. But Brett. Something about Brett . . .

With a funereal air Stan Breckshire approached the television. He studied the frozen face onscreen, then trailed his eyes to Darren Welk, pulling the stares of everyone in the courtroom with him. Welk flushed, averted his eyes to his grasped fingers. Suspicion, cloying and rancid, steeped the jury box.

"Your Honor," Stan Breckshire pronounced, the words dripping with meaning, "I have no more questions."

Terrance Clyde cross-examined. When defense was through, Stan pushed out of his chair with an air of finality and leaned across the table on spread fingers. "The prosecution rests," he announced.

THIRTY-EIGHT

Sweat trickled between Rogelio's shoulder blades as he weeded in the hot sun, his fingers automatically moving, mind far away.

Tomorrow evening Milt planned to air his story. The reporter had gotten a lot of information from Tracey, but there were still a few loose ends, he'd said. He needed this evening to try to put it all together. Exactly how Milt had gotten Tracey to talk remained a mystery. Rogelio wasn't sure he wanted to know.

Mama Yolanda still knew nothing. Rogelio had first wanted to hear from Milt. But he couldn't put off telling her any longer. He'd have to talk to her tonight. Kristin too. His heart skipped beats over *that* thought. All he could do was hope and pray for the words to make Kristin understand. Surely she would feel differently once she heard all he'd learned about the man who was raising their daughter. Surely all this would work out. Somehow.

God, he prayed silently, fingers grasping and pulling, *don't forget our bargain.*

"YOU CAN SEE THE guilt in every move of Darren Welk's body," Lynn Trudy declared to reporters as they gathered in the hall after lunch. "That videotape says it all."

Milt Waking watched Bill film happily away. The guy's tongue was practically hanging out of his mouth. Milt slithered a gaze to Lynn and shuddered. Today her pants were spangled with glitter, her too-tight knit shirt a hot pink. Not a good combination with her long purple nails, which continually scuttled through the air like crabs as she spoke. She'd apparently rinsed her spiky hair over the weekend, its new hue a deep red. Milt wondered about a woman who'd think of changing hair color in the midst of her sister's murder trial.

"Ms. Trudy, what's your latest thought on the phantom caller?" a reporter asked.

She turned to him, eyes flashing. "My thought is, why in the world haven't they caught who did it?" She glared at the reporter as if it were his fault. "It's obviously someone who wants Darren Welk found innocent, even when he most assuredly is not. How many people like that do you see attending this trial?" She cast a meaningful look across the hallway at Brett Welk's back. The reporters' eyes followed hers.

"Are you suggesting his son is behind the calls?" Pens dangled with anticipation.

"I will say no more." Lynn Trudy's plucked eyebrows rose. "Look at the facts before you. They speak for themselves."

Milt hung back, viewing the scene. Same old questions day after day. Oh, the questions he'd soon be asking this woman. *Ms. Trudy, did you know your sister sold a baby to a man of highly questionable repute? Did you know that your niece was involved?*

He couldn't wait to see the look on her face.

STAN BRECKSHIRE REPRESSED a smirk as he listened to the first two witnesses for the defense. Past boyfriends of the deceased. This second one, all muscles and tan and hair, looked a good fifteen years younger than Shawna Welk. What a slut she'd been.

Ol' T. C. and smarty-pants Erica were certainly dragging the trenches. They had so little of a defense to present. The most they could do was try to poke holes in his case, and Stan knew they'd managed to do little of that. So Shawna Welk had gone through a slew of boyfriends? Her husband had cheated on her, hadn't he? Stan could see the argument coming. If she'd been with these men, she'd probably been with more and perhaps had run off with one of them. Stan's comeback for his closing argument already ran through his head. So she'd run off with a supposed boyfriend, had she? Who was he? How come no one knew of him? Why was no man missing, as Shawna was?

Stan tapped the prosecution table. He wondered what other shenanigans T. C. would try to pull. He remembered the infamous story of a former murder case sans body. The defense attorney, in his closing remarks, had dramatically declared to the court that the "deceased" was not dead at all and would in fact enter through the courtroom doors in the next moment. All heads had turned expectantly toward the entrance. Of course, the dead woman did not enter the courtroom. But the defense attorney had made his point. Any of the jurors who'd looked, he emphasized, could not vote guilty, for they'd harbored just that much doubt.

How very cunning. Except for one thing. The jurors had noticed that only one person in the courtroom had not turned to look toward the door—the defendant.

Verdict: guilty.

Stan smiled to himself. It just didn't pay to get too cute.

He slid a look at his jury. Clay and Henry were dutifully taking notes. Other jury members took notes, too. Funny how Chelsea Adams had all of a sudden decided to join them. But these two men seemed in control, influential. One of these would be his foreman. And he had 'em both; he'd bet on it.

Young Mr. Macho left the stand. T. C. called his third witness. Another boyfriend. Stan drummed fingers against his leg. Ho hum.

KERRA SQUEEZED BRETT'S HAND in empathy as Barry "Buddy" Hottsteter assumed the witness chair with a tinge of defiance. He looked about six foot two, with black hair in a ponytail and a leathered face. Not a man Kerra would want to meet in a dark alley. How Brett must feel, seeing this parade of his stepmother's "other men." Kerra stole a look at the back of Darren Welk's head, wondering what he was thinking. Did he even care? He, the husband who'd apparently had a string of women?

He leaned over and whispered in Terrance Clyde's ear. The attorney whispered back. Erica Salvador rose to question Buddy, her ever present high heels clicking. Buddy watched her approach with a mixture of wariness and superiority—*I can handle you, Miss Lawyer.*

"Mr. Hottsteter." Erica stopped in front of him, hands clasped at her waist. "Good afternoon. I understand you're not too happy about being here, is that true?"

"You could say that."

"And why would that be?"

He gave her a look. "I don't like talking about my affairs in public."

"Hm." The corner of Erica's mouth turned up slightly. "Interesting use of words. Let's talk about your 'affair' with Shawna Welk. When did it begin?"

"Three months before she was killed."

Erica's face hardened at the word. "And did it continue right up to the time she disappeared?"

"Yes."

"Where did you manage to meet with her during these three months?"

"In my apartment in Salinas."

"You live alone?"

"Yeah."

"Was this during the day or evening?"

Buddy Hottsteter shrugged. "Both. Whenever we could."

"I see." Erica shot Darren Welk a glance of empathy. Kerra noticed Brett's hand twitch.

"Where were you on the night of February fifteenth, Mr. Hottsteter?"

He assumed a bored look. "Like I told the detectives, I was in my apartment, asleep."

"Anyone who can confirm that?"

"No." His eyes narrowed.

Erica folded her arms. "Isn't it true that three nights before Shawna Welk disappeared, a neighbor of yours heard you two fighting in your apartment and called to ask you to keep your voices down?"

Buddy glared at her. Wild hope flared in Kerra's chest. Her lips parted as she looked to Brett in surprise. His face remained impassive. She sent a piercing look toward the jury, Aunt Chelsea.

"It wasn't much of an argument."

"Really?" Erica walked with determination to the defense table and picked up her notes. Her finger slid halfway down the top page, then stopped. "Your neighbor, a Mr. Allen Foxmeyer, did not call you and say"—she consulted the notes—"'You are shouting so loud, my pictures on the wall are rattling'?"

Buddy flicked his eyes. "He's an old man; he's easily rattled."

Erica tapped a nail against the papers. "What were you arguing about?"

"Can't remember."

The defense attorney sighed. She read her notes again. "According to the police report, Mr. Foxmeyer said he heard you shout, 'I'm not rich enough to leave your husband for, is that it?' True, Mr. Hottsteter?"

"I don't know."

Erica tossed the papers on the defense table. "You sure? I could always call Mr. Foxmeyer to testify. And do remember you're under oath."

Buddy's mouth worked, the expression on his face venom.

"Can you remember?"

"Fine. I said it."

"You wanted Shawna to leave her husband?"

"Yeah. So what?"

"And you were angry when she wouldn't?"

No answer.

"Mr. Hottsteter?"

"Yes, okay? I was mad. It passed."

"When did it pass?"

"When Darren Welk killed her!"

Erica stared daggers at him. "Your Honor," she said in quiet malice, "I request that the witness's unwarranted remark be struck from the record."

"Granted." Judge Chanson instructed the jury to ignore the statement.

"Let's try again," Erica said. "When did your anger at Shawna Welk 'pass'?"

Buddy glanced from her to the judge, uncertainty flicking across his forehead. In a heartbeat it was gone. "When she was killed," he said, drawing out each word. He cocked his head in contempt.

Erica smiled knowingly. Her eyes slid over Buddy Hottsteter as if he were scum. "Did *you* kill her?"

"Of course not; that's ridiculous!"

"You just said your anger was quelled once she was gone, isn't that so?"

"I didn't mean that! I just meant . . ." He shifted in his seat. "I just meant that once she was dead, I felt sorry for her, that's all."

"Once she was dead," Erica repeated.

"Yeah."

The attorney nodded slowly, her gaze at him piercing. "I see. I have no further questions then."

She returned to her seat with a meaningful raise of her eyebrows.

Stan Breckshire stood to try to redeem the witness as much as he could. Kerra hardly noticed. She tugged at Brett's hand, casting a questioning glance to Buddy. "Please," her expression begged, "tell me, could he have killed Shawna?"

Brett's face slackened. His eyes filled with empathy, as if he realized for the first time the extent of her fears—for his dad, for him. For them. He tried to smile but his lips twisted. Slowly he raised a shoulder. Then patted her hand.

Sickness roiled through Kerra's stomach. Clearly, he wanted her to cling to her hope. Even though he had none.

THIRTY-NINE

. . . after the revealing video of the defendant, an obviously defiant boyfriend of Shawna Welk's testified for the defense, opening up questions regarding his own motive for her murder . . .

Milt's evening news report flowed through his head as he pulled into the parking lot of Tracey's seedy apartment building. With his recent scoops about the case, no doubt his number of viewers had increased significantly. And when he'd privately told his news director, Ron, about the story he was working on, the guy nearly choked.

Milt jerked off his tie and smoothed his hair. He'd phoned Tracey, saying he wanted to see her again. His gut told him she was holding out on him about the money. By the time this night was over, he expected to have a few more answers.

As Milt started to open the door, a familiar spike-haired figure stomped into the parking lot from the direction of Tracey's apartment. Lynn Trudy's head was bent, her arms pumping as she hissed what had to be curses under her breath. Milt ducked down in the seat. Seconds later he heard a car start. Cautiously he raised his head in time to see her screech out of the lot and in front of an oncoming truck. The driver's horn blared.

Milt sat a moment, puzzling.

At Tracey's door he rapped twice and heard the scurry of approaching feet. "I told you I'm not going to talk to you anymore!" Tracey yelled from inside.

"Tracey? It's me, Milt."

Immediately he heard the door unlock. Tracey opened it and stood breathing hard, clad in a clingy black dress, her legs and feet bare. "Oh, I'm so glad it's you." Her eyes closed in relief.

Milt took her in his arms. "Did I just see your aunt scorch out of here?"

"Yes." Tracey laid her head against his shoulder, still trembling in her anger. "I kicked her out."

"What did she want?"

Silence.

Milt pulled back and looked at her. "Come on, what is it?"

Tracey backed out of his arms, her face darkening. "I've *had* it, do you know that? Had it with people telling me what to do. I'm tired of it, really, really *tired* of it!"

Milt spread his hands, nonplussed. "Okay. Sorry."

"No." The lines smoothed from her face. "Not you. Other people."

He put his arms around her again. "Tell me what the trouble is."

"I don't want to talk about it."

Milt started to push further, then thought better of it. "Okay then, we won't."

As she leaned against him, his eyes fell on her computer across the room. It was on, apparently again to an email in-box. Milt pressed Tracey against his chest, squinting at the monitor. No way could he read it from that distance. As he lifted her chin and kissed her, he wondered who would be writing her. She relaxed as their lips lingered.

Tracey led him to a seat on the couch. "Want something to drink?"

"That would be great."

She turned with all the grace she could assume and glided across the room, her short dress swishing against her legs. Milt's eyes took in the sight, then rose to her computer. Tracey passed the monitor and snapped it off without slowing. She disappeared into the kitchen.

Milt puffed out air.

She returned with two glasses in hand and placed them on the coffee table. Then settled beside him on the couch.

"Been writing something?" He pointed his chin toward the computer.

"Just typing some emails to friends. Until Lynn showed up." The name edged her voice.

He rubbed a strand of her hair in his fingers, hoping she would say more. She focused on her lap.

Apparently, she needed a bit more loosening up. "How about if I take you to dinner?"

"I can't be seen with you."

"Mm, true. Wouldn't want anyone to know about us." He let the word dangle, play with her head. "We could slip into a back booth at a restaurant away from here. Near Monterey, perhaps."

Tracey bit her lip. Her longing was palpable. "No. We can't take the chance."

"Okay, I've got it. Let's do dinner on the beach. We'll stop by some take-out place and I'll go in alone. We'll take a blanket, watch the stars come out." He laid fingers against her neck. "Just the two of us."

Her thin cheeks flushed. "Sounds wonderful," she whispered. "Just let me get something warmer on."

"Okay. But don't worry about that too much. I'll keep you warm."

She slipped from his grasp with a "Five minutes." He made a sound in his throat loud enough for her to hear as she hurried down the short hall into her bedroom. She laughed. The door closed.

Milt tapped an impatient finger against the couch. Then a thought sped through his brain. The computer. Swiftly he crossed the room and stood before it. Punched on the monitor, glancing over his shoulder. A Flying Windows screen saver appeared. He smacked the mouse and up came Tracey's in-box. One new arrival, unread. From Maria, email address Bananas4U@starmail.net. He hesitated, then clicked it.

A noise sounded from Tracey's bedroom. Milt spun around, heart revving. Silence. Water ran through the apartment pipes. He licked his lips and turned back to the computer. Read the email.

And froze.

He read it again. Blinked. Read it a third time. Breath puffed from his mouth as he scrambled to make sense of it. What was this? It was crazy! Excitement and revulsion sucked up Milt's veins. Think, think! But he had no time to think; he had to do something with this email—*now*. With a trembling glance at Tracey's bedroom door, he punched some buttons and forwarded a copy of the email to himself. Then he clicked the reply button. His legs shook as he bent over the keys, fingers flying.

> Maria,
>
> I don't want to hear any more from you. I'm dumping this email address right now. Don't bother to write me here again; I won't get it. When I'm good and ready, I'll contact you.
>
> Tracey

He jabbed the send button, trashed Maria's email and his reply, then emptied the trash. Smacked off the monitor and lurched toward the couch.

He heard the bedroom door open. Milt gulped in air, forcing calm, his brain skittering to think, think, think. The implications of what he'd just seen numbed him from head to toe.

"I'm ready," Tracey declared in a silky voice as she slid to his side and placed a hand on his chest. She drew back, feigning disapproval. "My, Mr. Waking, your heart is racing already."

He swallowed. Smiled his charming smile. "Just anticipating, that's all," he managed. "Just anticipating."

FORTY

Brett gazed over the rolling hills and the bay beyond, the large, flat rock upon which he and Kerra sat still warming his legs. It was their second evening in a row at the vista point. He knew Kerra was just as frustrated with him as she'd been last night, even though she was trying to hide it. Brett blew out air. This silence between them could not continue.

Face it: his life was a train wreck. Yet miraculously, Kerra had come along to help him pick up the pieces. He knew she agonized about the truth of Shawna's death, fearing for him should his father be convicted. Their weekend talks about his past and hers had been good but not good enough to sustain them. They needed to talk about what was happening now. Brett's eyes drifted toward the darkening sky. How ironic this whole mess was! Kerra offered him hope. And he offered her healing. But if they couldn't surmount this wall of silence, their relationship would go nowhere.

Kerra laid a hand on his arm. "What are you sighing about?"

"Nothing." The word sprang automatically to his lips. He shook his head, angry at himself. Weariness washed through him. He turned to her, took in the blue of her eyes, which were filled with concern. His throat tightened. "Everything."

Pain tripped across her face. "Tell me."

He traced a finger down her cheek. "Do you realize we met only a week ago?"

"I know. Seems more like forever."

"And you go back one week from today."

She studied a ridge in the rock. When she looked up, her eyes were misted with tears. "I don't want to go."

"I don't want you to go, either. I don't ever want to let you go."

She stilled. Brett watched her consider the words, accept them. Embrace them. "And I don't want to be without you," she whispered.

He pulled her to his chest and stroked her hair. Out of nowhere his father's face rose in his thoughts. That silent, stoic face, smoothing with the recognition of Brett's love for him. For twenty-two years that relationship had been one of unspoken words, of frustration and regret and boyish yearnings turned to adult complacency. He was headed the same way with Kerra if he didn't find a way to open up to her. What a waste that would be. A total, sickening waste.

"Brett, what are we going to do?" Kerra breathed, almost as if she'd read his thoughts. She raised her head, fixed her eyes upon him. "We have to talk. I can't stand this. I don't know what you're thinking about the trial and your dad. I want to help you through it all, but how can I?"

He nodded but remained silent.

"Brett, say something!" She pushed away from him. "I've gone against my aunt to be with you. I've stood with you publicly with all the media watching. I've even been called to see the judge because of you. I deserve to have you talk to me. Please!"

He swallowed hard, images of that February night, of his dad's arrest and all their awkward jail visits, flickering in his head like some old horror movie. "I'm afraid I'll lose you," he heard himself say.

Surprise wrinkled her forehead, then faded into apprehension. She stared at him, as if realizing for the first time there may be more to the story than she'd ever guessed. "You won't lose me," she whispered. "I promise."

He flexed his jaw, fighting the fear. "First I want to ask you something. Why is it that every time I ask you about God in your life, you act like you don't want to talk about it?"

She seemed taken aback. "I don't know. I guess I have a few questions myself, after everything that happened."

"Well, I want to talk more about it. I can't forget what you told me about God reaching out to man. Right now I'm feeling like I could use all the help I can get. I'll bet you could, too."

Kerra lowered her eyes. He sensed she was making an important decision of her own. Then she nodded. "Okay." She was silent for a moment, then reached for his hand. "Now. Talk to me."

Brett took a deep breath. And told her his story.

FORTY-ONE

Mama Yolanda stared at Rogelio, a mixture of shock and wonder on her wrinkled face. "*Mi Jesus!* This is why God called me to pray for the trial!" She sucked her gold tooth, a faraway look appearing in her eyes. She slumped back on the couch as if weighted by the realization, crooked fingers working wrinkles into her dress.

Rogelio watched her in dismay. Didn't she understand the risk he'd taken? What faced them both when the story was aired? As the hours counted down to Milt's news report, Rogelio grew more and more anxious. Would reporters soon find their home, bang on their door night and day? Kristin's door, too? Would they be on Kristin's side, as Milt had promised? Or would they point at her new car and accuse her of horrible things?

Such unknowns they faced—and all Mama Yolanda could think about was God calling her to pray?

She turned to him suddenly, reached for his hand. "*Mijo,* I see the look on your face. Do not be afraid. God is watching over us. He has heard my prayers for you and for Roselita. He is changing your heart, and he is protecting her, since she is not in a good home. You think you have done this thing alone. No, *mijo*. God has led you. He will lead us out of it."

Rogelio frowned. How could her words be true? He'd never asked God to change his heart.

"Mama Yolanda," he said, squeezing her hand gently, "can you forgive Kristin for what she's done? When we have Roselita, I want Kristin . . ." He could not finish.

"You want Kristin to be her mother." His grandmother nodded in understanding. "You want me to accept her."

"Yes," he whispered.

"*Mijo*, I did not want any of this to happen. Still, I forgave Kristin long ago. It is the Christian thing to do. I would love her as I love you and Roselita. But who can know now what she will do? You go see her. Talk to her. I will stay here and pray."

ROGELIO KNOCKED ON Kristin's door, his stomach in knots. Of their own accord his eyes pulled toward the fancy black Mustang in her driveway. Her mother's battered car was nowhere to be seen.

The curtains moved. Rogelio caught a glimpse of a hand.

Silence.

He knocked again.

"Go away, Rogelio; I don't want to talk to you!"

Her voice, thick with emotion, came from just the other side of the door. The tone told him so much. Rogelio's heart constricted. She didn't mean those words. She wasn't mad at him; she was mad at herself, sick with all she'd done. Longing for her surged through his chest. Even if Roselita never existed, he realized, he'd be right here on her doorstep, trying to get her back.

He gathered his courage. "Kristin, I'm not leaving. I love you. And you love me. I'm tired of this. We're going to work things out, once and for all. Now let me in."

Nothing. He squeezed his eyes shut, praying she would listen.

The door clicked open.

She looked at him and her face crumbled. Before he knew it, she had her arms around him. He hugged her back, surprised.

"I've missed you," she whispered.

She led him inside and to the couch, still holding on to him. Rogelio could hardly believe it. "What happened?" he asked.

She sniffed. "I just don't want to go on like we are—with you mad at me for everything. I just want us to be the way we used to be."

"We will be, Kristin." He swallowed. This was going too well; he didn't want to ruin it.

She stilled, almost as if she'd heard his thoughts. Pulled back and looked deeply into his face. Her expression slackened.

"It's okay, Kristin, it's okay."

She shook her head and looked at her lap. "You haven't changed. Have you?"

The question ran so much deeper than she could know. He thought of Mama Yolanda's words. *God has led you.* And of that day—was it only last week?—when he'd thrown down his waxing rag and determined to set things right. "Yes," he said. "I have changed."

She raised her chin. "You don't want the baby anymore?"

He told her then. Everything. About his grandmother's pain and his guilt. How Mama Yolanda had been praying for the trial. About Delgadia. How afraid he was for Roselita, having such a father. How he'd gone to court and ended up talking to Milt. His words sped up, his muscles tensing as he tried desperately to explain to Kristin, holding her shoulders and forcing her to listen. Her green eyes grew wide, then filled with tears. Rogelio wasn't sure if they were tears of weary anger, grief, or both.

By the time the words ran dry, his throat ached. Kristin huddled against the arm of the couch, quietly crying. "I don't *want* the baby, Rogelio. I don't know how to be a mother."

"But you said you were sad to let her—"

"Of course I was sad! You weren't there. You haven't seen everything in here." She thumped a fist against her heart. "You don't know what it's like to have a baby and then give her up, and miss her and be glad she's gone at the same time! You don't know how many times I wished she was with you, so I could see her. The only thing I could tell myself was that she was in a better home than you and your grandmother could have given her. Now you tell me that's not true at all."

"That's why I had to do something."

She shook her head. "You shouldn't have talked to that reporter without asking me first."

"I didn't have time, Kristin. As soon as I heard how awful Delgadia is, I had to do something."

Kristin hid her face in both hands. He slid next to her and drew her close.

"I'm scared," she said, sobbing. "Tell me everything is going to be okay."

"It will," he replied soothingly, rubbing her back. "Everything is going to work out just fine."

BY TEN O'CLOCK ROGELIO had returned home. Mama Yolanda informed him that he'd had no calls. A disquieting doubt wormed through Rogelio's brain. Where was Milt? The guy should have phoned long ago.

He waited until ten thirty, then dialed Milt's cell phone. Four rings. The answering message clicked on. "This is Rogelio, man; where are you? I've talked to my grandmother and Kristin. They know about your report tomorrow night. After all this, you'd better come through. Call me."

By eleven thirty Rogelio's muscles ached for bed. He'd called two more times—with no answer. Had Milt turned on him? Gotten his story, then left him in the dust? Heaving a sigh, he dialed once more. Milt's recorded voice grated in his ear.

Rogelio banged down the handset in frustration.

FORTY-TWO

Milt scurried through the door of his Menlo Park town home after midnight and headed straight for his computer. Despite his amorous evening with Tracey, he'd failed to extract one measly bit of information about her aunt's visit or her email friend Maria. As for Delgadia's money, Tracey continued to insist she knew nothing about it. The girl was lying through her teeth. But then she was apparently lying about a whole lot of things.

Oh, she was all neediness and lost waif on the outside. Milt could even believe that was not an act. But what vile choices had she made to put herself in that position? Milt wondered if she'd been trapped by her own greed.

He threw himself into his office chair and fired up the computer, hoping his fly-by-night scheme had worked. As he logged on to his email, he considered scenarios. Worst case, Maria had ignored his warning and written Tracey again. If the two of them continued hurling accusations through cyberspace, it might be a while before they figured out an extra email had been thrown into the melee. Even if his cover was blown, he already had enough to write one whopping story.

Best case, Maria hadn't written and Tracey hadn't decided to write her. And he could now become Tracey.

Please, oh, please. He hit the keys with impatience.

Maria's forwarded email from "Tracey W." appeared in his inbox. Milt clicked on it, scarcely breathing.

> HOW many times do I have to write before you'll GET it?? Think!! He's a REPORTER! Don't you understand that after all these months everything could be lost? What if he really is only out for information? What if he gets suspicious about the rest of it? You could end up in jail! Darren could get off. Think! No insurance money! All the horrible things you've had to do—for nothing! All your plans to come to Brazil, ruined!!
>
> See what you've made me do? I'm so sick with worry, I've gone and written you without disguising all the words. THAT should show you how upset I am! Erase this letter now. And write back. PLEASE!

Milt read the email four times, then stared unseeing into the dark night beyond his office window. His mind whirled. What if . . .

He swiveled in the chair, pawing through the stack of paper on his desk until he found the stapled pages of Tracey's testimony. Pored over his notes. Then stared out the window some more.

No one could back up all of Tracey's version as to what happened the night Shawna Welk was murdered. Tracey could have mixed a lot of fiction with the facts. Suppose Tracey had gotten greedy and somehow intercepted Delgadia's payment or perhaps demanded a good portion of it from her mother. Then came the fateful night on Breaker Beach. Shawna called her daughter, asking for help. Tracey went to the beach. They ended up fighting as Darren Welk lay passed out on the sand. The fight escalated and Tracey pushed her mother. Maybe Shawna's head hit a rock and she passed out. Tracey left her. She floated out to sea. . . .

Milt dragged a hand across his scalp. Whatever the exact scenario, the most amazing part was not that Tracey had done it but that she'd gotten away with it for so long.

He turned back to the computer, narrowing his eyes at Maria's email. This gal lived in Brazil, of all places. Had Tracey met her in some chat room? Or maybe "Brazil" was a code word for some other place. At any rate why, with so much to lose, would Tracey confide in her? He turned possible reasons over in his mind, landing on Tracey's inexperience and obvious fear. She'd found herself mired in the muck of deceit and murder and couldn't stand the smell. She'd probably gone half crazy keeping her secrets to herself week after week, month after month. Women were like that. They always had to talk to somebody. Maybe Maria had started it by first confiding secrets of her own.

Whatever had happened, Milt aimed to get to the bottom of it.

His DSL server offered three email accounts, available under different names—a good incentive for a family who wanted individual email addresses. And perfect for his unexpected need. Fortunately, he'd only activated two accounts, one for personal use and one for business. Quickly he logged on to the home page of his server and set up a third address under the name of Tracey W. Then positioned his fingers over the keys, formulating his message.

Maria,

Okay, I've calmed down now. Guess I shouldn't have gone through the trouble of changing my email address. But I want you to understand that I'm falling in love with Milt—already. I've just never met anyone like him. So once I get the insurance money, I'm not sure I want to come to Brazil right away. Milt and I have talked about going on a trip.

Milt's fingers hung over the keyboard. Should he say more? He had to get this just right. He hunched over, reviewing the words.

Then signed off.

Tracey

He clicked the send button and breathed a prayer to any god in the universe that Maria would respond.

Before going to bed, he called his news director's private line at the station and left him a message. "Milt here. Listen, we can't air the story tomorrow as planned. We'll have to wait a day or so while I run down some new information. I've stumbled onto something you're not going to believe. . . ."

WEDNESDAY, AUGUST 14

FORTY-THREE

"Yes ma'am, they were screaming at each other."

The witness chair practically swallowed the tiny Hispanic woman. Chelsea watched her fingers latch and unlatch with nervousness, her thin brown lips forming a small O as she perched before Erica Salvador.

Lupe de La Roca, one of the weekly crew who had cleaned the Welks' house, was the fourth defense witness of the morning to testify about hearing an argument between Shawna Welk and another person, this one being her daughter, Tracey. Two others had told of arguments with ex-boyfriends. And the first, an electrician called to a repair in the Welks' household, had told of hearing a bitter argument between Shawna and Brett. The way defense counsel apparently wanted it to sound, Shawna Welk did little else *but* argue. Chelsea wondered at that. Shawna was turning out to be quite different from what she'd expected. Anyone who ran an adoption agency would have a soft side, would care about people. Maybe Shawna had cared for others. But more and more Chelsea was seeing her selfishness.

Lord, help me know what's true.

"What did they do when they saw you in the hall?" Erica asked. Chelsea thought her voice sounded unusually warm. She was obviously trying to put the woman at ease.

"Mrs. Welk pushed Tracey into her bedroom and slammed the door."

"Whose bedroom, Tracey's?"

"No, Mrs. Welk's."

"Did they continue to argue?"

"Yes."

"For how long?"

Lupe de La Roca frowned at her hands. "A few minutes."

"Okay. How far were you from the room?"

"At first I was down the hall, but I was cleaning the baseboards and came closer."

"Did you hear anything else as you got closer?"

"Yes ma'am. I heard something that sounded like a slap."

"A slap?"

The woman nodded. "Like a hand against a cheek."

Erica looked shocked. "Then what happened?"

"The door flew open and Tracey stumbled out. She ran right by me. Her cheek was red and she was crying."

Erica let the words hang in the air. "When was this, Mrs. de La Roca?"

"Wednesday, February thirteenth."

Two days before Shawna's murder, Chelsea thought. She wrote down the date in her notes.

"Are you certain of that date?"

"Yes. I know because"—the woman pressed her lips together until they nearly disappeared—"that's the last time I saw Mrs. Welk."

COURT BROKE FOR LUNCH. Milt hustled toward the hall, mind running in a dozen different directions. Phone messages, emails, and the testimony. Tracey arguing with her mother so soon before Shawna's death. Wasn't that interesting. But most important right now—had Maria emailed him back? And had Tracey written Maria?

Milt found himself behind Kerra and Brett, the couple of the year. He drew even with them. "Sounds like you're not the only one who didn't like Shawna." He raised an eyebrow at Brett. "Care to comment?"

Kerra turned on him like a wildcat protecting her young. "Get *out* of here!" she hissed, raising a hand.

Whoa. Milt melted back. He'd expected a reaction, but what was that all about?

"Milt Waking!" a caustic voice sounded from behind. He turned to see Lynn Trudy, eyes narrowed into slits, bearing down upon him in obvious wrath. She cornered him against the wall and away from others, raised a long-nailed finger and pointed it at his nose. "You better stay away from my niece," she hissed. "Or I'm gonna tell everybody what you're doing."

Milt stared at her, brain scrambling. Tracey had told her about them? Why?

Why not? She'd obviously yakked to at least one email friend. Talk about the kiss-and-tell type . . .

"You hear me? I know what you're up to. I know you're just using her to get information. I'm warning you—I'll ruin you and your career if you don't stop."

Easy does it, he told himself.

He set down his briefcase. Raised his shoulders in a slow shrug. "So I'm attracted to her; what's that to you?"

She cursed at him, her voice like gravel. "You don't care about her. You are the lowest, most disgusting form of scum on this earth."

Anger knocked around Milt's chest. He drew away from the wall, forcing her backward. "Who I choose to date, Ms. Trudy," he declared in a chilling tone, "is none of your business. But since you brought up this delectable subject, just what information are you so worried I'll discover?"

"There's nothing to discover," she shot back. "You've heard it all in court."

"Then I repeat: what are you worried about?"

Her face flushed to the roots of her spiked hair. "I'm telling you to leave my niece alone! Or I'll go to the other reporters right now and tell them how you're using someone half your age."

"You do that, Ms. Trudy." Milt flicked at an imaginary piece of lint on his suit coat. "You go right ahead. Maybe they'll consider it nothing more than a salacious piece of news to drop into their stories. Which, of course, would reflect as much on Tracey as it would on me. More likely"—he gave her a twisted smile—"they'll figure I'm on to something. They'll start watching. Real closely. And the next thing you know, Tracey will have a dozen reporters camped on her doorstep. Is that what you want?"

The crimson on Lynn's face crept down her neck. For a moment Milt thought she was going to hit him. He stepped back and picked up his briefcase.

"I'm going to forget we had this conversation, Ms. Trudy." He glared down at her, adjusting his tie. "This case will be over before long, and I expect you'll see the conviction you so heartily desire. In the meantime if you really want what's best for your niece, you'll keep her name out of the papers."

Before she could answer, Milt brushed past her and headed for the escalator.

He reached the first floor before he could breathe again. Briskly he walked outside and to his car in the parking garage. Leaning against the hood, he tried to collect his thoughts. He sure was making enemies all of a sudden. Which could only mean he'd stumbled onto something big.

Milt buffed his jaw with the palm of his hand. Okay, back to the most important thing on his agenda. He pulled out his laptop and rested it on the car hood. Logged on to his email and checked his inbox, holding his breath. Four emails popped up. The top one was from Maria.

Anticipation spritzed his nerves. He clicked on the email and read.

I don't know what to say to you, I'm so worried. I've been thinking about this for hours. I can't believe it. You simply

CAN'T do this! Please write back and tell me you've come to your senses.

"Yes!" Milt whispered. He'd done it!

Now how to get any information out of her? He frowned in thought, then typed.

I'm going crazy. I can't think straight. Why's it so bad to take a trip with Milt before I come see you, tell me that? Don't worry about talking openly; nobody's even the least suspicious of me anyway. Just HELP me!

Don't wait so long to write this time.

Tracey

Milt clicked the send button and exhaled. Distractedly he considered his other emails, then checked his watch. His phone messages still awaited. With all that had happened, he hadn't remembered to check them even that morning. He pulled out his cell phone and dialed.

Messages clicked on. The first was from an anxious-sounding Rogelio, left last night. The second was from an even more anxious Rogelio, left at eight o'clock this morning. The third had been recorded just two minutes ago. This time Rogelio's voice was a loud mixture of anger and panic. Milt winced and yanked the phone away from his ear.

"I want to hear from you, understand me! I want to know what you found out and what you're going to say in your report tonight. Plus what I should do then! You told me we'd talk some more about everything. Don't leave me hanging, Milt; I've got too much at stake!"

Oh, great. Milt could have kicked himself. Not a good thing to forget to call Rogelio. What if the kid got tired of waiting and did something stupid like go to another reporter? He'd have to call as soon as Rogelio got home from work. Convince him to hang tight another day or two. This baby thing would have to wait; no way could he blow his cover with Tracey now.

At least Tracey hadn't called him. Now to make sure he kept her in line. He looked up her work number on a small notepad in his suit pocket and dialed.

"Halding's Dress Shop."

"Tracey. It's Milt."

"Hi!"

No suspicion in her tone. His eyes closed in relief. "I'm afraid I have some bad news," he said. "I don't think I can see you tonight."

"Oh."

"I've got to do some interviews on another story."

"When *can* I see you?" she asked in her lost-waif tone.

"I don't know. I'll call you back as soon as I can figure something out. I don't want to wait long."

"Okay."

"By the way," he said, allowing irritation to creep into his voice, "why did you tell your aunt about us? She came at me today with both barrels."

"I *didn't* tell her!"

"Then who did?"

Silence. "Okay," she said quietly, "I did tell her. It was a mistake."

Milt shook his head. This girl lied coming and going. "Yes, it was. You're making it more difficult for me here. I want to keep seeing you, but you've got to keep quiet about us, understand?"

"Yes." She sounded meek.

"Have you told anybody else?"

A pause. "No."

Milt gestured in frustration. She *would* neglect to mention Maria to him. "Okay. But let me just warn you that if you do, others are likely to respond as your aunt did. They'll only make you miserable and get in our way. For both our sakes, I hope you won't talk to anyone like that."

He cringed as he awaited her answer. Had he said too much?

"Milt, I'm not going to talk to *anybody* who's against you, believe me. I threw my aunt out, didn't I?"

"Yeah," he said, his tone softening, "you did."

When he disconnected the line a few moments later, he suddenly realized how hungry he was.

FORTY-FOUR

The afternoon had seemed interminable to Chelsea. Yet another witness had testified about hearing Shawna in an argument with Tracey. Then defense counsel had called Peter Chesterton, a former sheriff with Monterey County, who spoke at great lengths about the shoddy job the department had done in investigating the disappearance of Shawna Welk. They had prematurely focused on Darren Welk, he said, then never followed up on other possible suspects after their interview with him.

Stan Breckshire was fighting back hard in his cross-examination. Hadn't the witness been let go from the Monterey sheriff's department? Wasn't he in fact a disgruntled former employee who'd had a hard time finding other work?

During break Chelsea leaned against the sink in the women's bathroom and closed her eyes. Her mind swirled with the testimony. The video of Darren Welk certainly made him look guilty, but she could not shake her suspicion of his son. How could anyone know with absolute certainty what had happened to Shawna that night? What if someone else *had* killed her? Someone like Brett?

Oh, God, please give me wisdom! I don't know what to think. And Kerra is with him all the time! Protect her, Lord, protect her. . . .

When the jury resumed their seats for the last part of the day, Chelsea was still praying.

ROGELIO BANGED DOWN the phone and glared out the kitchen window. From the living room filtered the sound of the television, already tuned to Channel Seven in preparation for their anxiously awaited news report. Rogelio shoved to his feet, marched to the set, and smacked it off. Reeling back into the kitchen, he dropped into his chair.

Mama Yolanda did not even look up from her tortilla making. "Does not sound like good news," she said mildly.

"It isn't. Milt's not going to run the story tonight. Says he needs 'more information.'" The last two words were a sneer.

Mama Yolanda set aside one tortilla and began rolling out another. "You think he is not telling the truth?"

"I don't know *what* to think!" He ran a hand through his hair. "He doesn't care about Roselita; all he cares about is getting a story. He'll make decisions based on that, not on what's best for us."

"The story's gotten bigger than we ever imagined," Milt had told him. *"I have to run down more facts and put this all together."* From the way he'd made it sound, he may need another couple of days. Milt had pleaded with him to hang in there, even if the story did not air until the jury was deliberating.

"Maybe so." Mama Yolanda picked up the rolling pin and aimed it in another direction. "But God will watch over us."

Rogelio sighed in exasperation. How could she be so sure about everything? After all he'd gone through to prepare Kristin, now he'd have to tell her the story wasn't airing tonight. And he had no indication it would air tomorrow. Kristin's emotions seemed about as balanced as a little kid standing on one foot. How long was she going to put up with this?

"Well, God can do all the watching over us he wants," he growled, "but Milt Waking is watching out for Milt Waking. And I'll tell you something: I'm not going to wait for him much longer!"

Terrance Clyde stretched in his hard chair as he watched Darren drop into his seat on the other side of the glass. His client regarded him with silent suspicion, tongue pushed between his teeth and upper lip.

"You brought Brett into it again," he said at length. "I *told* you not to do that."

Here it came. Terrance shrugged. "Barely. There was far more testimony about arguments with boyfriends and Tracey than about arguments with him."

"One witness is one too many."

"What do you want, Darren?" Terrance's voice rose. "You want me to get you out of here or not?"

"What I want," Darren declared through his teeth, "is to walk out of this hellhole and go back to my ranch and my *son*."

"That's what I'm trying to accomplish."

"I don't want my son sacrificed to do it!"

Terrance leaned toward the glass. "Darren, hear me. For the hundredth time. Any suspicion laid on Brett or anybody else will go *nowhere* once the trial's over. But it could raise enough reasonable doubt to get you off."

"Suspicion follows you; it's hard to get rid of."

"What matters is that you'll both be free."

"Yeah, so's O. J."

Terrance shook his head wearily. Arched back against the chair. "That's hardly a comparison." They glared at each other.

"Let me testify," Darren said.

"No."

"Why?"

"I've *told* you why. Breckshire would kill you on cross."

"I'd handle him."

"Not in a million years. He'd dance and punch."

"I'd handle him."

"Darren!" Terrance smacked his palms against the edge of the table. "Fine then. Tell me, Mr. Welk, did you fight in public with your wife?"

Silence.

"*Did* you?"

"Yes, okay? So what?"

"Did you run around with women?"

"A few." Darren blinked in defiance.

"Did you hit Shawna that night on the beach?"

Darren's mouth hardened. "I didn't mean to; I was drunk."

"Oh, drinking makes you hit people, does it?"

"No!"

"You just said it did." Cynicism oiled Terrance's words. "Just how does drinking affect you? Are you nicer? Or meaner?"

Darren shoved his arms into a fold.

"Would you like me to call some folks to testify about how you behave when you're drunk, Mr. Welk?"

"Okay, so I get a little testy."

"A 'little testy,'" Terrance mocked. "Testy enough to make your wife bleed all over her silk blouse?"

"She was hardly hurt."

"How about the tooth? Did you knock that out, too? And—here's a great one—let's talk about the blouse turning up in your backyard."

"I—"

"And do explain, Mr. Welk, your very convenient loss of memory *after* your wife began to bleed. After that let's talk about the footprints in the sand. And while we're at it, let's replay the video of your interview sentence by sentence so you can explain all your lies! Let the jury see one more time all those guilty expressions on your—"

"All right, all right!" Darren threw out his hands. Futility slumped him in his chair.

Slowly Terrance straightened. "And that," he said quietly, "is why you will not testify, and why *I* am handling this case." He pushed back his chair and stood. "Breckshire will finish his cross-examination of Peter Chesterton tomorrow morning. I'll shore the guy back up on redirect; I think the jury's willing to believe his testimony. Then we'll go to closing remarks. I'll put it all together for the jury then. With a little luck you'll be out of here soon. But keep quiet while I talk, Darren"—Terrance pointed a finger at his client—"and let me do my job."

He turned away from his client, still hunched in the chair, and left the tiny room.

FORTY-FIVE

Kerra sat on the rock beside Brett and cried. Tears had filled her eyes the moment she'd slid into her car. The day had been agony. Holding herself together during court, forcing herself to appear impassive while that awful man testified about Brett's argument with Shawna. It seemed as if every eye in the courtroom had been turned on them, analyzing, watching for the least suspicious movement.

"Oh, Kerra, I never should have told you," Brett said soothingly.

"Yes, you should have. I don't know how you bore it alone for so long. You *had* to tell me."

Her throat closed. Brett hugged her as she cried against his chest. "I'm sorry," she hiccuped after a few moments. "You'd think I'd be done by now."

"It's okay." He smoothed her hair. Finally she sat up and wiped her face, sniffling.

"Do you know," she said, "that's the first time in over a year I've cried about anything other than Dave's death?"

Brett smiled sadly.

She exhaled, tried to steady her breathing. "Know what else?" She pulled away a strand of hair that was stuck to her cheek. "Ever since last weekend I haven't seen the accident in my head." She focused on the bay, dwelling on that fact. "Aunt Chelsea told me she felt sure God wanted me to visit so he could help me move on with my life. I think so, too. But I think he knew all this would happen and that I'd end up with you."

"You think he put us together?"

"I don't know. Frankly, I never asked him. All I know is, you needed me and I needed you."

"That's for sure." He gazed out over the tree-covered hills, utter weariness on his face.

It struck her then how self-centered she was being. So focused on her feelings, her fears. Brett needed her far more than she needed him right now. He was practically drowning in his own anxiety and guilt. In her heart she knew Brett needed more than just her to help him through. He was seeking spiritually, whether he fully realized it or not. How wrong, how *selfish*, she was to hold back her knowledge of that truth.

"You know what I think we should do?" she heard herself say. "I think we should pray." How rusty the word sounded on her tongue. She remembered how joyous she'd been after she found Christ. How she'd shared her faith with Dave. How they'd begun to pray together, laying a deeper, stronger foundation for their relationship.

Brett looked at her, nonplussed. "How?"

"Does that mean you want to?"

"Yeah, I guess. But I don't know what I'm supposed to say."

"Brett," she ventured, "we've talked about how a person can reach up to God in response to him. You can do that right now if you want. To tell the truth, I need to get back to him myself. I think we should do that, plus ask for his help in all this mess. Goodness knows we're not doing too well on our own."

He pondered her words. "Okay."

She took his hand. "I'll start." She hesitated, words snagging on her lips. It had been so long. "Dear Jesus," she began, "we need you.

Please lead us through this hard time. And as for me, I'm sorry for falling away from you. Help me be close to you like I was before."

She fell silent. "You want to say anything?" she asked Brett quietly.

"Uh, yeah." She heard him swallow. "God. Thank you for Kerra. Thank you for what she told me about you. If it's true—well, I mean, I'm sure it's true—help me to follow you. You reached out to me, so I'll reach back." He pressed her fingers. "I guess that's it."

"Amen," she said.

"Amen."

They looked at each other.

"Am I supposed to feel anything?" he asked.

"Not necessarily. But you will if you keep talking to him. At least I sure did."

He nodded. Then sighed. "It didn't exactly take away all our problems, did it."

"No." Kerra rubbed his thumb. "But I know it'll help us through them. Somehow, Brett, some way, God's going to see us through this."

MILT STEPPED INTO HIS town home with a sigh. He plunked down his laptop and threw his suit coat over the back of the couch, followed by his tie. It was seven thirty, his evening report had aired, and his stomach was grumbling. He'd been running on nervous energy and too little sleep.

He'd received two more emails from Maria. They hadn't been full of substance, but they'd sure been full of frustration and anger. He'd written her back, playing the confused, love-crazed Tracey. Hadn't been too hard, after he'd watched the girl in action two nights in a row. He hoped he'd said just enough to keep Maria on her cyberspace toes.

He poured a glass of wine and headed for his computer, chuckling to himself. And he thought he'd had a coup last year with the Chelsea Adams exclusive. That success, together with his scoops in this trial, wouldn't begin to match the glory he was bound for in the next few days. Once he got this all worked out, he would single-handedly bring the entire Salad King trial to its knees. His ratings would shoot the moon! Offers from television stations would whirl around him like Tasmanian devils.

Milt set down his glass and booted up the computer, idly pondering how ironic his future coverage of Tracey Wilagher's murder trial would be. He logged on to his email, making small popping sounds with his mouth as he waited. Ah, there it was. Another note from his lovely Maria.

He clicked it happily, brought a fist to his chin and read.

The fist slackened. His hand fell to his lap.

The words refused to sink in. He shook his head. Read it again. Read it a third time. And a fourth.

The message rooted him to his chair. Milt Waking's stomach sank to his toes.

PART 3 | PURPOSE

I am God, and there is no other;
I am God, and there is none like me.
I make known the end from the beginning,
from ancient times, what is still to come.
I say: My purpose will stand,
and I will do all that I please.

Isaiah 46:9–10

THURSDAY, AUGUST 15

FORTY-SIX

Milt dressed for court on automatic, exhaustion and excitement fighting in his veins. He had barely slept all night. For hours he lay thinking, figuring, putting the last pieces of the puzzle together. Finally, in the wee hours of the morning, he had formulated a plan. Whether it would work or not remained to be seen. The only thing he wasn't sure about was Lynn Trudy. But he would take no chances there.

One immediate thing to do. Before leaving for court, he fired up his computer and wrote a final email to Maria. It had been fun, but all good things must come to an end.

I've made my decision. It looks like the case will go to the jury by the end of tomorrow. They will deliberate through the weekend. Everyone agrees they won't take long to find Darren guilty—probably by Saturday afternoon. I'll be at the courthouse so I can get the death certificate from the judge right after the verdict. Then Milt and I are out of here. I'm not even saying where. He's paying for our trip. Somewhere along the way we'll have the insurance money wired to us. Two MIL-LION dollars. Small payback, wouldn't you say?

Don't bother trying to contact me anymore. I won't be checking emails. I won't even be home.

Been nice talking to you.

Tracey

Milt cocked his head, surveying the last line. He hadn't planned on it but he liked the sarcasm. He smiled, pleased with himself.

He hit the send button. Two minutes later he was in his car, headed for the freeway.

CHELSEA WATCHED STAN BRECKSHIRE pace, brow furrowed in concentration. The prosecutor's hair stuck out in all directions, from his frequent head scratching. His tie was askew. His closing argument had begun immediately after the morning break, and he was now summing up. He'd gone over every piece of evidence, explaining with waving arms and staccato words why the jury could do nothing else but find Darren Welk guilty of second-degree murder. Chelsea drank in the words, desperately hoping they would put an end to her questions. She was so close to believing Darren Welk was guilty, but something continued to nag her. Her pen was poised over the piece of paper she'd headed *Facts to Support Guilt.*

Stan drew up in front of the jury box and spread his hands. "As you can see, everything fits, ladies and gentlemen. Everything. We have Lonnie Broward's testimony about Darren and Shawna Welk's escalating argument. We have Tracey Wilagher's testimony, with quite precise timing as to when she received the desperate plea for help from her mother, when she arrived at the beach, and when she returned to the house. We have the bill from Shawna Welk's cell phone to support Tracey's testimony about receiving the phone call from her mother. All the timing, and Tracey's explanation of the partial footprints she saw on wet sand, coincides with the testimony of Dr. Gaston, the expert in currents and tides. He told you almost to the inch how far the water had receded between high tide and when those footprints were made."

Lonnie B., Chelsea wrote in her notes. *Tracey precise timing. Cell phone bill. Footprints.*

Stan's pacing resumed, his fingers jabbing the air.

"Then of course we have the blouse. Evidence clearly shows that it was transported underneath the seat of Darren Welk's car. DNA evidence proves that the blood on the blouse belongs to Shawna Welk. And we have a witness, Victor Mendoza, who has proved himself reliable and trustworthy through twenty years of service at his employment. He saw Darren Welk bury that blouse in his backyard in the middle of the night.

"You heard Dr. Gaston testify as to the hazardous conditions of the rip currents on Breaker Beach. In fact, he told you about the sign on the beach warning people of the danger. You heard further testimony as to the horrifying shark attack on Eddie Hunt in nearby waters. We have the remains of Shawna Welk's body, the piece of fabric and her tooth that washed up onshore. 'As good as a fingerprint,' her dentist said of that tooth, due to its unusual qualities."

Chelsea noted all these items.

Stan slid to a halt, leaning toward the jury with a confidential air. "Now. Defense counsel will try to convince you, even after all this evidence, that because Shawna Welk's body was never found, you can't be completely sure she is dead." He shook his head in disbelief. "He will try to convince you that she must have simply 'disappeared,' perhaps with some unnamed boyfriend. *I* say, given the facts that we know about Breaker Beach, its currents, the outgoing tide, plus the presence of a great white shark, it's little wonder her body was never found. In fact, it would have taken a miracle for her body to be discovered. Again, remember Dr. Gaston's testimony about the large sign on the beach, written in English and Spanish: 'Danger' in capital letters in a big yellow triangle. 'Wading and swimming unsafe.' Shawna Welk's body would have been swept out to sea in very little time."

The prosecutor's eyes cruised the jury, from Clay to Tak to Chelsea. She looked back without blinking.

"I may not have a grisly photo of Shawna Welk's remains. All the more fortunate for you. Who among you would enjoy seeing it? But in no less way, she is crying out from her watery grave to tell you what happened in the early-morning hours of February sixteenth. Through her blood on the last blouse she wore, she is crying out. Through the blouse itself, buried by her husband, she is crying out. Through a piece of fabric washed up on the beach, she is crying out. She cries out to you through the one part of her body that we do have—her tooth. She cries out through her half footprint that went into the water and, tragically, did not come out again.

"And who is the *only* person who could be responsible for her death?" Stan turned and pointed toward the defense table. "Darren Welk, her husband. Who argued with her on the beach in front of two witnesses? Darren Welk. Who hit her, made her bleed? Darren Welk. Who was the last person to see her alive? Darren Welk. Who admitted to police that he'd buried her bloody blouse? The man who had promised before God to love, honor, and protect her—her husband, Darren Welk."

Chelsea stole a glance at Kerra. Her face was pale but her jaw was determinedly set. Her expression spoke volumes. She'd cast her lot with Brett Welk, no matter the outcome. Chelsea felt sick as she imagined the effect of a guilty verdict on her relationship with her niece. Would Kerra ever forgive her?

Lord, what are you going to do about that? I don't want to lose my niece!

"I'm asking each of you," Stan concluded, "to heed the desperate pleas of Shawna Welk. And to find the man who hit her, killed her, and threw her body upon the wild waters of Breaker Beach in the middle of the night *guilty* of murder in the second degree. No other verdict would serve justice in this case." He ducked his head in a curt nod. "Thank you."

A collective breath sighed through the courtroom. Chelsea lay down her pen and flexed her fingers. She glanced about the room, noting reactions. Judge Chanson shifted in her chair. Reporters scribbled final notes. Hesta Naples coughed delicately, a fist to her mouth. One of the three gray-haired women who always sat in the second row whispered in her friend's ear. The other woman whispered back.

"All right." The judge fiddled with the chain of her glasses as she checked the clock. "We've gone a little overtime, so let's cut our lunch break short and be back here in forty-five minutes. Mr. Clyde, I assume you will be ready to begin at one o'clock?"

"Yes, Your Honor."

"Court dismissed."

ROGELIO DROVE TOWARD his house during lunch break, smelling his own sweat in the hot breeze through his car's open windows. He'd *had* it, his anger having built with every minute that morning. This waiting was about to drive him crazy! He parked quickly, got out and slammed the door. Inside the house he marched straight for the kitchen.

"*Mijo,* why are you home?" Mama Yolanda pushed herself up from the couch and turned off the TV. "I'll make you some lunch."

He picked up the phone, punching in the memorized numbers.

"Milt Waking."

Finally! "This is Rogelio," he spat. "What are you doin', man?"

A pause. For a second Rogelio wondered if the guy had forgotten who he was. "Oh. I've been meaning to call you."

"Yeah, right. Is the story going to be on the news tonight, yes or no? And don't lie to me, because I've had enough of it!"

"No, Rogelio. The answer is no."

He punched the air. "*Why?*"

"I told you before. I've found much more. Give me two days; that's all I ask."

"I don't have two days!"

"Yes, you do!" Milt sounded desperate. "Do you want your baby or not? If you do, you'd better just sit tight. Because if you do anything stupid, we could both lose everything."

"What've you got to lose? I'm the only loser here."

"Rogelio." Milt breathed into the phone. "Please. Do what I ask. Two days."

"Two days is *Saturday*."

"I know. Two days."

Rogelio slammed his fist against a cabinet. He didn't trust Milt, but what choice did he have? Who else *could* he trust anyway? He had no clue what to do.

Forgetting Mama Yolanda's presence, he cursed aloud and banged down the phone.

FORTY-SEVEN

Chelsea could see Stan Breckshire's nervousness in his silently drumming fingers. Terrance Clyde rose from the defense table with confidence and strode to the podium. He took his time there, positioning his notes before him just so. He rubbed his temple thoughtfully, eyes squinting above the jurors' heads, as if he were reading something on the back wall. Chelsea could feel the anticipation as all waited for him to begin.

She headed a new piece of paper. *Facts to Support Innocence.*

"This is a tragic case of a marriage," the attorney declared in a quiet tone. "A marriage based on lies and deceit. The husband running around with other women, the wife having affairs with other men. A marriage of volatility, jealousy, upheaval, and unhappiness, full of argument, strife, and distrust.

"This is *not* a case of murder."

Terrance Clyde looked to Gloria, Tak, then B. B.

"The prosecution would have you believe that the absence of any real proof that Shawna Welk is dead is of no consequence. That is absurd. The *very first* requirement in proving murder, as you will hear the judge tell you in her instructions, is to prove that, quote, 'a human being was killed.'"

Proof of murder? Chelsea wrote.

The defense attorney's voice boomed through the courtroom as for the next hour he tore down point after point made by the prosecution. Shawna Welk's constant stream of boyfriends proved she was unhappy in her marriage. Who could be absolutely sure that she hadn't linked up with yet another man and made her escape? There were no witnesses to this alleged murder. Terrance threw out one scenario after another. Darren Welk had admitted that he'd hit Shawna in the heat of an argument. Perhaps her tooth had been knocked out at that time as well. What if Shawna staged the footprint, wading into the water and coming back out somewhere along the edge of the beach in a place that Tracey could not easily see on a night with little moon? She could have torn her pants and thrown the piece of fabric plus her knocked-out tooth into the receding tide in hopes that they would later wash up onshore.

As for the question of whether Shawna would leave Tracey, apparently the mother-daughter relationship wasn't everything Tracey Wilagher had made it out to be. The two had been seen fighting. Shawna had screamed at her daughter, slapped her. Tracey was now an adult and didn't need the constant care of a mother. And Shawna was known to be manipulative, demanding. "Angry as she was at her husband," Terrance declared, "bleeding from a wound he had caused, she may well have thought, *This is my chance and I'm taking it; I'm out of here.*"

Chelsea's pen scratched over the paper. *Fight with Tracey. Mad at husband.*

He leaned over the podium, voice dropping. "Remember this: With all the possibilities I have posed as to what could have happened that night on Breaker Beach, if you find just one of them plausible, you cannot be assured beyond a reasonable doubt that Shawna Welk is dead."

Chelsea glanced at Victor Chavarria on her right. Victor was normally an avid note-taker, but he'd written not one word in the last hour. On her left Gloria too had set down her pen.

Reporters were certainly writing. All except Milt Waking, who seemed to stare right through Terrance Clyde, his mind a million miles distant. As if feeling her eyes, he glanced at her, then stared with intensity. Chelsea flinched. But she could not tear her gaze away.

I don't like him, Lord, but you say you're using him. Please continue to work your will.

One of Milt's eyebrows raised the tiniest bit, his expression mixing smugness with burning questions. Chelsea sensed him probing her face. For what? A hint of some divine knowledge about the trial?

Sorry to disappoint you this time, Mr. Waking.

She turned her attention back to the defense attorney.

Terrance Clyde sagely shook his head. "In addition to all that we have just discussed, there is another problem. Even if you somehow, in some way, manage to deny the fact that Shawna Welk may still be alive, you face the next hurdle. And this one is insurmountable. You cannot be absolutely certain who is responsible for her death.

"You heard testimony of numerous arguments in which Shawna Welk was involved. She argued with her boyfriends. She argued with her daughter. And she argued with Brett Welk, the son of her husband."

The grim tone of the attorney's voice as he spoke the last line betrayed his intentions. Pinpricks danced up Chelsea's arms. Here it came. She could see the path he would lead the jury down, as clearly as if he'd rolled out a red carpet.

Darren Welk pressed back in his chair. He began to slowly rub his hands.

"Remember, according to Tracey, there was no love lost between Brett and her mother. Since the day Shawna Welk moved in, he'd seemed to resent her trying to take his own mother's place." Terrance eased away from the podium and toward the jury box, as if preparing for a confidential conversation. "Let me tell you a few things that bother me. Do you remember Tracey Wilagher's testimony about that night? Do you remember what she said when I asked her if she'd seen Brett Welk's car as she drove away toward the beach? 'No,' she replied. Then when she returned to the house, upset over not finding her mother, Brett came out of his bedroom fairly quickly. Darren Welk appeared, still drunk. According to Tracey's testimony, Brett then went downstairs for about ten minutes and came back visibly shaken. After that Brett put both his father and Tracey to bed in their own rooms. And *no one* can testify as to what Brett did until around nine thirty the next morning, when Tracey woke up."

Chelsea glanced at Kerra. Her niece sat stiffly, face pale. She looked as if she hardly dared breathe. Brett's jaw flexed, his expression granite.

Where was Brett? she wrote.

Terrance Clyde reminded the jury of Victor Mendoza's testimony. How the man had mistaken Brett for his father in a photograph and had admitted that in fact he could not be sure who he had seen digging in the Welks' backyard in the early-morning hours of February sixteenth. Father and son were indeed built alike—same height, both stocky, muscular. And Brett's face bore a great resemblance to his father's.

"Now." The defense attorney lifted a hand, forefinger pointing toward the ceiling. "I want to show you something. I want to show you part of this video that the prosecution considers so important to its case."

With Sidney's help Terrance pulled the television monitor away from the wall and dimmed the courtroom lights. "Here are the final moments of this infamous interview." Using a remote, he turned on the monitor and the VCR and turned up the volume. Darren Welk's face, slack-jawed and worried, filled the screen. Terrance hit the pause button. "Now, the next voice you'll hear is Brett Welk's. This is the moment when he arrives at the police station. Notice the fright in his voice. Notice what he says. Most of all, notice his father's reaction."

Chelsea felt her stomach turn over. Again she looked to Kerra. *God, please let this attorney be wrong!*

Terrance Clyde hit a button and the tape jarred into action.

"Where's my dad?" Brett's voice demanded off camera. "I want to see him *right now!* I want to talk to the detectives!"

Darren Welk's eyes bugged. "No!" He grabbed the detective's wrist. "You're not talking to my son. You've got your man." He hit his own chest with a finger. "Leave Brett out of this."

Terrance paused the tape. "'You're not talking to my son,'" he repeated. "Look at Darren Welk's face. Know what I see? *Fear.* The intense fear of a parent trying to protect his only son."

The video moved to action once more. Chelsea watched the screen.

"We've got our man?" the detective mocked. "Is that a confession, Mr. Welk?"

Darren Welk's mouth opened, as if he'd suddenly realized the trap he'd set for himself. His expression changed to anger. He hit the table with his fist. "I want to see a lawyer!"

Terrance stopped the video, rewound it, then paused it again at the moment Darren Welk heard Brett's voice. His face froze with the click of a button. The attorney pushed the monitor a few feet back but left it on, and asked a bailiff to turn on the lights.

"Let me ask you," he said quietly, "does it make sense that Darren Welk, drunk as he was, allowed Brett to put him to bed, then got up again and buried that blouse? I say that while Tracey and Darren were sleeping, *Brett* buried that blouse." He raised his eyebrows. "When Detectives Draker and Kelly went to the Welks' house, warrant in hand, Darren Welk couldn't seem to understand why the detective asked questions about the newly planted bush in the backyard. Darren told him a gardener had planted the bushes on Friday. When the bush was dug up and the blouse found, Darren Welk gave no explanation as to why it was there. I suggest that was because he was shocked to the core. *He* hadn't put it there. And there was only one person whom he realized would have done it—his son."

At the defense table Darren Welk's hands rubbed and rubbed.

Dear Lord, Chelsea cried silently, *it's true, isn't it?*

"How did Detective Draker describe Brett's reaction when he drove up to the house and found out what had happened? 'His face turned a sickly white,' the detective said. Then Brett stood on the sidewalk as if in a daze and watched the detective drive his father off to the sheriff's department. Before long Brett barged into the department, demanding to break into the interview so he could speak to the detectives. That's when Darren Welk abruptly stopped talking.

"I ask you," Terrance said, eyes narrowing, "why was Brett Welk so anxious to talk?"

Of their own accord Chelsea's eyes drew to Brett. Spectators and reporters stared at him openly. Chelsea watched him swallow hard, his chest rising as he breathed. Beyond that he did not move a muscle. Kerra too seemed to have turned to stone. One thing their expressions lacked was surprise.

They'd been expecting this.

The thought sped like a bullet through Chelsea's brain.

Oh, Lord, you've promised me you're in control. I believe you. I trust you. But . . .

At that moment, Kerra turned to Chelsea with a determined stand-by-my-man blink. Chelsea went cold inside.

Terrance Clyde was not nearly finished. He continued to pound out his accusations against Brett. If Brett had buried that blouse—and it seemed highly likely—how could the jury convict Darren Welk? If Darren was covering for this action of his son, what else might he be covering for?

BRETT. Chelsea wrote the name again in all caps. Slowly, painfully.

The attorney moved to his final argument. Even *if* the jury could fully, unequivocally believe that Shawna Welk was dead, and even *if* they could set aside every question they had about Brett Welk's involvement, they faced a third barrier to finding Darren Welk guilty of second-degree murder. At the most, Terrance explained, they could only find him guilty of involuntary manslaughter, for the homicide would have been committed without malice aforethought and without the intent to kill. What's more, it had occurred in the heat of passion and while Darren Welk was intoxicated.

"My friends, hear me," Terrance pressed. "The prosecution's case amounts to no more than involuntary manslaughter. They have not given you one shred of evidence to indicate that Darren Welk went to that beach with the intent to kill his wife. Yet they ask you to convict my client of second-degree murder." His voice rose. "Nor have they given you proof beyond a reasonable doubt that Darren Welk, and Darren Welk alone, is responsible for Shawna's death. And in fact they have not even given you solid proof that she is dead!

"In light of all the holes in the prosecution's story," he concluded, "and in following all the judge's instructions that you will hear, I ask you—how can you do *anything* but find Darren Welk not guilty?"

As the attorney took his seat, Chelsea focused on her notes. BRETT. Her own handwriting mocked her.

Dear God, help us all.

MILT DIALED TRACEY'S WORK number during the afternoon break, mind swirling. He'd hardly been able to concentrate all day, and his notes on the closing arguments were sparse. He would really have to wing his evening report. But that was the least of his worries.

Tracey answered on the third ring. He laid charm into his voice. "Hey, there." *You lying little witch.*

"Oh, hi!"

"Missed you last night."

"I missed you, too."

"Look, I have an idea." He worked to keep his voice light. "The jury's going to begin deliberations tomorrow afternoon—"

She drew in a breath. "Really?"

"Yes. We've only got the prosecution's rebuttal and judge's instructions left."

"I can't believe it. I can't believe the day's finally here."

I'll bet you can't.

"I know you'll want to be at court when the verdict comes in," he said. "I'll need to be hanging around, too. Since the jury's sequestered, they'll deliberate right through the weekend if need be. So here's my idea. Get your boss to give you the day off tomorrow. Come up here tonight and stay with me in my town home until the verdict is in."

"Oh, Milt, that would be *wonderful.*"

"Of course, I'll have to be at court tomorrow and Saturday while you stay here. Bring something to read. But at least while you're here, no reporters—or your aunt—will bother you. When I hear the verdict is in, I'll call you, and you'll be able to get to the courthouse pretty quickly."

"Okay," she purred.

"Here's how to get to my place." Milt gave her directions. "Come as soon as you can after work. By the time you get here, I'll be home."

He clicked off the line and closed his eyes. It would take every ounce of acting ability he had to pull this off.

And to think he'd almost felt sorry for the girl.

FORTY-EIGHT

That evening, after Paul's phone call, Chelsea knelt beside the hotel bed, desperately praying. Words from the prosecution, from the defense, roiled inside her head until she thought her skull would burst. The rest of the jury had been escorted out to dinner, while she'd once again begged off. She could imagine the raised eyebrows, the judgments festering in the mind of each juror. Here she was, on the eve of their deliberation, further distancing herself.

So what? she countered. It didn't matter what they thought. She *had* to pray.

She gripped the bedspread, speaking aloud. Asking God for grace, for strength and wisdom during deliberations. She could not shake the sense that she was preparing for an unknown and unpredictable battle. Meanwhile, she knew, God was continuing to work his will through others.

How am I supposed to vote, Lord? I'm so confused about what I've heard. I suspect Darren Welk, and yet I think Brett was involved. I'm scared to deliberate with that jury, especially if I disagree with them. Help me deal with Tak and Hesta and Latonia . . .

How many of the jury members knew about her niece's relationship with Brett? she wondered. How many, in their phone calls from loved ones, had listened to the whispered tales they were not supposed to hear? If she voted not guilty, would they suspect she was doing it for Kerra? Yet they wouldn't be able to voice their suspicions, because they weren't supposed to know. What kind of strange standoff would result?

And if she voted guilty, wouldn't Kerra hate her?

God, I know I shouldn't worry about these things. Help me just to do what's right.

Her worst concern lay with the rest of the jury. Perhaps the judge's instructions would help. Perhaps after hearing them, she'd find that the doubts she carried weren't "reasonable" enough for a not-guilty vote.

Lord, I don't want to disagree with any juror. They dislike me enough as it is. Be with me. Be my Dread Champion.

That verse. Jeremiah 20:11. She'd memorized only a phrase of it, but Chelsea sensed she may need to cling to it during deliberations. Pushing up from her knees, she reached across the bed to slide her Bible off the nightstand. Turning to Jeremiah 20:11, she read the verse.

The LORD is with me like a dread champion;
    therefore my persecutors will stumble and not prevail.
They will be utterly ashamed, because they have failed,
    with an everlasting disgrace that will not be forgotten.

Chelsea repeated it aloud, again and again, until she knew it by heart.

FRIDAY, AUGUST 16

FORTY-NINE

Judge Carol Chanson plucked her black robe from its brass hook and shrugged it on. She couldn't have been more glad that this crazy case was nearing its end. The best thing that could happen right now, she told herself, would be for the jury to return a verdict that very day. Not likely, but she sure could go for a weekend of sailing on the bay. She glanced at her wall, where there was a photograph of a large sailboat, its spinnaker flying. She imagined the breeze, the wind.

Well, maybe on Sunday.

Her phone rang and she picked it up automatically, still focused on the picture. "Judge Chanson."

"Jed Trutenning here. You're almost done, huh."

"Hi, Jed." She sat down in her chair. "We'll finish up this morning. What's going on with you?"

"Just wanted to keep you informed about our investigation. Remember I told you we staked out the phone booth? Believe it or not, we got a hit."

"You're kidding."

"Nope. And we'd almost given up. We questioned a teenage girl who used the pay phone last night. She informed us that she'd made a call from the phone on the evening of August seventh and that as she was walking toward it, someone else was finishing a call."

Judge Chanson raised her eyebrows. "Really. That's quite a memory for a teenager."

Trutenning chuckled. "Apparently, she's taken up with some boyfriend her parents don't approve of, and when she can't sneak calls to the guy from home, she uses the public phone. It's just around the corner from her house. She remembered the date because it happened to be the day after her birthday. And he forgot."

She frowned. "Who forgot what?"

"The boyfriend forgot her birthday."

"Oh." She sat back in her chair and sighed. "So could she give you a description?"

"Yup. One you'll probably recognize."

Her chin dropped. "Oh no. I'm not sure I want to hear this."

He told her.

"IN DECIDING THE FACTS," Judge Chanson read, "you must not be swayed by mere sentiment. . . ."

Chelsea tried her best to pay attention to the judge's instructions, even as her mind whirled with concerns over Kerra, suspicions of Brett, and worries about the dreaded deliberations. Thoughts of sitting around a table with so many people who disliked her chilled her to the bone.

"Remember also," the judge continued, "that you are not to place any significance upon answers that were stricken by the court, even though you heard them. . . ."

Lord, I feel so unsettled. I don't know what's going to happen, but I'm scared.

"As for witnesses, it is in your purview to decide who was telling the truth and who was not. You may take into consideration the fact that a witness has lied or made inconsistent statements. If you determine that a witness has lied about material facts, the veracity of all his or her testimony may be held in doubt. . . ."

I don't want to focus on my worry, Jesus. Just help me do what you want, minute by minute.

"You are not to draw any negative conclusions from the fact that the defendant did not testify...."

Chelsea glued her eyes to the judge's face. These instructions were of vital importance; she *had* to listen.

"The defendant is presumed innocent. In order to find for a guilty verdict, you must be convinced beyond a reasonable doubt and to a moral certainty of the truth of the charge. 'Reasonable doubt' extends to more than mere possible doubt and does not require that the proof be so clear as to eliminate the possibility of any error, for under such a standard no prosecution could prevail...."

Were her doubts reasonable? *Were* they?

Lord, help me see through this.

At ten fifteen Judge Chanson finished her instructions. All at once the case was over. The judge wished them well, banged her gavel, and swept from the courtroom. Chelsea stood with the other jury members, her gaze falling one last time on Kerra.

Suddenly the room dimmed. A vision was coming. Chelsea inhaled deeply. She hung on to the chair in front of her for support, trying desperately to appear as normal as possible. Her eyes closed.

With instant clarity the man's face sprang into view—that same man with the jet-black hair, the cold, narrowed eyes. He brought a hand to his chin, the raised scar jagging with a rough sheen between his thumb and finger. One corner of his hard mouth lifted in a satisfied, evil smile. He turned and looked straight at Chelsea, his lips flattening. She couldn't breathe.

Then he vanished.

"Chelsea?" Vaguely she heard Gloria's voice.

Blood pounded in her ears. She drew in a ragged breath, tried to relax her grip on the chair. *Lord, why do I keep seeing this man?*

A voice responded within her. *Pray against his plans. Pray!*

"Chelsea?" Gloria jiggled her arm. "What's the matter?"

She forced open her eyes. "Sorry," she managed.

The whole thing couldn't have taken more than a few seconds. Just long enough to shake her to the core. Somehow Chelsea picked up her purse from the floor and followed Victor out the courtroom door. Jumbled prayers already flowed through her head.

KERRA STOOD BESIDE BRETT ON the escalator. "Want to take a walk or something?" he said. "We might as well get out of this place for a while."

"Sure."

Four more days here, she thought. Maybe she should change her plane ticket, stay a few days longer. How could she leave Brett, especially if his father were found guilty? Deep in her heart she expected that. Maybe if the jury hung . . . Kerra wondered how Aunt Chelsea would vote. But even if they did hang, Darren Welk would stay in jail. Brett would have to go through a whole new trial, waiting, dreading.

The enormity of it weighted Kerra's feet as they stepped outside into hot sunshine. She winced. No way could this turn out well. No way at all.

TOO LATE, MILT SPIED Lynn Trudy lying in wait for him as he stepped off the escalator. "What have you done with Tracey?" she hissed, blocking his path to the exit.

He feigned a bewildered look. "I don't know what you're talking about."

"She wasn't home last night." Lynn leaned toward him with an evil eye. "And she's not at work today."

Milt drew back in distaste. "How am I supposed to know where she is? What am I, her keeper?" He started to slide around her. She stepped in his way, pointing a red nail at his nose.

"I don't trust you for a second. You're nothing but—"

"I believe we've already had this conversation," Milt spat. "Now get out of my way."

"Miss Trudy." Detective Trutenning suddenly materialized at her side and laid a beefy hand on her shoulder. "I need a word with you."

Saved! Milt sneered at her as the man guided her toward the wall, her face still flushed with anger. The detective said something to her in an undertone.

"Why?" she demanded loudly.

Milt couldn't make out the answer.

"I've already told you everything I know, which is nothing!" Lynn gestured impatiently. "So what's the point?"

"Everything I know." Milt knew Trutenning was investigating the jury phone calls.

"I repeat: we have further questioning," the detective said, his voice rising.

"So question me right here!"

What was this? Milt wondered. *Why come back to Lynn?* With mounting curiosity he watched them argue. This couldn't possibly fit. The phone calls had demanded a not-guilty vote.

Trutenning had apparently had enough. He wrapped his fingers firmly about Lynn's arm. "We're going to the station *right now.*"

Lynn opened her mouth, then snapped it shut. With a look of pure venom first at him, then across the way at Milt, she stomped beside the detective out the door.

Milt stared after them, stunned.

FIFTY

Chelsea's fingers trembled as she filled a small cup from the bottled-water stand in the deliberation room. The evil look on that man's face in her vision haunted her. *Lord, whoever he is, thwart his plans. Protect your people. And help me, Jesus; I need to be calm!*

She moved aside for Sylvia, who waited with cup in hand. B. B. had already sunk into a chair, laughing throatily over a comment from Latonia. Hesta sat near one end of the table, fingers laced, back straight, waiting. Tak was across from her, also silent, his greenish brown eyes tracking the movements of various members.

"Well, finally, here we are." Clay sauntered to the head of the table and pulled out a chair. He sat down, thumping a fat pile of notes, stapled into separate documents, in front of him. Henry claimed his place at the other end of the table. His notes were on a pad of yellow lined paper.

Chelsea willed her face to be impassive as she seated herself between Antonio and Gloria. Slowly she brought the cup to her lips and drank.

Sidney bustled around the table, setting a pad of paper and pen at each place. "Okay," he declared when he was through. "You all need anything, you know I'm just outside the door." He smiled at them, showing teeth. "Feeding time will be at one o'clock. That'll give you a little bit of time to get started. We have caviar and oysters on the half shell today."

"Hm." Latonia Purcell inclined her dark head elegantly, as if such delicacies were her daily fare. "Don't forget the chilled wine."

Sidney chortled. "Oh, don't you worry." He sidled toward the door, his expression turning serious. "Now, God's blessings on you all." He nodded once, his gaze falling on Chelsea. Then he stepped outside and shut the door. They heard a gentle click as he locked them in.

They looked at each other. Chelsea took a deep breath. *Lord, I have to focus on these deliberations now. Show me what to do.*

"Okay." Clay slapped his palms on the table. "Let's get down to business. The first thing we have to do is choose a foreman."

"That's right," Henry put in. The two men eyed each other.

"I don't think it matters much who's foreman," Sylvia said, her tone businesslike. She leaned on an elbow, two fingers under her chin. "Our votes are all equal here."

"You do it, Clay," B. B. suggested. "You're at the head of the table."

"I think Clay or whoever would be just fine," Hesta declared with an air of chilly dismissal. "We have more important things to discuss."

Clay gave her a look of distaste, then blinked away. "Anyone else have a comment?"

Chelsea remained silent as they discussed the issue. After ten minutes they agreed to take a vote. Chelsea went along with everyone else, voting in Clay as foreman. *If only the rest could be so easy,* she thought.

"All right." Clay assumed control like a general over his troops. "As you know, we have two different issues here. First is the issue of guilt or innocence. Second, in the case of an agreement of guilt, is the issue of exactly what crime was committed. I imagine at this point you each have a sense of your belief as to the first issue. I suggest we take a vote right now to see where we stand."

Here it came. Once and for all, where did she stand? Chelsea ran the possibilities through her head. The suggestion that Shawna Welk simply disappeared into the night was a defense tactic that she could easily dismiss. There simply was no indication as to how Shawna could have managed that or where she could have gone. In addition, Chelsea could not believe that she would choose to walk away from her daughter forever.

So many pieces of evidence pointed to Darren Welk's guilt. Who else could possibly have killed Shawna on a deserted beach when the very trip to that beach had been unplanned?

And yet there was Brett. Chelsea did not know the extent of his involvement. She only knew that as long as she suspected him, she could not fully grasp a vote for guilty. But as she searched for a logical explanation as to how Brett could have killed his stepmother, she found none.

Lord, if you want me to vote not guilty for now, how am I going to defend myself?

"I agree; let's take a vote." Henry drummed pudgy fingers as others murmured their assent. "On paper."

"Anything anybody want to say first?" Clay asked. He hunched over the table, leaning on his arms, chin thrust forward. They all shook their heads. "Okay then." He put his pad of paper on top of his notes. "Let's write our votes on a piece of paper, fold them, and hand them down this way."

Chelsea's hand grew damp as she picked up her pen. Even as she wrote her answer, she prayed God's victory over the man in her vision.

FIFTY-ONE

Jed Trutenning stuck his tongue in his cheek and surveyed Lynn Trudy's defiant features across the table. They'd been questioning her for an hour and had gotten nowhere. His partner, Gary Welch, sat between them, arms folded and impatient. "I want you to hear something, Ms. Trudy." Trutenning drew a sheet of paper from his breast pocket and unfolded it. Slowly, almost lovingly, he smoothed its creases against the table. "California Penal Code Section 95. 'Every person who corruptly attempts to influence a juror, or any person summoned or drawn as a juror, or chosen as an arbitrator or umpire, or appointed a referee, in respect to his or her verdict in, or decision of, any cause or proceeding, pending, or about to be brought before him or her, is punishable by a fine not exceeding ten thousand dollars, or by imprisonment in the state prison.'" He raised his eyebrows at her. "*State prison,* Ms. Trudy. And you'll have not one count against you but two. In other words, you won't be going home anytime soon."

He watched her swallow. She was trying to keep up a brave front, but he knew she was scared spitless.

"For the hundredth time," she said through gritted teeth, "I didn't do it. Why would I threaten two jurors to get them to vote not guilty? I want Darren Welk to *pay* for killing my sister. If I could, I'd strangle him myself!"

Trutenning tapped the paper with his finger. "We have the call records from the phone booth to both houses. At the right times. Our witness just identified you. You're dead in the water, Ms. Trudy."

"I didn't do it."

"Like I told you, it may go easier for you if you'd just tell us who gave you the contact information."

"*I didn't do it.*"

Welch leaned back with an exasperated sigh. "I'm getting tired of this. Put her in a cell. Maybe she'll talk tomorrow."

"You can't keep me!" Lynn's face turned crimson.

"What planet are you on?" Welch shot back. "Because of you, a whole jury's been sequestered. You've caused a lot of people a whole lot of trouble. We didn't gather this clear evidence against you to let you hit the streets and disappear. You're not going anywhere."

Lynn let loose a string of curses, followed by, "I want a lawyer."

Trutenning's heart sagged. "Fine." He pushed back his chair and stood, Welch following suit. "I've had enough of you for today. You call yourself a lawyer, Ms. Trudy. He'll tell you just how much trouble you're in."

HER HEART THUMPING, Chelsea watched Clay gather the folded pieces of paper in a small pile. All she could hope at this moment was that she wouldn't be the only one.

"All right, here goes." He picked up the first piece and unfolded it. "Guilty." Carefully he placed it to one side. Picked up a second. "Guilty." Chelsea's mouth ran dry as he continued down the pile. Guilty. Guilty. Then four more in a row, all guilty. He picked up the ninth, unfolded it. Gazed at it for a second. "Not guilty." Chelsea heard more than one disappointed sigh. Well, so what? she wanted to say aloud. How often did juries agree from the outset anyway?

The tenth vote was guilty. And the eleventh. Chelsea held her breath as Clay picked up the last one. "Guilty."

"Hey, not bad," B. B. commented with a nervous laugh. "Eleven to one."

Clay leaned over the table. "Quite amazing for a first vote, I'd say." He cast his eyes around the group. "Would the person who voted not guilty like to come forward? Maybe then we could discuss your reasons."

Heads turned, eleven pairs of eyes searching for a move, an indication on someone's face. Chelsea took a deep breath. "It's me."

Silence. Chelsea felt the stares, the accusations.

Sylvia waved a hand. "Oh, okay." Did her voice carry a forced lightness? "What are you thinking, Chelsea?"

What *was* she thinking? Once again, desperately, Chelsea searched for clear logical reasoning behind her choice. *Help me know what to say, Lord!* She gripped her pen. "I think Brett Welk buried the blouse."

B. B. gawked and Latonia pulled her chin back in surprise. Mike Bariston surveyed her with his protruding eyes. The expressions on these and other faces told Chelsea all she needed to know. They'd heard about her niece and Brett, all right. They'd probably half-expected her not-guilty vote. But now she'd thrown them a curve ball in accusing Brett himself.

Henry spread his hands. "How'd he do that?"

Chelsea put her pen down, forced her mind into clear thinking. "I think it's as Terrance Clyde suggested. Brett put his father to bed. Then he buried the blouse."

"But where did he get it?" Sylvia asked.

"He probably found it under the seat in his father's car. Remember what Tracey said? Brett went downstairs after his father showed up, and he came back 'visibly shaken'. The defense reminded us of that. I think for whatever reason he went to check his father's car. He saw the bloody blouse and it really shook him up. He knew it was evidence staring him in the face. After he put his father and Tracey in their beds, he buried it to protect his dad."

"Then why wouldn't Darren Welk say so?" Tak demanded.

"Because he didn't want to get his son in trouble." Chelsea shook her head. "The ironic thing is, Brett would have buried the blouse to protect his dad, but that very move caused his dad's arrest, because Victor Mendoza saw him."

"Okay, wait a minute." Clay held up a hand. "You know what, I can see the logic in that. I think it's plausible. Still, it doesn't change one fact. Darren Welk killed his wife. Brett may have tried to help cover it up, but in the end, so what? Sounds to me like your very argument supports Darren Welk's guilt."

Chelsea searched for an answer. "Well, we don't know where Brett was at the time of Shawna's death. What if he *was* at the beach?"

"How could he have been?" Clay replied. "First of all, there was no way for him to know his dad and stepmom were going to that beach. It's clear from testimony that the trip was Darren Welk's last-minute idea. Second, I have it right here in my notes. . . ." He shuffled through his stack of papers until he reached some stapled sheets near the bottom. He lifted them up, flipped through them. "Here it is. Tracey said that when she was driving to the beach, she did not see any cars coming from that direction. If Brett had been at the beach, he'd have passed her coming home."

"What if he went home a different way?"

Clay dropped his notes. "That beach is pretty remote. Doesn't sound like there are too many ways to get there."

He's right, Chelsea thought. So why couldn't she change her mind?

"You know, there is one thing about that blouse that bothers me." Victor Chavarria smiled self-consciously. "You have to forgive me; I'm retired, you see. And one of the things I do in my spare time is read mystery novels. Now here I am, in a real-life mystery. Anyway, here is my question. Where was the blouse when Tracey went to the beach?"

Clay tilted his head, thinking.

Sylvia frowned. "It was in Darren Welk's car, right?" She looked around the table.

"But when did he put it there?" Victor pressed. "As you can see, I took lots of notes, too." He riffled his pad of paper. "And I remember very clearly that Tracey said she saw a half shoe print in the wet sand coming out of the water, which led to a trail in the dry sand that went over to the campfire area, where Darren was asleep. Now, he supposedly followed Shawna down to the water when she went to wash her blouse. What I believe happened is just the scenario the prosecutor gave in his closing remarks. At that point they continued fighting. Darren hit her more. And he ended up killing her. She fell into the water, and the pull of the tide plus the rip current quickly drew her out. By the time Tracey reached the beach, Shawna probably wasn't that far adrift, but just far enough not to be seen in the dark waters with a crescent moon. Sad, thinking about that." He rubbed a thumb against the table. "At any rate, Darren, obviously very drunk and now spent of energy, then staggered over toward the fire, fell into the sand, and passed out. So I ask you—where was the blouse?"

"I don't think it happened that way." Henry Slatus shuffled through his notes. "I figure Darren saw what he'd done, saw the blouse left in the shallow water as evidence, and was of sound enough mind to stuff it under the seat of his car."

"Then why would he go back to the fire after that?"

"How does one explain a drunken mind?" Henry said. "You say his energy was spent when he was in the water. I say it was finally spent after he'd hidden the blouse. He shuffled back to the place of warmth near the fire and passed out."

"Drunks don't need warmth," Chelsea commented. "The alcohol makes them feel hot enough."

Hesta stared at her with pursed lips, as if wondering how Chelsea might know. Chelsea could have kicked herself. The argument had turned away from her; why hadn't she just kept quiet?

Sylvia leaned back and folded her arms. "Well. I suppose you have a point there, Victor."

"But what difference does all this make?" Tak demanded. He looked at Victor. "Even with your questions, you still voted guilty."

Victor nodded slowly. "That's true. Because when I weigh all the other evidence, it points to Darren Welk's guilt. We simply have no indication that anyone else was at that beach when Shawna was killed. Still"—he shrugged—"this is a point that bothers me. One of those little Agatha Christie points."

B. B. and Gloria smiled at him. The room fell silent again, save for Henry's knocking one knuckle against the table.

"Okay." Clay looked to Chelsea. "So you believe Brett buried the blouse, which maybe he did. And we don't know where he was at the time Shawna was killed. Can you give us some reason to believe he was at the beach? Like how he knew to be there and how he got back?"

Chelsea swallowed. "Not really."

Clay raised a hand, palm up. "Then what's the problem?"

"Brett knows something," she blurted. "I watched his face during the trial. He just looks guilty of something."

"Fine," Clay shot back. "At the most, he's guilty of burying the blouse and trying to protect his dad. Does that change Darren Welk's guilt?"

Chelsea bit the inside of her lip. "I still just don't think I can vote guilty," she said quietly.

"Why?"

"I . . ." Chelsea could hear the blood whoosh through her head. "I wish I could tell you. There's . . . something."

As soon as the words were out, Chelsea wished them back with all her might. She sounded so vague, so lame, even to her own ears.

"Is this about one of your visions?" Tak demanded suddenly, derision coating the last word.

The air chilled. Chelsea felt it and knew everyone else did, too. A line had been crossed, the unspoken now spoken. And it certainly hadn't taken very long. It was almost as if Tak had been waiting to accost her. In that moment understanding hit Chelsea like lightning. In that moment she realized that God had far bigger plans in this deliberation room than merely deciding the outcome of the trial. For these plans he had placed her on the jury.

The Lord is with me like a Dread Champion . . .

"No," she said.

"Really?" His eyes pierced hers. "Then why can't you explain yourself?"

"I just have to get my thoughts in order. Maybe I will be able to—"

"Are you telling us your vote has nothing to do with thoughts from your god?"

Chelsea's spine tingled. "I'm voting my conscience. I'm voting what I feel."

"It has to be based on some logic." Tak laced his long, thin fingers. "Just what would that be?"

"What about what happened after we were dismissed?" Gloria turned to Chelsea accusingly, as if she'd been waiting for the most opportune moment to mention the subject. "You almost seemed to go into some kind of trance for a couple seconds when we all stood up. You even had your eyes closed."

"So what? She probably got up too fast," Sylvia put in. "Can we get back to business here?"

"We *are* talking business," Tak insisted. "We are talking about the one person who was most questioned by the judge, because of her beliefs, before this trial ever began. Now this person votes not guilty. That would be fine in itself *if* she had a reason. But she cannot seem to give us one." He leveled a glare at Chelsea, waiting.

She couldn't respond.

"Chelsea," Clay said, an edge in his voice, "you need to answer."

Irritation swept over her. She did not care for the man's tone. And she wasn't going to stand silent before the accusations of some college student. "I have voted not guilty because I feel it's right, at this moment in time. If you want to change my mind, please, let's keep discussing it."

She leaned back in her chair, hoping they wouldn't see the pulse pounding in her neck. *Lord*, she silently begged, *give me the strength to stand firm.*

MILT LEANED AGAINST HIS car and dialed his home number on the cell phone. All during lunch he'd thought about Lynn Trudy. He still couldn't figure out why Detective Trutenning would hone in on her. Made no sense at all.

The phone rang once in his ear. He knew Tracey would be checking the Caller ID for his cell phone number. She answered on the third ring.

"Hello."

"Hi." He painted softness into his tone. "Guess who I ran into this morning." He told her about Lynn's confronting him in the hall. "It's a good thing you're hiding out," he said. "She'd be all over you if you were here."

"Yeah, I guess so." Tracey sighed. "I'm *sick* of her. I'm sick of everybody. Except you, I mean," she added hastily.

"Mm. Well, just hang in there. The jury started deliberating just before lunch. I don't expect anything to happen today, but I have to hang around just in case."

Tracey rattled off questions and he answered halfheartedly, his mind on other things. Milt did not tell her about Detective Trutenning. If Lynn had been involved in the jury calls, he had no idea how much Tracey knew. No use getting her out of kilter just yet. She could just hear it on his newscast that evening. By then he'd be home to keep an eye on her. Heaven knew, keeping Tracey Wilagher calm for the moment was his main concern. Keeping her calm . . . and setting his trap.

FIFTY-TWO

As the afternoon wore on, Chelsea floundered to defend her position, back ramrod straight and head pounding. The air in the jury room hung thick and tense. All eyes were on her, all arguments thrown her way. Beside her, Antonio seeped animosity. So did Hesta and Tak and Latonia. Clay took to speaking to her as if she were a half-witted child. Henry just shook his head. She couldn't believe how impatient they were with her. From their reactions, one would have thought she'd been the only holdout for days.

Her prayers had become simple, desperate cries. *Help me, Lord, please!*

Finally Clay suggested—no, demanded—that they go over the testimony, witness by witness. "Something in there," he informed her, "is bound to change your mind."

During the afternoon break Chelsea hid out in the bathroom, clinging to the sink and praying with all her might. "What's the point of all this, Lord?" she whispered aloud. "Nobody's changing their opinion. Am I supposed to fight like this the rest of today? And tomorrow? When can I stop? Just a few hours and already I'm so tired."

Break over, they all took their places once again. Chelsea sat woodenly, awaiting the onslaught.

Clay leveled his eyes at her. "Do you have anything you want to say before we take up where we left off?"

Chelsea felt the hardness of the chair against her back. A vise gripped her head. She forced her voice to remain level. "Only that I'm sorry. Believe it or not. I don't mean to cause problems. Like all of you, I just want to do what I think is right."

A small *tsk* emitted from Antonio's lips. Tak's eyes were cold. Hesta leaned forward and looked at her down the table, mouth in a thin line. "Right," Clay said with a slow blink. He consulted his notes. "Okay. Where were we?"

"Tracey's testimony," Henry replied. "She's kicking Darren Welk to wake him up."

"Yeah, okay." Clay read his notes. "He gets up, stumbles around, denies he knows where Shawna is. They both start searching the beach. Then Tracey goes back home, convincing herself she'll find her mother there, which of course she doesn't. Apparently, she makes enough noise to bring Brett out of his bedroom—"

"Do you realize how long this is going to take?" Tak's long fingers drummed the table. "I really don't see the point of going through every witness's testimony." He pointed at Chelsea. "I say you tell us your version of what happened, since you're so sure of yourself. *You* tell us who killed Shawna Welk."

Every nerve ending in Chelsea's body prickled. She gazed at Tak, feeling his scorn, his hatred. This was not just about the trial, she knew. This was about her Christian beliefs, which he apparently held in utter contempt. Others around the table may not have possessed his level of derision against her faith, but that was changing in the face of her perceived obstinacy. She had no proof of what she believed about the murder, no rational argument upon which to rest. She had only the knowledge, deep within her, that she was doing what God had asked her to do.

"I can't tell you that," she said.

"Because you won't or because you can't?" Tak pressed.

"Because . . . because I can't."

"Then you have no argument." Tak's face hardened. "No basis for your opinion. Which says to me that you are not listening to the evidence you heard in the courtroom, as you promised the judge you would. You are instead listening to some imagined voice in your head—that voice you claim comes from 'God.'" He slid his eyes around the jury table. "Can't you all see that? Why are we letting her get away with this?"

"*I'm* not letting her get away with it," Latonia declared. She wagged her head at Chelsea. "You think you've got a corner on God? I grew *up* in church. My grandfather was one of those Bible-toting preachers who rose up on his toes when he yelled about hell. I believe in God just like you do. But one thing I *wouldn't* do is let him make me look the fool. Which is what you're looking like at this moment!"

"I—"

"Well, I frankly don't care what *anybody* around this table believes." Hesta's voice burned like ice as she cut Chelsea off. "We're not here to discuss religious beliefs. We're here to decide on the guilt or innocence of a man charged with murder."

"That's exactly what I'm saying!" Latonia threw out her hands, palms up. "Yes, we're here to discuss a man's guilt or innocence, based on the evidence in court. But *she*"—Latonia pointed a perfectly groomed, short red nail at Chelsea—"is turning it into some sort of religious cause."

"That's not what you're doing, is it, Chelsea?" Sylvia prompted. "You simply have some questions, right?"

Chelsea's mouth dried out. She raised a water bottle to her lips with trembling fingers and drank. "I'm trying to tell you," she said, emphasizing each word, "I simply feel that something's wrong. I don't know what it is. Maybe if we continued discussing—"

"So this has nothing to do with your Christianity." Tak glared at her.

"Well—"

"It has nothing to do with your 'listening to God.'"

Dread unwound itself and slithered through Chelsea's stomach. Every eye around the table focused on her, full of scorn. "How can I answer that?" She wanted to melt into her chair. "In everything I do, I try to listen to God."

"There, you see!" Tak slammed a hand onto the table and Chelsea jumped. He hunched forward, his face livid. "You told the judge you would consider nothing but the evidence. You *lied!* Now you are in contempt of everything this jury stands for! If we had an alternate behind you, I'd report you to the judge and throw you out!"

"Yeah, well, we don't have an alternate." Clay's voice was layered with disgust. "And if we twelve can't come together, this whole trial goes down the drain. That's not going to happen, not on *my* watch."

"Not on mine either," Henry declared.

"Or mine." Hesta's voice nearly shook with rage.

"Wait a minute, wait a minute!" Sylvia held up both hands, as if blessing the room into calmness. She turned to Chelsea, face grim. "Things have gotten out of hand here." Her words were distinct, controlled, like that of a negotiator's. "Now. Chelsea. Just tell us what we need to hear. Tell us that you are basing your opinion on evidence you heard in the courtroom, evidence that we can then discuss. Assure us that your vote is *not* based on something you feel God is telling you to do, when you yourself don't see the reason for it."

Chelsea stared at her, throat closing. How could she possibly answer? She *had* promised to base her vote on evidence. Wasn't she doing that? Hadn't the evidence simply failed to convince her? She was voting her conscience, as God had commanded, wasn't she?

"When you yourself don't see the reason for it."

What was her reason? What did she believe? Could she deny she was basing her vote on what God told her to do?

What do you want from me, God! she cried. *They're all against me!*

She opened her mouth. Looked Sylvia squarely in the eye. Then gazed at Tak, at Clay and Latonia. A settling hovered in her chest, like kicked-up dust drifting back to solid ground.

"My opinion," she heard herself say, "is based upon my conscience of voting as I think is right. There's no doubt in my mind that this is what God would want me or any of the rest of you to do. My vote is based upon the judge's instructions regarding reasonable doubt. I cannot bet my life on the fact that Darren Welk, and only Darren Welk, killed his wife. Because I absolutely believe Brett, his son, buried that blouse."

She gazed around the table defiantly. Tak, Henry, and Hesta all hurled back their responses at once.

FIFTY-THREE

Brett's watch ticked past five o'clock with no word from the jury. Wearily he pushed to his feet from the hard bench. The hallway filled with people emptying out of various courtrooms. Most of the reporters who'd hung around for a possible verdict had already left. Milt Waking and his cameraman were headed for the escalator. Brett felt his face harden, watching Milt. Sorry excuse for a human being.

"Might as well call it a day." Brett held out a hand to Kerra. She gave him a sad smile as she rose.

Neither of them wanted to eat much. They bought sandwiches and drinks, then for the third evening in a row drove up Skyline to their vista. Brett sat on the rock and gazed without seeing at the bay, his arm around Kerra. His whole body felt weighted. After the long afternoon this night would seem interminable.

"They're going to find him guilty," he said, breaking the silence.

Kerra's head moved slightly. A breeze ruffled the hair around her face.

"But then why shouldn't they?" His voice thickened. "It's what God wants, isn't it—justice. The guilty don't get off."

"Oh, Brett, don't."

"Why not?" He pulled away from her, propelled to his feet. "It's true and I might as well face it. Still, he doesn't deserve second degree. You know he was drunk; he didn't mean to do it." Brett swung around toward the bay, shoulders sagging. He heard the swish of clothes as Kerra clambered off the rock and to his side. She wound her fingers around his arm. "If I just hadn't—"

"You have got to stop blaming yourself, Brett."

He shoved a hand into his pocket, blinking hard.

"Can you see what's going on?" Kerra squeezed his arm. "You and your dad are protecting each other. At a high price. I'm not saying that anything that happened was right. But I do know God can work through the horrible mistakes we make. Whatever the verdict is"—her voice tightened—"it seems to me you and your dad ought to be able to start talking. Whether it's at home or at the jail. The *actions* of love are all there. You two just need the words."

MILT SHRUGGED HIS SUIT coat into place and smoothed his hair. *One last time of standing on these courtroom steps,* he thought. *One last time.* By tomorrow, if everything went as planned, he'd have a story that would blow the whole Bay Area away.

He focused on the anchorwoman's introduction to his segment, coming through his earphone. The cameraman signaled him.

"Yes," he said to the camera, "as you've heard, things are winding down in the highly watched Salad King trial of Darren Welk from Salinas. Nevertheless, the case continues to surprise us all. As the case was sent to the jury late this morning for deliberation, I learned that Lynn Trudy, sister of the victim, was taken in by detectives for a second round of questioning about the illegal phone calls to two jury members—and is still being held. By telephone, her attorney, Dave Nugan, made this statement: 'I am certain that this misunderstanding will soon be straightened out. Throughout the trial of Darren Welk, Lynn Trudy has made it very clear that she believes in his guilt. She would have no reason to call two jurors and demand not-guilty votes. She will continue to cooperate in questioning with the detectives until the real culprit in this jury tampering is found.'"

Milt raised an eyebrow. "Despite Nugan's comments, by late this afternoon Ms. Trudy's situation had not changed, and according to sources, she has refused to answer any further questions. Back to you, Cindy."

"All right," the anchorwoman responded. "Thank you, Milt. This case does seem to get stranger and stranger."

Milt nodded at the camera, a little smile on his face.

You ain't seen nothing yet, babe.

SATURDAY, AUGUST 17

FIFTY-FOUR

Brett eased into a space in the near-empty parking garage. Clearly, the courthouse would be quiet, given that it was Saturday. As he locked his car, he spotted Kerra driving in. She caught sight of him, and her face broke into a smile that squeezed his chest. He walked toward her car. When they met, he pulled her into his arms. The fresh smell of her hair, the feel of her body, swirled him with comfort. Kerra hugged him tightly, then stepped back. "Are you okay this morning?" Her blue eyes searched his face.

"I am now."

She brushed fingers against his jaw. "Whatever happens, know that I'm with you."

He nodded, throat suddenly tight.

They fell in step toward the courthouse and more long hours of waiting.

Chelsea had barely slept. As she dressed for another day with the jury, her limbs felt as though they had weights attached. Before falling into bed at midnight, she had alternated between pacing the room, reading the Bible, praying, and just plain worrying. Every time she caught herself giving in to her anxiety, she'd tried to turn it into a prayer. Sometimes it worked; sometimes it didn't. Sometimes all she could see were her problems. She believed the Lord was at work. But at this moment, as she waited for the escort's knock on her door, she just wanted to climb into bed and pull the covers over her head.

I can't do this, Lord. I know you want me to keep holding out. You've made me sense that very clearly. But I just feel so weak. I can't last much longer.

A knock sounded on her door. Steeling herself, Chelsea walked toward the dresser to pick up her purse.

The vision came with no warning. It flashed through her mind, strong and vivid, gut-wrenching. That same evil man . . . and Kerra, her face pulled into a rigid mask of terror.

Immediately the vision vanished. Chelsea's blood turned to water. She threw out a hand and hung on to the dresser, eyes squeezing shut. Trying to tell herself that she hadn't seen it, she had *not*. This was not real.

She slid to her knees, prayers tumbling from her lips. Prayers for Kerra's protection, for her own wisdom and strength, for God to show her what to do. She needed to be with Kerra, warn her of coming danger, maybe save her from it. She'd have to change her vote quickly, do anything to get herself out of there.

Show me what to do, God!

The knock sounded harder on the door.

"Coming!" Chelsea called. Trembling, she pulled to her feet. *Lord, what do I do? Let me change my vote; let me go home!*

She snatched her purse off the dresser and headed for the door.

JANET CLINE CHECKED THE time as she chewed the last of her bagel. Ten o'clock. In fifteen minutes she needed to be out the door, and her hair wasn't dry. Even though it was Saturday, her calendar was full for the rest of the day. Four interviews plus a stack of paperwork. And since she'd be the only one in the office, she'd have to answer the phones.

She washed and dried her small plate at the kitchen sink, then returned it to the cabinet. As she hurried toward the bathroom to brush her teeth, the phone rang.

"Oh, forget you." She kept moving, then slid to a halt. Maybe it was her daughter, Caroline, who often called on the weekend. Pivoting toward the counter, she snatched up the receiver. "Hello."

A male voice grated in her ears. "Ms. Cline."

"Yes?"

"Enrico Delgadia."

Janet's heart froze. For a moment she couldn't move. Then slowly she reached for the counter and steadied herself.

"I have a little problem I thought you might help me with." Delgadia spoke quietly, as if he expected her cooperation at the mere raising of his little finger. "It has come to my attention that a number of days ago you requested some paperwork about the adoption of my daughter, from social services in Sacramento."

"Who told you that?" Janet blurted. Surely not Pat, her friend and colleague who'd sent the paper.

"I have friends in many places," he replied, oiling the words with meaning. "My friend has been unable to discover the reason for your curiosity about these papers, however. And it does seem odd to me, after so much time has gone by. I would be most grateful if you would tell me the reason for your inquiry."

She gripped the phone, searching for an answer.

"Ms. Cline?"

"I just wanted to follow up on a few things, that's all."

"I see. And you found nothing amiss, I hope."

"Of course not. Nothing at all."

He made a sound in his throat. "Why is it that you first requested only certain papers of the file? Namely the father's relinquishment form."

"Really, I—"

"Surely you understand my concern. We have had the child for seven months. My wife adores her. Shawna Welk insisted everything was in order. I would be most upset to hear that there is a problem."

Janet's heart pounded. She opened her mouth but no sound would come.

"Are you there, Ms. Cline?"

"Yes," she croaked.

"Good. I have no doubt," he continued in a mild tone that would cut steel, "that you will tell me the truth. So I can let you get to work. Such an attractive building your office is in, by the way. Your home is attractive also. Lovely flowers out front. You obviously take great pride in your house." He exhaled slowly. "But surely not as much pride as you take in your daughter, Caroline. Moved to Fresno with her new husband, hasn't she? Lives on Baker Street?"

Janet's veins turned to ice. Her head seemed to detach itself from the rest of her body. This could not be happening. She swallowed, snatched a breath. "What do you *want*?"

"Information, nothing more," he replied. "Now, please. *Why* did you want to see the relinquishment?"

Janet's mind whirled with a dozen lies, but none that could assure the safety of her only child. *Oh, Rogelio*, she thought. *What am I about to do to you?*

"The birth father came to see me with his copy. There were . . . some issues."

"Oh? First you say no problems; now you tell me there are issues." His voice turned to flint. "I do not care for people who play games with me, Ms. Cline. I suggest for your sake that you tell me all you know."

Any resolve she had left drained out her feet. In a trembling voice Janet told him, without giving him Rogelio's name. When she finished, the line was deadly quiet.

"You are quite sure the father has told no one else?"

"I'm sure. As I said, I convinced him to wait."

He gave a low laugh that chilled her to the bone. "That was wise of you, Ms. Cline. But hear me. My wife is fragile. I will not allow her to be upset by this unfortunate misunderstanding. I will do anything to protect my family, do you understand? *Anything.* Now. I have a copy of the father's relinquishment right here. Your signature is on it." He paused. "Of course, you *do* remember signing it."

It was not a question. Janet closed her eyes. How had he gotten a copy of that paper in a closed adoption? Images of Rogelio's determined face flickered through her mind, followed by the realization of all she had to lose. Her fingernails dug into her palm.

"Ms. Cline? I really must insist that you respond."

"Yes," she whispered. "I signed it."

"Ah. I knew it. You'll not hear from the father on this matter again, by the way. He has realized how complicated a baby would make his life."

Janet closed her eyes, sickness for Rogelio mixing with relief. No doubt he'd been threatened, too. Still, she rationalized, he had his whole life ahead of him. How much easier to just let this be.

"However," Delgadia continued smoothly, "on the off chance that this question should arise again, I stand assured that you will remember your signature?"

She thought of Rogelio's little girl, being raised by this despicable man. For a moment she wanted to stand up to him, make him pay for what he'd done. Then she thought of her own daughter.

"Yes. I'll remember."

"Very good," he said oh-so-pleasantly. "I will not forget your kindness."

Nausea rolled through her stomach.

"You have a nice day, Ms. Cline." The dial tone sounded in her ear.

Janet dropped the phone like a firebrand, stumbled to the sink, and threw up.

FIFTY-FIVE

"All right." Clay thumped his hand on his notes. The sound seemed to shoot right through Chelsea. "I wanted to start off easy this morning, go over some of the basic facts just to get today's discussion going on better terms than we did yesterday. Everybody seems a little calmer after a good night's sleep, and I hope it stays that way. Before we move on, anybody have anything to add at this point?"

Silence. Eleven pairs of eyes glanced at Chelsea. They all knew what was coming next.

Why, Lord? Why can't I change my vote? As soon as she sat in her chair an hour ago, she'd sensed God's strong leading to stand firm. She could not understand it. Surely she wasn't hearing God right. Why would he send her a vision about Kerra in danger, only to leave her stuck in here?

To guide you to pray, came the answer.

No. Chelsea didn't want to pray. She was sick to death of praying day after day while she was stuck and unable to *do* anything. And while she was at it, she was sick to death of visions and being used by God and . . . everything.

"Well then." Clay turned his full attention upon her. "Ms. Adams, we now come back to you. You are still the only holdout."

Fear and weakness frothed hotly through Chelsea's veins. She could not do this. "Could I just have a quick break first?" she asked. When the reluctant nod came, she aimed a smile around the table, then headed for the bathroom.

She locked the door and sagged against it. *Please, God, just let me go home. I need to help Kerra! Please talk to me.*

She pressed her palms together and brought them to her lips. She waited for a different answer than she'd heard before, but none came. Truth was, she *did* still have doubts about exactly how the murder happened. If she changed her vote, she would not be following her conscience, only her fears.

So what? she cried silently. Who cared about Darren Welk and this trial? *Her* first concerns were for Kerra.

That wasn't true. Her first concern was doing what God asked her to do.

"No, it isn't!" she whispered aloud. "Or yes, it is, but I'm just hearing him wrong!"

She leaned her head back against the door, fighting with herself and fighting with God. For the life of her she could not understand why God would place her in this position.

Help me, Lord! I've had all I can take.

In the next moment a calm began to settle over her. Chelsea stood warily, still pressed against the door, afraid to believe too soon that God was covering her with peace. But as her breathing steadied, she sensed also a strength and focus of will. She gave herself over to it, letting it carry her along like a warm river current.

Thank you, Lord, thank you! Give me more!

The strength continued to flow through her. Chelsea reveled in it, filled with thankfulness. Then she began to pray. For Kerra, for herself, for Brett and Milt. For the deliberations she now needed to continue.

When she resumed her seat at the jury table two minutes later, she rested placid eyes momentarily upon the hard gaze of Tak.

"Thanks for that time," she said. "Okay. I'm hoping we can resolve this, as I know you all are, too."

MILT LEANED AGAINST A PILLAR in the quiet courthouse hallway, trying in vain to appear his normal, collected self. He'd have liked to have enjoyed a better night's sleep, but keeping Tracey calm had nearly worn him to a frazzle. She'd met him at the doorway the minute he got home last night, fuming and stomping about his report on Lynn Trudy. When had he found out? Why hadn't he told her right away? Had Lynn really called those jurors? Why would she? Tracey stormed around his town house until he was sure she was about to break something. Took him a while to figure out she wasn't mad at *him*. She was furious to think what Lynn might have done. "It doesn't make any sense!" she kept yelling, which matched Milt's sentiments exactly.

One thing seemed sure. Tracey had known nothing about those calls. Which seemed logical, the more he thought about it. Milt had lain awake in the night trying to run down possible scenarios of Lynn's involvement. The only thing he'd come up with is that the detectives must be chasing a red herring.

Milt shifted his position against the pillar. Vaguely his eyes cruised over the scattered groups that waited. The Three Fates perched on the nearest bench like a trio of vultures, greedily eyeing every bit of motion. "We'll sit here all week if we have to," one of them had told him. "Never missed a day yet. Not about to miss the ending." Brett and Kerra waited fitfully like a pair of chugging engines at the end of the farthest bench, away from everyone. Now and then a reporter sauntered in their direction, only to be turned away with an apparent "No comment." Numerous television reporters loitered impatiently, but Bill was the only cameraman present. The other teams were no doubt hanging around the news vans lining the curb outside the courthouse. Stan Breckshire paced the other side of the hall like a caged tiger. Erica's high heels clicked in her own pacing, although she tried to be more suave about the whole thing. At the moment Terrance Clyde was nowhere to be seen.

Milt's cell phone rang. Ron was on the line.

"I just called to check," his news director said. "It's on time."

Milt exhaled in relief.

"I'm sending Gary to keep an eye out. I've made sure he'll be able to get through security. He doesn't know what's up. But I've told him what to look for. And that his job depends on doing this right."

Gary was the station's newest eager reporter. "Okay. I'll be waiting."

Milt disconnected and checked his watch. Ten thirty. In a little over two hours, if things went according to plan, he'd call Tracey to the courthouse. How serendipitous that Lynn Trudy was presently indisposed, he thought. He wouldn't have to worry about keeping her away from Tracey in that short time span. On the other hand, it was a shame Lynn couldn't be around to see the show. Milt would have loved to see her face.

In sheer nervous energy he checked his watch again. He was almost home free. *Come on, jurors, just keep at it for two more hours. . . .*

FIFTY-SIX

Salad King Trial Goes to Jury

Rogelio read the story, then thwacked the paper angrily on the table. The article said the jury might decide a verdict as soon as today, and still Milt was doing nothing. Rogelio paced about the kitchen, muttering under his breath. Milt was not going to come through for him; he might as well face it. He was going to have to do something on his own. Brett Welk's words flitted through his mind: *"Don't trust that guy."* He should have listened.

The phone rang. Rogelio jumped for it, hoping it was Milt.

"Rogelio Sanchez?"

"Yeah."

"This is Enrico Delgadia. You and I have a little matter to settle."

Rogelio's knees nearly buckled.

Delgadia got right to the point. Janet Cline had "graciously" told him everything. She had assured him that Rogelio was wrong about the witness signatures. In light of her story, Rogelio had no recourse but to drop the whole foolish notion of trying to undo a seven-month-long adoption. And by the way, Delgadia was certain that his grandmother, Yolanda, and Kristin, the baby's mother, would be most grateful for him to make this "wise decision."

Fear rose in Rogelio with every word. What had he gotten his family into? His heart turned over, then hammered against his chest. Had Janet really turned against him?

She'd probably had no choice.

"As much as you want to protect your loved ones," Delgadia continued in his ice-cold tone, "understand that I will protect mine. This is far from a business matter. You have crossed the line into my personal life. I intend to resolve this *today*. I want that form that you have."

Rogelio was speechless. In desperation he slammed down the receiver.

Seconds later it rang again.

Mama Yolanda shuffled into the kitchen, her slippers making a soft *shoosh shoosh* against the tile. She took one look at his face and halted. *"Qui es, mijo?"*

He stared at the phone, its shrill rings jangling every nerve. What to do, what to do? If he ignored Delgadia, what might happen to Mama Yolanda or Kristin? It rang again and again until Rogelio's ears nearly burst with the noise. He snatched it up, then put it to his ear as if it were a snake.

"I make a very bad enemy, Rogelio." Delgadia's voice was deadly.

Rogelio breathed hard into the phone.

"I will only say this one time. Bring the form to my office right now. If you do not, I have any number of friends who would love to pay your old grandmother a visit."

Rogelio's eyes flew to Mama Yolanda. She gaped back at him, face draining white. He gritted his teeth. What was he supposed to do? This man, this *monster*, had his daughter.

"Do you hear me, Rogelio?"

"Uh." He swallowed. "Yeah."

"Do not make the mistake of going to the police. That would be the worst thing you could do. Understand?"

"Uh-huh."

"I'm waiting. You have fifteen minutes." Delgadia crunched the phone in his ear.

Rogelio threw down the receiver, shaking. *What should I do, what should I do?* He had to keep a cool head. *Think!*

He closed his eyes, blocking out his grandmother's questions. Could he choose between Mama Yolanda and his daughter? Could he just cave in, leave Roselita to be raised by this man?

Could he put his grandmother in terrible danger? Or Kristin? *God, are you there? What do I do?*

"Rogelio!" Mama Yolanda shook his shoulders. "What *is* it?"

His eyes flew open. His grandmother's face blurred before him. He had to get her out of there.

"Come with me, now!" He pushed her toward the door. "We have to leave!"

"Why?" She grabbed his shirt.

"Just go; there's no time!"

The form. Get the form! Rogelio flung himself down the hall and into his room, snatching it off his dresser. Then ran back to Mama Yolanda, pulled her outside, and practically shoved her into his car. He fired up the engine and took off like a madman, Mama Yolanda gripping the dashboard for dear life. *Help me, God; show me what to do!*

He started to head out of town, then realized he had to protect Kristin. He screeched to her house, flew up the steps, and banged on the door. No answer. He banged harder. An eternity passed before she opened the door, a pink robe tied around her waist, her hair disheveled. She stared at him.

"Kristin," he gasped, "I need you to come with me." A warning shot through his head. No. Delgadia didn't really want to hurt these women; he wanted the relinquishment form. Maybe the worst place they could be was with him. Rogelio rubbed his forehead hard, forcing himself to think. Suddenly he knew.

"No. I need you to take my grandmother and go to a friend's house and *stay* there, understand?"

"What—"

"Just *do* it; you're in danger! You know where you can go?"

She nodded, eyes widening. "Uh-huh."

"Okay. I'll get her into your car. Quick, go write the phone number where you'll be."

"I have to get dre—"

"You don't have time! Just go!"

He jumped back to Mama Yolanda and threw open the car door, hustling her into Kristin's Mustang. Kristin appeared a moment later, shoving a piece of paper into his hand. "It's about the baby, isn't it?" Fear stood in her eyes.

He nodded. "Do *not* leave your friend's house until I say so. Don't tell anybody where you are. And put your car in her garage."

"Rogelio, where are you going?" she wailed.

He pressed his lips. "I'll call you." He pushed her toward her car, then ran for his own. Kristin backed out of her driveway and drove off.

Rogelio raced as fast as he dared toward the freeway, hands gripping the wheel. Telling himself he was doing the right thing. Once he put that relinquishment form in the hands of somebody else, Delgadia would be powerless. *God help me through this. Help me protect us all.*

Despite the prayers, as he headed north on the freeway, doubts washed over him. What if Delgadia found the women? He could hurt them before he realized his threats were too late. Rogelio would never be able to forgive himself.

He had to draw Delgadia away from Salinas.

Rogelio neared an exit and impulsively veered off. He found the nearest gas station and ran for the pay phone. He fumbled for the phone book and looked up the number for Chef Mate. His finger trembled as he ran it down the page. *There.* He read the number silently, dropped a quarter into the phone, and dialed.

"Delgadia."

Rogelio drew a deep breath. This was it. He'd better make the man mad enough. "It's Rogelio. Your daughter's real father."

Venom seeped through the phone. "You are going to be so sorry."

He willed his voice to be steady. "You can have the paper you want. Come to the courthouse in Redwood City to get it. I'm going there to wait for the verdict on the trial."

"The—" Delgadia chuckled low in his throat. "I don't have time for your nonsense. What have we to do with that trial? You come here."

"No." Rogelio pressed a fist against the phone booth glass. "You know how many reporters are hanging around that trial, looking for a story? If you don't show up, I'm heading for the first one I see and telling him *everything.*"

"If you don't show up here," Delgadia hissed, "certain people in your life will be most unhappy."

"They're gone," Rogelio shot back. "No point in going after them or my house or anything else; it'll be too late! By the time I get through talking to reporters and the defense attorney for Darren Welk, there's no *way* you'll get to keep my baby!"

Dead silence dragged over the line. "Defense attorney? What's *that* supposed to mean?"

Now he'd done it. No turning back. "Shawna Welk's death sure was convenient for you, wasn't it."

Delgadia exhaled with slow precision. "You are very foolish, Rogelio. Very foolish indeed."

The line went dead. Rogelio pulled the receiver away from his ear and stared at it. Fear gnawed his stomach as he thought of Mama Yolanda and Kristin. He could hardly believe what he'd done. He told himself they were safe. Delgadia wouldn't know where to look. Besides, Delgadia would come after him. What choice did the man have?

God, please!

Breathing more prayers through gritted teeth, he dropped the receiver onto its base. Then he ran back to his car and headed north toward Redwood City.

FIFTY-SEVEN

The calmness in the jury room hadn't lasted ten minutes. Chelsea found herself right back where she was the night before, with eleven jurors in various stages of frustration and anger, all of them doing their best to change her mind.

"I do not understand your reasons, Chelsea." Even Sylvia looked peeved. "We've gone over the buried blouse thing five times now, and every time we come to the same conclusion. Okay. Maybe Brett had a part in hiding the blouse. But *no one* other than Darren Welk could have killed Shawna."

"You don't understand her reason because she doesn't *have* one," Tak put in. "I'm telling you, this is some sort of religious thing with her."

"How about addressing *me*, Tak." Chelsea's voice was level but cold. "I'm right here."

Help me, God; help me hang on.

"Wait a minute, everybody." Clay hovered over the table like a vulture, his neck cocked at an angle toward Chelsea. "Ms. Adams. Doesn't look like any of us is going to change our mind. You stand alone against everyone else on this jury, and because of where you stand, we are going nowhere. Unless you can really imagine changing all our minds, I suggest you rethink your opinion."

Chelsea searched for a response.

"Do you think you can change our minds?"

"I . . . I don't know. I'm not really looking at it like that. I'm more looking for you all to convince me beyond the doubts I have."

"What doubts do you have?" Antonio flapped his large hand in the air. "Other than you think Brett wanted to cover up for his father. Hear the words—*cover up.* Meaning the dad did something that needed covering up."

For the next hour the jurors threw arguments at Chelsea, tempers mounting. Their voices collided with each other, leaving little room for Chelsea to answer. Soon she thought her mind would burst. Desperate prayers whipped through her head until they became one-word pleas. *Protection. Strength. Kerra! Milt. Brett.*

"I've had enough of this," Hesta snapped finally. "This is just getting us nowhere."

"Haven't we all had enough." Latonia glared daggers at Chelsea. Her red blush seemed to pulse right off her dark cheeks.

Weariness washed up Chelsea's throat and she fought to push it back down. What had happened to the peace that God had given her? How long did he expect this to go on?

"You know what I think?" Gloria declared. "I think we should go back to court and tell 'em we're hung." She skidded back her chair to stomp toward the water dispenser, furiously sweeping her hair behind her ears.

"Are you kidding?" Clay protested. "We've only been at this a full day now."

"So? We're not getting anywhere." Gloria snatched a paper cup.

Clay rested narrowed eyes upon Chelsea, then looked around the table. "You all don't want to do that, do you?"

Victor shook his head. "Won't matter if we do. The judge will be upset that we thought of giving up so easily. She'll only tell us to come back and try again."

"Maybe that's exactly what some of us need to hear," Tak said, sneering at Chelsea.

"I agree it hasn't been that long," Hesta said, her tone clipped. "But Gloria's right; we're not making any progress. I say we send the judge a message. Tell her it's eleven to one with Chelsea Adams as the holdout, and she'll give no reasonable explanation as to why."

Chelsea focused on her twisting fingers in her lap.

"What do you say to that?" Clay pressed her. "You think we should tell the judge what you're up to?"

Suddenly Chelsea had endured enough. She raised defiant eyes to his. "Go ahead if you want. But I don't see where that's going to get us. Instead of wasting your time trying to intimidate me, maybe we ought to stick to our discussion."

Henry Slatus exhaled in disgust. "What exactly *is* our discussion? What's it going to take to convince you?"

What do I say, Lord? I can't even clarify to myself what it will take!

The room settled into silence as they waited for her response. Chelsea stared at the table as if searching for an answer to appear written upon it. "What it all would have to come down to," she managed at length, "is Tracey's testimony. She's the key witness. She places herself at the beach, sees the footprints that are later washed away, and on and on. And I just ... maybe something isn't right about her testimony. After all, she stands to gain a great deal from a guilty verdict."

"We *know* that," Mike Bariston said with impatience. "But every part of her testimony has fit with evidence."

"Maybe not. Maybe we've missed something."

"Okay, fine, we've missed something." Clay wagged his head as if she'd taken his last ounce of strength. "What do you want to go over as we 'stick to our discussion'?"

Chelsea fidgeted with her pen. In the next moment an answer popped clearly into her head. "I want to hear her testimony again."

"We've got it all in our notes," Clay objected.

"No. I want to hear *her* words read back to us."

"How?" B. B. frowned.

Victor flexed his back tiredly. "We'd have to send word to the judge. She'd call everybody back into court and have the testimony read."

Clay considered Chelsea with half-closed lids. "How about this: We'll have the testimony read back. But if nothing *very specific* jumps out at you, you'll be left with no argument. You'll have to change your vote."

Chelsea felt a catch in her chest. *Is this what you want, Lord?* Surely it was. What other choice did she have?

"Agreed," she said.

A collective sigh rose from the jurors. Tak tossed his pen down and surveyed the ceiling.

"Okay," Clay declared. "Let's do it."

MAMA YOLANDA SAT ON the couch that was too soft for her back, ankles crossed, staring mindlessly at the television. She could barely think straight. A soap opera was playing in English. Kristin slumped in a chair to her left, wiggling a foot. Her eyes were glued to the TV, as if it were her only lifeline to the world. Still, Mama Yolanda knew she heard none of it. They were alone in the house. Kristin's young friend had scurried out the door an hour ago, headed for work. The girl's parents were nowhere to be seen. Yolanda guessed they worked on weekends, too.

Awkwardness hung between the two of them like a thick curtain. How to break through it? So many layers. Yolanda wanted to turn off the television, try to talk to Kristin. They both were scared to death, not knowing what was happening, waiting for the phone to ring with some news. Mama Yolanda's muscles felt as though they might snap at any moment.

She shut her eyes, wishing she could also shut her ears to the TV. Soon a stillness began to settle over her, the television voices fading until she heard them no more. *Rogelio. The trial.* These words overtook her, claimed all her thoughts. She focused on the sense within her, feeling it deepen, grow stronger. *Rogelio. The trial.* She must pray for them both as she never had before. *Now.*

She blinked open her eyes. Pushed her fists against the soft cushions and scooted her body forward. With effort she stood. Kristin looked at her questioningly.

"I go . . . ," Yolanda said in English, then pointed toward the kitchen with her chin.

"You want to eat?" Kristin asked.

Yolanda shook her head. "I pray, *mija*."

Kristin could not seem to answer that. Her lips parted and she nodded.

Yolanda made her way quickly to the kitchen table, pulled out a chair, and sank into it. Resting her elbows on the wood, laced fingers to her bent forehead, she began to pray.

TWELVE O'CLOCK. Milt jingled coins in his pocket, nerves frayed. Almost time. Thank God, the jury still huddled. Now they'd be breaking for lunch.

He was going to do it!

The courtroom door opened. A bailiff emerged and headed straight for the defense attorneys. Stan Breckshire immediately hustled over. Brett was on his feet in an instant. Milt's back straightened. Other reporters' heads snapped around. "What's going on?" two of them asked at once. The Three Fates got up, shuffling toward the bailiff to hear.

Milt hurried over. "What's up?" He hoped his voice didn't squeak.

Erica threw him an irritated look. "Not much. The jury wants to have some testimony read back."

"Now?"

"The judge is going to wait till after lunch." She turned to Terrance with a dramatic sigh. "I *hate* the waiting."

Milt's heart shriveled. *No!* Everyone would be in the courtroom at the wrong time. Who'd be able to jump to his aid if he needed it? Negative thoughts ping-ponged him right and left. He simply hadn't reasoned every scenario through. What had he been thinking? This plan was crazy from the start; it would never work. Besides, he didn't even know if he'd calculated right. What was he, an imbecile?

As everyone else moved in murmuring groups toward the escalator, he sank onto a bench next to Bill. Vaguely Milt registered the conversation between Brett and Kerra as they passed.

"Let's get in the car and drive somewhere," Brett said, sighing. "I'm tired of the places down Broadway."

Bill took one look at Milt's stricken face and shrugged. "It won't matter if they're all in court. If everything works, I'll be here."

"If everything works, you'll be *filming*."

"Yeah." He sniffed. "I'm gonna park the camera in the van and walk over to the coffeehouse for some lunch. Wanna come with me?"

"No." Milt rubbed his forehead. As if he could eat. Bill could afford to be calm; it wasn't *his* career on the line. "I'll get moving in a minute, stash my laptop in my car. Doesn't look like I can afford to have much baggage on me."

As Bill sauntered off, for no reason at all Milt thought of Chelsea Adams. At the moment he almost envied her faith. Right now he'd give practically anything to be a praying man.

FIFTY-EIGHT

Rogelio drove through Redwood City as fast as he dared. His head pounded from the constant flicking of his eyes to the rearview mirror. He'd seen no sign of Delgadia. Was that good or bad? Rogelio couldn't decide. He'd gotten perhaps a ten-minute lead on the man. He needed time to get his adoption paper into the proper hands. But then what? If Delgadia didn't come, where might he be? What would he be doing? What if coming here had been a terrible mistake?

Please, God, I'll do anything. Just protect Mama Yolanda and Kristin.

Rogelio checked the clock on his dash. Five after twelve. He had little time. What if everybody had scattered for lunch?

Fingers clenching the wheel, he turned into the parking garage. It was nearly empty. On the other side, near the pedestrian walkway that led toward the courthouse, two people were approaching a car. Rogelio's eyes widened. Brett Welk and that blond girl! Rogelio's foot punched the gas. His tires squealed over the pavement as he lurched the car into a nearby parking space. Brett and the girl turned abruptly, startled. Rogelio grabbed his adoption paper and leaped from the car.

"Stop! Wait!" He pounded toward them, heart beating in his throat. "I have to show you this. I have to show you this now!" He thrust the paper into Brett's hands, words spilling from his tongue. "You need to take it to your lawyer before Delgadia comes. *If* Delgadia comes. If he gets hold of it, I won't have proof to get Roselita. And Milt said it would help your dad. Please help me."

Brett ogled him. "What—"

"Just go!" Rogelio shouted. "We don't have much time."

"Go where? I have no idea what you're talking about."

Rogelio's hands futilely chopped the air.

"Just calm down," Brett commanded, grabbing Rogelio's arm until he held still. "Now what?"

Rogelio's explanations tumbled out. Twice Brett had to slow him down. As their meaning began to dawn on Brett, his mouth sagged open. The blond pressed a hand to her lips. Brett stared in shock at the adoption paper. "See, that signature's forged." Rogelio punched a finger on Janet Cline's name. "And Tracey wasn't a witness, like this says she was."

"Milt Waking *knew* about this?" the girl breathed. "All week?"

Brett's features blackened. "Terrance could have done something if he'd known. Now it's too late." His fingers made dents in the paper. For a moment Rogelio thought he would crumple it like trash. "I swear I'll kill Milt Waking."

"It's not too late; it *can't* be." If it were too late, what would happen to Roselita? Would no one even care? "We have to *go!*" Rogelio jerked toward the street, the hairs on his neck bristling. "Delgadia could be here any minute."

"I don't think so," Brett mumbled, still gawking at the paper.

"Yes, he will. He will come!" Rogelio threw himself in Brett's face. He could not bear to think where else Delgadia might be. Brett abruptly pushed him away, then locked eyes with him, the lines on his forehead unraveling as if he realized Rogelio's plight for the first time. His fingers loosened from the paper and it fluttered to the ground. The girl picked it up.

"Okay, you're right." Brett's voice sounded shallow. "We both just need to ... Right now I can't even *think* straight." He blew out air, collecting himself. "Okay. My dad's attorneys have probably left for lunch. We'll have to find them."

Rogelio's head nodded as if it were barely attached to his neck. The girl held out the adoption paper to him. He folded it twice and stuck it into his jeans pocket. With another glance back toward the street, he turned alongside Brett and the girl to head for the courthouse.

Delgadia has to come. Just give us a few minutes, God, then please let him come.

Rogelio slid his fingers into his pocket, double-checking that the paper was secure. He heard a car on the street and spun around, nerves tingling. The other two halted, watching. The car drove by. Rogelio exhaled in wild relief. "Come on," Brett urged. In the instant that Rogelio turned again, he heard Brett inhale sharply. Brett and the girl stopped abruptly and Rogelio almost knocked into them. His eyes whipped to the walkway and his lungs curdled.

A figure materialized in the open doorway.

THE JURY ROOM PULSED with grim expectation as each person picked up a lunch bag. Chelsea knew she could not eat. Jurors talked in small groups, their voices low. Most of them sat at the table. Some walked around, glad to be on their feet for a few minutes. Now and then someone emitted a nervous chuckle. She stood back from the table, feeling their antagonism. They had her now and they knew it, reveled in it. Bitterness swept over her as she imagined the next few hours. What if she heard nothing new in Tracey's testimony? She'd have to switch to a guilty vote, and they'd go on to discuss which crime Darren Welk was guilty of—second-degree murder or less. What if she couldn't agree with them on that either? Right now she couldn't begin to sort out those questions. What if today ended with no agreement? Would they take Sunday off? How long would this go? Monday? Tuesday?

God, what about Kerra all this time? Please protect her!

A pang of guilt struck Chelsea. What was *wrong* with her? How could she be thinking at all about herself after the vision she had that morning? She needed to be praying, not worrying.

"You going to eat?" B. B. motioned to the last bag sitting on the table. Tak and Hesta fastened Chelsea with frosty stares.

"No. Thank you," she said. "I think I'll just take my chair over there for a while and . . . think."

"You do that," Latonia commented just loud enough for her to hear.

It was a nasty remark that Chelsea knew she should ignore. But it shot right through her. *Dear God, my nerves are such a wreck. I'm never going to make it through this day.*

Wordlessly Henry slid her chair away from the table. He would not look her in the eye. She grabbed the back of it and dragged it near a corner, angling it away from the table. She hoped she could clear her mind of imagining the glares at her back.

She sat down and stared sightlessly at the wall. Without warning another vision, white-hot and intense, seared itself on her brain. Kerra. The man with the scar. A knife. The vision sizzled with urgency, imminence.

Chelsea raked in a breath and held it. Fear exploded within her, and every muscle in her body locked. Her thoughts leaped wildly, then flattened. For a second she could think no rational thought.

Pray now! The knowledge seemed to split her skull. *Pray!*

The jury room, the trial, the smell of sandwiches and chips, all faded as she jerked clasped hands to her mouth and launched into desperate prayer.

THE MAN STEPPED FROM bright sunlight into the garage. Brett processed the suit, the briefcase, the familiar, hated face. Rage, pure and frothing, surged through his veins. His body kicked into motion before he realized it. All the days, the sleepless nights, all the moments of guilt and fear and pain, propelled him in fury toward Milt Waking.

"Brett, no!" Kerra cried.

With a growl in his throat, Brett leaped the last few steps. He let his fist fly, catching the surprised reporter squarely on the jaw. "Ungh!" Milt lurched sideways, briefcase spinning out of his hand. Brett jumped for him, grabbed him by the lapels.

"Get out of the way," he heard Rogelio cry to Kerra. From the corner of his eye he saw her fade back.

Milt slapped a palm against Brett's chin and shoved. Brett's head snapped back but he hung on.

"Wha—" Milt vainly tried to wrench free. Blood smeared the corner of his mouth. Rogelio darted in to help Brett, face contorted with his own anger. He caught one of Milt's arms and pulled it back.

"You sent my dad to jail," Brett said, seething.

The three of them yelled at once, their voices intermingling, bouncing off the walls of the parking garage.

"I don't know what you're talking about—"

"All you care about is getting some story—"

"You lied about helping me—"

Milt threw a strong punch into Brett's temple. Dark spots danced before Brett's eyes. He heard Kerra shouting at them to stop. Rogelio emitted a string of curses.

"Wait!" Milt cried. "Listen to me!"

"I've listened to you *enough*." Rogelio ground the words through his teeth as he swung at Milt's head. The reporter ducked.

A car's wheels squeaked against the pavement of the garage. Brett barely registered the sound. Milt backed up toward the wall, flailing at both of them wildly. "Let me—" Rogelio's fist shot out, blocked by Milt's upraised arm. Brett heard the car screech to a halt, engine running. Kerra cried out. Milt jumped backward, puffing. "I'm-going-to-get-your-dad-off!" The words streamed from his bleeding mouth. "I'm-going-to-get-your—"

Kerra wailed. The panicked sound kicked through Brett's head. He and Rogelio swung around at the same time. Milt stilled.

Brett caught sight of a nightmare, and a trap door opened in his stomach. His mind reeled. *This isn't happening, this isn't happening!* His knees weakened and he stumbled. Then pulled himself upright. Enrico Delgadia hulked behind Kerra, pressed against her back, one beefy arm viselike around her chest. Kerra's arms had frozen midair, fingers spread. Her eyes were bugged and wild. Delgadia held a knife at the base of her throat.

FIFTY-NINE

Tracey flipped disconsolately through television channels in Milt's living room. Cartoons, a sitcom in Spanish, documentaries about animals and World War II. Friday was bad enough, but *nothing* was worth watching on Saturdays.

She threw down the remote and pushed off from the leather couch to pace the room. Oatmeal. Everything was colored oatmeal in here. Oatmeal carpet and walls and furniture. She shouldn't complain. The town home was a million times nicer than her apartment. And sleeping next to Milt had been like a dream. But this news about her aunt, plus waiting for the verdict, was about to drive her crazy. As if she hadn't waited months already for the trial. Then who knew how long she'd have to wait for the death certificate and the insurance money. Days? A week? Maybe longer? And that's if Darren Welk was convicted.

She couldn't begin to think what would happen if he was not. She could not allow herself to even remotely imagine it. What would she do? Go to Brazil anyway? With what money?

Besides, she hadn't sent an email to Brazil in days and still didn't care to. Why was she so narrow-mindedly focused on going there anyhow? If she got away with everything, got the money, maybe she should just cut and run. She had the whole world to see.

Could she do that? She stopped near a bookcase, idly fingering the spine of a novel. Go somewhere totally on her own, without knowing anyone? Even with two million dollars, Tracey had to admit the thought scared her to death.

She slid the novel out, pushed it back. Slid it out, pushed it back. Or for that matter, she thought, she could stay right here. Who said she had to leave California? She could afford a great place in the Bay Area. Near Milt.

Her hand stilled. Maybe she could even live with Milt.

She swung away from the bookcase and went toward the kitchen, hope rising. That's what she'd do! Move in with Milt. They could buy an incredible house. Just think of the vacations they could take with all her money! She could buy him presents, buy herself a new car, a fancy wardrobe. They'd go to parties and swank restaurants. She'd *be* somebody.

As for her lying, deceitful aunt . . . Tracey smacked her palm against the kitchen tile. Could she have called those jurors? What could she have been thinking? Tracey knew one thing. Ever since the trial had started, Lynn had proven just as bad as her sister. Manipulative and selfish. If Lynn had called those jurors, Tracey hoped they stuck her in jail for a long time.

How nice to be happily rid of her mother *and* her aunt.

Tracey wandered back to the couch. She sank once again onto its buttery leather, telling herself everything was going to work out. Milt had said they'd find Darren guilty.

Guilty. One little word. And she could finally start living.

"CHELSEA."

Vaguely she heard Sylvia's impatient whisper. She ignored it as prayers streamed through her head. *Protect Kerra, Lord; don't let this happen. . . .*

"Chelsea!"

"I'm sorry, I can't talk now."

Be the Dread Champion you promised you would be. . . .

"You have to talk now."

Chelsea shook her head. "No, please."

Send your angels. Send someone to help. . . .

"Listen to me."

Distractedly she turned away from Sylvia, eyes still squeezed shut. *Use people around her, use anyone—*

"You've got to *listen!*" Sylvia's insistent voice cut through her prayers. The woman shook her by the wrists until her eyes flew open. Sylvia stooped before her, face inches from her own. "You shouldn't be sitting here, praying like some fanatic," Sylvia hissed. "Don't you see what trouble you're causing? You've already got enough enemies here."

Chelsea pulled out of her grasp. "It doesn't matter; something's happening and I have to pray!"

"What's happening?"

She tossed her head. *God, please guard Kerra—*

"What's happening?" Sylvia shook her again, harder.

Panic sucked up Chelsea's veins. What was this woman trying to do? "Please just give me a minute." *Do anything, God; send a mira—*

"Chelsea, *stop.*"

"No!" Chelsea burst. "Go away!" Her voice filled the jury room. Suddenly she realized all other noise had ceased. She could feel the jurors gawking as if she'd gone mad.

So what? she cried silently. *I am mad! I'm going stark, raving mad, God. Kerra's out there and I'm in here with these people. You're asking too much of me; I can't do this anymore!* A sob caught in Chelsea's throat. She jumped from her seat and ran for the bathroom, then locked the door and hunched against it, forehead shoved against the cool wood.

Lord, I'm sorry. I just . . . No matter what happens in here, please just protect Kerra. . . .

COLD PINPRICKS RIPPED ACROSS Brett's body. He could not move. He could only stare at Delgadia's scarred hand, holding the knife against

Kerra's pulsing neck. In the sudden silence of the garage, Brett heard blood pounding in his ears.

"Sorry to break up your altercation," Delgadia spat.

Brett could feel rage burning off the man. Delgadia was not one to be taunted, especially in his private affairs. Rogelio had made a ghastly mistake.

"This is real simple." Delgadia's eyes narrowed into slits. "I want the adoption paper; then I'm gone."

Kerra's fingers jerked. Tiny sounds spilled from her lips until Brett thought he would rip apart. *God, help us!* Frantically he searched within himself for strength. Somehow he found his voice. "Delgadia." He swallowed on a dry throat. "*Think.* Have you gone crazy?"

"This isn't about you, Brett."

"Yes, it is!" he shouted. "You touch Kerra, it's about me."

Delgadia's eyelids flickered. "If you care about her, then you understand what a desperate man I am."

Desperation Brett knew. It catapulted through his limbs like a pinball, smacking at reason. Desperation could drive Delgadia to do anything. Briefly he imagined all three of them rushing the man. Could they get to him in time? They couldn't give that paper up; his dad *needed* it.

How long did it take to slice someone's throat?

"Give him the paper," he heard himself command Rogelio. The kid looked sick. With shaking fingers Rogelio pulled it from his pocket.

Delgadia's car door gaped open. He dragged Kerra away from it, their shoes scuffling against the floor. "Place it on the seat," he said brusquely.

His face stricken, Rogelio looked from the paper, to the knife at Kerra's throat, to the paper. "I . . ."

"Give it to him!" Milt barked.

Rogelio shot him a look of pure hatred.

"Do it *now*." Delgadia pressed his arm tighter around Kerra. She whimpered. The sound unleashed craziness in Brett's head. He snatched the paper from Rogelio's hand and flung himself toward the car.

"Here! Take it!" He threw the folded paper inside, then hunched facing Delgadia, breathing hard. "Now let her go."

"Back off."

Brett slid toward the front of the car.

"More. All the way over there." Delgadia jerked his chin toward Rogelio and Milt. Brett backed across to them, heart skidding in his chest. When he was close enough to touch Rogelio, Delgadia flicked the knife away from Kerra's throat and shoved her in the opposite direction. With a cry she stumbled and fell. Delgadia dove into the car, slammed the door, and revved it around the corner, tires squealing. Brett flew toward Kerra. As he reached her, he heard Delgadia speed out of the garage and away. His vision blurred as he pulled Kerra, limp and trembling, to his chest.

She clung to him, then erupted in sobs.

SIXTY

Milt wiped the blood from his mouth with the back of his hand. In a half daze he heard Kerra's crying and Rogelio's garbled moaning about what to do now. Milt's jaw throbbed; his clothes were a mess. The two rage-filled lunatics here wanted to kill him. Brett was preoccupied, but any minute now Rogelio could snap out of his whining and come gunning for him again. Milt's laptop was probably cracked in two in his briefcase. Which was ... Milt searched the ground. He spotted it near the open doorway and shuffled over to pick it up. The movement racked his arm with pain.

Most of all, he was running out of time.

He checked his watch. Twelve twenty. He stared mindlessly at a piece of litter on the dusty floor, trying to get his mind into gear. Why had he even come in here?

Laptop. Car.

Milt breathed deep enough to hurt his lungs. Then dragged himself to his car. *The cell phone!* The thought jolted him into clarity. What if it was broken? *Oh, please, please, no.* With scrabbling fingers he pulled it from his briefcase. The lights were still on. Relief flooded him. He punched a few buttons, automatically dialing Ron's direct line. As the phone rang, Milt kept his eyes on Rogelio. The kid was pacing, hands gripping his head.

"Where have you been?" Ron demanded. "I've been trying to call you."

Milt looked down at his suit. He wondered if blood had dripped on his white shirt collar. "Indisposed."

"Well, this is a fine time to be indisposed. We checked again ten minutes ago. It's going to be early."

"Early!" Milt sagged against his car, frustration and fear welling up in his throat. "What are you trying to *do* to me?"

"Hey, I don't schedule these things!" Ron exhaled loudly. "What's going on with you? Is something wrong?"

Milt almost laughed. "Are you kidding? I'm having the best day of my life." He glared at his right hand, flexing the fingers. They hurt like crazy. Brett Welk had a hard head.

Kerra's sobs were dying down. Brett still held her as if she were going to fly away.

Focus, Milt, focus!

He pushed away from the car, straightening. "Okay," he said tersely. "What time?"

"Twelve thirty."

His chin dropped. He looked a wreck. He *felt* a wreck. How could he ever pull this off? And that's if he was right to begin with.

"You there?"

"Yeah."

Rogelio yelled Milt's name, his arm raised, finger pointing. Angst and fright and the need to blame pulsed across his face.

"Gotta go; call me." Milt snapped off the phone and slid it into his shirt pocket, which was amazingly intact. He threw his briefcase into the car and locked the doors. Then collected his wits. Suddenly he knew what to do.

"Rogelio, you have to listen to me." He moved forward slowly, as if he were approaching a bomb about to explode. "You don't need that paper. I promised you I'd help you get your baby. And you will. *If* you and Brett and Kerra will do exactly what I tell you."

THE URGENCY DISAPPEARED. Chelsea felt it lift from her shoulders as if she'd sloughed off a heavy blanket. Weakly she leaned against the bathroom door and waited. Opened her eyes, fixed her gaze on the tile floor. She searched within herself, trying to feel the fear, the oppression. She couldn't allow herself to be wrong.

Lord, what's happened? Has the danger passed?

She waited, her unseeing gaze traveling the floor.

Nothing.

She breathed out slowly, bringing a shaking hand to her forehead. *Thank you, God. Thank you, thank you.* She lacked the strength to pray any more than that.

Chelsea could stand no longer. She sank down upon the closed toilet lid, feeling her ankles tremble. Her muscles felt soft, like cooling melted wax. Minutes ticked by as she rubbed her temples, allowed herself to breath, collected the scattered marbles of her emotions. She flexed her back and her spine cracked.

She knew she would have to go back out into the jury room. It wasn't fair for her to be occupying one of only two bathrooms. Besides, she'd need to face the jurors. The trial wasn't over yet.

Chelsea pulled to her feet and surveyed herself blearily in the mirror. She looked as if she'd been hit by a truck. Well, she *had*.

Lord, help me. Please.

Five minutes later she emerged from the bathroom. All conversation stopped, every eye warily upon her as if she were schizophrenic. Hesta raised her chin, her expression screaming disdain. Tak sat with arms folded, and Latonia openly sneered. Clay broke the silence with a foreman's bristling resolve.

"Are you going to be able to continue? Or is all our work going to end in a mistrial?"

She locked eyes with him. Only then did she realize her utter calm. After what she'd just been through, what could these people possibly do to her?

"I am fine," she replied levelly. "No mistrial here. Sylvia, please forgive me."

She walked to the table and reached for an unclaimed water bottle near Antonio. "May I?"

He picked it up with reluctance and handed it to her, making sure their fingers didn't touch.

TWELVE FORTY. MILT DRUMMED nervous fingers against Brett's car. He felt like a fast-talking salesman after the spiel that had gushed from him in the last ten minutes. At least nobody had hit him again. Brett's tanned face had faded to a pasty mud, save for his purpling left temple. He'd hardly been able to absorb Milt's words. Understandable, thought Milt, given the events crammed into the last half hour. Kerra seemed equally stunned. Her tears had dried, leaving tracks through her makeup. Mascara smeared under her eyes. Only Rogelio looked the better for wear. With Milt's explanations, wild as they sounded, the kid's hope had returned. He nearly trembled with anticipation.

Milt gazed at each of them, then felt his jaw. What a motley foursome they made. This was too bizarre.

"It may not work," he said for the third time. "I've done my best. I've done everything to make it happen. But the next part's out of my control."

"It's not out of God's," Kerra blurted.

Milt gave her a look. *Oh no, not another one. Wouldn't Aunty be proud.*

Brett nodded sagely. So did Rogelio. Milt turned his head from one to the other, mouth twisting with surprise. What *was* this, a conspiracy?

"Yeah, well, if God doesn't come through, don't kill me, all right?" He ran a hand down his tie, then puffed out air. "Trust me, you won't have to."

"If this doesn't work," Brett retorted, "if my father's found guilty and has to wait months for another trial because you wanted your exclusive story"—he sneered the words—"you'd better watch your back."

Milt tensed. For a minute he thought Brett would take another swing. Kerra wrapped both hands around Brett's upper arm and tugged gently until he calmed down.

The cell phone rang. All four of them jumped.

"Answer it, answer it!" Rogelio's eyes nearly popped out of his head.

Milt yanked it from his pocket and punched a button, heart turning over. "Yeah."

"I think we got a hit." Ron sounded breathless.

His eyes closed, relief washing over him once again.

"What, what?" Rogelio cried.

Milt turned away, cramming the phone against his ear. "Tell me." He listened, envisioning Ron's description. "How long does Gary think the line will take?"

"Not long. Maybe twenty minutes."

Calculations ran through his mind. Twenty minutes there, plus another twenty . . .

"Everything all right there?" Ron asked.

Milt swung back to his trio of cohorts and gave them a thumbs-up. Kerra gasped. "The jury's going to be in the courtroom, listening to testimony," he told Ron. "And you wouldn't believe the folks I've recruited to help me."

SIXTY-ONE

In Milt's kitchen Tracey filled a glass with ice water from the refrigerator, television droning in the background. The phone rang. She almost dropped the glass. Her heart tripping over itself, she slowly reached out to place the glass on the tile. Three sideways steps and she stood at the counter where the phone lay. She stared at it, reading the i.d. number. It was Milt's cell phone.

Another ring pealed through the kitchen. She snatched up the receiver. "Hello."

"It's Milt. Come down right now. The jury's in."

She sucked in a breath. Suddenly she felt light-headed. "I'll be there."

In less than a minute she pulled out of the town home parking lot and onto the street.

ROGELIO USED MILT'S CELL phone to quickly call Kristin as they walked to the courthouse. His heart constricted at the sound of her voice. "Are you okay? And Mama Yolanda?"

"We're fine. But I'm getting really tired of this, Rogelio. You have to tell me what's going on."

"Just stay there. I don't think you'll have to wait much longer."

"What's *happening?*"

"Kristin, I'll tell you everything. But I don't have time now. Just promise me you'll stay there and wait for my next call."

She made an impatient sound in her throat.

"*Please.*"

"Okay, okay."

"Call you soon." He punched off the phone and handed it to Milt. The reporter's shirt was pulled out, his tie all out of whack, and his hair a mess. "You'd better stop in the bathroom," he said. "You look like someone's just made your day."

ONE O'CLOCK.

Milt had gotten strange looks from the guard and deputy sheriff who'd been assigned the unusual task of running courthouse security on a Saturday. Once inside the bathroom, he'd managed to clean himself up remarkably well, save for the bruise on his jaw. At least no blood had stained his shirt. He almost wished the bruise were darker. It would only heighten the drama on camera. He touched the area and winced.

He hung back as other reporters shuffled through the courtroom door, followed by the Three Fates. Stan Breckshire appeared on the escalator. The attorney bounced off the top step and skittered inside. *Oh, buddy,* Milt thought, *you think you're nervous now.* He peeked into the courtroom. Terrance Clyde and Erica Salvador already hovered about the defense table. Chairs squeaked and papers rustled as people settled. A bailiff escorted Darren Welk to his seat, then walked to the courtroom door. "You coming in?"

Milt angled his bruised jaw away from the man. "Maybe later."

"All right." The bailiff closed the door.

The hall fell eerily quiet. Only he and Rogelio remained. Brett and Kerra huddled in the tiny conference room at the far end of the hall, the door slightly ajar. Best for Brett to keep out of sight, as his presence might be too intimidating for certain people. Milt wished he weren't so far away, but at least he was well hidden. No doubt he'd cover the distance in a heartbeat if he was needed.

Amazing, Milt thought, how all these pieces were falling into place.

Now, where was Bill?

Rogelio flexed his jaw, casting expectant glances toward the escalator. The kid was making Milt even more nervous. "Go sit on a bench on the other side, with your back to the courtroom," Milt told him. "Lean forward, stare at the floor like you're waiting for somebody." Rogelio nodded, then hitched himself away.

Bill appeared a moment later, lugging his equipment. "Channel Five's still around out front," he said. "Guy asked what on earth I thought I'd be filming. I said, 'Not a thing. But Milt Waking thinks he owns me.'"

Milt managed a wan smile. His heart thumped around in his chest. Tracey should be here. He'd figured out how to keep her from going into the courtroom. She was so pliable, really, for all she'd done. Half mush melon.

He checked his watch. Two minutes after one.

His cell phone rang and he nearly dropped it in answering. "Milt here."

"Everything's clear," Ron said. "You've got about twenty minutes."

CHELSEA FELT THE BRIMMING tension of every jury member as she followed Gloria Nuevo into the courtroom. The calm she'd experienced twenty minutes ago had faded, leaving her nerves worn and prickling. Her ankles felt weak as she lowered herself into her seat.

Brett and Kerra were absent.

Fresh fear bubbled in Chelsea's stomach. Did this mean anything? Maybe they were just at lunch. Maybe they didn't think hearing testimony all over again was important.

That couldn't be it, she argued with herself. Surely Brett would think *anything* occurring in the trial significant.

Oh, Lord, I thought the danger had passed. Please let her be all right!

Judge Chanson entered. Chelsea wrenched her thoughts away from Kerra as everyone rose, then sat again. She *had* to listen to this testimony. Surely the Lord would show her something. If not, she prayed for peace about changing her vote. *Give me wisdom, God; let me hear with your ears.* Judge Chanson examined the jury with intensity, trying to read their expressions. She wouldn't have to try very hard, Chelsea thought fleetingly, given the black looks on most of their faces.

Chelsea's eyes pulled back to the spectators and reporters. She couldn't stop thinking about Kerra. Then she realized with a start that Milt Waking was also gone. The knowledge snagged her breath. No way would he choose to miss any piece of news about this case.

Unless more exciting news was happening somewhere else.

She dropped her gaze to her lap, considering. That had to be it. Slowly understanding seeped through her. Hadn't God told her that he'd chosen to work through Milt? Hadn't he warned her that when she could not act herself, her prayers would be critical? Hadn't God clearly led her to pray for Milt and Brett and Kerra? God was working. While her emotions had swayed her this way and that, while she'd alternately prayed and complained, God had been at work.

Thank you, God, thank you. I never should have doubted, not for a minute.

"All right," Judge Chanson announced. "I understand that you want to hear certain parts of Tracey Wilagher's testimony. We have brought up the part of the record that you're interested in, and the clerk will now read it to you." The judge's eyes caught Chelsea's, then blinked away.

The clerk began. "'I'd been sick with the flu,'" she read from her computer without emotion. "'I'd gotten it three days before, and after a day of having a fever, I'd finally gone to bed. . . .'"

TRACEY SENT HER PURSE through security and scurried up the escalator. Everything seemed so deadly quiet. Spooky almost. As she neared the second floor, she spotted Milt outside the courtroom. Only two other people were on the entire floor—a man with a television camera, and some guy she barely noticed, sitting on a bench. Milt met her halfway in the hall.

"Are they already inside?" she huffed. Her stomach felt tied in knots.

Milt squeezed her shoulder. "Yes, but they haven't decided on a verdict after all. They just wanted to hear some testimony read back."

Tracey's lungs deflated like a punctured balloon. "Oh." She rubbed her forehead. "Oh."

"I'm sorry," Milt said soothingly.

She surveyed him wearily. He seemed a little on edge himself, running his fingers up and down his tie. It took her a moment to register the large bruise on his jaw. "What happened to you?" She reached out her hand.

Milt pulled back before she could touch him. "My clumsy assistant over there." He indicated with his head. "Bonked me with his camera."

"Oh," she said again. Tracey half-turned away, staring mindlessly at the floor. She must sound so stupid, but her brain would hardly work.

"Look, since you're here, you might as well stay." Milt put an arm around her. "You look exhausted." He urged her into motion, guiding her to a seat near the far end of the hall. "If you stay down here, when folks come out of the courtroom, you won't be bothered."

"Maybe I should see what's going on."

"Nothing but boring testimony." His lips twisted in a half smile. "Or believe me, I'd be in there myself."

"Okay." She slumped on the bench.

"You know I can't stay with you. I'll go talk to my cameraman. Just sit tight now. If I hear anything, I'll let you know."

As he moved away, she saw him check his watch.

STAN FORCED HIMSELF BACK in his chair, feigning calm, wondering what the problem was with Tracey's testimony. What had he missed in his questioning?

As the clerk's voice droned through the courtroom, his eyes roamed over the jury. Something was definitely up. Tak's typically stoic expression was laced with anger. Latonia's jaw was set, her forehead creased. Henry sat straight in his seat, arms crossed. Clay leaned forward, head ducked, looking up at the clerk.

Clay's the foreman, Stan thought.

His gaze slid to Chelsea. She looked worn, beat up. The thought hit him like a brick over the head: she was fighting the jury. Stan couldn't be sure she was alone. Maybe she had one or two on her side. But if she did, he certainly couldn't pick them out based on their body language.

Did she know something?

For the first time since he'd first laid eyes on Chelsea Adams, fear of her supposed ability flashed through his veins. What if she really could see things? What kind of damage could she do?

Just as suddenly the fear vanished. *Nothing,* he told himself, *that's what.* If Chelsea Adams could "see" anything with divine knowledge, she'd see Darren Welk killing his wife. Besides, this God's power stuff was ridiculous. The strange mix of rationality and emotion—that's what ruled the courtroom. Ruled the world, for that matter.

Purposely Stan fixed his eyes upon the clerk, even as his back muscles tightened and anxiety edged down his right arm.

ONE TEN. MILT SWEATED bullets as he walked away from Tracey. He felt soaked in his suit, his shirt plastered to the white T-shirt underneath. His eyes swung to Rogelio, who faced the opposite direction, neck and shoulders arched. The kid looked like a cat ready to pounce.

He angled over to Bill, who was sprawled on a bench with an arm on the back. "How much time?" Bill asked in a barely audible voice.

"Maybe ten minutes?"

Bill smirked. "Too bad I can't use lights. A dark picture won't do much to show off your injury."

"Yeah, well. You ought to see the other guy."

"Really. Didn't think you had it in you, Waking."

One eleven.

Milt was about to split a gut. Soon it would be all or nothing. A rocket to the moon or the end of his career.

He glanced back at Tracey. She was staring at her lap. What a great move, getting her to sit all the way down there. All the more floor space for luring. Plus she wasn't that far from the conference room. *That's it, babe, just sit. Just play decoy for ten more minutes....*

"Bill, go over and talk to her, keep her occupied. Sit so you can keep an eye on me. I'm going to watch the bottom floor."

"Right, Boss." Bill spoke in a gruff voice, like some Mafia underling.

Milt ignored him. He waited until Bill had settled next to Tracey. Then he sidled toward the top of the escalator and glued his gaze to the bored security duo below.

CAUTIOUSLY BRETT EASED THE conference room door farther open and peeked out. His temple throbbed where Milt had punched him. A minute ago he and Kerra had heard voices close by—Milt and Tracey. Now he heard another man's voice. There was Tracey. Sitting on a bench in profile, not twenty feet away, talking to Milt's cameraman.

He drew back inside.

"Is she there?" Kerra mouthed.

He nodded.

Kerra bit her lip, then hugged him, quivering with nervous energy. He held her tightly, resting his cheek on the top of her head.

Brett could barely grasp what was happening. He'd so quickly assumed that his father was guilty, thinking he'd pieced together the events of that night on the beach. Obviously, his father had believed the same, the glaring evidence filling in the missing elements of a drunken memory. In the last hour, Brett had gone through enough emotions to last a lifetime. Anger, relief, and elation still swirled in his chest like brittle leaves in a dust storm. To think of the months of guilt he'd felt! All those times he'd beat himself up for burying that blouse. All the sick remorse over his dad's refusal to point the finger at his stupid cover-up, just to keep him out of jail. Kerra was right—their actions, however skewed, proved they loved each other. If this worked out, Brett declared to the heavens, he'd shout to the whole world what God had done for him. And for his father.

Kerra drew back and gave him a weak smile. His heart lurched at the concern on her face. She'd been through so much herself, yet all her thoughts now focused on him.

God, thank you for her most of all.

"Promise me something," he whispered. "Promise that I can visit you every month in Kansas."

Her eyes filled with tears. "I can't leave you."

"Yes, you can. Your teaching commitment's only for a year. After that I won't let you out of my sight again."

The meaning of his words played across her face. She wrapped her arms around him once again, fingers pressing into his back.

MILT SPOTTED HER. Stepping through the security scanner, carrying nothing. Whatever she'd brought through customs at the airport had probably been left in a waiting taxi. Coal black hair, cut short. The face was still lean and tanned but far different from her photographs. Jeans and a long-sleeved navy shirt, tucked in at the waist. Nothing to make her stand out. She could have been anybody.

His heart slammed against his chest. He jerked his head at Bill down the hall, then at Rogelio. *Easy, easy; don't spook Tracey.* Bill drew himself up, sliding his fingers into place over his camera. Vaguely Milt heard his voice drift down the hallway. "Nice talking to you." He started ambling toward Milt. Rogelio caught Milt's eye and came to attention like a soldier hot for battle.

Air snagged in Milt's throat. His entire body shook. He forced himself to look off into the distance as if deep in thought. In his peripheral vision he saw the woman ask the deputy sheriff a question. He pointed to the second floor.

She stepped onto the escalator and began gliding up. Milt glanced toward Tracey. She was rising from the bench.

No!

Tracey stretched, shooting him an impatient look. Then began pacing aimlessly.

The woman hit the top of the escalator. Her eyes locked on to Tracey like a laser beam.

Come on, come on, Milt begged silently.

Features hardening, she propelled herself into stealthy motion, a lioness stalking her prey. Milt's mouth dried out. Quietly he followed far behind her. He saw Rogelio pull to his feet and aim for the top of the escalator. When the woman was fifteen feet away from Tracey, Milt flicked his thumb upward at Bill. Immediately Bill raised his camera and began filming her back. Tracey glanced up, saw the woman, the camera. Her face creased with surprise, then blanched. She froze, her bottom lip sagging open.

The woman pulled up, shoulders tensing. She stared at Tracey's ghosted cheeks, then swung a startled look over her shoulder. Milt sped up, closing the distance. She reacted, then cringed like a cornered animal. He slid to a halt beside her, turning so Bill could film his profile. He'd rehearsed his line for the last two days.

"Right on time," he sneered. "Just as I planned."

For an instant nobody moved. The camera whirred.

The woman launched into a run toward the escalator, flat heels clacking like an accelerating freight train. Bill jumped out of her way, still filming. "Brett!" Milt cried as Tracey swept after her. Milt caught Tracey's arm and yanked, jerking her off her feet. She went down with a thud. Brett catapulted out of the conference room, saw Tracey scrambling up, and grabbed her shoulders. She kicked and fought like a banshee. Brett locked both arms around her waist, teeth gritted.

Rogelio blocked the escalator. The woman rammed into him as if her life depended on it, nearly knocking him down the stairs. Milt lurched behind her, threw his arms around her waist and pulled. She jabbed both elbows into his stomach. "Oof!" His grip loosened. Rogelio leaped for her and they tumbled to the floor. She shot a knee into his groin. He yelled in pain and rolled off. Milt caught one of her flailing legs, then fell on top of her. She squirmed violently beneath him. Teeth sank through his jacket into his wrist. Rogelio scrabbled toward them like a crab. Purple-faced, he lifted his victim off the floor, yanked her arms behind her back, and held on.

Milt swayed to his feet, holding his wrist. Off to the side he could see Bill filming. Somebody was yelling inanely—"I got you, I *got* you!" Milt realized the voice was his own.

On the first floor the deputy sheriff and security guard leaped toward the escalator. "No, no!" Milt called down. "She's mine!" The woman struggled against Rogelio, kicking wildly. Milt jumped out of her way and grabbed her shoulder, all reason falling from his head. "Into the courtroom, into the courtroom!" he screeched. He dragged her across the floor with Rogelio's help. They reached the courtroom door.

The deputy sheriff and security guard hit the top of the escalator.

Milt let go of her with one hand and yanked open the door. "Stop!" the deputy cried. The three of them fell into the courtroom like a bundle of feuding cats. Every head in the room snapped in their direction. The Three Fates gasped as one. Stan Breckshire shoved to his feet. The heavyset bailiff sprang forward.

The deputy burst through the door, Bill filming at his heels.

"Your Honor!" Milt yelled, lungs puffing like billows. "I bring you Shawna Welk, risen from the dead!"

SIXTY-TWO

Jed Trutenning sauntered into the small interrogation room with the swagger of a gunman in a saloon. His partner, Gary Welch, followed close behind. Lynn Trudy slouched in her seat, surveying them with narrowed eyes. Her hair spikes were askew, her lips pale, and the remnants of her makeup smeared. Apparently, jail didn't agree with her. The thought almost made Jed smile.

Gary chugged out a seat and sat down. Jed opened the manila folder in his hand and extracted a stack of papers. He placed them on the table, then smacked them with his palm. He pulled out his chair and sighed into it. Sniffed. Regarded Lynn Trudy almost with indifference.

"Congratulations. Nothing quite like a resurrection in the family."

Lynn's mouth slacked. She held herself very still.

"You remember Shawna. Your dead sister."

She swallowed.

Jed had to admit she was good. He cleared his throat with a rat-a-tat. "She was booked right here in our fine county jail this afternoon, along with your niece. We've made sure to keep you all apart. Wouldn't want the party to get too loud."

Lynn's resolve melted like wax in flame. She dropped her chin to her chest. Jed let her sit a minute.

"You're looking at all kinds of new charges, this time from Monterey County. Insurance fraud, false—"

"I didn't know anything about it!" She yanked her head up. "Not one thing!"

Jed exchanged a glance with Gary, then picked up the top piece of paper in the stack, held it out far enough to read it. "Email," he informed Lynn. "From Shawna Welk, a.k.a. Maria, to Milt Waking, a.k.a. Tracey Wilagher." Lynn's eyes bugged. "Wednesday, August fourteenth. 'For the last time, *think what you're doing!* Lynn says she tried to set you straight, and you threw her out of your apartment like some maniac. And don't be mad at me for telling her. I did it so she'd keep an eye on you. But *never* did I expect this! You *cannot* be with that reporter! Do I have to come back from the grave myself and knock you straight?'"

Jed flicked the paper across the table. "You can keep this copy; we've got plenty. In fact, we've got all the other emails from Shawna, courtesy of Milt Waking. We've looked at his email account. All the electronic originals are still there. We'll be looking at 'Maria's' too. In short, we've got all we need to prove you were a part of your sister's little scheme."

Lynn jerked her head to stare sightlessly at the floor, lips pressed. Jed waited her out. Gary tapped a forefinger on the table.

"I didn't do any of it," she said tonelessly. "I only knew a month before the trial. Shawna called me."

As the hidden camera recorded, Lynn eventually told what she knew. Cornered as she was, she didn't bother asking for her attorney. A mistake for their side, Jed thought.

Shawna had called Lynn only once, Lynn said. From then on, she and Lynn had corresponded by email, Shawna using the name Rachel. Tracey's emails were beginning to worry Shawna. Only a month to go before the trial, and Tracey seemed about to break under the strain. Shawna wanted Lynn to come to the trial. Keep an eye on Tracey *and* on the case.

"What was in it for you?" Gary asked.

For a moment Lynn balked. "A hundred thousand dollars," she said quietly. "*If* we got a guilty verdict."

The money would come out of Tracey's two million dollars. Tracey meanwhile had no clue that Shawna had contacted her aunt.

Lynn kept her gaze on the table. "When Shawna told me Tracey had taken up with Milt Waking, I had to try to stop her. That's when Tracey found out that I knew."

"Her insurance money," Jed pressed. "Going to you and her mother."

Lynn shrugged. "Shawna had Tracey under her thumb. Tracey never could think much for herself."

As for the details of staging the crime, Lynn claimed she knew nothing. Shawna had never wanted to write details in an email. As with Shawna's emails to Tracey, until things started to fall apart, the posts between her and Lynn had been carefully worded. "Shawna was always worried about them falling into the wrong hands," Lynn explained, "even though we deleted them immediately."

Jed shot a disgusted glance at Gary. Weren't these women some trio? All the lies and deceit, each one looking out for herself.

He switched subjects with a detective's ploy—assuming facts not yet admitted. "How did you get the two jury members' names and numbers?"

A smug expression flicked across Lynn's face. *Idiot,* thought Jed. *She's half proud of herself.*

"Stan Breckshire and I talked about the jurors. Who we liked, who might be a problem. I don't even think he realized he used their names. But there were too many Lowes and Brackens in the phone book to find the right numbers. I followed Candy home one night and Irene the next to get their addresses."

"Why'd you do it?"

Lynn shook her head. "Those women looked too soft." She glared at him as if he were to blame. "Obvious defense jurors. I had to get them out of there."

Jed ogled her. "Out of there? You told them to vote not guilty."

Her eyes rose toward the ceiling. "How stupid do I look? I knew they'd go running to the judge, and all she could do was kick 'em off."

"So . . . you were just trying to cover your tracks. Thought you were smarter than the system." Jed couldn't resist the sarcasm. "Smarter than the D.A."

She lifted her chin, eyes ablaze. "Had you fooled for quite a while, didn't I."

Jed stroked his jaw. He hoped the two detectives who'd come up from Monterey were having as much luck with Tracey. She'd probably bleed confessions about Shawna like a stuck pig if they offered to drop some of her charges. "The only fool in this room," he declared to Lynn Trudy, "is sitting in your chair."

"I COULDN'T *HELP* IT!" Tracey screamed as tears tracked down her flushed cheeks. She jumped out of her seat, paced to the wall, and pounded it. "It was all my *mother's* fault. She told me what to do every second!" She leaned her forehead against the wall and broke into fresh sobs of fury. "I hate Milt Waking. I *hate* him!"

Stan Breckshire was about to come unglued. He tapped his pen against the table, exchanging glances with the two Monterey County detectives. Douglas Draker's muscular arms were folded, his face grim, as he watched Tracey's tirade. Les Kelly's expression exuded impatience. Bad enough, Stan ragged to himself, that his case had just exploded like a heap of dynamite. Bad enough that the detectives had been yanked from their days off to tear up here from Salinas. That, and the ruin of their murder investigation, hadn't exactly made them pleasurable company. *Now* this loony bin girl—who'd once been his own witness—was wearing Stan's nerves to a complete frazzle. She'd already signed the deal he offered her. Given the circumstances, what choice did she have? Stan couldn't let her sashay out a free woman, but he had lessened numerous charges, even though he'd just as soon lock her up and throw away the key.

Now all she had to do was *talk*. And all she was managing to do was convulse.

He raised his eyebrows at Draker with the silent message, "You going to do something about this or not?" He knew Draker's M.O.: wait 'em out. Well, Stan had endured all the waiting he could handle.

He shoved back his chair. "Tracey!" He stalked to her side and poked her hard in the shoulder. "I'm leaving and I'm taking my deal with me. What do I care about details? I've got living proof in a jail cell!"

He swiveled back to the table and snatched up the papers. Tracey's cries died like a wounded animal's. He scowled at her. "My, aren't we quiet all of a sudden. You going to talk to me?"

"Yes," she said in a pitiable voice, sniffing. Stan detested her.

"Then sit down." He pointed to her chair. "I want it from start to finish."

Tracey huffed into her seat. Stan started to pace out of sheer habit. Draker gave him a look and he sat down.

For the next half hour they listened to Tracey's halting story.

Her mother, she told them, was already looking for a way to disappear. Mom knew she'd botched the papers for Delgadia's adoption, and feared for her safety should he ever find out. Plus she was miserably unhappy in the marriage. Who wouldn't be, married to Darren Welk? Then there was the two-million-dollar life insurance policy. She wanted desperately to fake her own death but didn't know how.

Then came the night at the beach. When Darren hit her mom in the jaw, she fell and cut her forehead on a piece of metal in the sand. In fury she flung the metal into the ocean. The wound bled a lot, dripping onto her blouse. She took off the blouse to wash the blood away in the water. Darren followed her and they kept arguing. He hit her again in the jaw, almost knocking a tooth out. The blouse fell from her hand. Then, drunk as a skunk, he veered away toward the fire and passed out on the sand. Mom was livid. And scared. His drinking problem was leading to worse and worse problems.

That's when the idea struck her.

She stood in the water, thinking everything through. She studied the tracks she and Darren had made through the sand, and their wet footprints. Couldn't spoil that. She splashed through the shallow water to the far end of the bay before heading back up the beach. Then she called Tracey on her cell phone and told her to bring the money Delgadia had paid for the baby—four hundred thousand dollars sitting in a locked box in her office.

"*All* of it," Tracey spat. "I had to beg her to leave me a couple thousand just to live. And besides that, I was sick that night."

Her mom also told Tracey to bring a change of clothes, a baseball cap, and a pair of scissors. While Tracey was driving to the beach, her mom stuffed the blouse under the seat in Darren's car, tore her pants, and worked her loose tooth until she could pull it.

She went back into the water at the end of the bay and waded to the area near her footprint. She threw the piece of fabric, her underwear, and the tooth into the quiet inlet protected by the rocks, hoping they would wash up on the beach in a day or two. The underwear must have gotten pulled out to sea.

Tracey twisted her mouth. "She made me drive her to a bus station on the outskirts of Monterey, talking all the way. Planning her story for the police and making me repeat it again and again. An overnight bus happened to pull into the parking lot when we got there. Mom sort of fell in step with the passengers so she wouldn't stand out. She went to the bathroom in the terminal, cut her hair really short, and flushed it down the toilet. Then she put on the baseball cap. The bus was going on to Los Angeles. She got a seat on it." Tracey's voice nearly faded away. "And that's the last time I saw her."

"When did she go to Brazil?" Draker pressed.

"I don't know. Maybe a month later. She had to find a new identity, get a passport. She also dyed her hair. In Brazil she had plastic surgery. Why not? She had all that money," Tracey added bitterly. "While I crimped for every penny to move out of the Welks' house. But it wasn't supposed to be for very long. We didn't know there had to be a body to get the money. Mom thought she'd left enough evidence and that would be it. So I was stuck waiting for the trial. All those months. And having to testify."

Testify? More like lie through your greedy little teeth. Stan didn't feel one bit sorry for her.

By the time Tracey was done, his arm throbbed like mad. This case had done him in, body and soul. He'd be famous in Salinas for sure—for all the wrong reasons. The deputy D.A. who prosecuted the crime that wasn't. He might as well pick artichokes. Stan snorted. And to think that not two weeks ago his biggest worry of the day had been Chelsea Adams's direct line to God.

What a joke *that* turned out to be.

EPILOGUE

On Monday, August 19, Chelsea found herself in a standing-room-only Salinas courtroom to witness the arraignments of Shawna Marie Welk and Tracey Ann Wilagher. Reporters crowded into every niche of the room, more spilling into the hall. Chelsea, Kerra, and Brett had seats only because Darren Welk insisted to the bailiff that he save three on the end of the front row for them. Darren Welk's seat had been allotted by the judge himself.

Chelsea had not wanted to come, but Kerra had pleaded until she'd given in. "On one condition," Chelsea had told her obstinate niece. "The minute that arraignment is over, we're out the door. We're *not* going to be inundated by reporters."

The arraignments lasted only minutes apiece. Cut and dried, uneventful, belying the intensity of emotion swirling about the events that had led to them. Shawna Welk pleaded not guilty to her myriad charges. Tracey pleaded no contest. According to the newspapers, she'd cut a deal with Stan Breckshire.

Tracey was led away in handcuffs, out the same door through which her mother had disappeared. The courtroom filled with a cacophony of rustling clothes, squeaking chairs, and conversation. Chelsea rose quickly. "Okay." She tapped Kerra's arm. "Let's get out of here."

"I'll meet you outside," Kerra whispered to Brett.

They hurried up the aisle, beating most of the milling crowd, and pushed through the doors. In the hall, news crews readied for filming. Automatically Chelsea ducked. "Come on!" They scurried toward the stairs.

"I want to watch," Kerra declared suddenly, veering away.

"Kerra, no!"

"Oh, good grief, Aunt Chelsea." Kerra grabbed her arm and pulled. "We can just melt into the wall clear on the other side. The reporters have far bigger targets than us."

Helplessly Chelsea allowed herself to be propelled across the floor. She would not leave Kerra alone. They turned in time to see Brett and his father exit the courtroom, surrounded by a mass of reporters. Lights flicked on, throwing their shadows onto the wall. Cameras whirred. Reporters shoved microphones in their faces.

"How do you feel, Mr. Welk?"

"Will you be called to testify against your wife?"

"Are you filing for divorce?"

A smiling Darren Welk held up both hands, clearly enjoying his moment in the sun. "Yes, I am filing for divorce. As for how I feel, well . . ." He gave a short laugh. "I am glad my soon-to-be ex-wife rose from the dead to exonerate me." The crowd chuckled with him, then shouted more questions, one voice tumbling over another. Darren waited until all was again quiet. "Most of all, I am glad to be reunited with my son, who stuck by me all this time." He placed an arm around Brett's shoulder. "We're going back to our ranch now, where we'll work side by side, bringing our products to tables everywhere." Darren grinned, pointing a finger at the nearest camera. "When you eat your salad at dinner, remember the Salad King."

Laughter bubbled from Kerra's mouth, wrenching into a stifled sob. Chelsea reached for her hand and squeezed. Kerra had cried in wild relief the better part of the last two days. As Brett and his dad had immediately returned to their ranch, she had clung to Chelsea like a child adrift. Kerra knew Brett needed time with his father, and was glad to allow them their privacy. But the need to talk, to think out loud, to pray, had overwhelmed her. Secretly Chelsea was glad for her neediness. Kerra talked to her like never before, spilling the story about the growing relationship she shared with Brett and how they had prayed.

Kerra hung tightly to Chelsea's hand. "I'm just so glad for Brett," she said, her voice shaking. "Glad enough that I'm able to leave him tomorrow."

Chelsea would be taking Kerra to the airport in the afternoon. Two days later Paul would come home, followed soon by their boys. Chelsea could hardly wait for their family to be reunited. As for Kerra's last evening in the Bay Area, Chelsea knew she'd be spending it with Brett.

Chelsea was silent for a moment, watching Darren work the crowd of reporters. Despite what Kerra had told her about Brett's decision for Christ, she still worried. The thought of Kerra around Darren Welk left her cold. "He's not exactly a nice guy, Kerra."

Kerra withdrew her hand. "God will work on him through Brett," she said firmly. "You'll see."

MILT WAKING BROKE FROM the mass of bodies and strode across the hall toward Chelsea and Kerra. Even from a distance he could see the distaste on their faces when they saw him approach. *My, my,* he thought, *such ingratitude.* No matter. Since his breaking-news exclusive footage had aired midafternoon two days ago, he'd been the Man of the Hour. Make that Man of the Year. He'd already had a preliminary phone call from one major network. He imagined there would be more after Channel Seven aired its unprecedented hourlong special about his single-handedly dissolving the Salad King trial. The program was slotted for prime time on a Friday night, two and a half weeks away. Milt had already been scrambling for interviews with the attorneys and jurors.

He drew to a halt in front of Chelsea and her niece. "Kerra. Ms. Adams."

Kerra regarded him with grudging deference. "Hi."

Chelsea clasped her hands at her waist. "Well, Mr. Waking. Once again congratulations are in order."

"Thank you," he replied. *And well I deserve them.* He pulled a mask of humility over his features. "Ms. Adams, as I mentioned to you earlier, I'm putting together a one-hour special about the case. I've already had a few jury members admit they gave you quite a time in the deliberation room."

He paused. No response.

"I'm still hoping you'll tell your side of the story."

"Why do you need me, Mr. Waking?" Chelsea's voice was as light as lead. "Your reports have already been full of your incredible exclusives. You must be very proud of yourself."

He tilted his head in self-satisfaction. "All the same, Ms. Adams, I need your story. I heard about the last day of deliberation. How you did nothing but pray." He narrowed his eyes. "I'll bet you had a vision, didn't you? You knew *something*. That's why you fought the jury so hard in deliberations. You gave me time to reel in Shawna Welk like a fish." He spread his hands. "So what exactly did you see in your vision? Shawna on the beaches of Brazil?"

She considered him at length, a little smile on her face. "I'm sorry to say, Mr. Waking, that you are wrong. I did not know Shawna was alive, and I had no visions concerning Darren Welk. However, I will tell you one thing. And you can quote me. If you dare."

Milt worked to keep the smugness from his face. He was actually going to get Chelsea Adams to talk! "I'm waiting."

"God *did* speak to me—before the deliberation and during it."

"And what did he say?"

"That he was sending me his chosen servant. That in good conscience I was to stick to my vote until that servant accomplished what God had called him to do."

Milt sifted through possibilities, rejecting them all. "Who was that?" he asked, frowning.

"You."

He blinked. "No way. I never consulted God about anything. I did it all on my own."

That little smile on her faced twitched. "Ever read the Bible, Mr. Waking?"

"No."

"Well, here's the rest of my answer for your one-hour special. First, Jeremiah twenty, verse eleven. God is a Dread Champion, bringing about what he will. Second, Isaiah thirty-seven, verses twenty-four through twenty-eight. This is the Lord's word to the Assyrian king, who was boasting of all he had done 'on his own.' Verse twenty-six is God's particular quote for you. *If* you should dare use it." She took a deep breath. "Good day, Mr. Waking."

In unspoken assent the two women stepped around him and headed for the exit. Nonplussed, Milt watched them go.

Thirty minutes later Milt headed up the freeway for the long drive toward the news station. When he passed Redwood City after an hour and a half, on the spur of the moment he veered off the Edgewood exit toward San Carlos. He had some vague memory of a Christian bookstore on Laurel Street. He cruised slowly up Laurel, reading signs. Ah yes, there it was. The Door. He pulled into a parking space and slipped inside the store, keeping his head down. He walked through a card and gift section, spotting an area of Bibles in the center of the store. Reaching the nearest Bible, he picked it up. Now, where was the book of Isaiah? He thumbed through the front, consulting a table of contents, then found the book in the middle of the Old Testament. *"Verses twenty-four through twenty-eight."* He read the boasts of the Assyrian king. "I" this and "I" that. The guy sure was stuck on himself. Milt ran his finger to God's reply in verse twenty-six.

Have you not heard?
    Long ago I ordained it.
In days of old I planned it;
    now I have brought it to pass.

The words had a strange effect upon him. They seemed to seep into his chest like a warm salve. For a moment he stood there, staring at the verse.

Then came to his senses.

No way, he huffed. *God could not have planned what I did.* He slammed the book shut. He had done it alone—*all* of it. Milt reached out with purpose to plunk the Bible back on the shelf. Of its own accord his arm stilled. He let it hang there, thinking, staring at the smooth leather. Trying to make sense of what he was feeling.

Then abruptly he pulled back the Bible, swiveled, and headed for the checkout counter.

"Come on, come on, it's almost time!" Mama Yolanda cried in Spanish, shooing her houseful of friends and neighbors out of the kitchen. "Where's Kristin?" she asked Rogelio breathlessly.

"In the bedroom, trying to put Roselita down."

"Ay! She cannot miss the program! Tell her to come out, Rogelio. The baby can sleep in her arms."

Rogelio loved the sound of those words. "Okay."

He led Kristin out, placing her in a seat of honor beside Mama Yolanda on the couch. Roselita lay against Kristin's shoulder, whimpering softly. Mama Yolanda rubbed her back. "Shh, shh, *chiquita.*" Roselita quieted. Rogelio's heart nearly burst through his chest. The baby was slowly getting used to her new mamas. And he fully believed that in time Kristin would move into their home as his wife.

Thank you, God, the prayer welled inside him, *for keeping our bargain.*

Smiling from ear to ear, he plopped on the floor at Kristin's feet.

Music rang from the television set, fading into a voice-over. "This is a Channel Seven special. Tonight, the breathtaking, exclusive story of the Salad King trial, Enrico Delgadia's desperate secret, and how the truth was brought to light by one determined reporter."

Collective oohs resonated through the room. Excitement plinked up Rogelio's throat. Now that it was all over, he couldn't wait to see himself, Kristin, and Mama Yolanda on television. With their baby. *His* family. He swung his head toward Janet Cline, their special guest. She smiled at him in anticipation.

Milt had been right. The news stations *could* make things happen. Plus Terrance Clyde and Erica Salvador had offered their help for free. A court hearing had been quickly scheduled, and Rogelio and Mama Yolanda had been given custody of Roselita Nicole. Delgadia had been arraigned on charges of baby trafficking. Mama Yolanda said they should pray for him. Rogelio just wanted him to rot in jail.

Milt Waking's face filled the television screen. He was seated in a restaurant Rogelio immediately recognized, at the very table where they had eaten lunch. "'I'll tell you my story,'" Milt began, looking straight into the camera. "'But I want something in return.'

"Those were the words of twenty-year-old Rogelio Sanchez of Salinas," Milt declared. "Little did I know that Rogelio's story would in the end bring back three hopelessly lost people—his illegally adopted baby, a man imprisoned for a crime that was never committed, and a scheming 'murdered' woman who frolicked on the beaches of Brazil."

The baby cried. Rogelio looked over his shoulder to see Mama Yolanda holding out her plump, willing arms to help. Kristin gently placed Roselita in her great-grandmother's arms.

"Stay with me for the next hour and I will tell you the tale," Milt continued. "But first, just how could such an extraordinary sequence of events have occurred? One answer comes from Chelsea Adams, a jurist for the Darren Welk trial, and the woman who made headlines last year with her visions about the Trent Park case. Calling God a 'Dread Champion,' she quotes the Lord's words from the book of Isaiah: 'Have you not heard? Long ago I ordained it. In days of old I planned it; now I have brought it to pass. . . .'"

EYES OF ELISHA
Brandilyn Collins

The murder was ugly.

The killer was sure no one saw him.

Someone did.

In a horrifying vision, Chelsea Adams has relived the victim's last moments. But who will believe her? Certainly not the police, who must rely on hard evidence. Nor her husband, who barely tolerates Chelsea's newfound Christian faith. Besides, he's about to hire the man who Chelsea is certain is the killer to be a vice president in his company.

Torn between what she knows and the burden of proof, Chelsea must follow God's leading and trust him for protection. Meanwhile, the murderer is at liberty. And he's not about to take Chelsea's involvement lying down.

Softcover: 0-310-23968-0

ZONDERVAN™

GRAND RAPIDS, MICHIGAN 49530 USA

COLOR THE SIDEWALK FOR ME

The Bradleyville Series
Brandilyn Collins

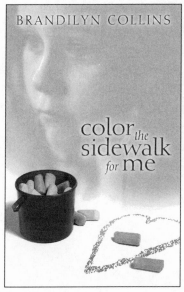

As a chalk-fingered child, I had worn my craving for Mama's love on my sleeve. But as I grew, that craving became cloaked in excuses and denial until slowly it sank beneath my skin to lie unheeded but vital, like the sinews of my framework. By the time I was a teenager, I thought the gap between Mama and me could not be wider.

And then Danny came along. . . .

A splendidly colored sidewalk. Six-year-old Celia presented the gift to her mother with pride—and received only anger in return. Why couldn't Mama love her? Years later, when once-in-a-lifetime love found Celia, her mother opposed it. The crushing losses that followed drove Celia, guilt-ridden and grieving, from her Bradleyville home.

Now thirty-five, she must return to nurse her father after a stroke. But the deepest need for healing lies in the rift between mother and daughter. God can perform such a miracle. But first Celia and Mama must let go of the past—before it destroys them both.

Softcover: 0-310-24242-8

GRAND RAPIDS, MICHIGAN 49530 USA